ADDITIONAL PRAISE FOR **BRAND NEW CHERRY FLAVOR**

"**Brand New Cherry Flavor** is pierced, tattooed, mirror-shaded, and as far off its face as the L. A. it depicts is off the planet. It simultaneously combines to be hideously, hilariously believable and dream-logically scary. What's more, it's cool, nasty fun... Enjoy!"

~Charles Shaar Murray, author, *Boogie Man*

"Darkly magical. The pages fly!"

~Patricia Briggs, NYT Bestselling Author of the "Casey Thomson" series

"**Brand New Cherry Flavor** is, hands down, one of the most spectacular novelistic events of the '90's!" **~The Oregonian**

"Cool and funny, visceral and paradoxically detached, **Brand New Cherry** Flavor seizes its subject matter and does it justice. With a vengeance. Lisa Nova's the sexiest, most striking new heroine in dark fantasy since Sonja Blue—Or anti-heroine." **~Locus**

"Avant-garde horror writer Grimson...leaves one thrilled if feeling rather unclean."

~Kirkus Reviews

"Witheringly funny in its satire against cinema, stardom and celebrity, Grimson's novel performs a gleeful demolition job on the mindlessness of American 'slasher' movies. Working within the tradition of John Updike's 'The Witches of Eastwick,' the book blends subject matter and a realistic technique to explore what one of its characters calls 'the metaphysical strangeness of existence.'" **~The Daily Telegraph, UK**

"A hectic pursuit of narrative force by any means is allied to verbal wit and ingenious games in **Brand New Cherry Flavor**, Todd Grimson's spectacular novel of Hollywood and the occult... a foul-mouthed, extravagant novel, combining a strong sense of the demonic with some snappy one-liners. Grimson...has produced a novel of vitality and promise."

~The Times (of London) Literary Supplement

"A gang of zombie bikers, ancient Aztecs, designer drugs and bucketloads of horror movie glamour take **Brand New Cherry Flavor** on a hallucinogenic, Hollywood trip. One highly hip, extremely bizarre and darkly humorous read—buy it!" **~Company, UK**

BRAND NEW CHERRY FLAVOR

Also by Todd Grimson

Within Normal Limits (Novel)
Stainless (Novel)

BRAND NEW CHERRY FLAVOR

TODD GRIMSON

First Printing in the United States: November 1996
First Schaffner Press Edition: October 2011

Published in the United States

This book and all Schaffner Press titles are distributed for the trade by Independent Publishers Group (IPG): www.ipgbook.com.

Special thanks to Chuck Denman, L.A. Detective, and Jim McLennan, editor of "Trash City," London.

For further information or to obtain permission from the publisher, contact: Permissions Dept.
Schaffner Press, Inc.
POB 41567
Tucson, Az 85717

For Library of Congress Catologuing-in-Publication Data, contact the publisher.

For B., Lise Raven, and Christopher Schelling

PART 1

~

Morality was a word my parents never used. *Truth* was the word. Truth and facing things like an animal.

NASTASSJA KINSKI

ONE

So the whole thing started in a restaurant. Ferns, cut flowers, glass, and mirrors. Lisa had the white-bean rapini salad, olive bread, white wine, while the vice president in charge of development at a major studio, tall, fifty-three, tanned and aerobicized, known in select Hollywood circles for his net play and crosscourt backhand, had marinated lamb with vanilla-bean vinaigrette, Persian *taftoon* and *lavash,* halved figs, iced mint tea.

The rich asshole told her that no, sorry, the job of assistant to the director he'd promised her, her dream job, the chance to work with and presumably get tight with Selwyn Popcorn, whose films she had always admired, cult-worshiped way back before film school—now, after two and a half fruitless, generally fucked-up years out here, getting nowhere, ending up going to bed with this guy, whatever the hell his name was, Lou Greenwood, Lou Adolph, Lou Burke, Lisa meanwhile not getting any younger at twenty-six, totally broke at the moment too, just everything—Lou said sometimes things came up, he couldn't help it, somebody's daughter had been promised, it was a fait accompli . . . so would she like to be a second second AD on the project? "I can get the DGA to waive the written," he said, but Lisa wasn't having any of that. They were sitting next to each other, and he'd been complacently fondling the inside of her nylon thigh; presumably he already had a replacement girlfriend lined up, he never fucked his wife anymore—mutual consent, he'd said—whatever, who knew? What difference did it make?

Lisa forced herself, it was terrible but she managed, in a flat voice, to get out, "Listen, I'm fucked up, I'm really broke. . . ."

"This happens to you, doesn't it?" he said, consulting his brown leather wallet, and—this was all so humiliating, she could kill him—

he *counted it,* it looked like, coming up with a hundred or so, in that neighborhood; she took it but it was nothing, pocket change, in effect. She hated him for putting her in this position.

It was like her eyes glazed or something for a moment, and she *suddenly* stuck the sharp-tined fork in his thigh, hard, stabbed him with it . . . and it stayed there, stuck in his flesh. After the initial moment he nodded and said, "I understand." Other than an initial flicker, like a video tracking badly for a nanosecond, he took it well. Did he know she was capable of murder? Did he understand that?

No, probably not. He didn't have the capacity to understand. He thought he was handling her violence in an ultracool ultraworldly manner. She should kill him, then he'd know. He wrote a phone number on the back of one of his cards from the studio, a number in medium blue Papermate ink.

"You want some money, try this."

Lisa took the card from him and went outside. As she came out she raised her arm to shield her gaze from the whitish yellow blurry sun. Fucking L.A. She had believed that gradually, diplomatically, without seeming to ask for any favors, she could have manipulated Selwyn Popcorn into really desiring to see some of her work. The black and white art film she'd done in New York, or the Cubism-versus-Godzilla video. . . .

This would have been the job to have. As first assistant director, for instance, you just yelled, "Hey everybody, places," all the time. Second unit director, you went around shooting close-ups of door-knobs or planes landing, shit like that. Assistant to the director, you called up Chuck Suede and he took your call. Now all this was lost.

Damn. She'd left her sunglasses inside, her favorite pair. Foot traffic: two guys who looked like Hong Kong action-movie gangsters, very cool, gazing at Lisa, one saying to the other something hidden by the language difference—out of it emerged "Nastassja Kinski." Lisa heard it clearly, it wasn't exactly the first time since she'd been in L.A. that she'd been compared to the actress. The resemblance was noticed, or hyperbolized, as it never had been in New York. It was a compliment out here, whereas in New York it would have been cooler, probably, to look like someone more cultish, say the fifties *film noir* femme fatale Jane Greer, who had been in only a relatively few movies (most memorably Jacques Tourneur's *Out of the Past,* opposite Robert Mitchum).

Nastassja Kinski, especially in her early films, had huge, hypnotic eyes, full, pouty lips, dark hair . . . and she eventually ended up nude in almost every film. Later on in her career she had become more ethereal, and blond. Lisa didn't know what to think or what to say in return when the resemblance was remarked upon. She had become good-looking only when she was seventeen or so. In fact, she had been chubby as a child. It was weird, therefore, to be told she looked like someone famous, and famously beautiful. She didn't look *that* much like her.

At home, after trying to call her best friend, Christine, and getting her machine, Lisa, petting her Burmese cat, decided to call the number Lou had given her. It was mysterious, and Lisa could never resist mysteries. Curiosity. It would be tacky if Lou was just trying to pass her on to some friend of his. It didn't seem like that, though.

OK. What the fuck. She'd screwed someone to advance her career, and now she was behind on the rent. So why not? She felt reckless and despondent, and this was at least action of some kind.

"Who's this?" a woman's voice said.

Lisa pronounced her name.

"Oh, yeah. Sure. Are you ready to do it?"

"Do what?"

"We'll pick you up around eight. Don't worry about what to wear."

Click. Lisa frowned. But then the touch of her cat's body and smooth fur cheered her up. He knew her hand. The human-animal bond. He purred, closing his eyes. She gazed around at her apartment, slowly, like a stranger to her own life.

Then she sighed and thought again about that fucking Lou. He wasn't stupid, wasn't a philistine or an accountant like so many of the men out here she'd met. He was married, with two kids. He had viewed all her material, said he liked most of it, said what he thought were film school–art school conceits. He knew she needed money; it was getting to the point where she couldn't afford either to stay in L.A. or to go back to New York.

Music. She needed to hear some noise. Some of her friends were in a band called the Painkillers, for whom she'd done the Cubism-versus-Godzilla video, in which cubism defeats the monster, driving it into the bright blue Japanese sea . . . but Lisa wanted to listen to something harsher, so she put in a CD of a new local band, Feed My Ego 3.

Later, as she ate something for dinner, she channel-surfed from a commercial (a woman in a white bikini emerging from the sea, glistening slo-mo droplets on tanned golden skin, just a glance, perfect) to a kung fu movie dubbed into Spanish. The choreography was fun for a few minutes, the sound of the blows exaggerated with electronic snare-drum handclaps, *yi! ho! hiyah!* A girl in a red kimono turns her back to the assailant, executes a forward somersault, then poses, almost Egyptian, freezes, then barely moves, not even glancing behind, so that the guy walks right into what turns out to be a punch.

Lisa went down at eight. She waited in her battered old black leather jacket, untucked white shirt and faded jeans, sensible shoes, semi-anonymous, smoking a cigarette while she leaned against a palm tree by the street. Defiance expressed by not dressing up. Anguish at feeling betrayed by the world. She did, however, have some makeup on. Dark red vamp lipstick, blush . . . and she had three little gold earrings decorating each ear.

A limo pulled up. The driver, in uniform, was wearing sunglasses. In the backseat, a blond crew-cut woman beckoned Lisa inside, giving her a knowing, coolly friendly smile.

I am in a pornographic situation, thought Lisa Nova, one hour later, in a mansion surrounded by woods and manicured green lawns, somewhere in Bel Air.

TWO

Floating slowly, like fish in an aquarium, following almost mechanically precise geometric paths, in a big, big room, bigger than a gymnasium . . . eyeballs like nude cephalopods, swimming around without their shells, a cloudy white, filmed with red. The eyes seemed unnaturally large, brown irises, blue, and dark electric green, opening to the retina, behind this—or somewhere—the invisible, theoretical rods and cones.

There were also some robotic insectoid eyes on flexi-metal stalks, moving about to examine her from this angle or that. An impression of protozoan, amoebalike shapes, as Lisa, anesthetized with a synthetic endorphin derivative, well-being and contentment riding through her bloodstream, knew that everything was fine, for instance, in the blue vein under the smooth pale skin there in her foot.

The ceiling was so high. Some eyes had ascended, evidently studying the solar system painted way up there, orbits described on neutral zinc white with dotted lines. The ciliary muscles moved the gazes this way and that, soft creatures whom she was not afraid of at all . . . though she was not completely without fear. Fear of the general state of things, of the blind spot, of surprise.

The stark yet intimate transaction: money for flesh. It had been explained to her, and she understood. If she experienced some disquiet behind the medication, that was nothing to shiver about, nothing to depress.

Voyeurism. Exhibitionism. I'm weak. I have been paid. Painless, she looked too. Pinkness. Wet flesh mirror, or monitor, slowly melting mirror.

THREE

"Then you're a whore," pronounced her best friend and collaborator, Christine Rien. "Just 'cause it's thousands of dollars doesn't mean it's not prostitution."

"I know that," Lisa said somewhat crossly. Then, a moment later, after taking a sip of sweet café au lait, "Nobody touched me."

Christine sighed and shook her head. She had silky golden blond hair, darker at the roots. She looked very Gallic. She'd written articles on cinema for *Artforum,* the history of the femme fatale for *Auteur,* women in melodrama, all of that. "I can't believe you'd do something like this."

Lisa shrugged. "It's just skin."

"You let him turn you into a bimbo. It excites you, doesn't it, in some perverse way."

They were at Christine's sister's house, in Manhattan Beach. Nobody else was home. Lisa yawned. She hadn't slept much the night before. Almost a year ago, when she had first come out here, she had had a part in a horror movie, *The L.A. Ripper,* a small role in which she had played a victim and appeared nude. She had been offered the part because of a series of personal connections, and it had appealed to her as an exercise in intentional bad taste. She appreciated that Christine did not now bring this up.

"You don't understand," Lisa said quietly. "I'm going to get revenge. He lied to me, fucked me over, and he's gonna pay for it. You'll see."

Christine looked at her, trying to gauge her level of conviction. Lisa was too impressionable, she thought, always too open, too liable to change her mind. Sometimes this led her to do dumb things. She was impulsive and unpredictable.

"I'm serious," Lisa said. "I don't know what exactly I can do, but I'll get him somehow." She spoke implacably: passion cooled into will. A good part of her motivation here was to prove something to Christine, though she would not have wanted her friend to realize the power she possessed. She needed some form of payback. It was all so plain to her now. Her conscience would be clear.

"How many others might have seen you?" asked Christine dispassionately.

"I don't know. At one point, I thought I saw Roy Hardway."

"Really?"

"Just a glimpse."

Hardway was the thinking man's action star. His films included *Slammer, Dieability,* and the remake of Fritz Lang's *The Big Heat*. Lately he'd been in a couple of bombs, but he was still huge.

"I thought about brain transplants," Lisa said. "I was imagining a brain hooked up to wires, lying in fluid, like in those movies from the fifties, where the brain starts controlling guys, hypnotizing them, killing people with death thoughts . . . if there *was* a transplant, no way they'd get everything hooked up right. All those nerve endings and things would goof, you'd try to open your mouth and your leg would kick out straight . . ."

"Was there music playing?"

"There might have been. It wasn't a big item."

"What exactly did you do?"

Lisa thought about it, then said, "I did something to myself."

"Did you make any noise?"

"I might have, yeah. I don't know."

"But you got paid?"

"Yes."

The film they'd cowritten, *Girl, 10, Murders Boys,* still played sometimes in New York. Christine had produced it, and she'd helped with everything from production design to lighting. The subject, one very close to Lisa's heart, was the true (well, semifictionalized) story of a ten-year-old girl named Mary Bell, from a bad slum in Manchester, England, who had murdered, a month apart, first a three-year-old boy and then a four-year-old, strangling them with her small hands.

The film had been shot in sort of a Tarkovsky-influenced visual palette, toned down, timed for a blood red cast . . . and Lisa and Christine had used Godardian tactics, flashing back and flashing forward, showing questions in white block letters on a momentarily black screen, like *DO PARENTS OWN THEIR CHILDREN?* or *IS MOTHER-CHILD LOVE AUTOMATIC? WHAT HAPPENS WHEN IT'S NOT?* or, when Mary experimentally half-strangled one of her playmates, laughing after she'd been pulled off, *DO OTHERS FEEL THE SAME THINGS WE DO?*

"What if you're on a video?" Christine said, breaking the silence, changing her position, looking concerned.

"*Tasteful Nudity II:* the sequel to *Tasteful Nudity*?" Lisa rejoined, but she was shaken. I'd have to kill him, she decided. Mary Bell would.

"What exactly did you do?" Christine asked again.

"I don't want to talk about it," Lisa replied in a lower, less accessible voice, like a sulking child who's done something wrong and already confessed.

After a while, not looking directly at her, Christine said, "Freud presented the fetishist image of a woman, vulva displayed, punished and humiliated, often by another woman plus penis, or dildo, penis substitute, or whip. The pornographic gaze."

Lisa looked at her with a look that said, Shut up. Now. I'm not kidding.

Christine got the hint and talked about something else. A new photography show. Lisa was wearing black cotton tights under this special pair of ultrademolished shredded faded jeans, and a NO FUN black T-shirt. She had on a couple of bracelets, along with an expensive watch Lou had given her when he'd been infatuated, at the beginning—he'd probably found a way to have his accounting firm write it off. Christine had on a crayon-bright overlarge green and yellow top, a blue skirt, and red tights. No shoes. She stretched out on the couch as Lisa sat there in the bamboo chair, frowning, plotting revenge.

She couldn't let herself be fucked with in this way. It was important that Lou understand. She should have stuck that fork in his face. Gone for an eye. Fuck. The glass coffee table reflected the afternoon rays of tired sun.

FOUR

That evening Lisa drove over to see Code. He knew a lot of people; maybe he could help. He was one third of the Painkillers, who'd had two dance-club hits: "Imitation Ho Chi Minh," the remix, and "Gilded Youth," with its timely chorus *"jeunesse dorée."* The band's sound was synthesizers, sequencers, samples, and drum machines, though Code had actually started out as a guitar player. Their first album was old news, though it continued to sell. But now the future of the band was in jeopardy: One of the others—Wendy Right, who sang on a few songs and who had been Code's girlfriend for a while—had hired a lawyer, trying to keep the trademark and get rid of Code. Wendy had hated him since they'd stopped sleeping together; lately she'd been working on the one in the middle, Sterling Music, who worked out most of the drum programs.

Lisa had once had a crush on Code, and they'd fucked nearly every day for a month or so, at one point spending a week together in Jamaica. Code wanted to get more work in commercials or films. He was a fairly gorgeous young man. Lisa liked him; they were still good friends.

Recently it seemed like he just hung around Hollywood or West Hollywood, bringing young girls up into his rented pad. He had the whole top floor of a seven-story building, and he was doing demos there, waiting to see if he'd still be part of the Painkillers or not.

Outside, on the street, everyone was glam, the S&M hurt-me look a constant. Rouged children, baby-faced under the makeup, the metal fatigue girls in mesh hose and garter belts and microminiskirts, guys with wild teased hair. All this ready flesh like bruised raspberries, glazed, unborn faces, faces waiting to be born in twisted noise.

Lisa had a key to Code's building. After she'd parked her beat-up red Trans Am, she went up on the big freight elevator, wondering what kind of scene she might find. More than once she'd come in on weird stuff.

Tonight there was no sex scene in progress when Lisa came in. But Code was with some friends. It was a long walk, through a maze of sound baffles and abandoned office furniture, big wooden crates, to the space Code had made his own. He had brightly colored sci-fi sheets and pillowcases on his queen-sized bed, and he sat there wearing a padded-shoulder pearl gray corduroy jacket, no shirt, white trousers with a drawstring, bare feet.

"Lisa," he said, "I want you to meet Freak, and that's Alvin Sender, and uh, Vladimir One. Vladimir Two went out to get an effects box. What are you up to? Hey, I like your T-shirt. Can I have it? Trade? Look in the closet: anything you want."

"You told me once," Lisa said, taking off her jacket, heading to the closet, pulling the T-shirt over her head, "about some guy . . . who, if you ever wanted to do harm to somebody . . ." She threw the T-shirt at him. He smiled and took off his jacket to put the T-shirt right on, see how it felt. Lisa was now naked from the waist up, but not flaunting herself, not really giving anyone a good look at her—she picked out a conservative sports-shirt, good fabric, dark blue. Italian disco was playing. Cool beat. Lisa turned back to them, buttoning up as Code gave her a knowing little leer.

"We've just been arguing about spilling paint on the floor," he said, and did not elaborate, as Lisa went to the brand-new refrigerator and came back with a crimson can of Coke.

Freak was a lanky model type, with short pale blond hair, a seventies-style silver minidress, whitish silver metallic stockings, silver high heels. Bare arms. Beautiful, sure. Alvin Sender was maybe thirty-seven, thirty-eight, artistic but probably not an artist, thin, with delicate bones. It seemed like she should know more clearly who he was. Vladimir I was tan, maybe twenty-five, good-looking in a Red Army kind of way, wearing a jumpsuit that might have been the favored uniform in some science fiction film in 1973, canary yellow with a red zipper, red belt, and red hightop athletic shoes. Maybe he was a musician.

"This material feels great," Code said, rubbing his hand over the surface of the tee. "It's kind of funky, 'cause you were outside and it's warm. I love it."

Lisa was not about to be embarrassed in front of these people. She'd perspired in her leather jacket, and Code dug it. That was OK.

"What about this guy?" she asked, not to be distracted from her point.

"What guy?"

"You told me about this guy. He has a 900 number or something. 1–900-I Kill for Cash. Something like that."

Vladimir I laughed. Freak continued to kind of sulk, stretching her long legs on the bed so the juncture of her silver tights came into view. Alvin Sender smiled, a little too observant but very relaxed. Lisa decided she didn't like him, no matter what drug he was on.

"I'm just doing research," she announced.

Code nodded and said, "Oh. Sure. Well, I think I know who you mean, but I don't know how to get in touch with him directly. You know Zed, don't you? Zed might know. Tell him you're looking for the cat who does the psychic tattoos."

"Where's Zed doing business these days? Pomona?"

"Zed, uh—shit, go see Ultra Jim at Overplus. That place is a trip, but Ultra Jim is, like, the distributor for a lot of hardware, software, mood elevators, and reality softeners. You ever had Stairway to Heaven? It's pretty new. You should try it. Freak here would give you a testimonial, but she's using Candy 2000, and that's not a very verbal type of experience."

"Stairway to Heaven is great," Vladimir I testified. "It doesn't leave you stupid, and as soon as it's over, it's over. I've used it and logged on, and I was fine, I did some interesting work."

"I've seen you in something," Alvin Sender said, and Lisa had the impression he'd known this all along.

"She was the third hooker cut up in *The L.A. Ripper,*" Code helpfully remarked.

"That's right, and then you're in the morgue," Sender went on; Lisa flashed for a second on that scene. "You were good," he said. "We're very sympathetic to you . . . your murder is the one that hurts the worst."

"Thanks," Lisa replied, eyes flashing dark at Code, wishing she'd had a drink. Maybe it was worth going to Overplus just to have some vodka on the rocks. Without being alone with him, she couldn't tell if Code was on one of these new wonders of chemistry or not. Most likely they all were. Waiting for Vladimir II to come back with some kind of a box. She got up and left.

It was about eleven o'clock. Ultra Jim was one of the DJs at Overplus. It was supposed to be a total experience, and it would probably have a life span of about two months. The clientele was mostly gay and lesbian, and Lisa'd heard there was a fair amount of S&M action in the back rooms. You could easily end up getting fistfucked on a trapeze. You could have a life-changing experience. Anyway, going in by herself, it might be assumed that she was looking for . . . uh, love.

There wasn't any real reason to go through with all this. But if it was reasonably easy, she'd like something to disturb Lou's orderly ride. She didn't like the idea that he thought he knew her limits and had written her off. It only demonstrated his lack of fucking imagination.

Iggy Pop said that one time he had met Raquel Welch, backstage at Letterman or something, and that it was like trying to have a conversation with Hitler; seeing two people having what looked like an unsatisfactory exchange, Lisa thought of this for one brief, disconnected instant as she paid to go into the club, presented with the loudness of the music and the kinetic, kinaesthetic reality of the crowd. She *felt* more than heard the vast, wide thud of the bass drum, silver-crisp splat of the hi-hat circuit, smack of the snare, dancers moving from side to side, up and down, heads bobbing, shoulders dipping, heads shaking, elaborate little pantomime routines at hyperspeed, same-sex couples for the most part, gyrating and contorting, as if the ceremony really meant something to them, like they'd remember this moment tomorrow, it fulfilled some intrinsic need . . . the lighting went hot pink, gold, hot turquoise, and otherworldly, blinking science fiction double red.

In the Old South, during slavery, drums were banned because they could be used, the slave-owners reasoned, to signal revolt. Now that simple rebellion in the U.S. meant nothing, the fertility beat invoked some much more complex conditioned response.

Lisa had a vodka and asked the bartender where she could find Ultra Jim. The bartender said, "Is he expecting you?" and she said, "Yeah, sort of." The bartender gestured toward a stairway that she had not noticed before.

Ultra Jim was not the kind of DJ who talked much. He was known for his interesting mixes, but tonight he was just creating an environment, sort of on automatic pilot, maybe as a gesture in reverse. He seemed to recognize Lisa, beckoning for her to sit down next to him. From the window in his booth and a couple of video monitors one could oversee different aspects of activity within the club.

"Code called me, said you might drop by. You're looking for a hit man or some bad-ass medication. I couldn't really tell. Ever chewed on actual fresh-cut coca leaf? It's a lot more subtle, but it makes you solid with the Incas, and you never know when you might need that in your life."

"Do you know where Zed lives?"

"I'll write down his address. Here, try this. It's very light. Instead of a hundred-watt bulb, it's like, soft white, forty or twenty-five. See, it's a green Chiclet."

Lisa put it in her mouth. It didn't taste minty. She took a sip from Ultra Jim's iced tea, if it was iced tea. He segued into a new Interpol computer handcuff beat, a spunky clone of African buzz-tones and sampled rhythmic yelps. He had a chain with a padlock around his neck and a pullover in a Stuart Davis pattern of vibrant yellow, red, white, and black. The chain went down to around his waist. He had a little mustache. Lisa couldn't see his eyes. He was of Hispanic descent, a mixture, maybe Venezuelan or Brazilian mixed with Minnesota strip. Lisa's father, Dr. Nova, lived in Brazil.

"I was chastised today," Jim said. "I can't say I didn't deserve it, but I didn't really enjoy it. Or maybe I did. Tell me, Lisa Nova, Nova Lisa, is every sadist really a masochist, secretly desiring to have the tables turned? I really have no idea. I don't know. I'm asking you."

"I'd just be making a guess," Lisa said flatly, seeing something in one of the monitors that caught her eye, something she'd never thought of anyone wanting to have done.

"All this urban riffraff," Ultra Jim mused, his attention following hers to the same scene. "I like to look at them, though. I want to watch these total strangers, all the time. I don't really know why, except that it's there. Exhibitionists want to see themselves as others see them, right? It would be nice to gently detach their eyeballs, set them down on the table, on a napkin, they could watch themselves and go from there. I have no imagination, Lisa, none at all. Look at that. What is it? I have no idea. What I do is, I make people dance."

This sounded sinister. Lisa took Zed's address, thanked him, and said goodbye. Down among the dancers she felt a strange euphoria coming over her. A beautiful black woman in a velvet bustier gave her a challenging but seductive stare. The lights went to strobe white, and she felt crazy, crazed. By the time she made it out into the night, it seemed an empty elsewhere, a vacuum after a plenum, like she was on the streets of Pluto after cruising the steamy pubic Venusian maze. The cassette deck had long ago been stolen from her junky car. Someone had now left her a statuette, on the passenger seat, of the Virgin Mary. Only this Mary was hot. Mass-produced down in Mexico, sexy, wanton, breasts falling out of her vamp's dress. Lisa held it, savoring the plastic contours in her hand. After she started the car, she put the figurine under her seat. A mohawked kid with a thin chain going from his nostril to his bare nipple walked past with his friend. There were other strangers all over, like personalized bacteria, which was OK. The night for most was young.

FIVE

The sky the next day in Pomona was the color of bleached bones, and a lot of buildings and homes and stores seemed to be painted orange. Lisa saw kids wearing lime green, fuchsia, tangerine, black, and cerise. Skinheads and airheads, innocents and dorks. Spray-painted on a low cement-block wall, interspersed with gang shorthand and satanic graffiti, was the message *Debbie is a dickhound,* which Lisa thought was unkind. Unfortunately she found herself recalling how she had willingly sucked the penis of Lou Greenwood, Lou Adolph, Lou Burke. And then she had allowed her body to be visited . . . she blushed faintly to herself, glad she had on sunglasses, feeling embarrassed, rather a slut. One hand on the steering wheel, wearing an embroidered linen shirt and amber necklace, brown skirt, chocolate brown stockings and lace-up shoes with a backward heel. Some touches of makeup, since she wanted to look businesslike but not butch.

She had a vaguely scheduled appointment later that afternoon with Jerry Dolphin at his office, but he'd put her off and rescheduled her so many times that she felt like standing him up. None of these meetings ever actually led to any work. Just more promises. All false.

She reached the address in Pomona, took off her shades, and got out of the car. She had bought the Trans Am used, after it had been in a wreck; since then she had given it some hard use herself. The engine was good, though she wasn't so sure about the transmission. Still, she was used to it; she liked shifting gears and accelerating, velocity for its own sake when she could find some open road.

The lawn was scorched yellow and brown; a big pastel blue aluminum trailer stood in front of a smallish pink house that was blackened and almost burned down to the ground. A dog, some kind of ugly, mutant dog, was tied to the door of the trailer, he was growling . . . and then he started barking, frightening her. She really did not like mean, threatening dogs. This dog was white, with pink skin showing through.

Zed came out, smiling at her and telling the dog to shut up, wearing tartan plaid pants and a plain white clean T-shirt with a pocket, a skinny guy with blondish hair and a darker beard. The dog behaved itself, and Lisa slipped past it into the trailer, smelling what turned out to be grilled cheese and catsup sandwiches, served by a tall, spectacularly proportioned woman named Joey—who had a completely bandaged head and face. She asked if Lisa wanted a sandwich, and there was something funny about her low-pitched voice. Lisa declined the offer, lying that she had already eaten lunch. She sat down with them, a kind of booth situation, like a minimalist diner, across from Joey and next to Zed. Lisa figured out that Joey was a transsexual.

"When the bandages come off, she'll look like Daryl Hannah," Zed proudly proclaimed.

"Cher wasn't built in a day," Joey intoned cheerfully, the only things not wrapped in gauze being mouth and eyes and a slit at nose level for breathing. It was a little creepy, but Lisa continued to look.

"I haven't seen you since you broke up with Code," said Zed. "How have you been?"

"Oh, not so bad. I was hoping to be AD on Selwyn Popcorn's new film, *Call It Love*. I got screwed out of it, though . . . and I was wondering, I remember you mentioning once some guy, some weird guy who would, like, help you get revenge?"

"Sure. Boro." Zed took another bite of his sandwich. "I don't know if you want to mess with him, Lisa. Why don't you just nod out for a few days, take a vacation in your own apartment? I've got some great new items, you can hardly keep up with the chemistry majors these days. Nonaddictive, very few side effects. If you haven't done it before, try Stairway to Heaven. That's a greatest hit. Or Obsession, if you want to have sex. Wait a second. There's also Joy Division, which is great, Heaven 17, or MC^2."

"Sometime I'll really score a pharmacy's worth from you, but right now I just want to see this Boro, see if he can come up with anything. Code says he does, what, psychic tattoos?"

"Some deep background here. Boro is way, way fucking out. He's from the Amazon jungle, and he's got all these very strange vines he grows, he eats flowers and shit. He's a flat-earth expert, I'm telling you. And his gang!"

"Listen, honey," Joey said, "you'd be better off, if you've got a hard-on against some guy, let's call him up, get him to come over here, and we'll cut off his dick and stick it in his mouth. And then when the cops come, we'll say, 'That's the way he came in!'"

Lisa laughed, liking Joey more, stubbornly intrigued, however, with the concept of Boro, more intrigued the more they tried to put her off.

Zed digressed. "There's a rumor, I mean I'm hearing it from three-four different people, that there's this new procedure they can do, they discovered it from fucking around with chimpanzees and baboons . . . they stick a thin gold wire in your brain, directly into your pleasure center . . . and then it just stays there. Unless they X-ray you or do a magnetic scan, it's just invisible, and you activate it by running a little electric current in with a remote control. It's supposed to be, uh, indescribable."

"It feels real good," Joey explained as Zed nodded, and Lisa just smiled. She remembered when Zed and an earlier partner had been selling star memorabilia, secret photos of Drew Barrymore on the toilet, or her used tampons, stolen dirty panties, all kinds of stuff that fit under the broadly defined rubric of celebrity skin. Lisa was curious about how the little pink house had burned down.

"We can't talk about that while it's under litigation," commented Zed. "Some jokers . . . well, if you really want to see Boro, I'll send you to him. Don't blame me if he turns you into a zombie biker chick with three hundred tattoos."

"Come on, he can't be so ridiculous that he can't just do some straight-up business now and then."

"Yeah, I guess he does get things done. You know, for a while I had the patent on a new kind of mouse. I bought it from some kid at USC."

"So where are all your mice?"

"Well, I've got to look that kid up sometime, get him to clone me some more. They were doing fine, then we got a new microwave . . . "

"Honey, you don't know for sure that's what did it," Joey said, her voice showing evidence of time with a speech therapist. A voice can be low and still sound feminine—it's the delivery that counts.

"Anyway, it was depressing to see all those dead mice. OK. Maybe Boro will just fill your order and that'll be it. I know he does a lot of nice jobs for the Laotians and Cambodians. Let me draw you a map."

SIX

Boro was so ugly he was distinctive, not ugly-handsome but certainly memorable, with long dreadlocks and all kinds of tattoos all over his body, symbols and signs rather than screaming skulls or lions or names. He had a motorcycle, a Harley-Davidson low-rider, and there were six other bikers hanging around with him, keeping their distance, strange dudes, moving very slowly, *very* slowly, not saying a word.

His teeth, when he smiled, looked like dentures; he wore a braided vest, no shirt, a little leather bag hung from a string around his neck. He had on very old dirty jeans and beat-up black boots. He was sitting on a sawed-in-half oil drum with a woven reed seat, as if waiting for Lisa, expecting her, the motorcycles parked near him in this odd, dusty hollow, while a ways back there was a bright green Astroturf lawn and a brightly painted green and red house, surrounded by artificial bushes, plants and flowers, as well as some blossoms and growths that seemed to be real. There was a cat that was really a sculpture, welded out of stainless steel, and what looked to be a mechanical facsimile of a big black dog.

Lisa was a little tired, and there was no way she could possibly make it to see Jerry Dolphin. Oh well, so what. She was curious but wary, keeping her sunglasses on as Boro said, "When were you born?"

She told him, and he wanted then to know the time of day. Although in obvious ways he was sort of a repulsive variety of being, she found him not without an odd little spark of charm.

"Who sent you? Are you from the government?"

"No," Lisa said. "I'm here because I've heard . . . you can do things. I want to pay you—to do something to somebody for me."

"Ah, cast a spell. You're a jilted, jealous lover."

"No. I was cheated by someone. He promised me a job, a job I really wanted, and so I did things for him, but he gave it to someone else. He lied to me."

"You prostituted yourself."

"Yeah, I did," Lisa said, his eyes or charisma or something indefinable making her not want to mince words.

"Your brother's a violinist," Boro said, lighting a cigarette, lean muscular dark golden-brown arms cording, tendons flexing, a silver engraved band on one wrist, tight little Indian beads and leather on the left. His face was clean-shaven.

Lisa nodded, sitting on a wooden crate near him, not even wondering how he knew. Her brother, Track de la Nova, was well known in certain avant-garde circles. He was brilliant, with a huge ego, a shit. She loved him dearly, even if she could hardly stand him most of the time.

Boro said, "Your oppressor—I need some of his pubic hairs to start the spell. You want minor irritation or the whole works?"

"The whole works."

"Yes, I thought you would." He smiled, and she thought that he liked her. This was all so weird, she was in it and she couldn't imagine being outside, coolly civilized, objective, in an office or at a screening, any of that again. She had taken her sunglasses off and was thirsty. She licked her upper lip, and Boro snapped his fingers at one of his gang, saying something in an unfamiliar language. The fellow went into the house and came back, still walking slowly and stiffly, somnambulently, with two cold bottles of an imported soft drink.

Guarana. Made from a rain forest berry. Something vanilla and different. It tasted good.

"I'll do his whole family," Boro said, introspectively. "That's what I feel like. Is that OK?"

"Sure," she said. Already things seemed slightly out of control. She was playing tough to please him, to play at being what she sensed he wanted her to be. But it seemed fun, a goof.

He laughed. "I like women who can be cruel. We'll get along. What do you want to pay me?"

"Money," Lisa said.

Smiling, holding his *guarana* bottle in one hand, Boro strolled over to his nearby chopper and unhooked a leather bag, bringing it back to where she sat. He opened it up and carelessly spilled out the contents onto the dusty ground in front of her. Shrunken heads, with sewn-up eyes and mouths, long hair. They looked real. One was female, with blond hair.

"Hey, Pierre," Boro called, tossing down the bag. The fellow who'd brought the carbonated beverages returned, expressionless, his eyes unblinking, terrifically pale, filthy, patches of his skin sort of bluish, clad in jeans and an ancient, tattered T-shirt, kneeling down to put the heads back in the bag. Lisa felt sickened, though afraid to show her disgust. Boro put his arm around her shoulders as she stood up. He smelled strongly of bitter chocolate, something like chili peppers, and deep, dark earth. "Come back tomorrow night."

There were several messages on Lisa's answering machine. Toni,

Jerry Dolphin's assistant, had called to say Jerry couldn't make it, something came up, but he would still like to meet with her and she should give his office a call.

"Fuck you," Lisa said without passion, eating take-out black-bean salad from a little carton with a white plastic fork.

"Hi, this is Adrian . . . I heard about Alison Hand getting to be the assistant for Popcorn. What a drag. Call me if you feel like it." Adrian Gee, whose pleasantly modulated, unmistakably gay voice cheered her up a little, just hearing it. He was a freelance writer, doing pretty well, writing on fashion, films, celebrities, whatever, for the upscale slicks. He knew all the gossip and was endlessly supportive: a good friend, but she didn't think she'd call him tonight.

Christine: "Some film festival up in Seattle wants to feature *Girl, 10, Murders Boys,* and they want us to be there and introduce it, take questions and be on a panel. They probably haven't seen it . . . I don't know. Bye."

Then another beep, and a male voice Lisa almost recognized—there was something familiar about it, the confidence—said, "We don't know each other, but I've seen you . . . and you'd probably recognize me. I'd really like to meet you, I think we could have some serious fun together, I see possibilities in you I haven't seen in anybody for a long time. I want to see if you taste as good as you look. No, forgive me. I'll be waiting for you. Put the wheels in motion. If you need money, I've got money I don't know what to do with . . . I hope that you'll call."

Who was it? It sounded very much like Roy Hardway. That face . . . she could see it, match it with the voice; she rewound and listened to the message once more. It was too weird. Wasn't he supposed to be fucking Trish Featherstone?

There was one more message: Code, saying, "Hey, I'm here, gimme a call. Let me know what's going on."

She didn't call anyone. There was an ad she had seen once, someone had pointed it out to her as amusing, or unique, existential, years ago in New York. In black and white, the shot was from above the navel to midthigh, the thighs parted but not so far as to make the vulva gape; the dark pubic hair formed a neat triangle, not really hiding the labia . . . the notable thing was the message: *I Exist.* A phone number below. And that was all. Lisa remembered it very well. The others had had full-body poses, with faces, explicit promises of dirty deeds. *I Exist.* This is my cunt.

Lisa took a shower. Once dry, she sat down on her bed with her legs stretched out. Her slightly cross-eyed Burmese cat, Casimir, came to her, wanting some attention, to be petted and massaged.

Caz was careful with his claws when she was naked, he knew the difference; he lay now on her thighs, stretching out, purring, adjusting himself to fit. She lightly caressed his back, down to his tail. She was thinking. She had a semblance of a plan. There, in her bed, she picked up the phone from the nightstand and dialed Code. When he didn't answer after three rings, she hung up just as his machine was about to come on. She'd get him later. She wanted to talk to Christine, but Christine would be able to tell from her voice that stuff was going on.

Lisa sort of wanted to play the piano, as doing so sometimes induced a meditative state that calmed her and wiped her mind clean—but right now she didn't want to move Casimir. She closed her eyes. No, she definitely didn't want to speak to any more progressive cinema aficionados, that was out. There was nothing to gain. She never thought about that project anymore. She wanted to go forward. Maybe, if it really was Roy Hardway, she should fuck him, or pee on him, satisfy whatever creepy or semicreepy desires he had. It was hard to know what was the correct and gainful move.

After some time Caz roused himself, stretching and yawning, going off to attend to some feline errands, check his bowl, and Lisa got up, also yawning, reaching up as if to touch the ceiling above. She had had plenty of piano lessons but no great talent; still, it had been fun to accompany Track until he got too good. She enjoyed the tactile sense of her fingers on the keys. The dexterity that had been arduously drilled into her had a memory of its own, in her hands, independent of her conscious mind. She played softly, halfway to Debussy, somewhere near easy Poulenc.

Just before midnight she called Code. She told him she needed a favor, and decribed it to him. He had to call her back. It took about twenty minutes, but then he said it was all set up.

"What's this all about?"

"Trust me."

He just laughed. "You too," he said, and laughed some more.

SEVEN

In her dream, she was high on a cliff above a beach and ocean she'd never seen in real life, blue sky and panoramic view as if the Andes were right next to the sea, she was at a tremendous height, it was beautiful, she was in awe . . . but then things changed, and she was in her own apartment. Looking at the Turkish rug in the living room, which her father had purchased in Ankara. She lifted up this rug and found a trapdoor. She opened it and saw wooden stairs, leading down to where? To what? She was afraid, but also rather excited, adventurous . . . she turned her head and saw a row of skulls across the closed piano lid. The room was lit by candles, it was different, it had changed, and now her first wish was to escape. A huge scimitar was raised up, ready to flash down in an instant—

She awoke. She was sweating, her pulse was racing. Her cat, who usually slept all tangled up with her, was down at the foot of the bed, sitting in an Egyptian position, observing her with half-open eyes. When she started to speak to him, he turned and jumped off the bed.

The worst part of the dream was the trapdoor. It was ridiculous, but she had to check, make sure it was not there under the rug.

EIGHT

OK. Reality, so to speak.

There needed to be at least one man about forty, and as it turned out, Lisa got two in that range. Code introduced them to her as Ralph and James. They were actors, struggling actors. Code drove them all in the borrowed van. He didn't know what it was all about, but he was enthusiastic. James and Ralph seemed more dubious, and Ralph gave indications of not thinking fifty bucks apiece was enough. They were types. Lisa didn't recognize them, but they had actors' voices, presence of a sort. She was hopeful they'd be fine. They wore suits and ties. Lisa, meanwhile, had on black-rimmed prop eyeglasses and the most unassuming dress and shoes she had been able to find.

It was early for Code. Anything before two or three in the afternoon was too soon for him to be up, but here he was. Lisa appreciated his help. James seemed oblivious and obedient, but Ralph had to be reassured several times that she was not going to steal anything; he kept trying to figure out the appropriate potential legalese. Impersonation of federal officers. Were immigration agents really federal officers? Lisa said, for no particular reason, "I think that's just the Secret Service, or the FBI." Icy silence, then Ralph went on: unlawful entry, criminal trespass, what else? He asked James, but James just shrugged.

The routine of the household was pretty familiar to Lisa. To make sure none of the family was home now, Code had called and asked to speak to Veronica (Lou's wife); and then, claiming to be a cousin from Connecticut (they did exist), to the son, Jonathan. No, Mrs. Gonzales said, she could take a message, but no one would be available until later in the day.

Flashing a phony badge, Ralph led the way. As soon as Mrs. Gonzales answered the door she was cooked. They all came inside. Ralph's irritable, overbearing manner was perfect, he said they were from immigration and had a report some Salvadorans were in the house. Lisa knew that Mrs. Gonzales's English was not so good, it had its limits; her nineteen-year-old daughter's was better, but she was very timid and shy. They were going to search the house, Ralph said severely, and Mrs. Gonzales protested, concentrating on Ralph, while James went upstairs and Lisa slipped away down the hall. It would be Ralph's job to keep the woman away from a telephone until they were ready to leave. Code stayed out in the van, keeping the motor running, ready to honk if anyone drove in.

Lou was at the studio; Veronica was most likely at the gallery she owned on La Brea, near Melrose. Maybe Veronica didn't like to give her husband blowjobs anymore (Lisa had this impression) but for someone in her mid-forties or so, she didn't look too bad. Ash blond hair (no doubt to solve the problem of gray), maybe or maybe not a little eyelid work with the surgeon's scalpel, Lou never said—Lisa didn't have enough status to be the recipient of such confidences, because of her position, the very fact she was trying to make it, as well as her youth. Veronica went to some kind of trainer, or a personal trainer visited her, Lisa wasn't sure. Was Veronica intelligent, given her interest in art? What did that mean?

Jonathan, twenty-four, lived in Glendale, back from a year in France.

The other offspring, Celia, was herself away in Israel on some fellowship, maybe working on a kibbutz, planning to write a paper about it when she was done. Lou had never talked about his children much.

Lisa knew that Lou kept the door to his study locked. That was where he read scripts late at night, or watched films on his VCR, if he felt like doing such a thing (new product, of course, he had screened on the lot). Lisa had come here once and fucked him while the Gonzales mother and daughter (the husband was dead) attended a wedding somewhere. Veronica had been out of town as well.

Code had called someone today, at the last minute, and come up with a skeleton key. He said it would open seventy-five percent of known locks. This one stuck a little, and Lisa had a cold moment of panic, but then it found its purchase, and she opened the door. The big leather couch in here folded out into a bed. Lou slept here sometimes, and Lisa didn't think that the sheets were necessarily changed as often as those in the rest of the house.

Yes, there were some pubic hairs in the fold-out bed. Lisa didn't think any of them could be hers—the Saturday she'd been here was a long time ago, or it seemed like it—but, just to be on the safe side, she examined each one before putting it into the envelope, making sure she selected only coils tinged with gray.

NINE

After dropping off James and Ralph, in that order—at the last moment Ralph blackmailed Lisa for twenty dollars more, saying he knew who lived there and who she was, that he'd call anonymously and inform on her—"You're an asshole, man," said Code, but Lisa paid him—and after returning the van to its owner, Code running back from dropping off the keys, smiling, blond hair that's really golden, all kinds of shades of gold . . . they stopped by Lisa's apartment and she changed her clothes, she put on some light earth-tone makeup, a little brown eyeshadow and dark brown mascara, bright fresh blood semimatte lipstick, wooden jewelry, and a sleeveless short linen tank dress, with bare legs and thong-style sandals . . . and then, with Lisa still insisting that all she'd done was collect a personal item in order to put a spell on old Lou, a story that Code politely disbelieved, they went to a restaurant on Santa Monica Boulevard at Sepulveda. After they'd been seated and had their menus, it was two-thirty in the afternoon by now, Code said, "I wish things were simpler. Remember when we were in Jamaica? If we're still around by the time we're thirty, if we're still just fucking around by then, you and I should get married . . . I know what you're thinking, but I'm careful, you can get a blood test on me anytime you want. Now tell me, are you serious? You mean this shit about casting a spell?"

Lisa shrugged. She had felt sort of romantic when he'd mentioned marriage—not that she'd ever do it, not with him, he was too undependable—and she wanted to enjoy the little shiver of sentimentality and regret, which probably wouldn't have been so poignant if they were still having sex together. He was smart, she liked his music; they could talk about things. He shared some of her anticinema, antistardom, anticelebrity feelings, yet they were both trying to make it; she had once thought she was purer but, as it turned out, she was undoubtedly worse.

"I was in a commercial with Ralph and James," said Code after a few moments. They were sharing Vietnamese food: Lisa was especially interested in a piece of fried fish with a spicy, vinegary sauce.

"What product?" she asked.

"They haven't started them yet, but it's this, uh, computerized psychiatric program. You dial it up on your touch-tone phone, and it asks you questions, with one of those mechanical voices . . . it's being offered, you see, as an entertainment service. An understanding voice in the night, at a few dollars a minute. No one says that it's really therapy—there's a big disclaimer at the end—but there really are a lot of options, it's not just Mickey Mouse."

"You played a patient?"

"Yeah. My girlfriend just broke up with me, and I'm depressed. I call up the computer. It tells me to cheer up, let's see, to get more exercise and some other stuff . . . I just remember it said to try walking two miles a day."

"It's not for L.A., in other words."

"Well, that particular suggestion isn't, but the service, I don't know, I think it might catch on. 'Let's talk about me.' And we personify these machines pretty easily; in no time at all you wonder if it likes you or not, what it really thinks of you."

"It's probably sort of like being with Freak," Lisa said, making fun of the supermodel, a little catty, and Code replied, "It's like being with anyone." He was pensive, sort of, drinking an iced coffee with condensed milk. "I talked to Adrian," he said. "He told me that Alison Hand got your job."

"Adrian should keep his big mouth shut," Lisa remarked.

"He told me about a lawyer, incidentally, if Wendy's serious about this stuff. It doesn't seem like she should be able to force me out of my own band. The Painkillers were my idea, I put the band together, but Sterling's not talking to me, so I'm sure she's fucking him, she can get him to sign anything. I was hoping we might get to do the soundtrack for an orange juice commercial."

Lisa considered giving him the phone number she'd been given by Lou Greenwood, Lou Adolph, Lou Burke. Code was certainly good-looking enough, they'd find some use for him, the techno-whorehouse atmosphere would probably really turn him on. The only thing was, he might go in and never come out. She wouldn't go back herself, though she could see how one might rationalize it to oneself.

The funny thing was, she had really liked Lou; usually it had been enjoyable to spend time with him. He knew things, he was informative, he had one of those warm, gravelly, intelligent western voices like they use as voice-overs for giant multinational PR. The sex had been ordinary but no worse. He was considerate and had gentle hands.

It was hot outside. Sunglasses went back on. There was a hum that turned circling faraway birds into police helicopters making a daylight assault; at a distance the pops of gunfire were harmless and indistinct.

TEN

The sun was going down in ultraviolet flamy orange, a spectrum of unnatural, vivid colors and a sucking wind, the streets near the address blowing torn newspapers and rolling an empty red Coke can past shards of polychromatic, brightly reflective broken glass. Lisa had stopped at a drive-in and gotten a double chocolate milk shake; as she drove she suctioned up the sweet coldness through a straw.

At first no one seemed to be around. There were a few choppers parked over by the artificial leaves of the fake hedge. Lisa carried her big leather purse, the strap over her shoulder—she felt dirty and fatalistic, both somewhat frightened and ready for the worst, for the big ugly to kiss her on the mouth. Taste of ashes, that was OK.

One of the zombies (for that's all they could be) came around from the side of the garish green and red house. He moved slowly, and slowly raised his arm to her, motioning, so Lisa followed him as he turned and walked away along a crunching gravel path. Shadows were lengthening quickly now, purplish and dark reddish brown, extinguishing the lurid vermilion light. Sweat ran down Lisa's face. She was sticky, the dress stuck to her. She was thirsty again. It seemed more humid than before.

Some distance away, she could hear voices speaking Spanish, laughter, an accordion, a dog barking—here there was silence. She and the zombie came to a greenhouse and went inside, the perfume of the flowers having an immediate, mildly intoxicating effect. There was hardly any light, so she couldn't see the plants very clearly, the colors were dimmed. . . . At the end of the long passage between exotic blossoms and vines there was a clearing, and here sat Boro, surrounded by his gang. The zombie who had led her in took his place in the line. Boro sat on a director's chair, and Lisa was glad he was not adorned with feathers or anything strange, a bone through his nose or something like that.

"It's good to see you," he said. "Why don't we get on with it? I promise, nothing will hurt."

She handed him the envelope from her purse containing the gray pubic hairs.

"Good. These will be fine. But now you must undress. Give me your necklace."

She started to protest, but said nothing. She had to fight against involuntarily showing her powerlessness and fear.

Boro, meanwhile, revealed the possession of a male figure, some kind of red wax with a skeleton perhaps made of wire, maybe twelve inches tall, with its cock sticking straight out like a broom handle. Boro kneaded some of the pubic hairs into the figure, saying some indistinguishable syllables under his breath. He draped Lisa's wooden bead necklace over his own head, and she sensed that he intended to wear it from now on, she would never be getting it back.

Reluctantly she took off her clothes. The zombies didn't really even seem to be aware of her.

"Who are they?" she asked. Boro chuckled and pointed at each one in turn.

"This is Chris. Pierre. Brian. Sean. Alvaro. And Greg." They all looked both ancient and no older than twenty-five, some maybe having expired still in their teens. Brian was particularly muscular, like a big surfer.

"Where did you find them?"

"I reanimated them," Boro said. "I'm just borrowing them for a while. They can talk and follow instructions . . . I just have to keep them supplied with a certain substance, or they fall apart. Here, rub this ointment over your body. It doesn't haven't to cover every inch, but be generous with it. Smells good, doesn't it?"

Lisa nodded. It was like before: Being naked like this, she became dissociative. The conversion of personal nakedness into impersonal nudity. A removal, a split.

Boro lit a little fire with a small bundle of kindling and sticks, adding some dried leaves and a resin that burned green-white, flaring and hissing. He pricked his finger with a sharp knife, the drops of blood falling into the flames; then he handed the knife to Lisa, without speaking, and bade her do the same. She did, cutting her left index finger more deeply than she intended, the blade was so sharp.

"I must write on you," he said, and he was so relaxed that it seemed easy, she felt languid and curious, he held her face up by the chin and began drawing, with a soft crayon, on her cheek. On her forehead. Lisa closed her eyes. Then he daubed blue paint on each of her breasts, her belly, and into her sex.

"We're almost done," he said, making a motion with his hand that caused the zombies to begin chanting a repetitive, low verse. They gently swayed back and forth. Boro handed Lisa the wax figure of Lou. "Hold him over the fire until he's just beginning to get soft. You must spit on him, and then pee on him, and then toss him into the flames. After that, you can get dressed. We'll do the rest."

Lisa followed his instructions, finding it difficult, however, after spitting, to initiate the stream of urine—only a few straw-colored droplets spattered out, but they fell onto the voodoo doll's head, and Boro nodded, smiling, one of his false teeth completely gold, an earring visible beneath a dreadlock, and he said, "That's good. Now throw him down."

As soon as she tossed the figurine into the fire, Boro, with almost inhuman quickness, plucked it out of the flames, so that it was only partly melted and distorted; apparently he did not burn his hands.

Then Boro spat on the tiny man and placed him in the jaws of what looked like a Venus flytrap.

Lisa had on her underwear, and was putting on her dress, when Boro said, rather indifferently, "When you see some results, then we can negotiate the fee. Don't worry about it. I don't have the conquistador's insatiable greed. Besides, I like you. Go home and take a bath, and don't drink any milk for a couple of days. The signs on your face . . . they disappear by the time you are home. Pierre, walk with her out."

Lisa didn't thank him, common empty politeness seemed stupid, she just looked at him, and looked at the figure, stuck upside down in the wide-open lips of the man-eating plant, glistening droplets of secretion on the slippery, brilliantly colored inner leaves.

ELEVEN

Dr. Nova was known, within his field, for having discovered (or invented) an infinitesimally tiny molecule without any conceivable medical, military, commercial, or popular implications. Other researchers continued playing around with it, under the aegis of the company for which Nova had worked, trying to find some conventional application for the heretofore useless but "beautiful" product of his unfettered imaginings.

Lisa, at nine: Her father stood in a white lab jacket as Track, the child prodigy at twelve, violently played the violin. Right there in the lab. Lisa adored her big brother then. Dr. Nova glanced over at his assistants, who were giving the music their entire attention. The place was bugged, Track told her later, and some of the assistants worked for the FBI. Track didn't like the way he looked with a violin tucked under his chin.

There was another sister, Andrea, two years younger than Lisa. She was their mother's favorite and was now in a modern-dance company, following the path that Lisa had not. Lisa had been too clumsy, injury-prone, and, by her mother's stringent standards, too fat.

At sixteen, Lisa discovered an acute natural prowess in the backstroke and joined the swim team, winning some exciting races, quitting the team the next year when the coach would not stop pushing her to develop the butterfly kick.

Suddenly Dr. Nova was in Brazil. There was a divorce. Lisa's father called her from São Paulo and invited her to come take a look at a local species of ant. In Mato Grosso.

Lisa attended the School of Visual Arts. She went from painting to photography to film. She met Christine.

Track was not on good terms with his father; they just never seemed able to talk. He treated his mother rudely, but they basically understood each other. Track had gone to Rio once, for a concert, and spent a weekend with his father and his new wife, but he'd told Lisa he hadn't had a good time. At that time he was a member of the Berlin String Quartet.

Lisa had been down there twice. She had in fact observed, with interest, the activities of those highly conspicuous ants. Her father had surprised her on the second visit, not too long ago, by having in his possession a video of *Girl, 10, Murders Boys,* which he must have gone to some expense and trouble to obtain.

Isabel, his second wife, was very nice. For some reason it had crossed Lisa's mind that Isabel had been provided by the company to care for Dr. Nova. It was not out of the question that he would accept such an arrangement as a perfectly natural, neutral-to-positive phenomenon, never giving it another thought.

TWELVE

In the morning Lisa had something like a mild sunburn all over her body. Her first thought was that it was from the ointment, but the slightly painful redness was general, not limited to the areas where the ointment had actually been spread. In the shower, the hot water stung, so she turned it down to lukewarm, and then all the way to cold, which felt pretty good.

She was tired, with an unfocused headache somewhere behind her eyes. The time spent with Boro seemed like a dream, but what memory ever really did not?

There were slim green tendrils in the bed of the grand piano, she noticed. They were connected, coming up from the soundboard, between the tautly strung wires, and she could not see where it all began.

Casimir meowed at her, a question mark, and she picked him up as an answer, cradling him in her arms, one hand under his back feet so he would feel secure. He purred. Perhaps he could sense her disquiet; nevertheless he continued to purr.

"Oh, Caz."

There were messages on her machine.

An unknown voice, female: "This is Daphne Stern." She went on to say she was from an advertising agency: Lisa's name had been recommended to them as "a young director with energy and flash." She said she'd be in a meeting most of the morning; if Lisa was interested, please call sometime in the afternoon. 822–4552.

Then, again, Roy Hardway. "I hope you understand that I don't do things like this. But I can't stop seeing your face. Your face is a sexual organ, I want to see it in a close-up. Your skin . . . mmm. I want to be there with your naked face." A long silence before he hung up.

Lastly: "Lisa Nova, Alvin Sender. We met the other night at Code's. Whether you know it or not, you've come into my sphere of influence. I think we should talk. 858–6522."

What was it that he did? She couldn't remember. She dressed hurriedly—she was going to be late for breakfast with Adrian and Christine.

This was something they tried to do every two weeks or so. Today Christine was accompanied by her boyfriend, Oriole, an actor whom Lisa didn't much like. His mood swings tormented Chris, and of course Lisa usually heard about it, so her impression of him wasn't very good. He was critical of how Christine dressed, critical of her forays into "the business" . . . though he himself wasn't exactly yet in demand. He was quirky-looking. He could seem ugly or handsome according to the light and his mood.

Adrian Gee was often (though not today) accompanied by his longtime lover, Brad, a curiously unambitious but intense fellow who worked at a cutting-edge architectural firm. The two lived together in Long Beach. Adrian, born in San Jose, was half Chinese.

He was wearing, this morning, a white canvas sailor shirt that set off his golden complexion and the perfect teeth of his generous smile. Christine had on a unitard with a sarong-style miniskirt, while Oriole was dressed all in black.

There was sliced fruit on a platter: kiwi, mango, papaya, strawberries, orange sections, and pineapple. A pot of Sumatran coffee and some fresh croissants.

Adrian, who treated Lisa most of the time like an adorable child, told her that last night, at some awards dinner, her old friend Lou had been stricken by an unstoppable nosebleed and forced to leave the event. Cocaine was out of fashion in favor of the more exotic chemical compounds now on the scene, but the swift rumor was that Lou had stuck with the white powder, wearing out the mucous membranes of his nose until they just broke down.

Lisa stopped herself from putting cream in her coffee, remembering what Boro had said about milk. Somebody mentioned that it looked as though she'd been out on the beach. She smiled and said something noncommittal, thinking instead of Lou with a big red stain down his front.

Oriole was talking about the usual pretentious things—he had gone to Yale, though he'd never gotten a degree—and today Lisa found him more insufferable than usual, maybe because her sunburn stung.

Somebody was waving at her. Adrian nudged Lisa's arm. She looked across the room and saw Jules Brandenberg, who'd directed her in *The L.A. Ripper*. Fast on his way to becoming another Wes Craven, Jules's latest hit was *Abra-Cadaver*. Lisa waved back, wondering if he actually remembered her name. He was leaving money, preparing to go. Standing up, with his companion. Since Brandenberg was still gazing over, smiling, Lisa decided to go see if he had anything particular in mind.

"It's Lisa, isn't it?" he said.

"Yeah, it is."

"I'm casting for a new project . . . do you think you might be free?"

"I don't know," she said. "What is it, *L.A. Ripper II*? Can I be killed again?"

"This is something different. It's called *My Evil Twin*. *Ripper II* is still way back in preproduction—I haven't got a director nailed down yet. It needs a script doctor something bad." He laughed. He had wire-rimmed glasses, a receding hairline, a barely grown beard. He looked OK.

"So you're just producing it, is all, the sequel?"

"Yeah."

"Why don't you consider a woman director? I've done a film in New York, with no budget, that people didn't hate."

"You're serious. Cool. Sure, I'll be happy to take a look—now, what about *My Evil Twin*? You say yes right now, Monica'll pencil you in. That's completely separate from if I like your other work."

"OK. How do I die?"
"You really care?"

THIRTEEN

At Code's, Lisa couldn't believe it, Freak was in the bed, masturbating with some dildolike device. How gross. If it was attention-seeking behavior, it was stupid, because Code couldn't even see her. He was playing his electric guitar for a change, the monster riff for "No Fun" over and over again, altering a foot pedal here and there. A minimalist all-day sucker of a song. Freak's pubic hair was dark brown, in contrast to her platinum blond head; she had on a peach-colored lacy half slip up over her pelvis. Lisa was fairly certain Freak was trying to prove some point to Code, something was going on between them; maybe this was why he kept on playing the guitar.

It sounded good to her. Lisa went to his amp and took off her jacket, dark brown flannel with golden stars, she used to wear it a lot when she went out with him in New York. She smiled at him; he barely acknowledged her, but she could tell he was glad she'd come by. She wanted to use his phone, but that could wait.

In the meantime, she played a game that they used to play—he kept playing the riff, varying an emphasis here and there, a dynamic, while she slowly altered the sound by turning the tone knobs or messing with the effects box, adding echo and distortion, turning the midrange down to three and boosting the bass and treble to nine. Adding some superflange. A bite of fuzz.

In the old days, she might have played an assigned part on the synthesizer, but right now it was better just with guitar. Code had been in a band called Lepers Sing and played guitar and sang, but things were different now. If Wendy's lawyers kicked him out of the Painkillers, though, maybe he'd put on another style.

About twenty minutes later, after fooling around with feedback for a while, Code ceased.

"Hey, that was fun," he said, and this might have been a joke, since the song he'd jammed on for so long was "No Fun."

Freak, without either of them noticing, had put on some clothes and left. She was gone, anyway.

"What does Alvin Sender do?" Lisa asked as they shared a can of Coke.

"He does business. Sells shit. Lies. Runs scams. Why?"

"He left a message on my machine."

Code said, "Let me guess. There's this rumor going around—that there's this bootleg porno video of Nastassja Kinski that Roman Polanski once did, for kicks. Now, I doubt it. But I heard that there's this fabulous whorehouse where they can come up with Madonna look-alikes—"

"That's easy."

"—or blasts from the past, from Lauren Bacall to Veronica Lake. Boys, too. James Dean. Montgomery Clift. Fuck the stars. Now, I've seen, like, *Cat People,* and *Exposed,* with Rudolf Nureyev, which is really awful . . . except there's this MTV three-minute thing where Nasti dances around. There *is* a resemblance, as you know. The early Kinski. So I wonder what you've been up to. Does that answer your question about what Alvin does?"

"Shit."

"He probably wants to give you some money. Take it. You're already fucked, so you might as well get your licensing fees, or royalties, whatever."

"I didn't give anybody a blowjob or anything. Nobody touched me."

"You were just supposed to be, what, like a model?"

"Yeah. I'm kind of sworn to silence, but yeah. I thought I saw, uh, Roy Hardway—I caught just a glimpse of him."

"So?"

"He's been calling me, leaving messages. He wants me, I guess, to sit on his face."

"Do it," Code said. "He can probably help your career. A lot of people never get a chance to lay down on the old casting couch—but you seem to really be in demand."

"Shit," Lisa said. "You think I'm a total prostitute."

"We're all prostitutes. The only difference is in how shameless you are."

Before Lisa could digest this or respond, the phone rang—Code made a motion for her to answer it, so she did. It was Adrian, who said, "I thought you might be there. You know Lou's wife's art gallery? The Horizon? It's on the news, but here's what really happened: Some guy came in while everyone was occupied, or anyway no one noticed, but whoever it was left a life-sized figure. Sort of, I guess, like a Duane Hanson, remember those? Or some of those guys by Charles Ray. Anyway, so after a few minutes the figure started spinning around, I mean rotating three hundred and sixty degrees at the waist, spraying out black indelible ink. All over the walls and the paintings on the walls—it was a mixed show, with new faces, that kind of shit. Then a voice comes out of a tape recorder, warning them that the figure's going to explode. Some kind of warning siren, and a countdown, and then *blam*! It wasn't kidding, the thing blew the fuck up. Veronica and some other woman were slightly injured in the blast. Duck and cover, you know? An LAPD spokesman's saying it might be some kind of art terrorist stunt that got out of hand. Or some disgruntled artist they wouldn't represent. I thought of you—Lisa, are you still there?"

"Yeah, Adrian, I'm here."

"Do you know anything about this? I'm not doing a story, I'm not going to turn you in or anything, but I thought you seemed different this morning. Like maybe something was going on. I shouldn't even ask you, should I? I'm sorry. I could hear the explosion from my window, though. Turn on the television."

"I will. Thanks. It's not me, Adrian."

"OK. Sure. Goodbye."

"Bye."

Lisa and Code watched the coverage of the incident on TV. The weird thing was Lou's nosebleed last night, and now this—could be some artist, it probably was, there was no reason to feel sure it was the spell. Seeing the rubble, though, the firemen, suddenly it was like clouds clearing and no longer disguising the sun, and Lisa started to smile. It was, she knew, a wicked smile. Veronica was hardly hurt at all. Scratches and cuts.

FOURTEEN

There are times in your career as a person when you just start fucking up, and even fuck up on purpose. When Lisa Nova got home and saw that there were tiny crimson buds on the vine growing in her piano, she was shaken, the more so because she was already somewhat fazed by Code's attitude—before she'd left his place, he'd said, "You're up to your ass in something. You found that guy, didn't you? You think you can handle it?"

"Yeah, sure," she'd said defiantly, "look," and out of false bravado she'd picked up a publicity photo of Code, Wendy Right, and Sterling Music: the Painkillers. Lisa drew a black felt-pen *X* over Wendy's face. "There; pretty soon your troubles will be over." It was on this note that she'd left.

After a shower—her skin was not so tender now, though it still felt warm and tight—the ritual petting of her cat served to relax her; Casimir's expression made her laugh. After a trip to the kitchen, she just climbed into her unmade bed. It was only seven-thirty. Lisa told Caz, with her hand on him, that she didn't know what to do. He was real, a member of the animal kingdom: Lisa had the feeling that the things he knew, his philosophy as an animal . . . this was more how she should strive to be.

Her usual ambitions and desires seemed misguided, sordid, a bore. She sighed. The love she experienced for Casimir, by this point in their relationship pretty much unconditional, made her realize, or gave her an inkling, of what it must be like to have a baby, flesh of her flesh . . . the responsibility might be huge, but it was a bullet that at some point had to be bitten if one was to participate in the full range of human experience. She didn't want to wait too long.

She recalled, suddenly and unwelcomely, maybe suggested by a half-second shot of a perfume ad on TV—she had been disgusted by Freak, and hadn't wanted to consider it, but now couldn't help wondering what she herself looked like, God, if this story of the video was true. Lisa had done the thing for money, there was no other way to look at it. At the time it had seemed as though once it was done, it was done, and she could forget about it; if she had no recollection, then it didn't happen . . . she could train herself that way. At the same time, something about the illicitness of it had appealed to her—she simply hadn't thought it through. She hadn't, in some emotional sense, "thought" about it at all. Not at the time. And she really didn't want to now. Out of nowhere, she was absolutely certain that if there was a video, Lou had seen it, he might even have commissioned it—she was glad now, again, that she had gone to Boro, the shit that had happened seemed unplanned and unpredictable, but cumulatively, perhaps he'd feel the full measure of her willed revenge. She needed to behave like Casimir would behave. Fuck with me and you die. It was a power she had often aspired to;

maybe now, even if indirectly, she could strike back like a panther, without mercy or regret.

The traditional means of feminine violence and payback were poison and witchcraft. Since she had been compared again to Kinski, Lisa indulged herself in thinking ultrabriefly about *Cat People* (the graphic remake), in which the best part is when Nastassja, nude, chases down a rabbit at night, a predator in the woods. But Lisa didn't like to dwell too much on her appearance . . . the unlovely, round fourteen-year-old was still within her, however sleek and nearly beautiful she might have become.

Lou had told her once, after watching her walk naked to look out the window, "I like your breasts the way they are, they're perfect, but if you want them to really jump out of the screen, you should maybe have just a little augmentation job—I would pay for it, as an investment." He'd smiled then. "Producers are morons, baby, they're fixated on big tits. They're like twelve-year-old boys." Lisa had frowned at this—just because she'd been in one sleazy exploitation film, Lou always seemed to think she harbored secret dreams of becoming a big star.

Madonna had tried so hard to look like Marilyn Monroe, to invoke that dead star's luster and add it to her own, like Hitler constantly comparing himself to Frederick the Great, or Prince finding his image in an amalgam of Little Richard, Jimi Hendrix, and Sly Stone. One of Lisa's professors at art school had written a book on something like this, on fame and the use of images—the first half of the book had been absorbing, until he started trying to fit it all within the confines of his ideology. Then it got too "deep."

The professor had barely passed her. She heard later that he didn't like her film.

FIFTEEN

More and more hot sauce, red salsa, and diced green chiles. Boro and Lisa sat at a yellow-painted picnic table, shaded slightly by two palm trees and a billboard with an elaborate Virgin Mary with child. The sun was very warm. Lisa wondered how Boro could stand so much peppery fire on his tongue and in his stomach; she liked hot things too, but Boro's predilection was extreme.

She took another bite of her burrito. It pleased Boro to see her eat.

He had shown up at her home while she was making some phone calls; there seemed no reasonable alternative to accompanying him to lunch. She hadn't realized that he'd lead her so far into the barrio, but a little sense of danger was OK. No *cholo* would bother her when she was with Boro, in this she felt sure.

One funny thing he had done, before they left her apartment, he was smiling but insistent, so she let him: With an ink pen, he drew a cross on her right bicep, a cross with short little lines radiating out from it, like rays of power . . .

while on her left bicep (now tan, the sunburn had worn off and she now had an allover tan) he drew a simple jaguar, shading it in.

"This will help," he said, and then added, "I've been very busy. They're a nice family. You'll see more shit is happening to them today."

The ink marks were dark blue, like pure tattoos, and being here in a lavender print, cotton halter dress with Boro did not feel very innocent. She slipped her thongs on and off her feet, as Boro, while smoking a cigarette, saying, "We'll rest a while before having some flan," began telling her his life story, or some version of it, his "legend," as they sipped at cold Tecate beer. Lisa had on turquoise-and-gold dangling earrings and a loose skirt, no doubt already dirty, and as she watched children and local citizens go by, low-riders with their custom paint jobs, children on bicycle or foot, an old guy with a cane and a Panama hat, she realized that she didn't seem to be drawing special attention; the new tan perhaps made her pass, at a glance, for Latin. She listened to Boro without really concentrating, there in the heat, the beer's effects slowing her mind.

Some workers arrived in a pickup, laughing and talking in swift Spanish, in gunmetal blue clothing, sleeves rolled up or not, some wearing beat-up Day-Glo orange hard hats. They noticed Lisa, sure, but they seemed more interested in her parked, dusty car. They went to the restaurant's take-out window and ordered, then ate while hanging around the bed of the pickup. With the tailgate down Lisa could see shovels and lengths of shiny new pipe.

At a certain point, as Boro spoke, she found herself, while still hearing him, staring up with wide eyes at the sky and this one large formation of clouds. The clouds were gleaming white on top, where the sunlight hit, the lower halves shaded, white merging into gray, difficult to distinguish from the neighboring pale blue of the naked sky.

"I was born the son of a stonecutter, and in those days that was it. There was no way to become anything else. It wasn't such a bad job, but I was ambitious, I had all kinds of crazy ideas. See, I had heard this story about a white jaguar way off in the jungle, on the other side of the mountain—if you could ride this magic white jaguar, she'd give you all these powers, you see, man . . . what made me do it was this one time, this big ceremony, I saw the princess Xtah and I just couldn't believe it, I was mesmerized by her. She looked so perfect, so calm. Like she knew everything. Nothing could bother her, ever." Boro laughed, shaking his head. "I wanted to get next to that. So I went to this wizard, and he checked out my birth date—and then he wanted to give me my money back, he didn't want to tell me anything. Well, I was just a kid, but I knew I'd never get anywhere if I didn't find out what he knew, so I jumped on him, I cut his throat a little, and he finally talked. He said that if I rode the white jaguar, I could rule our people, I could lead them in war against the Imtecs, I would never lose. I could change a seven into a three. But if you try to cheat the jaguar, he said, you'll come to a bad end."

Boro paused, cupping his cigarette as though it might blow out in the wind, though there wasn't much of a wind, while Lisa, looking beyond him at a graffiti-covered wall across the street, heard the sounds of traffic as if from far away, she was trying to remember something, or understand, when he continued, "I was taking a big risk by going. Nobody who had ever gone out to seek this jaguar had ever come back. And once I left, I couldn't change my mind and return after a couple of days—the overseer would punish me, it would be better to be eaten by the wild animals or bitten by a snake. So I waited, I was thinking it over. The wizard, to keep me from cutting him, might have lied to me, told me anything. Then there was another special number day, and when I saw Xtah this time, after the sacrifice, as she gave the stiff-armed blessing to the young girls carrying the flowers, I was smitten, that is the only word . . . I left that night."

"How long did it take you to find the jaguar?"

"I don't know," Boro said, seeming pleased that Lisa was listening, "maybe a couple of weeks. I saw other jaguars—I had to sleep in a tree at night, to keep from being eaten. Jaguars are the worst cats in the world at climbing trees. I just had to fight with the monkeys."

He took another drink of beer. It occurred to Lisa that she didn't know a single one of her friends who would come into the barrio like this, just as no one white and sane would venture into Compton or Watts.

"The white jaguar was on the prowl around the Big Lake," Boro said. "That was what we called it. I didn't know anybody who'd actually been there, though you heard rumors—merchants and warriors, from time to time—anyway, I saw her, oh, such a beautiful animal, and *big!* A huge albino, soft as silk, the most dangerous animal in the jungle. I told myself that I mustn't act afraid. If it tore me apart, I didn't want to die cowering like a Mec.

"She probably caught my scent before she saw me, but it was daylight, a sunny day like today. The blue waters of the lake were beautiful too. I was hungry and tired, but suddenly none of that mattered—I was filled with radiant joy."

"Why didn't she eat you?" Lisa asked after a few moments, to prod him on.

"I had a very musical voice in those days, and I was handsome and young—I just kept on telling her how beautiful she was, I was so honored to be in her presence, I kept talking, approaching her very slowly, with my hands held out to my sides to show that I had no weapon. I don't really know. Later I had it figured out that this was a lucky number day for me, all the signs and influences were perfect . . . when I tried the first time, she snarled and swiped at me with her paw, but I was unafraid, in fact I laughed. She liked that, I think. It was all preordained."

"So you rode her?" Lisa said uncertainly, when his pause stretched on and on.

"I fucked the white jaguar," he said, "and lay with her; we hunted together and tore apart the prey—I thought I was turning into a jaguar myself."

Lisa flashed on *Cat People* again; the association struck her as disturbing. She shifted her seat on the wooden bench and scratched her left calf with her right big toenail, which was painted red.

"Using her claws," Boro said, "she delicately scarred me, giving me powers and knowledge—which, except for one day, I'll never forget . . . well, a few days there, bad days—other than that, I still have everything Zaqui Nima Balam ever gave me."

"The white jaguar? That's her name?"

Boro said, "That's not really what she was called. I change all the names." He sounded apologetic but playful, hard to read.

"What happened next?" Lisa asked. "You must have returned to your people?"

"Yes, I did. Zaqui was somewhat jealous, but she let me go on the condition that once every month—we had thirty-day months, with five unlucky days at the end of the year—I had to bring a young, healthy sacrifice to her, at a prearranged spot, tied to a tree. She said she preferred female flesh, because of the fatty breasts and buttocks and thighs."

"How did she communicate with you?"

"Through the eyes. We'd look at each other, for a long time, and then I would know. Do you want some flan? It's very good here."

"Sure."

"OK. Good."

With the first taste of the rich custard upon her tongue, Lisa heard Boro explain, "I was changed when I returned home. I wasn't unrecognizable, but I looked very different than before. To be brief, I made a spectacular impression, never mind how, and I took over. I made everyone afraid. I announced that I had been sent to deliver us from all wickedness, and the priesthood proclaimed that my coming fulfilled the prophecies. It was inevitable. Whenever anyone thought about it, they realized they'd been expecting me for a long time."

"Sort of like Jesus."

"Yes. A killer Christ. People were happy, and I was soon engaged to marry the princess Xtah, and we were making preparations—happily, with great patriotic joy—to conquer our neighbors and take over their wealth. But . . . there was one thing very wrong. The princess I had fallen so in love with, seeing her at a distance . . . she existed, but she was so different, she had no tranquility, she was not placid. She accepted our engagement as a political necessity, but she could tell from my manners, from certain things I said, that I was poorly born, and she hated me for this. And I discovered that the being I had viewed was her double, a perfect double whom they used for ceremonial occasions. Because such occasions were tiring and boring, and Xtah was a bitch. This double—I never did find out if she was Xtah's twin or a girl they'd snatched away because of the resemblance—this twin was retarded and mute, she could hear but she could not speak. Even so . . . it was Xtah I wanted, the more she despised me the more I was determined to impress her, I was sure I'd win her over in the end. She was just spoiled, but basically good. This was what I told myself. The qualities I had seen in the other, they were in Xtah too, eventually they had to win out. I would show off my powers. So I led us into war. Against the Bird House People."

"Were you married yet?"

"Not until we returned. Victorious, with all kinds of booty and slaves. The warriors loved me because I was invincible and, without letting them know it was magic, I made them invincible too. I confused our enemies' vision, caused their leader to be attacked by a black bird, which was a terrible omen . . . I had all kinds of tricks."

"What happened with Xtah?"

A yellow jacket was hovering near Lisa, annoyingly; she waved at it, and it fled her hand but then came right back. Boro pointed his index finger at it, mouthed a silent "bang," and the insect dropped lifeless to the ground.

"I was married to Xtah in a magnificent ceremony, and then I fucked her and fucked her, she was very hot and I thought she was liking it, but afterward she'd roll onto her side and say it hurt, that my penis was too big. I told myself that she really enjoyed it . . . the cries of pain in a woman are sometimes hard to tell from cries of pleasure . . . it's a hard thing for a man to ever know. Maybe my penis had developed a secret barb like the male jaguar has, and it only comes out inside the female."

"What about your monthly sacrifice?" Lisa asked, drinking from a glass of iced limeade the old fat woman had brought out to them without a word, taking away the flan cups and spoons.

"That went along fine for almost a year," Boro said, "and then, just before the five unlucky days, Zaqui came to me, it was time for the next sacrifice, and she said, 'Give me your wife.' That was the hidden part, I saw, of the bargain. She was jealous . . . cats can be very jealous—like your cat in your apartment. If he saw you petting another cat, talking to it in your private voice . . . he'd be, oh, *mucho furioso.*"

"So what did you do?"

"I was an idiot. Xtah still hated me; I could have kept the dummy and nobody but her family would have known the difference, and I could have taken care of them . . . what I did was, I left the twin in Xtah's place, tied to the tree. I felt terrible, for even if Xbaquiyalo was a dummy, she was innocent, she had never had an evil thought in her head, she always smiled when she saw me. I left her there and then came back and raped my wife, and once again Xtah screamed like I was murdering her. I felt ashamed that the servants could hear. She cursed me then, and said she knew that I was a sorcerer, she said I could kill her if I wanted to, or put her under a spell, but she despised me, I was a lowlife . . . she spat on the floor, which back then was the worst insult you could do. It was too late to take her out to the tree and make an exchange. The next day, going against the number—because usually during the unlucky days you just took it easy, stayed inside, tried not to get in trouble, not to cross the path of a big green snake or anything else—I said that it was unlucky for the Chavin, that we would be unexpected, and I forced the royal astrologer to announce that it was all preordained, they invented some new math to make the numbers come out right. But it was doomed.

"We got our asses kicked. My magic was gone, and I was seeing things that weren't there, that nobody else seemed to see . . . ghost warriors, I don't know. We were driven all the way back, taking heavy losses all the way. The Chavin chieftains just wanted *me,* I was famous by then . . . and my own people had turned on me, there had been rumors about the sacrifices and they had feared me, but now Xtah saw that my magic was gone, so she denounced me. I was a witch who had changed the numbers and led them all to blasphemy, and so Ahcucumatz had me put in a cage and given to the enemy, with my hands and feet cut off, my tongue ripped out, castrated . . . the Chavin kept me alive, they wanted to take me south to show me to the emperor. On the way down, following the Yellow Road, Zaqui came one night and killed whoever stood in her way, dragging me away like a dead monkey, carrying me in her mouth. At the Big Lake, Xbaquiyalo was there, Zaqui hadn't eaten her, she'd known what I was up to all along. My people were now under the administration of the Chavin . . . Zaqui came back with body parts, and Xbaquiyalo patiently sewed them on. Look," Boro said, and pulled off the bands over first his left wrist and then the right, then pulling up his pants legs to show his ankles—all the terrible scars. Lisa saw that the skin tones did not quite match.

"So how," Lisa said, her voice quavering just a little, "are you still here? And what happened to the jaguar?"

"Don't you want to know what became of Xtah? She had helped them cut me up. You can guess what she chopped off. But she was pregnant and didn't know it; later on she gave birth to twin were-jaguars. They killed her on their way out of her belly. Sort of like *Alien*, you know. And Zaqui, many years later, when she was tired and sick, was killed and skinned—the last I heard, someone had made her into a couch. A couch that still exists, with great powers, by the way. If you knew where it was . . . well, forget that. As for me, well, if I told you, then you'd know. And I kill anybody who knows. I've told you a lot, Lisa Nova, more than I've told anyone for years. I like you."

"I like you too," Lisa said. "It's very weird, but I do. I'm a little afraid of you, though."

"You should be," Boro said. "You don't act like it much, huh? That's good. Did you like the flan?"

"I liked the whole meal."

"Good," he said, almost as if he were a bit drunk, waving his hand, then holding his face in both hands for a few moments, hiding his eyes. "You go now, and I'll see you again."

Lisa nodded, although he couldn't see her, said OK, goodbye, feeling uneasy about the way his mood seemed to have just turned. His dreadlocks, his wristbands, his rings, his fading, thin-lined tattoos on ageless burnished bronze skin.

Now, as she drove in her car, the residents of the barrio all seemed to be noticing her, a stranger, and she didn't want to get stuck in traffic here in East L.A.

At a red light, she could see workers at a construction site. A man in an orange hard hat looked down from above. There was the giant echoing buzz of some machine. Then hammering noises. The honk of a horn. A blue elevator, not part of the building but a temporary external addition, began to ascend. The big noise started again, drowning out all other layers of sound.

SIXTEEN

Lisa greeted her cat, glad to deal with him on his level, directly—she didn't want to process all of this other stuff.

Daphne Stern had called her back about doing the commercial. It looked good, they wanted something stylized, she needed to meet with Lisa soon.

The next message caught her off guard, it was Code but she almost didn't recognize his voice at first, she didn't know what his problem was but it was disturbing to hear him say: "Lisa? You fucking bitch." He said it halfway as an endearment, laughing. "I can't believe it. Maybe it's just a fucking coincidence . . . if it is, it's too bizarre. Talk to me. Are you there? Hey, Caz. Meow. What's Lisa up to, man? What the hell is going on?"

Lisa stopped the machine and punched his number, more puzzled and concerned than mad. When he answered, she said, "You tell me what's going on."

"You don't know?"

"What?"

"No, I guess you don't. OK, get this: Wendy got stabbed, this nineteen-year-old hustler boyfriend of hers got mad because she wrote him checks that bounced, and so he stuck a steak knife in her chest. She's in critical condition in Beth Israel. Sterling called me . . . I guess I might wrap things up here and go back to New York. No lawsuit has been officially filed, and Sterling says we can go to France and do some gigs, he claims now he was fed up with Wendy anyway, she was just being a bitch. . . ."

"Oh," was all Lisa could say. Implicit in Code's tone was the vivid memory of how yesterday Lisa had X'd out Wendy's face in the picture of the band.

"Yeah. 'Oh.' And Adrian called me . . . the cops arrested Lou's son, Jonathan—whom Adrian knows, or he's met him a few times—supposedly he's the one who blew up his own mother's gallery. I don't know what their evidence is."

"I bet he's already out on bail," Lisa said, considering all this, wondering when something was going to happen directly to Lou.

"You *are*!" Code said. "You're an evil fucking bitch!"

"I don't have to take that kind of jazz from you," she replied.

"No, I'm sure you don't."

"Listen, I don't criticize *you*, Code. If you got in trouble, I'd stick by you without any questions."

"You would?" Code said, mock disbelievingly but realizing, perhaps, that Lisa's emotions might be a little frayed.

"Yeah, I would." She dramatically sighed.

"Uh-oh, I've got company. I shouldn't have given a key to Freak. Talk to you later," Code said, and hung up.

Lisa was trying to cope with a lot of raw information. She wished she hadn't come home. It might have been soothing to have spent some money, bought some stuff, some music or new clothes, accessories, maybe some semirare movies she meant to study, somewhere around here she had a list.

The phone rang, and she answered it at once, unthinking, maybe reflexively assuming it was Code again, or Christine. It was Roy Hardway.

"I'd like us to get together," he said in his seductive actor's voice.

"No," Lisa said. "I don't think we should."

"I—"

"What do you think you saw?"

"I saw you, I recognized something in you. . . ."

"That wasn't me."

"How do you mean that? That you were acting? I don't care. I saw you beyond all masks."

His voice, coupled with her mental image of him, was hard to resist: It was a Pavlovian, scientifically tested response. The power of the personality expressed on the big screen.

"You don't even know me."

"I do. And you know me. You do. What you've seen is what there is. Decipher it. The message is all there. It's in the eyes."

"Please don't call me anymore."

"All right," said Roy Hardway, as if thoughtfully, and hung up.

God. Jesus.

What the fuck.

The last message on the tape was from Christine, asking if Lisa was sure she didn't want to go to Seattle. It sounded like Christine wanted to, for whatever reason, and without analyzing it, Lisa called her and said OK, let's go.

Christine sounded like she wanted to talk, but some music was playing, Lisa sensed Oriole's presence, so they just ran down the plan and said goodbye.

Then Lisa erased all the messages, poured herself a glass of iced tea, put on a CD of some interesting music her brother had sent her, a piano in "just" intonation played by one of Track's friends. She was afraid, and she didn't want to be. It would be too easy to be weak, to melt. She went out onto her veranda, put her bare feet up; Casimir soon followed, jumping up onto her thighs. The noises of the neighborhood blended in with the eerie piano music. Traffic, raised voices now and then, *thump-a-thump* bass beats from young males in their passing cars.

She wondered if Jules Brandenberg would be watching *Girl, 10, Murders Boys* tonight. Well, she didn't know, it was out of her control. At least she had some work. The perfume commercial, if it came off, could lead to other things.

She refused to speculate about Boro. It wasn't worth it. She didn't want to worry about the implications of what he had said. No interpretation. No conclusions drawn. It wasn't that she was incurious about the constellation of forces active all around her, but she thought it was wisest in this case not to think too much about what to do. Thought was an impediment, a snare. It would only make her more nervous than she was. She trusted her snap judgments.

Fear, by itself, can be lived with, like teenagers worried about Armani while living in downtown Beirut.

SEVENTEEN

"I was very impressed by it. You had that visual sense of something always about to be revealed, so that even a scene that seemed neutral enough played with my expectations. I kept thinking, What is going on here? What is this all about? And I really wanted to find out. Every shot was full of the draw of the future, of possibilities suggested . . . it kept me watching. All this momentum without any of the traditional narrative props."

"I want to do melodrama now," Lisa said, wanting to get this out and have it be understood, because despite the flattery she was afraid he was leading up to saying, in one way or another, that she was too "arty" to ever do a regular film.

It had been just an impulse that had made her call Jules Brandenberg's office; at 8 P.M. she expected only a machine, she planned to leave the possibly pointless message that she would be in Seattle for a couple of days. Once she began talking to the tape, however, Brandenberg himself picked up the phone. He said he'd watched her film the night before, he wanted to talk to her about it. He hadn't realized, he said, that he'd stayed in the office so late—would she like to meet him for dinner? Or, if she'd eaten . . . Sure, she said, and he named a place, Michael's, in Santa Monica.

So, out of nowhere, she had a date of sorts. A meeting. The revelations of Boro seemed somewhat distant now . . . she was excited by the fact that Brandenberg liked her film. She took a shower and changed into what seemed a pretty basic outfit: black minidress, black tights, her studded black leather jacket, a necklace that looked like it was made from spaceship wreckage, unidentifiable bits of hardware intermingled with cobalt blue marbles encased on wire spirals, one matching earring of pseudospaceship debris with a cobalt chip, the other ear with just its three gold little rings. She put on makeup and considered trying to do something about the ink tattoos on her arms, but she couldn't wash them off, even with an alcohol swab. That fucking Boro. Oh well. Given his films, one would think that Jules would be intrigued by intimations of excess.

Now he sat across from her, in warm and generous candlelight, eating grilled free-range chicken, while she had sautéed red snapper with ginger and thyme. He was well-mannered, he seemed intellectual but he had that corrupt-to-the-point-of-innocence air that basically translated as a kind of boyishness, like he'd perfected an act of not being anywhere near as worldly and wised-up as he really was.

"I was really taken by some of the images . . . like, ah, that unusually soiled T-shirt the girl was wearing when she was out on the fire escape. The compositions were tilted, angled, cropped . . . but it didn't seem gimmicky, it contributed, with the flashing camera, to the mood of vulnerability, or sexual vulnerability. Oh, and something that I'm personally obsessed by: the lighting. Do you know Selwyn?" Jules said, looking up and smiling. Lisa had been so absorbed in listening to her work being praised that she hadn't even noticed the master, the acknowledged "genius"—he had apparently just arrived, with his party of four, and he stopped by to say hello to a fellow pro.

"This is Lisa Nova," said Jules, introducing them, and she made eye contact with Selwyn Popcorn for only a microsecond, thinking that he probably thought she was Brandenberg's equivalent of rough trade.

"I've heard your name," said Popcorn, much better dressed than she had often seen him in casual shots. "Take care, Jules," he said, putting his hand on the younger filmmaker's shoulder, ambiguous parting words and an ambiguous parting gesture that made Lisa blush. She tried to hide her loss of composure by taking a long sip of white wine.

Then, when she had regained her poise, she saw, across the room, at Popcorn's table, Lou Greenwood, Lou Adolph, Lou Burke, his wife, Veronica, the blond actor Christian Manitoba, the Australian body-model-turned actress Polly Fairchild, and a young guy with longish hair whom she didn't know.

Lou didn't see her, but the unknown guy did: He stared at her, kept staring . . . Lisa stared back, then she shifted her gaze back to pay attention to Jules, as the waiter meanwhile had taken away their plates.

Oh yeah, Lou had noticed her. She felt suddenly brazen, fuck all this, she'd like to give him the finger but it would give too much away. He'd get his, she thought, and Jules Brandenberg must have noticed something in her expression, for he reacted, giving her a strange, shy little smile.

He had a little gold earring in his left earlobe, and he was wearing an expensive olive green shirt with khaki trousers and, when he put it back on, a khaki jacket.

"I'd like to see what you could do with *L.A. Ripper II*," he said as they were on their way outside, desiring neither coffee nor dessert. "The script is all fucked up, but maybe you'll have some ideas. I know you'd probably rather do something of your own, but the sequel's got to happen, I don't have any desire . . . I'd just as soon have somebody new give it an interesting twist. Can you stop by my place on the way home, pick up the script? And I should give you one for *My Evil Twin*. You're Ramona . . . you're in the big Halloween scene. I'm in Laurel Canyon—is that too much driving for you to do?"

She followed his Porsche. It wasn't all that far. His house was something else. The gate opened electronically, letting them enter the property. The house was white and well lit, quasi–Frank Lloyd Wright. Very modernistic.

"Do you ever hear anybody talk about this new drug called Stairway to Heaven?" he asked as they went in the front door. When she said yes, he said, "I'd like to try that." Lisa decided it was a request. The interior was impressive, but she hardly noticed. She was wondering if he was going to try to get her to stay.

She stood, jacket still on, looking at his oversized TV and enormous, luxurious couch. His relative shyness had reassured her about him, and the fact that he was sensitive enough not to push it made her want to do it—not really out of desire for Jules in particular, just a generalized will to have sex.

Lisa pressed the button on the remote control, knowing that by doing so she was making a decision. When *Girl, 10, Murders Boys* came on—he'd rewound it, there it was—it all became inevitable. Besides, for some reason she didn't want to go home to her apartment tonight.

She clicked out the videocassette and put in another, a French horror film she'd heard of but never seen. *Les Yeux Sans Visage* (*Eyes Without a Face*), directed by Georges Franju, 1959.

Jules put the scripts down on the glass-topped table and said, "Want to watch that? It's a classic."

"I've heard of it," she said.

He gestured toward the couch. Lisa took off her leather jacket, shivering for just a second, then remembering the samples from the place in Bel Air, in an inner pocket . . . she got them out while he was pouring brandy, and the black-and-white film was beginning, a woman driving in the night.

"If you want to get stoned," Lisa offered, "this is a new Swiss synthetic endorphin . . . I have some samples, I almost forgot."

"Are you going to take one?"

"Yeah."

Pretty soon they were more relaxed. The brandy tasted great, it occupied Lisa as they sat together, leaning against each other, on the comfortable couch. The lights were low. Some of the stuff in the film, Lisa didn't want to see. Usually she could be clinical, but right now she shut her eyes when she thought something gross was about to occur.

Slowly, gradually, her shoes came off, then Jules was reaching up into the waistband of her tights. Like a blind man. She accommodated him, raising her buttocks so that the tights could come off.

At the end of the film, her thighs on his shoulders, she opened her eyes and saw a cloud of white doves upon the screen, flying up from the evil scientist's daughter, who had no face. Her back to the camera, dressed in white, she took off her mask, and the *jouissance* was rendered kinky. Lisa didn't make an exaggerated noise, but her voice was heard, certain muscles clenched as she felt a vast liquid warmth that spread and gave her an immense sensation from her belly outward through her limbs. The feeling passed but left a residue in her musculature, her bones. Then Jules was lying up beside her, he kissed her and she tasted herself, her juices, she let him kiss her, as a sign of appreciation she squeezed him in her arms. It would have been OK but she was satisfied enough when he showed no inclination to want to fuck, thus avoiding the delicate condom issue, fine with her. He had not once touched her breasts, and she was still wearing her short black dress.

"Call me in two weeks or so and let me knew if you have any ideas for the script," he said in a drowsy murmur before falling asleep. Lisa was reassured. She slept for an hour or two, but when she woke up to use the bathroom and heard birds singing, though it was still dark, she decided to drive home. She collected herself and was alert enough as she left (the gate swung open automatically when she reached it), but once she was actually driving through the night, she yawned until tears came to her eyes. It was good to finally reach home and be with her cat. The piano vine hadn't grown much more. Her bed seemed safer now. Caz arranged himself against her thighs, under the sheet. She left on the light.

EIGHTEEN

Daphne Stern said she wanted it to have a classical element, not classical music exactly but a timeless feeling, upscale, perfection, a stillness that would draw attention, cut through the clutter; Lisa said, "I understand."

Thirty seconds. The model was already picked out. Daphne passed over the portfolio. OK, yeah. Afterward Lisa called her brother, wondering if he'd be home in his different time zone, however (besides playing and listening to music) he spent his time. He traveled a lot with his girlfriend, a dancer who was trying to put together a multimedia show. (Which meant, as always, slides.)

Track answered the phone. "Yeah?"

"Listen, I need some music. Send me a variety, but basically kind of beautiful tone-colors, lush—it's for a perfume commercial. You'll get paid."

"I fucking better. How long, what, thirty seconds?"

"Exactly."

"FedEx?"

"Yeah."

A pause, and then he said, loud busy atonal string quartet music in the background, "So how have you been?"

"Not too bad. Things are crazy, but I might direct *L.A. Ripper II*."

"What's that?"

"What does it sound like? It's an important opportunity. I could probably get you for the soundtrack."

"I don't know if I'd want my name on something like that."

"Call yourself Joe Blow. Don't be a shit."

"OK, you're right, it's an important opportunity. Mother and Andrea will be proud."

"Fuck them. I'm in a hurry, Track, I've got to catch a plane. Send me some music."

"Perfume commercial . . . OK, I'll rack my brain. How are you getting along with Christine?"

"Don't dog me, Track."

Adrian Gee was going to take care of Casimir for the weekend. Adrian loved cats, and Caz had stayed with him before, getting along reasonably well with the house Russian Blue.

Oriole was driving them to the airport. It was Friday, the flight was scheduled to depart at two o'clock. They would return early Sunday. In the car, Lisa sat in the backseat with her bag, sleepy, from time to time closing her eyes and leaning her head back.

On the plane, Lisa took out the script for *Ripper II* and was surprised to see, after Jules had so disparaged it, that he was the only author listed on the cover.

She remembered when she and Christine had been roommates for a while in New York, subletting an apartment on the Upper West Side. One time, when they had been out walking together on the endless path straight up through the center of Riverside Park, for some reason they had hugged, they were happy about their film or something, anyway then they had held hands for a little while as they walked along. Some teenage guys had noticed them and walked toward them, calling them lezzies and queers, all you need is a good fuck, stuff like that, and it had been humiliating and infuriating to turn and see them, it was broad daylight and there were other people around, but it felt like there was some danger of, if not actual rape, then of simple assault. The three guys all looked tough, they could have beaten up the two young women in about one minute flat and then just walked away.

The assholes had felt the fear vibrations and dug it, Lisa and Christine walked on and away, the boys stayed behind to play basketball or deal drugs or something, but the incident had made a big impression at the time.

Now, airborne, Christine said after a while, "It seems like you've got a lot on your mind."

"You wouldn't believe it," Lisa said a bit helplessly.

"I know Adrian's worried about you, and I know you said you were going to do something to Lou . . . and then you managed to pick up Jules Brandenberg."

"I went to this guy," Lisa began, thinking that there was no reason not to talk about it, "I wanted to get revenge on Lou. So we put a spell on him. I don't know what's gonna happen, if he's gonna die or what, but it's happening . . . the bad thing is, some stuff is happening to me too. I'm not sure what Boro wants, but I don't trust him, he might do anything."

"I heard about Lou's son. Adrian said he's been in therapy for years, he's got a real sick thing about his mom. I don't see how that was caused by any spell."

"I know how it sounds. It's not over, though. Boro's taking his time."

"It sounds like he really bowled you over." Christine's tone was solicitous, inevitably patronizing, but Lisa didn't blame her for this. She hadn't expected Christine to understand.

At the Sea-Tac Airport, they were met by two women and a man from the film committee. Raelyn, Shawn, and Andrew. Raelyn and Shawn were lesbians. Raelyn kept looking at Lisa, she seemed to be coming on to her. Andrew was straight, one of those types to whom avant-garde art is a kind of religion. Nothing could ever be too far out or too neo-dada kindergarten for him. It was a crowded car. Raelyn's thigh pressed against Lisa's.

The skies were gray, the temperature was much lower than it had been in Los Angeles. Lisa, who had consciously decided to be sullen and unforthcoming, was worried about getting a cold.

Once in the city, the guests were checked into what seemed like a fairly inexpensive hotel and then were taken to a Vietnamese restaurant.

Raelyn, who had an avid, mobile face, said to Lisa after the spring roll appetizers had arrived, "One thing I've never understood. Why did you appear in *The L.A. Ripper*? It seems inconsistent."

Lisa shrugged. "I was a warm body," she said, unable to refrain from sounding superior, snotty even. She had on her leather jacket, a T-shirt featuring the cover for *Dread in a Babylon* (an old U-Ray album), a photo in which the dread is enveloped in a cloud of ganja smoke, and then her ripped jeans, red cotton tights. No makeup. Raelyn wore a long violet-yellow-and-rose-on-white tie-dyed T-shirt dress. A dark crewcut. She ran her hand against the grain of the short hairs on her head, looking into Lisa's eyes, unoffended by the brush-off, the gesture succeeding in making Lisa wonder what it would feel like, how silky her short hair might be.

As it developed, not only *Girl, 10, Murders Boys* was to be on the program, but also, somehow, they had gotten hold of Lisa's shorter film, *A New Asshole,* and were very pleased with themselves over the coup.

Lisa inwardly groaned at the news. What had she hoped to express in that film other than flamboyant nihilism? She didn't know. The best part was when the main character, a black teenager, says, "We vegetabilized the motherfucker," and then, obscurely, disconnected from anything, "This shit is wrong, man," and everyone carries on as before, he's not innocent, he joins in. The message of the visuals was deliberately unwholesome.

Luckily, in the theater, the questions afterward mainly concentrated on *Girl, 10,* its collective vision of simultaneity, as Lisa slouched near the microphone, her hands in the pockets of the leather jacket, trying to get as deeply inside it as she could. She felt bored and shy but also defiant, looking out at the faces of the audience—more than two hundred, maybe three. She tried to count them at one point.

"Was Yvonne Rainer an influence?"

Christine answered, "No."

To another question, Christine said, "Well, when you don't have a lot of money, you have to hope for happy accidents, because you can't do multiple takes. The mistakes that happen are never the ones you expect."

Were they consciously seeking to make a feminist film?

They looked at each other, and Lisa said, "No." She spoke slowly. "If you have your own personal ideology, it'll probably come through unconsciously, and it's more effective like that."

The questioner, an intent rounded woman with rimless glasses and another very short haircut, pressed on, saying, "Karl Popper said that ideology determines what questions are asked . . . and therefore what answers are possible."

"We can't argue with that," said Christine, and got a laugh.

"What are the differences between the two of you?" asked a young pale guy with spiky dark hair and all-black clothes.

Christine: "We're very different." She hesitated, as if about to elaborate.

Lisa put in, "She's literary and literate, and I'm not." Again, some laughter at this.

Christine said, "We like a lot of different people. For instance, I like Eric Rohmer and von Trotha, while Nova here likes Chantal Akerman and *Near Dark,* by Kathryn Bigelow, which I found way too rough."

"It's the last great vampire movie," Lisa said, which again caused some laughter. They thought she was being ironic when she was not. Her delivery probably contributed to the misunderstanding.

More about influences, but not much more, and then some questions about what they were working on next. They looked at each other, and Lisa said, "I might direct *L.A. Ripper II,*" which was again taken as a joke.

NINETEEN

In the shared hotel room, Christine was already undressed and in her bed when Lisa came out of the bathroom, slightly drunk, in her underwear, and Christine remarked, "You don't have any tan lines. When did you start going to tanning booths?"

"I don't."

"Then what? You've been hanging out on the nude beach?"

"Yeah."

"Who with?"

"Daphne Stern. She's got an allover tan too. We're hard-core sun worshipers."

"I guess." Christine turned off the light.

"Raelyn wants to show me around tomorrow," Lisa said.

"No kidding."

In the morning, Christine got up first and had showered and gone out for a walk and come back before Lisa arose and took a shower. All she could remember of her dreams was a nude man lying on a couch or something, resting, his body painted completely blue.

When she came out of the bathroom and was starting to get dressed, Christine, looking up from reading a magazine, asked, "When did you get that tattoo?"

It wasn't either of the ones on her arms, which still wouldn't wash off. No, this was on her left buttock, a finely executed, vivid red heart with a dagger through it. Lisa could only glimpse a portion of it by looking back and down over her shoulder. To really appreciate it, she had to look at herself in a mirror.

It was hard for Christine to accept that Lisa didn't know, that Boro must have done it from afar.

"You think I've gone out of my mind," Lisa said, dressed now, still stunned, horrified at being so violated, finally starting to cry, big hot tears rolling down her cheeks. Christine hugged her and tried to reassure her, and Lisa didn't cry very long. Soon she had retreated into an unseeing daze, broken only by stony-eyed minutes in which she still seemed to be studying something far away. She was frightened, and felt whipped. Christine took care of her and sheltered her, so that Raelyn, when she came by, went away thinking the two were inseparable.

At some point in the afternoon they went for a walk, and Lisa sat in a green, grassy park by a lake and watched a blue jay take a bath in a big puddle; she watched it until it flew away into a tree. She was inconsolable.

TWENTY

By the time they got back to L.A. on Sunday, Lisa was feeling a little better, having decided to confront Boro and try to call off whatever he had put in motion. If he could give her a psychic tattoo, there was a chance he could also take it back.

She did tell Christine more details, including the part about how she had drawn an *X* on Wendy Right . . . who might by now be dead.

Christine's theory was that Boro had hypnotized her or given her drugs, tattooed her, and then she'd forgotten. The rest was merely bizarre, if suggestive, coincidence.

When they reached her address on Fairfax, Lisa hurriedly said goodbye, kissing Christine on the cheek and rushing off, carrying her bag—Oriole and Christine waited to drive off until she was inside the front door.

As she waited for the elevator, checking through her mail, she thought of Raelyn just for a moment, because she'd seemed full of spunk, the kind of fierceness you had when you were only twenty-one . . . it seemed like Raelyn might have been a good person to go with her when she went out to Boro's, it would be nice to have some backup, a bodyguard or just a psychological ally. Now that she was back in L.A., she regretted not having done something crazy. If she'd gone to bed with Raelyn, she wondered, how different would she feel now, and would such an experience have meant she was weak or strong?

It was too bad Code was the way he was. That odd comment of his the other day, about getting married if they both reached thirty and were still fooling around . . . he could be sentimental, but he induced it in himself as a kind of a drug. His will was not to be trusted. Whenever he made a decision, he was sorry later, buyer's remorse, he inevitably felt an attraction for the next Crayola color out of the box.

Her apartment had a different, empty atmosphere without Casimir. She opened the door to the veranda to let in the breeze. The vine with red blossoms now nearly reached the floor, winding down two of the piano legs. She looked under the raised lid, making sure there wasn't anything new there, an unpleasant insect or piece of meat. There was nothing but the flourishing vine, growing without water or soil.

The phone rang, and instead of letting her machine take it, Lisa moved quickly to pick it up.

"Hello?"

"Lisa, it's Lou. Will you talk to me?"

"What do you want?" she said, sitting down, curious but sounding suspicious, wanting to hear what he had to say but thinking that to seem innocent, she should play hard to get.

"Please talk to me, Lisa. I know you must despise me, and you're right, but . . . please . . . we were friends, at least, and I don't know who to turn to . . . I need to tell someone about what's going on, I feel like I'm going crazy. My tennis buddies, the men I'm friends with through my work—you know how it is, as soon as they smell blood in the water . . . "

"They'd eat you alive," finished Lisa, and then said, with a big, complicated sigh that did not mean what Lou thought it did, "You set me up when you gave me that number."

"I gave you a connection."

"Yeah, to fuck myself. That showed what you really thought of me. A piece of ass."

"I'm sorry. I always thought of us as friends, but you stuck that fork in my leg, and I thought, well, it was up to you. A lot of people make valuable connections like that. You'd be surprised. The business is much more irrational than most people know."

"I had to pay my rent, so I did it. But you've looked at me, haven't you, Lou?"

"Lisa, I just can't lie to you today . . . I'm sorry. I've missed our talks. I didn't treat you right."

There was a brief pause, and then she said, "OK, tell me what's wrong. I want to know. I'm interested. But why can't you talk to Veronica?"

"Veronica's outside with some Guatemalans she hired, painting a giant insect on the wall of our house."

"What else is going on?" Lisa asked, cautiously.

"You heard about Jonathan and the figure in the gallery? Well, everything points to him, the forensics guys found equipment linking him to it, but Jonathan swears he didn't do it . . . and I don't think he's capable of building something like that, to tell you the truth. But since then, he told me yesterday, he keeps having this dream that his right hand has been cut off and replaced with some kind of mutant hand grown in a greenhouse, he says he can see fifty or sixty of them, growing in pots, some black, some white, some incomplete or deformed . . . and the other night, oh this is so awful, this is the worst . . . "

"I'm listening, Lou. It's all right."

"Remember when we saw you in the restaurant? I felt terrible, because there you were, and here I was with Selwyn Popcorn, and I noticed you were with Jules Brandenberg, maybe you've got something going there, but I felt terrible. I don't expect you to forgive me, but listen, it was one of those studio things; I had you down, and F.W. crossed off your name. He hired Alison Hand and there was nothing I could say, everybody'd know and I'd look bad—and anyway, it wouldn't have done any good. Robert Hand's daughter. Shit.

"So, driving home that night, pretty late—these bikers stopped me, it looked like this one guy'd been hit by a car . . . from a distance, these two guys looked pretty clean-cut, but up close, there was something weird . . . they just plain hijacked us, they took us to this old house in the Hollywood Hills, just a few minutes away but secluded, I think Tuesday Weld used to live there once, or Dennis Hopper . . . "

"What did they want?"

"They raped me, Lisa. It was just . . . beyond belief." He was all choked up. When he spoke again, he said, "They were so strange, it was like it wasn't personal, or like they were just so spaced out from drugs they weren't even human. Their hands were so cold. But they used some lubricant, some Crisco or something, so I thought I could stand it, it wasn't the most pain I've ever felt, it wasn't like breaking your leg or a kidney stone . . . but the second one, this big blond guy, he put something up me, something hot, it burned me . . . it was like Tabasco sauce in your eyes, but this was up my ass. . . .

"Since then," Lou said, "I've been jumpy, but I've been trying to handle it. It was a degrading, horrible experience . . . but I think it was like a nightmare, and when a nightmare's over, you can survive, you can forget. But Veronica . . . won't talk to me, and she started doing this project. I didn't see everything, I know they put their hands on her, and one of them emptied her purse and lipsticked her face, I mean all over, thick . . . *I* was the one who was really traumatized, and after they left, Veronica drove us home, but ever since then . . . she won't talk about it.

"I'm going crazy, Lisa. How could these things be happening? Veronica's out there . . . will you meet me, Lisa? I don't mean to screw, I'm not that stupid, I just thought—can you hold a minute? I've got another call. It might be the doctor."

Lisa waited about three seconds, then hung up. It was faintly vindicating to hear how well the spell had worked, but this was enough. She had to get Boro to stop.

Other messages of interest: Roy Hardway, again, saying, "I can understand your caution. But if you want to see me, just to talk, this is my unlisted number. 274–8081. Tell Javier your name, and he'll get me, wherever I am."

And also, in the middle of a couple of other calls from Lou: "Hi, this is Alison Hand. Look, I've heard about you, and I'd like to have a conversation. I'm at 939–4554. It might be worthwhile."

Lisa wondered what she wanted. She automatically was ready to dislike her, because Alison was two or three years younger, and had connections, and of course had what should have been Lisa's job. What could she possibly want? Lisa didn't want to hear her voice.

Lou called again now, and she let the machine take it; he said, "I'm sorry, but that was Edgar, and it took a while. Are you still home? If you want to call me back, I'm in the study." He gave the number, in case she'd forgotten.

Instead of calling Lou, she had an inspiration, considered it for a long time—changing her clothes, making a fresh pitcher of iced tea—and then, at about four o'clock, the sun outside at its brightest, she called the Beverly Hills number: 274–8081.

When Roy came onto the line, his voice was confident and friendly, obviously delighted that she'd apparently changed her mind.

A little nervously, she began, "I was thinking about you, and since you've been wanting to spend some time together, I thought maybe, well, let's see if there's really any chemistry. . . . There's someone I'm scared of that I have to see. I don't want to go alone."

"What is it, a drug deal?"

"No, but he's done a favor for me . . . and I don't trust him, he's unpredictable. I need to tell him OK, I'm satisfied, you can stop."

"I don't quite understand," he said, "but then, I suppose I don't have to."

"Do you have a gun?"

"You're serious, aren't you?"

TWENTY-ONE

Roy Hardway came by at seven-fifteen. When he buzzed her on the intercom, Lisa said she'd be right down. It had crossed her mind that if she let him come up into her apartment, he'd try to fuck her before they went anywhere else.

She had gone to a bank machine and taken out several hundred dollars. For Roy's sake, she'd put on some makeup, red lipstick, and gold retro-Madonna-style cruciform earrings. A short print dress, bare legs, the studded black leather jacket.

"Hey, Roy." She came around and got into his gleaming white Jaguar sedan.

"You look great," he said. "Where we headed?"

God, he was handsome. He was tanned, and his face had little scrunching lines that gave him the look of more character than any actor could possibly have, especially one who seemed to be some kind of nympho. He showed her the shoulder holster under his charcoal corduroy jacket.

"A thirty-eight," he said, "just like the cops. With hollow-point shells. I've been shooting since I was a kid."

"Where'd you grow up?"

"You don't know my standard bio? That's OK. North Dakota. Just outside of Fargo. My dad was a drunken bastard, the only good times we had together were out hunting, too early in the morning for him to have drunk himself mean."

"If I was going to direct you, would you give me a bad time?"

He smiled. "Because you're a woman, or because you're young and don't know anything? Listen, I'd just do my job. If you had your shit together, we'd get along fine. If you fucked up, you wouldn't be able to blame it on me. I'd do the best I could. If you were a woman and an asshole, and I realized this early on, I'd give back the money and walk away. Why? Is that what you want to do?"

"Yeah."

The sun wasn't going down yet, but it was at such an angle that it made things look jaded and bright. Concrete. Suspended wires. Telephone poles. Electric blue, carmine red automobiles. A man and a woman, holding hands, waiting to cross the busy street.

Roy Hardway displayed no fear. He drove well, and Lisa relaxed. She told him about the trip to Seattle. She told him about herself, some version that to a man like him might make sense.

"What's the exact story on this fellow we're going to see?" Roy asked after a while, when they were starting to near the vicinity.

"This will sound unreal, but he put a spell on a guy for me. I want to have him turn it off. And Boro's doing other shit . . . like he drew on me, with a pen, my own pen, and it won't come off, it's like a tattoo."

"Why did you want to put a spell on someone?"

"He double-crossed me. Isn't that enough?"

"It could be, yeah. What should I do up here?"

"Turn left."

As the Jaguar came to a halt, then pulled a little off the driveway onto the shiny greener-than-green Astroturf lawn, Roy looked around and smiled at what he saw. The choppers were parked down past the house—which Lisa had not yet been in. They knocked on that door first, but nobody answered.

"He's probably in the greenhouse," Lisa said, and so they headed back there.

The door to the greenhouse was open. Sure enough, Boro and his followers were down at the other end, where the spell had been cast. It was as if they were waiting for them. Expecting them.

Lisa suddenly was afraid, it went through her like a splash of cold electric water, and she no longer felt as good about Roy Hardway, his easy confidence and manner as he walked in seemed no protection if Boro decided to be difficult or mean.

Boro smiled, with his dentures, and said to Lisa, "You read my mind. Thank you. It's a nice gesture for you to bring me someone. I appreciate the gift." He nodded, his dreadlocks bobbing, and he leaned forward to take a hit off a long wooden pipe. He still wore Lisa's beads around his neck.

"Your name is Boro?" Roy stepped forward, staring at the zombies who lingered around, staring blankly, like delinquents on a corner skipping school. Dum-dum boys. They did not blink, and there was nothing in their eyes.

Lisa saw, off to her right, beyond some of the meat-eating plants, a pile of what looked like soft, pale, imperfectly formed human hands. The fingers occasionally quivered and moved, slowly, contracting slightly toward a phantom fist, then flexing back out. Behind her she sensed some faint movement; she turned and saw that two of the zombies had been outside and followed them in.

"Yeah, I'm Boro; who are you? Superboy, that's what you look like to me."

"Why did you give me the tattoo?" Lisa asked, rather plaintively, at this point just thinking of the pierced heart upon her buttock.

"Don't you like it? I thought you would."

"I didn't ask you to do it, and I wish you'd take it off. And I have some money to pay you. I'm satisfied with what you've done to Lou."

"I've barely started. And to take off the heart, somebody would have to rip off half your ass. My boys here, they'd like that, they like it raw. I go for deep-fried, but everybody knows what they like best. *Dirty Harry*, you see that movie? I'm talking to you, man."

Boro seemed to have a contentious attitude toward Roy, who was so much taller, a big white man with a gun who'd played cops. It was still unclear to Lisa whether bringing him along had been a good idea or not. The atmosphere was menacing, but Roy had the gun; what if she'd come here all alone?

"What *are* you?" asked Roy, as if Boro offended him, taking an attitude.

"I'm a soul eater," Boro said. He attended once more to his pipe, then, without exhaling, conspicuously nodded to the zombies to his left, at which signal every single one of them began to slowly walk forward—and from behind (Lisa looked) the other two were coming. She could smell Boro, some other, deep earthy cavelike odor, and the flowers' sickly perfume.

"Roy," she said, bringing his attention to the ones at their rear, and Roy saw them, clenched his jaw, and reached into his jacket to come out with the gun, clicking something on it, choosing to point it at Boro, who continued smiling, a hot light dancing in his dark eyes.

"Shoot me, motherfucker."

The zombies quickened, Roy narrowed his eyes, and then—*boom,* deafeningly, he fired the gun. The impact of the shot knocked Boro over backward, but then he got back up, springing to his bare feet, laughing in a snarling way, there was a hole in the front of his shirt but no blood, he made an effort and then spat the spent bullet out into the palm of his hand.

"You missed," he said as Roy shot again, and the zombies suddenly all moved very swiftly, they ignored Lisa and overwhelmed Roy. He struggled, firing thunderous rounds at nothing until the gun was empty, some glass shattering, Lisa let out an involuntary shriek as they rode him to the ground. Biting him, one of them sticking a knife right into Roy's neck from the side, sawing, digging deep, his hand and the knife overflowing red, the blood leaping out and then, after this initial spurt, just flowing steadily. . . . Lisa saw Boro smile at her, and she turned and ran. At the doorway of the greenhouse she looked back and saw one zombie disengage and rise, as if he was going to follow her—the rest were busy on Roy, who seemed to be still alive, crying out horribly. They were cutting off his head.

Boro was coming after her, saying, "Thank you for bringing me this sacrifice. Don't run. Stop for just a second; then you can go."

Lisa paused, wide-eyed, looking all around to make sure there wasn't a trap, some zombie lurking too near. Boro reached down and then walked toward her, jingling Roy's car keys, holding them so she could see.

"I saw somebody who looked sort of like you in a movie once," he said. "How would you like me to turn you into an animal? You could be a strong, sleek leopard. I was with Simon Bolívar, the great man, when he executed seven hundred prisoners. That's the way it goes. Here," he said, and threw Roy's car keys at her. She caught them and realized she was crying, a feminine response to carnage, one which she despised.

"Take a ride in the Jaguar," he said, smiling at his joke. "It's too bad for you it's just a machine, not the real one. I *own you,*" he called in a louder voice as she turned and fled.

She didn't scream, she made an exclamation, she could hardly breathe. She reached the Jaguar and opened the driver's-side door—then she did scream. There was a shrunken head on the seat. She knocked it out of the car, hating to touch it, then she got in, started the motor, and drove away as darkness fell. Frantic, speeding, talking to herself oh no oh god oh shit, it probably helped to hear her own voice, she was trembling, her leg was shaking so badly she could hardly keep her foot down on the gas.

Colored lights. Circles, rectangles, stars, and lines. Lozenge shapes. Gleams of shiny reflective steel. Keep driving. Try not to speed too much. You don't want to be stopped by the cops. Oh god. God.

TWENTY-TWO

The drive back home took long enough that Lisa became cold. It coldly occurred to her that even if she wiped her fingerprints and ditched Roy Hardway's car, once his body was found in a citrus grove or something, or if he simply disappeared off the face of the earth, she'd be linked to him by his phone records. She had faith in her ability to lie, she'd told lies and gotten away with them since she was a child—even so, she thought she'd do better later on, after some time had passed. . . . She parked the Jaguar a few blocks from her building, wiping down any surface she might have touched, on second thought leaving the car idling, in neutral, windows rolled down, a Frank Sinatra cassette playing in the deck. Someone would *have* to steal it, you couldn't miss it, kids taking it for a joyride at the very least.

She walked home quickly and threw clothes and whatever else seemed of use into her suitcase and flight bag, the two scripts from Jules—on her way out, just as she was leaving, the TV came on, spontaneously, and it looked like Boro, there in the greenhouse—she went out the door, lugged the bags to her car, and drove away.

She drove to Code's, leaving the suitcase locked in her trunk, taking her flight bag up with her in the elevator, using her key, intending to change clothes and make some calls. She was dead certain that, back in her apartment, there was now a trapdoor leading down to a new, strange room.

As she came up she heard music getting louder and louder. When she pulled open the elevator cage, she realized that Code had a number of guests, there was a spillover into parts of this floor seldom inhabited.

"Welcome, earthling," Zed greeted her, and she acknowledged his greeting, making a note to herself that Jules wanted some Stairway to Heaven, Jesus, she saw Code at the mixer, smoking a cigarette, in the NO FUN T-shirt, looking like he'd been up for days, with dirty hair, next to a black guy—it was the rapper Huckleberry. Sterling Music was doing something with the synthesizer, the first she'd seen of him for a long time, wearing his typical goggles, like a Martian. Vladimir I was playing a bass guitar while a drum program slammed out the complicated beat. Alvin Sender came up to her and said, "Didn't you get my call?" She shook her head. "You've got something on your dress," he said, and it was blood. There were other people here, people she didn't know, she excused herself from Sender and tried to get into the bathroom, on the way she saw a person who from her figure must have been Joey, her Daryl-Hannah-to-be face still evidently not quite healed, concealed by a black rubber bondage hood, as the music surged, Lisa was next in line . . . the drum program started again, they were going to do this song over and over, Lisa heard a familiar voice on a sample saying, "Do it harder"—she didn't know where he'd got it, when he'd taped it, but Code was using a sample of Lisa's voice, that motherfucker—she got into the bathroom and saw in the mirror that she was messier than she'd known. She had her bag, so she changed her dress and rubbed water over a crusty patch of dried blood in her hair. She'd have to put the stained dress in a Dumpster somewhere.

There was a phone booth on the other side of some big crates. A biracial couple were kissing, oblivious, she had to shove against the girl to get by. It wasn't a pay phone in the phone booth, there was a long cord but Code thought the phone booth was cute, it had an ambiance, usually the phone was in his bed. Lisa called Track, at two-thirty in the morning New York time. He was still awake and she told him, "I'm in big trouble. This guy's got a spell on me, he says he owns me, and tonight I saw him kill somebody."

Track said, "Go to the airport and get on the first plane. Either come here or go to Dad down in Brazil. Can you hear me? It sounds like you're in a nightclub."

"I'm here at Code's. He's making a demo of a song based on a sample of some stuff I said while we were having sex."

"Just get to the airport, Lisa. Get the fuck out of there, OK?"

"Yeah, yeah, yeah."

PART 2

~

I descend
until
I touch the depths
black reflected in black black light
pollen in the dark

HAROLDO DE CAMPOS

~ ONE

Martinho Vidal's initial impression of Dr. Nova's daughter was that she was spoiled, a typical American rich girl, she seemed sullen when she got off the plane and stayed sullen, pouting, all the way in the car, driving through Rio to the house in the wealthy hill district of São Conrado, a house provided by the company and from which Dr. Nova was usually absent, as now.

Lisa looked out the window, but whether she was interested in what she saw or not, it was impossible for Martinho to tell. He wanted her to like him, but he was uncomfortable with her so far, which made him resent her a bit, for he was used to being liked. He was forty-eight years old, thickened some by the years, thirsty now, sweating when the traffic stopped, wishing he had taken off his jacket before he'd gotten in the car. It was a nice Mercedes, a company car. He sounded the horn—for no reason, but then afterward the cars in front of him began to move.

"You came here once before, yes?" As soon as he said this he felt foolish and irritated; he knew he was repeating himself, fishing for more of a response from this bored little bitch.

"I was here before, a few years ago," she said, turning to him. "I saw many things . . . that I did not really understand."

What did she mean by that? She struck him as the kind of girl who would like to be mysterious, to try to make herself interesting, and he didn't like her, she was the same age as his own daughter, but Solange was far more mature.

"You must be hot," he said. "Why don't you take off your jacket?"

Black leather. Underneath: a short skirt.

"All right."

Martinho could smell her, smell her body and the leather, some trace of perfume, as she moved around, slipping out of it, baring her arms. He looked again, unable to believe his eyes. God in heaven, she was tattooed. Like a whore. She was trying to look brazen, but she noticed his attention—so she was not yet completely without shame. Was it possible her father knew about this? No, it was not. Poor Dr. Nova. Even great men had their crosses to bear. She was a pretty girl, too. Tragically disturbed. There was probably a history of therapists and tranquilizers, special schools and lies and suicide attempts.

He became solicitous, almost without knowing it, feeling sorry for her now. He talked about Rio, the Botanical Gardens, and Copacabana Beach, more as a soothing ointment than to inform. She seemed to be listening to him. She would be alone at the house, with the cook and the maid, for three days, until Dr. Nova arrived; he was tied up in the laboratory in the jungle, way north, near Boa Vista. Special plant alkaloids, that's all Martinho knew. This poor creature. He wondered if she had a disease.

Once inside the gate, the air immediately felt cooler. It was shady, there was water spraying up out of the fountain, and when they got out of the car they were greeted not only by Celina, the black Bahian woman Martinho's age who ran the house and whom Lisa recognized (they hugged), but by another American girl he knew from the research site, a redhead, Martinho could not remember her name. "Caitlin," she introduced herself. Well, she was obviously here to show Lisa around, she could translate and ease the strangeness.

They went inside. It was a beautiful house. Yes, Martinho gathered, the tentative plan for tomorrow was still for Solange and some of her friends to accompany Lisa Nova north a couple hours up to Buzios, a beach famous for its perfection, "if that sounds agreeable—?" This Caitlin was professionally friendly and very organized, he could tell. He wouldn't know whether to tell Solange to expect her along or not. Caitlin must have just arrived herself this afternoon.

Martinho was relieved. He had anticipated having to hang around here, maybe even sharing dinner, so as to keep Lisa entertained. Now that this seemed unnecessary, he found himself wishing to linger nonetheless. Celina's cooking was excellent, and his curiosity about all of these people was aroused. When it seemed Lisa was going to her room, maybe to take a short siesta and a shower before the evening meal, Martinho excused himself and left, not before stopping to exchange a few words with Celina on the way out. Yes. In the

Mercedes, *sans* his jacket, taking off his tie, he turned the key in the ignition and once again took his pleasure in the fineness of this automobile. Then he thought about other things. His own family. His life, with its myriad cares.

TWO

In the shower, the water splashing her full in the face, on the top of her head, Lisa finally acknowledged, accepted, the full strangeness of the impressions she had imbibed, the sights and sounds and atmosphere that inescapably meant she was in a foreign country. Everything was different now: She was in Brazil.

She was so tired, so sapped of all vitality and energy for the moment, not only from the travel . . . usually she traveled well, changing time zones and weather didn't bother her, but . . . something else was troubling her, against her will she felt the pull of whatever spell Boro had put on her. Whatever he wanted of her, it was distant, she could forget about it for hours at a time . . . still it remained, some claim on her, the visible symbols manifest in the tattoos of the jaguar, the cross, and the heart.

One new symptom, it had started in New York, she was sure she wasn't imagining it or exaggerating—she felt herself constantly simmering with lust, she could resist it, but she wanted to come off with whomever she came in contact with, even the ugly ones, sometimes it seemed like anyone looking at her could tell. On the drive from the airport she'd considered fucking Martinho Vidal, and then seeing Caitlin, her red hair, Lisa'd immediately imagined them locked in a fervent sixty-nine. She was in heat, and it was a torment, it wore her out. In the shower it didn't take her long, if she moaned it didn't matter, she had to, it would have to keep her for a while. She had a fever. She was turning into an animal. Now she was hungry, all that mattered was getting some food. She cursed Boro, she hated him, knew he was influencing her from afar. Drying herself, walking into her room, she saw that there were freshly cut flowers, beautiful pale yellow blossoms next to the bed.

In New York, Track said that if it was all true, it seemed to him the key lay in the story of the white jaguar. Where one could go with that, he wasn't sure.

They had walked to the Strand bookstore, and Lisa got bored and went outside after a while. It was too stuffy in there. She sat down on a step across the street, and a black man walked by with a boa constrictor wrapped around his neck. He smiled at Lisa, so did his blond girlfriend, and Lisa wanted to go to bed with the whole menage, the serpent too. A stab of heat shot up from her ultrasensitive clit, so that there on the street, bare legs under her cotton dress, in the sultry air, she involuntarily gasped, and later had called up an old boyfriend, Rudy, hoping he could come over and fuck her, soothe this restless desperation of the flesh.

Now, dressing in new clothes, Lisa felt temporarily calm, looking forward to the simple pleasure of eating when hungry, resolving to learn more of the language this time, and tan but not burn.

The house was on the side of a hill, above the beach, with a beautiful view—Lisa sat out with Caitlin on the deck. A maid served them iced drinks, with crushed lime slices and *cachaca*, and Lisa took a good-sized sip, quite prepared to get moderately drunk. Why not? Her father wasn't here.

The São Conrado neighborhood is south of Ipanema and Copacabana, patrolled by a private security force, lots of nice houses with views . . . but, not too far from a huge *favela*, crazily jumbled and jammed-together shacks and alleys, such poverty always nearby. At night one would hear gunshots. There were *favelas* like this all over Rio, improvised shantytowns no one could tear down, always growing, full of malnourished children and ghetto blasters and young hoodlums, it all came back to Lisa as Caitlin explained why Dr. Nova had been delayed.

"What do you do?" Lisa asked.

"I'm a botanist." Caitlin smiled.

"So . . . you work in Boa Vista, usually?"

Caitlin said yes. Maybe she too was feeling the sugar cane liquor's effect. Lisa no longer felt lust for her; she liked her better as a result. It crossed her mind to confide that she had killed someone by drawing an *X* across a photograph of that person, but she refrained. She was a murderess. It could be neither contemplated nor forgotten. She hadn't decided what she should think. At last, here came the food. A Bahian recipe, with coconut milk, coriander, and shrimp.

THREE

The blue water came up to midthigh. It felt magnetic to Lisa, as though it possessed properties she had never been able before to perceive. One hundred fifteen miles from Rio, along the Costa do Sol, the beach was quiet, idyllic, all of that. Somebody in the party had a rich parent to have a weekend house here.

Even though Lisa thought Caitlin was really not all that interesting, she would have liked it if she'd come along. But it was never a question. Caitlin brought her two swimsuits to choose from, had coffee with her, and then Solange and her friends came along and off Lisa went.

She did remember Solange. They had hung out together some when she'd been here before. The others—Tavinho, Marisa, and then, greeting them here, Flavio, Jorge, and Bianca—seemed new, all good-looking, healthy, and tan, all with at least some English, though in ordinary repartee they unselfconsciously chattered in Portuguese.

In the stylish home here where they changed, Lisa asked Solange to come into the bathroom for a moment, and felt only slightly shy about the trimming of her pubic hair. The Brazilian swimsuit didn't cover very much, and she felt naked, but they would all be as naked as she.

Tavinho was attracted to her, she could tell. He was a couple years younger, a student, tight young body, serious despite his smiles. He rubbed sunscreen on her. She asked him to.

Flavio and Bianca were a couple—Bianca looked like a model, and seemed stupid or stuck-up. Flavio was the rich kid. Jorge complained about something, Lisa couldn't quite catch what. Solange was interested in him, they flirted, Solange was enamored of him, playing it cool. He had obviously pumped iron, but he wasn't gross. He stared at Lisa more openly than the others did. Solange, in English, explained that Lisa had made a film. She had actually seen it, it turned out. Lisa felt a new affection for her father, finding out something like this, that he'd actually shown off her work.

Marisa was political. Lisa liked something about her, instinctively, but sensed in return some disdain. In the unbelievably clear water, Lisa thought: This is a vacation. The cloudless azure sky, the white sand—this was what people worked all their lives for. She walked through the little waves, Tavinho tagging along. Maybe she'd fuck him. He thought she was a sophisticated, avant-garde little New York bitch with an attitude, and he liked this, it appealed to him a great deal. She could read his mind. This made for the illusion that he was sincere.

He had spent two years at Stanford, he told her.

"*Que bom,*" she said, mocking him, flirting with him. He was sweet and his English was good, a young Montgomery Clift type. She splashed him. Tavinho splashed back, and followed her when she swam out a bit, you could look down through the turquoise and see the sand and shells and rocks and unconcerned fish, the only worry was if her skimpy swimsuit would survive.

"What does the jaguar on your arm mean?" he asked, brave now that they were away from shore. Some scuba divers surfaced, fifty yards or so away.

"It gives me power," Lisa said, realizing for the first time that this might be literally true. They swam parallel to the beach. You couldn't swim in Rio. The water there was all fucked up. Tavinho (Solange had mentioned, earlier) was going to be an astronomer. Or a physicist? One of these.

Back around the ice chest, with a blue and yellow umbrella for vague shade, they drank cold beers and ate shrimp off toothpicks, shrimp that had been soaked in some sort of peppery vinegar solution. Bianca had been topless for a while, but now she put on a lavender T-shirt over her smallish breasts. It looked like Jorge had a pretty big unit there within his wet black bikini-style trunks. Solange ran a finger along his thigh. He still seemed in a bad mood, or perhaps constitutionally sulky as part of his concept of *machismo;* Lisa couldn't tell. The other males seemed more enlightened than that. The cold beer tasted good, especially with the shrimp. Marisa was without a partner, unless Tavinho had been hers; in any case, she didn't seem to mind. Now Marissa took off her top and leaned back, narrowing her eyes against the sun.

Tavinho dared rub an unsolicited ice cube on the back of Lisa's neck, and she let him, it felt good. She turned to him and smiled. Flavio said, "Don't go back to the city tonight. Stay here. There's room."

Flavio's house (his father was a big industrialist in São Paulo) was made of rose stucco, with vines and flowers and a terrace overlooking the rocks and sea. Lisa was impressed. Inside, a large screen showed Elvis Presley, the sound low, with Portuguese subtitles. It was one of those musical numbers where nothing quite matched, he lip-synched badly while one saw saxophones and trumpets, hearing only strings and a Hawaiian guitar.

Out on the terrace, the help served drinks: Flavio wanted everyone to have Coca-Cola and Jack Daniel's, "to Andy Warhol imperialism," he said. Jack Daniel's had been Warhol's favorite brand of booze. It made you confident, Warhol had said in one of his books, Lisa recalled. She'd been very interested in him for a while.

Because she'd been drinking, Lisa said something later about wanting to see how poor people lived here, even if this was a touristy kind of thing to do. But, being female, it would be harder, she thought.

"You want to see the *favela*?" Jorge said. "What do you think it is? It's shit."

Solange said, "They'd want to rob you. Even during the day it isn't safe."

"If you know someone, it's not a big thing," Tavinho said. "Especially during the day, when the sun's out. I'd go with you."

"Sure you would." Flavio smiled. There was something soft about him. He had blond curly hair. Everyone else was dark.

The maid's name was Giulietta. There must have been a cook someplace, but you didn't see her. Giulietta brought more drinks, and Flavio argued with Marisa about something.

Tavinho explained, next to Lisa: "It's *daimé.* Have you heard of it? It's like LSD. You extract it from the *ayahuasca* vine."

"Have you taken it?" Lisa asked in the shadows.

"No," he said, shaking his head. "I might do it sometime—Flavio says it makes you understand nature. It, ah, tells you things you can't find out any other way."

"And Jorge?"

"He says it makes you lose your will." Tavinho's tone was amused. Lisa imagined he knew his friends pretty well. "I'm sure your father knows all about it," he said, modestly enough.

It was twilight. All of them were half dressed. Bianca complained that she was cold. No one paid any attention to her. Giulietta brought out some plates, and then linen napkins, silverware.

They ate at about nine o'clock.

Bianca asked Lisa if she had met many film stars. She was very interested in Madonna and Drew Barrymore. Only Tavinho and Solange were not smoking cigarettes.

Lisa realized, looking into her nearly empty drink, now mostly melted ice, that she had to have her cat shipped down here, she needed him. She wondered, with great seriousness, if there were many obstacles to this, and if it was in Caz's best interest.

When it was time to go to sleep, she was paired with Solange. A half hour later, when she thought Lisa was asleep, Solange crept out. Lisa was in a room right off the terrace, which extended around two sides of the house. She could hear the ocean. It seemed to her that all the alcohol had left her mind; she felt wide awake. Solange had gone the other way, into the house, presumably to seek out Jorge. Lisa went out into the violet shadows, the ocean louder now. The cool air felt good. Her skin was slightly tender; despite the sunscreen, she had a minor sunburn. On the terrace, barefoot, she listened to the waves.

In the dark, she saw a figure, male. She stopped, remained still. He was looking at her. Her breathing slowed. The darkness was purplish and charcoal gray. Then, without being able to really see him, some rhythm, some chemical, some invisible signal told her this was Tavinho, and his silence, his stillness, struck her as beguiling.

"Tavinho," she finally whispered, her voice coming out low and hoarse. He made some movement, maybe a nod, yet still did not speak. She knew it was him.

"Como vai?" he said slowly, teasing her now with his use of Portuguese.

"Que bom," she replied gravely, and they were in complete accord. He stood up and came closer, taking his time. Then they embraced, somewhat formally, gracefully, and began to kiss. They kissed.

FOUR

On the way back to Rio, they had a slight car accident. It was the other car's fault, and nobody got too upset about it. They all got out and stood around for a few minutes. Lisa couldn't follow the conversation. The driver of the other car was a tall black man who didn't seem inclined to be pushed around, but he was reasonable, very handsome, Lisa had on sunglasses and she felt like she knew him. He glanced at her several times like he also possibly recognized her. She felt embarrassed, her lips bruised and puffy, her muscles sore from swimming and fucking.

Tavinho was in the other car, which had gone on ahead. At breakfast they had acted like nothing had happened. She knew, though, that he was in love with her, he would call her in Rio. Now Jorge and the black man were parting on friendly terms, no damage, no dents. The black man looked at Lisa again and made a little wave as they drove past him, Lisa turned and watched as they went around a curve and he was lost from her gaze.

In the midst of an explanation to Solange, Jorge said the word *Africa,* and so Lisa concluded that the black man was just over here from Kenya or Zimbabwe, or Johanesburg, but she liked Kenya somehow. She was disturbed by the force of the sexual attraction she had felt for him. It was scary, how promiscuous this spell might make her become. She wondered whether she had gone insane. In many ways that was an easier answer, and she seriously, painfully considered it, whether she might have hallucinated, suffered memory lapses, imagined things with Boro . . . she tried to give this alternative a fair shake. She pretended it was true, she was just crazy: OK, then what should she do? Psychotherapy didn't seem fast enough by a long shot—maybe electroshock treatments were the answer, run some volts through her head and see what seemed real then. Sure, right.

What had Boro said? Something about how Zaqui, the white jaguar, had ended up as a couch. But when, and where? It might have been four or five hundred years ago. Well, no, sometime after the conquest: As far as she knew, the Incas and Mayas hadn't had jaguar-skin couches. And an albino jaguar . . . that must be rare; she had never heard of it before. What good would it do her, even if it still existed and could be found? She didn't know. It was the only possibility for magic other than the ordinary selections down here, *macumba* and *candomblé,* which seemed to be awfully well trodden paths.

She said goodbye to Jorge and Solange and carried her bag into the house. Celina greeted her, asked her if she would like some lunch. Lisa said yes, and asked if Caitlin was here.

"No, she's out again, visiting the cemeteries."

Lisa looked puzzled; the black cook shrugged and smiled. It was a mystery, then. Halfway through lunch, Caitlin came in and was served a plate of spicy black beans over rice, with a small salad.

"You've been at the cemetery?" Lisa asked. She felt more poised with Caitlin now, seeing her as someone who worked for her father.

An employee. The perhaps basically vicious distinctions of class and household were beginning to sink in.

"Yes. Did you have a good time at the beach? You look like you got some sun."

"I had a good time," Lisa said, looking at her, waiting for her question to be more fully answered.

"Good." Caitlin took a bite of food. "I'm checking for a special vine that grows in certain cemeteries. So far no one has found one in a modern city . . . but I'm looking anyway. There are three or four cemeteries I should be able to see this afternoon."

"Can I come with you?" Lisa asked, after a moment of thought.

"It's pretty boring."

"I don't mind."

"OK, then, if you want to, sure."

If Lisa felt like she was including herself where she was not wanted, it didn't trouble her too much. She wanted to find out more about what Caitlin was doing, and she didn't want, at the moment, to ask a lot of questions. When she knew more, she'd know better what to ask.

Lisa yawned without covering her mouth. She hadn't slept much the night before. She wore jeans, sandals, a black-on-shiny-gold Alfred Jarry T-shirt she'd bought in New York.

Another Mercedes, with a younger Brazilian driver. He hadn't come in for lunch. Caitlin and Lisa got in the backseat, and Caitlin spoke to him in Portuguese. They were off.

Caitlin wore a white dress with flowers on it. There was a funny tension between them. After a few minutes Caitlin asked Lisa about film school, what was that like, perfunctorily, and Lisa gave her a perfunctory if rambling answer, telling about how you could get equipment easier in L.A.—Panavision, for instance, would let you use all kinds of stuff—while in New York you had to hustle for everything. . . .

The scenery on the drive, up past Ipanema, was wonderful. The driver, who with his high cheekbones looked very Indian, remained silent. They arrived at the first graveyard and walked through it, past flowers strewn on graves, past white crosses and burned-out candles, Andreas, the driver, waiting by the car, drinking from an already opened bottle of *guarana*.

Lisa looked at the names on the markers. A swarm of yellow butterflies danced around just overhead. There was a smell of smoke, a wood fire, or perhaps marijuana. One could look down and see the blue of the ocean. Nearby was a church. Apparently there was no sign of the corpsevine here. None of the characteristic little white flowers were anywhere to be seen.

~ FIVE

The next day, Lisa insisted she wanted to go to Copacabana, so she called up Solange and said, "I know it's crowded and all that, but I want to try it for an hour or so." Solange agreed, saying that you could see most of Rio on that beach sooner or later.

Tavinho had called Lisa the night before. Tonight she was supposed to go to a movie with him. She wanted a Brazilian film, in Portuguese, with a Brazilian audience. They had talked for an hour. He had spoken of the "metaphysical strangeness of existence," saying that people were always trying to break through, to feel at home in their own lives, at home in life. Lisa listened to him, feeling like she was fulfilling the typical passive role of a Brazilian girl.

Jorge and Solange drove over, and the three of them went down to the supercrowded beach. There was a lot of music, blasters putting out *sambas,* hiphop, reggae . . . there were thousands of people here. Jorge was in a good mood, looking at all the women's buttocks displayed by the tanga. Solange applied sunscreen to Lisa's belly and shoulders and thighs, they were on a big violet and crimson beach towel depicting some complicated, more or less psychedelic scene. Jorge was really very tan. *Machao.* Proud of his body, happy in it. The dreadlocked hustler beach bums assessed him and didn't bother him at all. Solange was restless, or excited for some reason, she couldn't keep still.

Lisa was animated, smiling, talking about her role in *The L.A. Ripper,* they were interested in hearing about how things worked in L.A. She described the knife with the retractable blade, the little bags of fake blood. It felt innocent, refreshing, to be talking so unguardedly, she didn't care if she seemed a little foolish or young. The crowd around them, the huge milling crowd, all the golden brown bodies, this atmosphere was exhilarating, there was always something to attract one's attention, the satisfaction of fitting in here, of having local friends of some sort, however skin-deep it all was. . . .

At some point Jorge went to get beer. Solange inclined her head to the right and said, "There are the businessmen, with their cell phones, they come to the beach and do their deals . . . over there are the gays, we have a lot of them here, some of them in drag are unbelievable. Best in the whole world. The kids from the *favelas* all come here, why not? Maybe they can steal something, get something to eat, or buy some crack. You like this song?"

"Yeah, I do."

"Gilberto Gil."

Jorge returned with the beer. He seemed to feel he'd done them quite a favor. The beer was cold, the first couple of sips tasted very good. Solange asked him a question; they got into a conversation, she sounded peevish, he barely answered. . . . During a lull, Lisa stood up and said politely, "I'm going to go for a little walk. Just down to those kites and back." She smiled, but whether they were disarmed or not, she left them. This was what, she realized now, she had wanted all along. To be alone, walking by all these people. Certainly no one would imagine she wasn't Brazilian, she pretended that she was, trying it on, to see how it would feel. She saw what there was to be seen, she was alert; at the same time she was quite self-absorbed. She drew stares, but it was all comparatively anonymous, she might even vaguely smile back at someone, it meant nothing; she had her mission, which was to walk down to the big kites, red or blue or green depictions of birds on white, shaped to demonstrate the birds' outflung wings. The sand was hot on her bare feet, she dug them in a bit, burrowing her toes some, taking her time.

It felt different from American beaches she'd known, all the near-naked bodies so terrifically vulnerable yet without more than very slight flickerings of fear in this social situation, the different bodies functioning as variations on a theme. All the cultural impediments of parents' lives, bank balance, employment, vocabulary . . . all seemed to waver and recede in the crucial physicality of these many bodies on the beach—and she felt a sheen, a glow, a radiance of the reflected collective gaze on her, in the warmth, the smell of suntan oil, as she existed in a movie, in the random moviegoing that fit together to compose the fractionated, brightly lit scene.

Then she saw him. At first she wasn't sure. It was the black man from the traffic accident. He smiled. It was obvious he recognized her. Or did he? She hardly knew what she was doing; she walked up to him and said hi.

"Como e seu nome?" he said, what is your name, and when she struggled to answer, fumbling the language, *"Meu nome . . ."* he

smiled and said, with a slight British accent, "Are you American? I'm over here from Nairobi. Sit down for a moment. My friends left me alone."

His name was Errol Mwangi. She told him she was Lisa. She thought he was dazzlingly handsome; she'd never been so attracted to a black man before.

"Are you here long?" he asked.

"In Rio? I don't know. My father works here—I'm staying with him."

"Do you want to have a drink sometime? I'm sort of at loose ends these days, just waiting, hanging around."

"Sure. When do you want to?"

"Tonight?"

"I can't."

"Well, I have something tomorrow—Friday, then?"

"Yeah, OK."

"Maybe we can see the inside of a couple of clubs. Do you want to meet somewhere?"

"Yeah, that sounds good," she said, helplessly.

"Well, then, Lisa, I'll be at the Ya Ya Club Friday at ten. There's a cover charge, but it's not much. I'll look for you at the bar. We can have more of a talk then. I'll see you, yeah?"

"OK."

Lisa stood up, sand on her haunches, brushing it off, thinking she didn't have to meet him, he'd made it an easy date to break, but she looked back at him, saw his eyes, his pensive expression breaking again into a smile, his blue trunks . . . she glanced back once more, and he was no longer there, or rather, he was standing up, shading his eyes, talking with two women in tangas and a man with a beard, the man holding a bottle of beer at chest level, then up to his lips.

The women were both tanned, nice bodies, one with her black hair in a single long braid down her back, the other wearing sunglasses, short hair, lanky and relaxed, also putting a beer to her lips. Lisa didn't look back again.

Jorge and Solange seemed not to be speaking to each other now; the change in their mood was obvious. In a few minutes Lisa suggested they leave. Jorge asked why. But then, five minutes later, he said, "Let's go." Lisa put on a tie-dyed, mostly purple T-shirt. She felt naked now, her buttocks exposed, walking back across all the expanse of sand, the boulevards, toward the car. All those white crosses in the graveyards, all those dead bodies, those skeletons, dissolving into the earth. She shivered.

Was his name really Errol? She sensed he'd lie to her without a twinge of guilt. He seemed intelligent, too, which only made it worse.

Tavinho, she suddenly thought, was too much like her. He was too knowable. She liked him, she could like him a lot, but his sensitivity, his way of thinking . . . she wasn't sure. Sometimes it was better to play dumb, even to oneself—especially to oneself!

She shivered again, from head to toe. How could she test the power of the jaguar? Maybe she could do more than kill someone with an *X* on their photograph. Yes, she rather thought she could. But no one had told her what, or how.

SIX

It had made a big impression on Alfred Nova (now most often called Alfredo) when Sandra, his first wife, told him he was inhuman. He had been shocked and hurt; he didn't think it was true. A cruel, unfair slur, but it stuck with him and troubled him, for there were certainly many times when other people's actions and motives were inscrutably mysterious to him.

Like now. He had known that there was some difficulty, yet it was vague to him, he had no conception—it was painful seeing the tattoos, to begin with, because he knew how his present wife, Isabel, however sophisticated and liberal she was, would react. Lisa was his favorite child, and the other siblings had sensed this, however fair he sought to be, but it was still difficult for him to show affection . . . with women there was sex, and they accepted this as evidence of affection, even if otherwise he seemed detached. Lisa, Lisa . . . it very nearly made him weep, the assumption was obvious: She was self-destructive, punishing herself. . . . In his study, he asked her, directly, "What's the story on the tattoos?" and she told him, with what seemed naive enthusiasm, a story he had difficulty following. He would remember and analyze every word, but while she told him about her dispute with Lou, her resort to Boro, this spell that got out of control—Nova, as he heard it all, was simultaneously conscious of all that was unsaid, the parts she'd glossed over, plus the parallel notion that the whole business was invention or hallucination—none of the extant possibilities was good.

Nova was tallish, slender, and ascetic-looking, balding in a distinguished way: the very picture of rectitude and intellect. Now that he lived in Brazil he had a tan; it was an irrationality, an example of vanity and a risk of skin cancer, but most of his life he had never been tan, and he still associated it with wealth and good looks. Isabel was naturally golden-skinned, she had to do very little to become beautifully bronzed. She too had been married once before, to an executive in the Brazilian recording industry who had died in a car accident when he drove off a cliff on the way back from his mistress's beach house late one night. Isabel had one child, Ricky, who was now in Paris, continuing his studies. He would be an economist, for the government or some big firm. His special concern, though, was the environment, and in this regard he was highly critical of the United States. His facts were incontrovertible. Ricky was pleased that he had raised Dr. Nova's consciousness in this regard. There was little tension between them, less by far than there was between Nova and Track, or between Lisa and Andrea for that matter. He had hardly known her at all.

Lisa had been the easiest for him to love. He considered himself a failure as a parent, but that disappointment was qualified by the conviction that children are basically resilient, their own animals, and that they seldom turn out how they are intended, if you send them one way they most often somehow rebel.

For many years (and still) Sandra considered Lisa to be imperfect. She was a good-tempered, imaginative child, full of curiosity, but Sandra was appalled by her impulsiveness, stubbornness, and for a long time, in contradistinction to Andrea, her tendency to roundness—Sandra was constantly telling Lisa she was too fat. Nova himself didn't see the problem. If Lisa was a little plump, he only found it more enjoyable to hug her than stiff, bony Andrea, but he had allowed Sandra to rule in this, as in so many other matters of daily life, for he certainly could claim no expertise in girls' dresses and bodies and first bras. He let Sandra enroll Lisa in dance classes she hated, let her restrict Lisa to celery and carrot sticks for days on end . . . but when Lisa bloomed, joined the swim team on her own, and absolutely refused to continue dance, Nova was on her side, and as time passed and she found her own way, he felt more pleasure in her accomplishments than in anything he'd done himself, he felt like he daren't let anyone see the true measure of his delight.

The things she thought of . . . he had no idea where they came from, what people she must have observed, how she processed the raw data to come forth with an artifact as assured and intriguing as her independent film. And now—a further reproof to Sandra, even if Sandra rarely saw her—she was so lovely, far lovelier than Sandra herself had ever been.

That's why the tattoos really disturbed him. How would others perceive them, what signal would be received?

"So you see, Daddy—I didn't *do* it!" she said, suddenly overcome, and began to cry. She didn't sob or contort her face for more than a moment . . . just a few tears rolled down her cheeks. Nova found this very hard to deal with, very hard. He was far from unmoved.

"It seems to me," he said, "there are two possibilities here. It's a complex story . . . an extraordinary story, as you must know."

"I know. It's unbelievable."

Nova resisted an urge to ask for more about her relationship with Lou, which was unclear. But maybe he could guess, or maybe he didn't really want to know.

"The first possibility, as far as taking any action goes . . . is that you're mistaken, and something else has happened—hold on—and maybe you need a psychiatrist.

"The second is that it's true, that is, you've told me the truth as far as you know, and you're a reasonably reliable observer . . . in which case . . . well, it's a long shot. But if there's any trace of this white jaguar . . . "

"Boro said she ended up being made into a couch."

"Yes. Well, we'll hire a detective, see if such a thing still exists. Antique dealers, museums . . . it's at least worth a try, don't you think? Because it may have been, on this Boro's part, a clue."

"Yes. And I thank you . . . if you want to send me to a psychiatrist, just to be on the safe side, I'll cooperate. I mean, if I'm crazy, I wouldn't know it, would I? Like, um, objectively?"

"I don't think you're crazy, Lisa," Nova said, touched, and he came out of his chair, came over to her and put his hand against her cool cheek, she held his hand tightly and pressed her face against it, closing her eyes. He could have easily improvised something on the theme of how there are strange things, strange powers, phenomena that we sense but cannot pin down . . . but he said nothing. Wordless, they were in communion.

SEVEN

As Isabel's first husband had been involved in the music business, and her brother was an executive at Polygram at the present time, she knew plenty of stories about Brazilian musicians, and Lisa had been exposed to enough music through Track that she knew the difference between, say, Caetano Veloso and Jorge Ben. Lisa had been curious enough while in New York to pay attention, and Track loved to tutor her on something new, so she knew enough, and it was still fresh in her mind, to ask plausible questions and be genuinely interested in the answers, as they ate dinner, another of Celina's Bahian-style dishes, with fish, coconut milk, *dendé* oil, and hot sauce on the side. Dr. Nova was very liberal with the *pimenta,* he liked it hot, and he relaxed when he saw Isabel and Lisa getting along.

The night before, Nova had heard from Isabel (who'd been told by Celina) that Lisa had been out until three in the morning with Tavinho Medeiros. Medeiros had at one time been a controversial name in Brazilian politics, Isabel told him. Was this Tavinho related to that branch of the family? he asked. She shrugged, and he took it for a yes.

Tonight Caitlin, perhaps discreetly not wishing to crash the family reunion, had accepted an invitation to dine with some friend up from São Paulo, someone she'd met through work. Nova appreciated the evident delicacy of Caitlin's instincts; tomorrow he'd have to find out if it was true what Lisa had told him, that there was no evidence here of the vine.

Up in the Roraima territory, in the wild area where El Dorado had for so long been thought to exist, a vine had been discovered growing in the remains of an ancient village that long ago had been burned to the ground, its inhabitants apparently slaughtered en masse; the vine had also turned up in an abandoned Spanish graveyard and at two other significant sites—one of which, it turned out, was the site of repeated massacres, of Indians by Indians, Indians by conquistadors, and vice versa. The fresh sap of this vine, when ingested in tiny amounts, provided the ingestee with a uniquely powerful experience.

The two volunteers who could talk about it afterward seemed, expressing themselves with difficulty, to believe that they had experienced someone else's memories, extremely foreign memories . . .

possibly from the bodies who had died at the spot. Three other volunteers had had very different, more decidedly negative experiences. One fellow, a German, had not spoken since and was still being treated with antipsychotics, to no apparent effect. (Naturally, he had signed a waiver beforehand.) The other two had demonstrated signs of terrific torment and screamed and struggled . . . and then remembered nothing, absolutely nothing of what had gone on in their minds. Otherwise they seemed unimpaired. The ones who remembered the effects also seemed unimpaired, and one of them wanted to try it again.

The Japanese component of Universo's research and development unit was greatly interested in the possible refinement of this substance. Dr. Nova wondered (crudely, he thought, but it was his instinctive response) if their interest had anything to do with ancestor worship and the like. The notion of a synthetic drug with which one could dare experience some jumbled portion of a mind from out of the past, however incoherent or unsettling this might turn out to be—well, the Japanese were very interested, and as a result the lab was well funded, replete with assistants and equipment. The problem now being that there just didn't seem to be much of the rare corpsevine around, and it didn't travel well at all. It lost its potency within a few hours of being cut. And it would not, as of yet, take root anywhere other than exactly where it was found.

In other words, there was a multiplicity of variables, and potential commercial gain from this vine was probably nil.

Nevertheless, Nova's prestige within the company was greatly enhanced. Once again he had found something where no one else had looked.

Tavinho telephoned. Lisa blushed slightly when told he was on the line.

She was a little nervous about having spoken to her father. Though what she had told Dr. Nova was essentially the truth as she knew it, there had been many significant omissions along the way. She had not told him, for instance, about the tattoo that had appeared on her ass while she was in Seattle. Nor had she mentioned how Roy Hardway had become zombie chow. And she had not even been able to imagine telling of her near-constant state of sexual arousal, the swollen ache she felt in her clit. But the conversation had turned out satisfactorily, she felt closer to him than in years, the blood bond was there, and no doubt those details and others really didn't add much to the picture as a whole.

EIGHT

The pervasive stink had an aspect of sickly sweetness to it, it was a complicated smell, incorporating many other factors within the dominant, deep, earthy odor of shit. Dead flowers, rotting fruit, papaya, mango . . . Lisa held Tavinho's hand, glad that she, physically, could pass for a Brazilian. Coming downhill they had passed teenagers listening to loud American rap, some of whom might be numbers runners, any of them might be thieves—Tavinho had told her about the death squads, hired by local businessmen, who cruised the downtown area at night and picked up conspicuous criminal-types or young prostitutes of either sex, at the lowest level, twelve-year-olds, kids without a home . . . they'd put a bullet through their heads. Almost every morning a few more new corpses were found. The death squads were unofficial, usually ex-military or police, maybe veterans of the years of torture and *linha dura* (hard-line) repression against whatever could be found (or invented) of the left.

It was a naive, touristy, American thing to do, to want to see the poor, and she was ashamed of her voyeurism, her curiosity, she should be handing out twenty-dollar bills or something, though that too would be patronizing, interfering. . . . She had hardly visited the rougher areas of East L.A., she had driven through Compton once, as a mistake . . . in New York, back in film school, she had been in a car with two blacks and her then-girlfriend Sukie, they had driven through areas of Harlem where it looked like a nuclear bomb had gone off; Jerome, the middle-class black from Long Island at the wheel, hadn't wanted to stop at a red light. They'd all been scared. Here too she and Tavinho got some mean stares, but no one followed them. Tavinho, serene, unhurried, casually spoke of the inflation and the decisions way back in the sixties, under the military, to opt for production but no redistribution, growth for the big companies, tax breaks, while keeping down the minimum wage.

That sound of angry blacks from L.A. promising to kill and fuck, that hard, smacking shuffling hiphop beat. Tavinho and Lisa turned a corner and came upon a group of ten young guys, two ghetto blasters on the same station—they were smoking dope, using a long bamboo bong. Tavinho greeted them, and one kid with dreadlocks replied to him, Lisa couldn't follow it, Tavinho answered, and the guy said something else, then grinned a big grin. A couple of the others laughed, one lightly punched his friend in the shoulder. The dreadlocked one wore an unbuttoned bright blue and cerise Hawaiian shirt over his café au lait skin.

"*Que bom,*" Tavinho said, and the kid gave him the peace sign. Lisa found herself smiling, as they went by—the grin was infectious—she gave him the peace sign in return and thought that he had no future at all. Nothing that anyone would consciously want or seek. Dead flowers on a garbage heap. Wasn't that a line from an ancient song by some punks?

Lisa wondered if anyone was worried yet about the disappearance of Roy Hardway. Were her name and number written down in his house? Oh well. She felt safe here. She should send postcards to Adrian and Christine. For a while now she'd been angry at Christine, holding an unspecified grudge, no doubt unfairly; she couldn't disentangle why.

Tavinho took her home after a while. Lisa felt a little bad, but then thought, Why should I? It's not like we're in love, and yet . . . she didn't want to be mean to him.

She had to let him know she had a date with someone else (Errol). He said, "I don't get jealous. That *machao* shit is so old."

When he pulled up to the gate and stopped the car, she came over to him and they kissed, innocently at first, then harder, tongue to tongue. His hand, under her blouse, located her tender breast.

When she got out of the car, she lingered for a moment, looking at his face, interested in him, not analyzing anything, feeling strangely defenseless, even sad. "Call me tomorrow, OK?"

NINE

Many years ago, at the state university in São Paulo, when he'd been a student, Ariel Mendoza had been confused with another Mendoza. They weren't related and they didn't resemble each other in the least. But the informant for the security police had pointed out Ariel . . . and he had been tortured, they wore hoods, he'd never seen their faces. Eventually they realized he knew nothing of subversive political organizations or mimeographed illegal newsletters, but once having suffered the parrot's perch, the dragon's chair, pleading as he had, seeing himself robbed of something dear—it changed him forever. When released, he did not go back to school. He eventually had to find work, but he no longer had ambition, he didn't care what he did as long as he could be left mostly alone.

He read books. Difficult books. Joyce, Musil, Proust, and Broch. But fiction, always. Once every few months he relieved the recurring minor urge in his mind and belly by visiting a whore. He moved from São Paulo to Rio de Janeiro, because in São Paulo he still ran into some people he knew, and he preferred to be a stranger, without risk. He eventually, after years of various employments, came to work for a detective agency. He was very good at following people without ever being seen, and he didn't mind waiting for many hours at a time, he was never restless or bored. He was thin, with electrical burn scars he did not want anyone to see. Except, occasionally, a prostitute. If they were disgusted, well, overcoming disgust was part of their job.

He was convinced he had cancer all through his bowels. It was pointless to go to a doctor; he would just go on until it was too late, and then he would die. They had done it to him, the specific introduction of negative energy via a cattle prod. They had actually laughed, it was a joke, as they put it in his ass. It was the worst thing they had done to him, and now, whenever he had diarrhea, or sudden, severe pains in his rectum, it was obvious what had been done. When it hurt, he resorted to heroin. The best painkiller known. They had murdered him, torturing him nine different times—senselessly, the wrong guy—and he had been a dead man ever since.

Ariel Mendoza could interact with people, he was attentive, polite, and, if suffused with an underlying melancholy, might also at times seem warm, with a sense of humor. He was very good at his job. He was the chief operative (or "research associate") of Oliveires Confidential. Manfredo Oliveires had been a lawyer; when he was disbarred, peripherally implicated in a bribery scandal, he had turned immediately (well, after a vacation during which he and his wife considered what options were available to him) to the detective business, where, with diligence, he had become highly successful. In the last few years, many of the cases involved industrial espionage, and Manfredo had an ex-CIA contact up in the United States, in St.

Petersburg, Florida, who supplied him with the latest in electronic gadgetry, from sophisticated bugging equipment to cameras that watched you from inside your TV screen. More and more information, of course, was entered into the computer. But still, in many cases, you needed a man on the street. And here, as Manfredo well realized, Ariel Mendoza was the best.

So when Martinho Vidal called him and asked for someone who could handle a delicate, possibly eccentric affair, Manfredo decided to offer it to Ariel, see if he wanted to deal with this scientist and his whims. It might involve travel, Martinho had said.

Dr. Nova received Ariel courteously, offering him a variety of beverages; Ariel went for iced maté. Nova requested that the maid bring two, and then he began explaining the nature of the proposed quest. He said (in excellent Portuguese) that he had reason to believe there might exist, somewhere in the world, a couch made from an albino jaguar skin. He did not know precisely how old this piece of furniture might be, but his guess was that it had originated in Honduras, Guatemala, or Yucatán. The obvious first focus of inquiries, it would seem, might be antique dealers or museums. Alfredo Nova shrugged.

"If it is findable, I want it found. If it can be purchased, I want to buy it. Any problems you might have with travel vouchers, expenses—you may contact me directly, it's not necessary, now that we've been introduced, to go through Vidal. This is a private matter, nothing to do with Universo. Either here in Rio or when I return to Boa Vista, I can always be reached. Naturally, I'll expect you to account for your activities and whatever you spend along the way, but I don't expect you to travel second-class or keep me informed of your every movement. If you find nothing at all, no trace within, say, three weeks, then we'll reevaluate the situation."

Ariel had a few questions. He lit a cigarette. No, Dr. Nova knew of no previous owner of this couch. In fact, he said, if Ariel heard of a large albino jaguar *skin*, perhaps made into a rug, that would be of interest as well. He realized it was an unusual assignment, Nova said.

He introduced Ariel to his daughter when she arrived late in the afternoon. Nova's affection for her was obvious, even though he was a man of natural reserve. Ariel observed her, unable to meet for more than a moment her burning dark liquescent eyes.

She rattled him a bit, just for an instant, he had no idea why. Nova informed her, in English, who Mendoza was, what mission he was about to undertake. Lisa took it all in at once, she must have known about it before. She asked, "Where will he begin?"

"Tegucigalpa," Ariel said, showing them his English. "Then Mexico City. Or, if you prefer, the other way around."

"The skin is very old," Lisa said. "Who knows? It may have been destroyed. But if there's any story of such a thing, any record . . . "

"Yes," Dr. Nova said. "A reference in an old history, anything."

"I'll see what I can find out," Ariel said, already detached, contemplating the many possible approaches, receiving the advance, in American dollars, lighting another cigarette as he said goodbye and left.

TEN

Lisa was thinking, in the taxicab, about this guy who'd been at the School of Visual Arts with her, two years older, how he'd done this half-hour documentary and sold it to London's Channel Four. Just like that he'd gotten hot, and the next thing you knew, he had a three-picture deal. She'd heard that since then he'd gotten fucked up. His first feature hadn't even been released theatrically, instead going direct to video and whatever it could do overseas. Males, though, if someone thought they had talent, tended to get that second and even third chance. If you were a woman, you could find yourself, very quickly, working as an office PA, taking people's cars to the car wash and shit like that.

She was lucky. The deal with Popcorn had evaporated, it had been a mirage, but she'd been given another break via Jules Brandenberg. She might still get a chance to impose her vision on the world. She wanted to seduce and subvert, jab a needle so irresistibly that they didn't even realize their illusions were being pricked, inflatable dolls collapsing into sad rubber husks . . . demonstrating—Tavinho's phrase—the "metaphysical strangeness of existence." Was that her wisdom? Was that something she knew well enough to illustrate via the play of colored lights and sound? If she couldn't really communicate it, maybe she could deceive them, play some tricks, fuck up their heads.

L.A. Ripper II was her big chance, if she could pull it off. Tonight, before dinner—which wasn't until about nine—she'd worked on the script. The basic premise was the same as in so many of these films: A young woman is stalked by a maniac, we see things mostly from her point of view; after the others are killed, she's the only one left. It looks hopeless. Things get worse and worse.

Lisa hadn't been so preoccupied with the screenplay that she'd been insensible to the disapproval her father and Isabel were trying not to show when they learned that she was going out this time of night. Surely, though, they knew very well that things started late in Rio. It was no big deal.

The Ya Ya Club was in Copacabana, some distance from the beach. When she got out of the cab, she saw some prostitutes; for transvestites, they were very good. She felt brazen—or rather, brave, adventurous—as she used her limited Portuguese to get into the club. Live music, a reggae band.

The lighting was red, sort of a bluish red, glints of purple . . . it didn't really change much. She was warm in here; outside it had been cool, there was an evening breeze. If Errol wasn't here, she'd have one drink and then go. The fucker, if he stood her up. Oh well, it was all material. Her eyes were adjusting to the crimson glow covering everyone, all the bodies, the mouths and eyes, the dark and lighter skin. This pseudoinfernal, easily erotic glow. The energy patterns. If you were stoned, it would be a productive place to hallucinate. All these bodies. She wasn't frightened, she was OK being here alone. It was cool, ordering a drink at the bar, using the language, putting out *cruzados*—the *caiprinha* (lime slices crushed with sugar, cachaca over ice) tasted great. The music . . . drew her attention. She found herself identifying with the keyboard player's part, it was simple—the real star was the drummer, with his little accents and offbeats, choking his hi-hat unexpectedly, expressively, once in a while getting around to eloquently smacking the center of the snare.

Someone spoke to her. Errol. He had a table, it turned out, over to the side of the band. She was glad to see him, it felt like they were already friends. She didn't know what she would have done if it had felt strange. No, he was as she had experienced him before, and she enjoyed just being in his presence, interested in seeing the elaboration of his personality, of who he was.

Power and Glory, from Jamaica, segued from "So Jah Say" into a cover of Black Uhuru's "What Is Life?"—a great song Track had once included on a compilation tape he'd sent to her, a song characterized by a stinging, smoky electric clavinet. She took another sip of the cold cane liquor and asked Errol about himself, sort of interviewing him. He cooperated, amused but seemingly telling the truth.

He was Errol Mwangi. He was a writer, a journalist, and a ghostwriter. Just now he was working on a novel. In London he'd ghostwritten a novel for some actress, using her tape-recorded memories, the diary they'd made her keep in rehab, and much that he'd simply invented, jokes that she now thought she'd made up herself. He'd been paid well, and part of the bargain was that he keep his mouth shut. When he'd seen her on the BBC, being praised for what he'd written, he found that difficult, and so he'd come down here. A publisher had given him an advance. The riots in Brixton? He'd been there, he'd covered that . . . his novel would be centered around that situation, the underside of British life.

They had another drink. He was smoking, so she asked him for a cigarette. At the break, as she was playing her part of the game, answering a few things about herself, telling about having appeared as an actress, one of the guitarists, the bass player, and one of the female backup singers came to sit down at their table. They knew Errol. Lisa just smiled and hung out, until after a while the band members went back up to play another set. She hadn't said much, but she was having a good time.

Errol's skin was so very dark.

"We could listen to some more music"—he gestured, a trifle drunkenly—"or maybe go somewhere else, hear some sambas, dance . . . "

"I danced the other night," she said. It wasn't true. She'd gone to a movie with Tavinho, but they hadn't danced.

"You did? Well . . . maybe we should do something else, then. We could go back to my room." He leaned over to her and kissed her, embraced her. She rested her head on his shoulder and sighed. The red lighting made everything different; all the shadows seemed alive. Looking up at some new people who had entered the club, Errol said something about how there were unusual people in the hinterlands, you wouldn't believe the unusual leatherwork, but she couldn't really understand, this set was a little louder than the last. She didn't think you could really dance to reggae . . . you could sway, and move your ass. That's what Sabrina, the backup singer, did. Sabrina had spoken to Lisa at the table, and Lisa had listened intently, though she had understood very little of the Kingston patois. Now, as they left, Sabrina gave her a big smile, and it felt like they were friends, like they'd known each other for years. Deceptive, beguiling impression. Lisa held on to Errol's arm.

There was a crowd outside, in the night . . . though not waiting to get in. To Lisa, it was unclear why they were gathering; not knowing the language made her feel dumb. A woman in her thirties, with an air of authority, stared openly at Lisa, looking into her eyes. She had long dark hair pulled back severely, too much makeup, false eyelashes, heavy earrings, a big cross on a chain around her neck, a low-cut top, a short black skirt, and then these little red patent leather boots. She was scary. Lisa clung more tightly to Errol, and they walked away from the mysterious crowd, which seemed to be waiting for something to happen or someone in particular to arrive.

"What's going on?"

"I don't know," Errol answered. He looked back too, he knew what she meant. "I don't know," he said again. They walked away. It was ten blocks or so to Errol's apartment. Lisa was slightly drunk. She yawned, and remembered kissing Tavinho that afternoon.

Errol's apartment was nice but messy, clothes lying around, empty bottles, newspapers, magazines, papers, and books. She sat on the bed. In a few moments Errol was next to her, touching her, their mouths were pressed wetly together, he was unbuttoning her dress. His bare chest struck her as enormously attractive, and when they were naked, lying on the pale blue sheets, she kissed his chest, lightly bit a nipple, tasting him, thinking: a big chocolate man. His mouth tasted of the sugar cane liquor, lime, and a hint of marijuana. . . .

He had very sensitive, gentle fingers. Stroking the lips of her labia, patiently, music of the nerve endings, up to touch the super-responsive place where the lips came together, and then the clit, so that she said, in a low voice, "Ohhh . . ." She would have been ready to fuck, but Errol moved so that his head was down where he could eat her, leaving it incumbent upon her to behave reciprocally, do the best she could. She looked at his penis, the throb of it in her hand, when she opened her mouth to suck it she closed her eyes. She kept hold of it around the base. It had always been a fuzzy concept to her, the notion of "giving good head." All she knew how to do was suck to please, to imagine what she, had she a cock, would like someone to do. Suction, tongue action, temperature—she did the best she could. Code . . . had liked her to suck him until her jaw was sore, until she was sick of it, while he lay on his back and stared at the ceiling; he said that was the most philosophical he ever got, the time when he experienced the most profound thoughts of which he was capable. And Lou Greenwood, Lou Adolph, Lou Burke . . . could never get hard without some preliminary sucking, though he didn't like to go down on her in return. Code had been selfish, but he'd been willing to trade places, to do whatever she wanted, for as long as she wished. Tavinho . . . just wanted to please, he was a little anxious about it, though once he got going he was fine.

What impressed her about Errol, as he fucked her, was his easy strength, the power of his body. Even relaxed, his physique seemed to radiate energy—and it now felt like he could move his penis around, independent of his hips or the rest of his body, to an extent she didn't think she'd ever known before . . . the waves flowing through her cunt drove her into hot, flesh-melting delirium, images flickered at hypervelocity, her eyes wide open, seeing visions, his face above her, all those excitable nerves firing, overfiring, like having a seizure . . . pinwheels and pulsing arrows, walk through the doorway into the secret room, all the colors at once . . . crescendo, decrescendo, an animal moan as the spent organ, in its wrapper, like a candy bar, contracted and withdrew.

In a while, perspiration beginning to cool, she left the bed to go to his bathroom and pee. When she returned, he said, "Look, you're bleeding. What happened to you?" She followed his eyes, seeing on her left upper arm, right at the mouth of the stylized jaguar, one single, dark, ruby red drop of blood. She had no idea what had caused it. It didn't hurt. The drop welled up—she touched a finger to it, then sucked the finger, tasting the salt of the blood, maybe its magnesium or zinc. A familiar flavor, bringing back some kind of inchoate, primal memory. Lisa smiled at Errol, feeling naked, young, not sure if he really liked her so very much or not.

"While you're up," he said, "would you mind getting me a beer? Why don't you have one too?"

Lisa obeyed. She didn't feel like drinking more alcohol, but she took a small sip to keep him company, reclining next to him in the bed. The jaguar bled no more. It had done Lisa some good to have come so hard. What a relief. The cells in her body had been craving the nourishment fed them by the energy released.

Errol said, "Has anyone ever told you how pretty these are?" studying and examining her breasts, hefting one as if weighing it, seeing how much of it he could hold in his hand, rubbing the erect nipple gently with his thumb. They fucked again, much more slowly, with

Lisa on top, Errol holding on to, fondling, the whole time, the soft meat of her breasts. Amiably, without too much attention, he asked her about her Brazilian friends. She didn't say much, but in between easy, slow plunges, revealed that her father worked for Universo. Conversation lapsed. He wanted to take her from behind. At first she thought he meant in the ass. No, in the cunt, with her on elbows and knees. To finish satisfactorily, though, he needed to be on top, her legs wrapped tightly around him. As the velocity reached a plateau, he pinned her knees down on the bed, which rocked and creaked . . . Errol was fucking her very aggressively now, they were both panting and drenched with perspiration, Lisa was in a daze, having completely lost all sense of time, hardly knowing where she was, her identity overflowing the boundaries of her flesh.

Soon after he had come, lying on her for a minute or two, and then going to the bathroom, Errol opened another beer, took a long swallow, and, lying on his side, his arm flung out abandonedly, he fell deeply, peacefully asleep. Lisa turned away from him in the bed. She was thinking. And then she slept, but only for about an hour. She didn't know what woke her up. In the bathroom, she saw in the mirror that her jaguar tattoo had bled again, it must have just happened, right in the mouth of the beast, one big, dark, red, unbroken drop. She checked her other arm, checked her ass: no blood anywhere else. Boy. Her face looked sleepy, sort of a blank pout . . . she could smell her sweat, her sex. She was sore.

In the entryway, the door opened, she could hear it. A lamp clicked on. Lisa came in to see who it was, ready to wake up Errol, to start yelling if it was a thief. So she was somewhat excited when she confronted the woman, who looked her up and down with open scorn, saying something Lisa could not understand. Well, she knew what *puta* meant.

The woman seemed at home here, and Lisa assumed the fact that she had a key was significant. So Lisa began to get dressed. The woman was quite pretty, even beautiful, with long hair, wearing a sexy dress . . . she could have been Miss Brazil. Errol was awake. He said, "Tereza—" and the woman interrupted him, she hadn't been too angry before, just scornful, controlled, contemptuous—now her voice rose, and she threw a glass against the wall. *Boceda*. That meant cunt. Since Lisa wasn't jealous or surprised that Errol would have other women, she found it unreasonable for Tereza to be so dramatic, so unrestrained.

Lisa was sitting down at the foot of the bed to pull on her tights when Tereza hit her. It was a punch, not a slap, and Lisa didn't expect it or see it coming; the shock of it brought tears to her eyes. Tereza was looking her right in the face now, demanding eye contact, as she spoke to her in a spiteful, vicious tone. Lisa made no attempt to listen or try to understand a word. When Errol stirred in the bed, Tereza suddenly brandished a stiletto, she must have had her hand on it in her purse. Histrionically, she seemed to threaten castration, and Errol was mad now, but frightened as well, he covered his vulnerable parts with a pillow. He kept talking to Tereza, trying to calm her down.

Tereza chose, however, to threaten Lisa with the knife, enjoying being dangerous. To intimidate, to see how much fear she could cause, Tereza held the knife very close to Lisa's face, almost touching her cheek with the point. *Puta. Piranha.* Then it seemed like she was asking, rhetorically, Do you want me to slash your face?

Lisa held up her hands, and Tereza pricked her palm, the pain bit her sharply. Suddenly, with decisiveness, Errol slapped hard at Tereza's wrist, so that the knife flew out of her hand. It hit Lisa, without seemingly cutting her, and she picked it up as soon as it fell to the carpet. Tereza rushed after her. Without thinking, Lisa rose and in a single fluid motion stabbed Tereza, hitting a rib, sliding the knife down and stabbing her again, meeting some resistance in the meat but pushing hard, hot blood springing onto her hand as Tereza screamed and the knife stayed *in.*

"Why?" Errol asked, truly not understanding, and Lisa shook her head. Errol called an ambulance. He put his pants on and tried to reassure Tereza, who was gasping and praying—Lisa walked out the door. Maybe she should have stabbed Errol instead.

ELEVEN

Across the street there was a tiny park featuring a statue of some famous man, flowers, a few palm trees, and some benches. Lisa sat there in sorrow, just letting the tears run down her face, as the paramedics and police arrived on the scene. There were many other people around, and a young couple sat on the bench next to hers, wondering what was going on . . . Lisa mourned what was happening to her, the unknown planets within the universe of her mind were colliding, wreaking havoc. She blamed the spell, she was turning into a creature she didn't know, and while not all of this was awful, at the moment the loss of control filled her with sorrow. . . . The ambulance took Tereza away, an IV in her arm. Lisa didn't think she had killed her, maybe she'd punctured a lung, but you could survive that if nothing went wrong.

A little later, when they brought Errol out, he spotted her; it must have been painful to him to have to point her out. The police came to her as the crowd murmured and stared. A policeman asked her, in English, if her name was Lisa. She said yes.

"Did you put the knife into that woman? Tereza de Souza, the dancer. Did you do this?"

"Yes."

Lisa stood, and her wrists were handcuffed behind her. She was taken away to the police station, to the jail. No one spoke any more English to her for a while. She felt serene. Gradually, however, realizing where she was, the history of how people had routinely been tortured—female suspects raped or violated with electricity—she began to tremble with fear. . . .

Lisa sat on a plain wooden chair in the interrogation room, before an old wooden table with scars, and she was conscious of her tattoos. Being American might not make a difference, she might seem accessible for anonymous revenge, something like that, fucking a black and then stabbing his other girlfriend, a stripper. . . . It was sordid, and she was helpless, nervous, sore, afraid. They had left her in this room, with the door open, only a matron to watch over her, a heavyset Indian-looking woman with an indifferent face, a face so indifferent as to be cruel. No doubt she'd seen it all. Every kind of pleading, tears, lies of betrayal. Every variety of human weakness exposed.

"Porfavor . . . onde e . . . banheiro?" Lisa asked. She had to empty her bladder, she was uncomfortable . . . she'd been working up her courage to ask.

The woman called into the hallway (*"Oi!"*) and another officer came along; it was no surprise that the door to the bathroom was left half open, the male officer outside, while the matron watched her pee.

"Muito obrigado," Lisa said, coming out, and the matron mumbled, *"De nada."*

TWELVE

It took longer than expected for Dr. Nova's connection with Universo to kick in. Lisa, in a cell by herself, had to stay in jail all weekend. She refused to eat the food, she was on a mini hunger strike. For her own private, dimly sensed reasons.

Hugging her father, she felt nine years old, faint, she thought for a flash of Mary Bell, the ten-year-old murderess, she stumbled and almost fell on her way out to the waiting car, somebody took a photo of her, only as she fully realized how truly hungry she was, how just a piece of bread would be a feast, only then did it occur to her that the sexual fever seemed to have passed, her incipient nymphomania had relented . . . maybe at the moment she had stabbed de Souza, fulfilling the omen of the bleeding jaguar tattoo.

At home in São Conrado, all she wanted at first was a piece of bread. Then, after a while, a mango. Celina, somewhat surprisingly, patted her on the shoulder and promised that all would be well.

Over the next few days Tavinho called several times, but she refused to take his calls. She was ashamed. Errol did not call, and she was somewhat hurt by this. She might have given him a chance.

A postcard arrived from Christine, saying that there had been a fire at Lou's house. It hadn't burned down all the way.

Meanwhile, Isabel, rather to Dr. Nova's helpless dismay, had contacted an *umbanda* priest she had met before, he was well-known . . . and he had thrown the cowrie shells, contacted Lisa's spirit, "like, you might say, her guardian angel," it had been explained to Nova, who said nothing to indicate disbelief. A purification ceremony was needed, they were told. Nova supposed it wouldn't hurt. This was a side of Isabel he didn't like to encourage, but now that matters with Lisa had definitely become irrational, he felt there was little choice but to indulge all this.

Lisa didn't seem to care one way or the other. She looked at the cards, sort of like a tarot deck, and slept in a room with white candles, and kept her thoughts to herself.

Tavinho showed up at the gate, but when Lisa heard this, she went into her room and locked the door. She told Isabel, "Tell him I won't see him, I don't want to talk to him. I won't come out of my room until he's gone."

Meanwhile, Lisa worked on the script to *L.A. Ripper II*. It was all clear to her now, she had plotted it out while in jail. Basic melodramatic principles. Terror and pity. Foreshadowing and payoff. A big surprise. The sex workers (whores) get the Ripper in the end. They castrate him. Caitlin faxed some of it to Jules Brandenberg, and Lisa talked to him on the phone, not a very good connection, but he was pleased, pleased too by the potential for American publicity in the trouble she'd gotten in. He wanted to know if there was anything on video of her arrest.

THIRTEEN

Ice cream. Although it was rather cool outside, there was a chill in the breeze, Ariel Mendoza wanted some ice cream to line his stomach. If it made his teeth chatter, that was OK. Tegucigalpa is situated at a higher elevation than one might think, and it can get pretty cold. Ariel had read a good deal about the Mayans, whose civilization perished, in large part, right around 900 A.D. for reasons no one yet understood. The Aztecs—and, down south, the Incas—were comparative latecomers to power, ruling for only a little more than a hundred years before Cortés (and, some ten years later, Pizarro) arrived upon the scene.

Just in what is now Mexico, the estimated population before the arrival of the Spaniards was twenty-five million people. By 1600 there were twenty-four million less. History, all well known.

He was on his way to visit the retired professor of Mesoamerican history (and advisor to the national museum) Saturnino Ortiz. Ariel had been in the city three days, had talked to several historians and antique dealers—if anyone would know anything about it, several agreed, it would be Ortiz. It had been difficult, however, to arrange to see the man. Saturnino Ortiz was eighty-four years old, and (this from his housekeeper) singularly uninterested in strangers by this time. No, he was in reasonably good health for a man his age. But he had been pestered by dumb questions long enough. Let some of these people just open a book.

And so Ariel saw no alternative. On the phone with the housekeeper, who did not sound mean or completely unsympathetic—his instinct was to tell her everything he knew, throw himself on her mercy—he said he was employed by a client who was looking desperately for an albino jaguar skin that might be several hundred years old. He didn't know the whole story, he confessed, but the client's daughter was somehow in trouble, something was wrong, and it was hoped that finding out if this jaguar skin existed . . . well, no, he didn't understand it, they hadn't told him the whole thing.

Hours later, the housekeeper (Señora Ramirez) called him at the hotel and said the professor would see him tomorrow at three o'clock in the afternoon. He should not be late. Ortiz had put up with enough tardiness in his time to have little tolerance for it now, when he could determine his own rules.

The day was cloudy. On the street, some children had set up a kind of puppet theater, starring toy skeletons with articulated limbs. The children chattered conspiratorially, their voices intermingled with the sounds of chickens and dogs. Ariel saw a motionless lizard on a rock.

Near the end of the Mayans' hegemony, they began carving, in stone, what are referred to as zoomorphs—strange, unknown animals, monsters, griffonlike creatures, mixtures of several animals in one beast. In the last few years of the empire, they had seen monsters. A clue, surely, to what might have been going on in the collective psyche.

Monsters, he mused, as he crossed a plaza toward the professor's address. Two fair-haired tourists, probably Americans, with cameras, good-looking, reminded him of something that had happened in the countryside near here. To the local Indians, red or blond hair is a sign that one is a devil. Two Dutch archaeologists had been working, digging in a special field, on a holy day, and twice refused offers of food or something to drink. Devils do not eat or drink. The Dutchmen, unable to express themselves well in the local tongue, kept on smiling and shaking their fair-haired heads. So they were murdered, with knives. The Indians, when brought to trial, were found not guilty. They had believed that they were killing devils. They'd acted in good faith.

The housekeeper was very ugly, but pleasant. For some reason she seemed to welcome this intrusion. Perhaps retired Professor Ortiz had been spending too much time alone. Into the parlor, and coffee with hot milk. Saturnino Ortiz sized him up, nodded impatiently as Ariel explained his mission, and then began talking, in such a way that it was not immediately apparent whether he was being responsive . . . but Ariel knew how to listen, and how to wait.

Ortiz had a histrionic manner, at least part of the time. He would slip into it, as if delivering his discourse before an attentive classroom, eyes far away . . . then coming back to Mendoza's face, making sure he was listening, lowering his voice.

He began with jaguars and jaguar-gods. Some general information on jaguars: how they differed from African lions, Bengal tigers, and other feline carnivores. Albino specimens were, he said, extremely rare.

"You've heard of Pedro de Alvarado? The most notoriously bloodthirsty of that first wave of conquistadors. . . . After the Aztecs were conquered, Cortés sent him down to Guatemala, where he killed and tortured indiscriminately, rapaciously looking for gold . . . always the gold. In 1533 he went to Quito, taking five hundred Spaniards and two thousand Indian and Negro slaves. None of the slaves lived to return. In 1541 Alvarado went north from Mexico, looking for the seven cities of Cibola . . . and finally died, falling from his horse on rough terrain."

Ariel waited. It was possible Ortiz knew nothing pertinent. Ariel was patient, enjoying the coffee and the cookies, which, coated in powdered sugar, reminded him of tasty little skulls.

"Alvarado had a friend," Saturnino Ortiz said. "This fellow—Orestes de Fontana—had the reputation, early on, of being very devout. He had an innocent air about him, some of the others thought he should have been a monk. He came to Guatemala after it was largely pacified, though there were constant problems with slave rebellions and the like. Since the Indians were not Christian, they were not human, so they had no souls. Orestes de Fontana was influenced, one might say, by his friendship with Alvarado. Who can imagine the conversations they must have had?

"In any case, it is mentioned in a letter of the time that in 1535 or so, Fontana came into possession of a very large white jaguar skin . . . it's not clear whether he himself actually killed the beast. He had by this time picked up Alvarado's habit of invading villages and massacring nearly everyone present, torturing the survivors to see if they knew where to find more gold. In this manner, he accumulated a lot of miscellaneous goods, including jade figurines, Mayan codexes—which, as a good Christian, he burned—and a large number of slaves. But evidently he differed from other, garden-variety conquistadors in that his mayhem gradually took on a more demonic flavor . . . there are documents that are locked up in the Vatican library . . . as Fontana, ah . . . gave himself over to the dark powers."

"What do you mean?"

"He evidently came to believe—it's said he formed an alliance with some renegade Mayan priest, who convinced him that by sacrificing children he could achieve magical powers, so that he would be led to the legendary El Dorado and be acclaimed there as their king. It was also necessary, apparently, to acquire a quantity of Spanish heads—enough to erect a small pyramid, atop which he would enact his final sacrifice . . . however, he was stopped before he could carry this plan out. The Indian accomplice escaped, and Fontana was judged to have been possessed by a demon. So they buried him alive, within an iron cage. Juan de Aparecido next came to own the white jaguar skin. We know this from the records of an auction some years later, after Aparecido had been murdered, poisoned, by his Indian concubine. A fellow named Arturo de Silveira purchased it—paying the money to the church—and departed, stopping in Hispaniola on his way back to Spain. But the ship was attacked by Dutch pirates, led by Lars Morning, who took the booty to Rotterdam, where the skin was auctioned again. Thereafter, it passed into oblivion for some two hundred years.

"But in Mexico, in 1802 Don Carlos de Bienvenida, a great landowner, one of the family who repeatedly helped put down the Tabasco Indians . . . Don Carlos had a large couch, made by a fine Italian furniture maker, the famed Pietro Volponi . . . and this couch was upholstered with a beautiful white jaguar skin. Now Don Carlos came to an untimely death, trampled by horses, and, as he had no heir, the church took over the hacienda. Bishop Quiroga gave the couch as a gift to Maximilian, the unlucky one, who in short order passed it on to Sebastian Velasco de Nuñez. And I believe it's been in the possession of the Velascos ever since. They've had some reverses in the last twenty years, so nothing is certain. But you, Señor Mendoza, are fortunate in having come to me. I have not taken a special interest in this skin, yet I have noted it, as I have noted many other little things. I could give you an educated guess, for instance, as to what became of Cortés's sword."

Ariel flattered the old man's memory and let Saturnino Ortiz entertain him with other, perhaps more often told, historical anecdotes. Professor Ortiz, finding a worthy audience, brought out a painstaking copy of one of the three surviving Mayan codexes—which Ariel was truly interested to see—and translated the hieroglyphs as well as he could. When the housekeeper came in to remind the professor of his siesta, Ariel was, far from being bored, sorry to have to leave.

Ortiz asked him if he would promise to tell him the outcome of the quest, by letter or by phone, or in person if he passed this way again, and Ariel said yes, he would let him know.

There was no guarantee that the couch still existed, none at all, but Lorenzo Velasco, in Guadalajara, was the one to ask.

Later, over a simple meal of *tapado* and a green salad, Ariel contemplated the story he had been told by Ortiz. It had come so easily, the old man could have had it rehearsed. This hypothesis didn't make any particular sense, but then, Ariel knew that he was far from knowing all the relevant facts. Indeed, he had not even been provided with a clear rationale for the Novas' odd quest. The story Ortiz had related might be true, or not. It did arouse his suspicious nature to have it all lead so patly to one man, this Lorenzo Velasco. Ariel would approach him with great care.

In the meantime, he smoked a cigarette, drank brandy, and considered whether or not it would be worth the trouble to have a whore sent to his room. Dr. Nova's expense account, under "miscellaneous services," would pay. But no, he wasn't really in the mood. In Guadalajara, he'd see. He'd been there once before.

In the darkness of his bed, Ariel plumped up his pillow. He was having a hard time getting to sleep. There was a bar nearby, and although it wasn't noisy, from time to time there was audible, flirtatious conversation before the people walked off or drove away. Ariel took another big swig of sweet thick red codeine cough syrup. He didn't have a cough, but he was in the habit of helping himself fall into sleep. By doing so he usually obliterated the possibility of a lurid, awful nightmare . . . or, for that matter, any other kind of dream.

FOURTEEN

Lisa shuddered. It was spooky, the constant drumbeats drove one a little wild, it was impossible not to sway, to move, to feel it take one over a bit, the regularity of the polyrhythms disrupted with the master drummer's emphatic blow, never quite when you expected it, just when your body thought it had comprehended the rhythm it changed, slightly but significantly, the repetition was important, sound waves going through your muscles, your nervous system, meat, tense and relax, you could not help but react.

There were several hundred candles burning, and the black *umbanda* priest, red and gold beads around his neck, danced around the tethered young white goat. The air smelled of some particularly fragrant, complicated mixture of rum, sweat, and big bags of fresh popcorn. They were near the beach, in early evening, shadows in purple shapes beginning to form, colors changing against the illumination of all these flickering, waving little flames.

Lisa wore a white dress: A black blindfold was tied over her eyes. There were many representations of the saints, the transformed African gods. The beats were too swift and sure to be counted or sorted into time signatures . . . the priest beat on an iron bell with a carved heavy stick, playing off the beat, behind it, the offbeat only complicating and talking to the central rolling surge. Layers of unstoppable wood, skin, stretched skin accelerating sonic hieroglyphs—as Lisa nodded, the priest was speaking to her, his sparse graying beard and yellow teeth, his yellow eyes, speaking into her ear as she took into her hand, still blindfolded, the sacred knife. The priest showed her the way, and she made one introductory ritual slice into the neck. The goat was screaming, struggling, kicking, feet tied together, Lisa's blindfold fell off as the animal was raised by two strong shirtless young black men over Lisa's head. The cut had been widened and the blood flowed freely, dark and bright bright red, like flowers, onto Lisa's head and down over her face, as she gasped and closed her eyes, the red staining the pure white cotton of the dress.

She raised her hands up then, as if in ecstasy, opening her eyes, uttering something—when suddenly the two fellows wielding the sacrificed goat were flung backward, simultaneously, as the goat carcass flew violently at the priest, knocking him over. The priest seemed then to be lifted up bodily and thrown down onto the ground, levitated involuntarily and then dropped yet again, as the drumming continued, now mingled with women screaming, disorder ensuing. The priest was lifted up high and thrown down once more, bruised and bleeding, and the crowd began to scatter. Tavinho, who had been watching, forced his way toward Lisa, who was transfixed. Gazing at her hands, or her fingers. The bloody white matted fur of the goat began smoking, smoldering, twitching, even as several birds fell from the sky, one or two at a time, just falling, apparently struck dead in midair. Birds just kept falling down from the sky.

At last the master drummer sought to halt his demon-possessed disciples . . . and Lisa sprinted away, barefoot, across the white sand to the blue-green foamy sea. She wasn't running from Tavinho, he was sure of that, and so he went after her, as she ran she stripped off the stained white dress with its delicate stitching, throwing it down as it burst into orange flames.

Into the surf, she was nude now, cooling herself in the saline waters, ducking under to wash away the blood. When Tavinho caught up with her she was wild-eyed, she didn't know him, he held her and, soaking wet, newborn in the sea, she wept, her face completely naked, more naked than he had ever known, she could hardly speak, shivering, she cried, "Look!" and showed Tavinho her hands.

On the back of each finger was tattooed a letter. The right hand (burning cross on the arm) spelled *L-O-V-E*. The left (jaguar on the bicep) said *H-A-T-E*. Tavinho understood that this had just happened, the dark blue ink was brand-new. Some bad magic had powerfully intervened, and the exorcism had been foiled.

FIFTEEN

The obvious allusion was a cinematic one, to *Night of the Hunter,* in which Robert Mitchum plays a demonically sleazy evil preacher, with *H-A-T-E* and *L-O-V-E* tattooed on his fingers in the same manner that Lisa now possessed. Obviously, also, many Hell's Angels and other bikers had the same design, as well as maybe some of the transformed zombies, so one could not be sure exactly what Boro meant, or if he meant for there to be any message at all outside of the message inscribed in the demonstration of his power and the fact that he was aware of what was going on so far away—assuming, that is, that he was still in Los Angeles . . . which, yes, Lisa assumed.

The other reference, just in her own head, and it hadn't occurred to her as it was actually happening, but only later, picturing what had occurred—she thought of *Carrie,* when at the prom a bucket of blood is poured over Carrie's head, how that had looked. . . .

In the hotel room, after showering (unfortunately there was only lukewarm water at this time of day, but she made do) Lisa emerged, in a white terry-cloth robe, using another towel, still drying her hair. She thought she was comparatively calm about everything, although Isabel was still upset. The ceremony had been Isabel's idea, after all. Tavinho . . . Lisa knew that he loved her, and he was gentle and understanding, she was afraid if she allowed it to happen he would get hurt. She didn't want to hurt him, maybe it would work out differently, but that was her first guess: that she would be responsible, and he would be hurt. He had learned of the purification ceremony somehow and followed them here. Knowing this now, Lisa thought his devotion was cool. She liked it that he cared.

Lisa had asked for coffee, with milk and sugar, and she poured herself some now, checking the backs of her fingers to see if the alien marks were still there. They were.

Isabel was on the phone to São Paulo, trying to get through to Dr. Nova, visibly rattled, trying to keep her composure with one underling after another . . . sending a meant-to-be-reassuring, uncertain smile to Lisa as the crazy stepdaughter sipped her sweetened coffee.

Lisa had *known* the dress was going to go up in flames, she'd had a prickly feeling on her back and between her shoulder blades, her breasts . . . she'd known it before the fabric even started to get warm. The dead birds falling from the sky had seemed inevitable, as natural and neutral as the rain that now poured down, steadily, not quite a monsoon, washing all the church spires and cobblestones and red tile roofs.

She felt modest, like a child, and like a child she had no volition or plan for the near future: Whatever she was told to do, she'd do. They would know best. The ceremony hadn't worked out so well, at least in its official goal, but on the other hand it had clarified some things, they could see it wasn't all just her imagination, and so, despite the new, tangible signs of Boro's power, she found some strange relief.

Tavinho came over to Lisa, and two black maids entered, bringing in trays of food. It was nine-thirty, and no one had had any supper. Isabel was irritably telling someone on the phone that she had to go. The maids regarded Lisa with something like kinship, an odd familiarity, mixed in with some horror and undisguised awe.

"Are you hungry?" Tavinho asked as Lisa got up to go put on some clothes, just a T-shirt and faded jeans. "No," she said as she walked away, closing the door. She was ravenous.

Tavinho scored points by ignoring the contradictions, the perversity. He didn't ask her, for instance, why in Rio she would never come to the phone after she'd been in jail, and Lisa noticed this forbearance, she saw that he wasn't even thinking about any of that. They ate shrimp in coconut milk, with peanuts, and spicy fried bean patties called *acarajé*, and some kind of firm white-fleshed fish flavored with coriander and garlic. Everyone was soothed by the act of eating. Isabel and Solange were soon laughing about something, which Lisa missed. Tavinho asked her after a while, thoughtfully, licking his thumb clean of *pimenta*, "So tell me . . . how are these strange things that are happening to you affecting your view of the world?"

It was a good question; it made Lisa wonder how much he knew, and she threw him a penetrating glance. He seemed impervious.

Accordingly, she answered, "Oh well, it all comes in, it all goes out . . . it's all material, you know. Experience."

"Really?" he said, challenging her. "It doesn't change you?"

"Who am I to say exactly *how*? Of course there are changes taking place, some good, some bad . . . some chemical, some—I don't know—*mystical*. What, you think I'm made of stone?"

At this outburst, Isabel said something Lisa guessed to be, "Don't upset her, Tavinho," in Portuguese—but Tavinho seemed unmoved by this, getting a reaction had pleased him, Lisa could tell, and she said, "It's OK if he bugs me, Isabel, *meu madre*"—she didn't know if she got that right, but went ahead anyway—"*que bom.*"

Everyone thought she was being ironic here except Tavinho, who was looking at her seriously, ready for anything, surprised by nothing now, asking her, "Do you have magical powers?"

"I don't know," she said. "Maybe. Some. Maybe I have some that I don't understand yet; I need time to find out what they are, get them under control."

Isabel was looking at her like she was out of her mind, or maybe not. Lisa felt embarrassed, but then, all she had to do was look down at her fingers to remember how she had *X*'d out Wendy Right.

Tavinho understood, she saw. Or he had the capacity to understand. Errol would, too, in a different way, but Errol wasn't here. She was aware suddenly, unaccountably it made her blush, that Tavinho could see her nipples through the fabric of the T-shirt. It was still raining outside, tirelessly, in the shimmering dark.

"Lisa Supernova," said Tavinho, teasing, in a low voice no one else could hear, and Lisa knew they had to fuck, and soon; she smiled at him and he probably understood the message, at least approximately. If it would take Tavinho climbing in her window like a suitor from a few hundred years ago, then that's what it would take. A dessert was served then that reminded Lisa of flan, she tasted it thinking of Boro and his taste buds, his tongue on the sweetness of the rich flan the afternoon he'd told her about the white jaguar and his ancient life. There was a prefuck aura in the room, a sweet taste in their mouths, melting saliva, and hidden places and caves.

SIXTEEN

Did this mean her left hand was now dangerous, the right one safe, like the Islamic belief in sacred and profane, the Latin *dextra* and *sinistra?* Lisa thought she should avoid grasping Tavinho's penis in her left hand, there was no telling what mischief she might spare him. The tryst turned out to be easily arranged. It was cold, so they got under the covers, kissing. She was glad it was dark, she didn't want to ponder all the marks on her body and what they were supposed to mean. The heart tattoo was on her left buttock—but that's the side of the body the heart is on, and one couldn't assume that Boro was designing all this as hieroglyphics to be decoded with care, it could as easily be sort of random. The jaguar and the cross were significant, but that was all she'd be willing to assume.

Now, in the dark, Tavinho's fervent kisses were a distraction, the warmth they generated diverted her from fruitless contemplation of her doom. Tavinho must truly imagine himself to be in love with her to have followed her up here, knowing, as he surely did, about Mwangi. From his demeanor it wouldn't seem to matter, but still, maybe he was saving his jealousy for sometime later, once he thought he had enough power to risk it. At the moment he was nonpossessive, fighting the Brazilian stereotype. She didn't know, couldn't guess, how much was for her benefit, how much was sincere. She was willing to accept his caresses, his tongue, his penis . . . tonight, in this old colonial town, a few blocks from the slave-trading headquarters. Up from the beach where the ceremony had failed, or been redirected. Tomorrow, early, they would get out of town. Before Lisa had to endure too many more people crossing themselves against her, fingering their amulets, their charms, against the witch. Hide your children's eyes.

SEVENTEEN

Lisa's hair was getting a little longer these days, and she liked it this way. Barefoot, wearing a simple cotton dress, she hung out with Caitlin on the wooden porch, both of them waiting for it to rain. They were at the experimental compound, somewhere in the vicinity of Boa Vista. In the northern Amazon, where the jungle still held full sway.

Caitlin's conversation wandered. Lisa wasn't perhaps fully paying attention, for the term "blocked energies" caught her without any idea at all of what it meant or where it fit in. She looked at Caitlin, and Caitlin seemed to accept the gaze as intelligently interrogative, for she went on.

A cerise bird landed in the branches of a tree, brilliant plumage disappearing in green leaves. There were seemingly infinite gradations of the color green, from blue-green through bronze- and yellow- and gold-green, green turning to silver, or purplish, greens that changed drastically when moistened or dry.

Now it started, more or less on schedule, raining like hell. Just a vertical, intense, silver-white yet somehow brownish downpour. Loudly beating the buildings, turning the earth temporarily into sepia mud.

There wasn't much here to do, but it seemed safe, she was with her father. She spent afternoons in a hammock, listening to her Walkman. (Tavinho had very thoughtfully, on his own initiative, sent her some tapes. Errol Mwangi, on the other hand, had made himself scarce.) She read books on the history of the region, mostly stuff about conquistadors, the search for El Dorado, Lope de Aguirre, all of that. It was very vivid at times to her, in her imaginings.

There was no TV. There was an old Bell and Howell projector, and her father had given her two metal canisters of film, totaling about ninety minutes, supposedly a classic documentary about Amazonian ants. Somehow she hadn't yet gotten around to watching it. It was funny how her father, benignly, had always assumed she was interested in ants.

Lisa yawned. She was hungry. Caitlin had gone "to sort samples." Lisa wondered sometimes what would happen if she came into close proximity to a jaguar. Was there some special affinity, via the jaguar tattoo or Boro's powers, originating as they had, at least according to his story, with this magic white jaguar?

She had certain powers, she felt strangely sure of this, though she didn't know what they were yet. Two days ago she had gone for a walk, not venturing too far away, and she began watching a large palmetto bug, bigger than any cockroach she'd ever seen in New York . . . and she suddenly had a wicked impulse, she wished she had a magnifying glass, she'd set it on fire using the sun. This was a fairly idle thought, but she had nothing else on her mind . . . the palmetto bug began to singe, to brown, and then it *popped*—its exoskeleton exploded, leaving nothing but a fine swirling poof of black dust, swirling like miniature, insignificant shrapnel.

She had found she could repeat this, once also focusing her "evil" attention on a pretty butterfly gliding by, which burst into flames and crashed into some leaves. She had begun to have a headache, and she was a little bit freaked out, she was scared. She didn't know what else she could do.

Maybe she wasn't strictly human anymore. No—human plus spell. The parameters of this remained as yet unknown.

A bird flew by. A snake crawled on the ground. Lisa tried to knock the bird down out of the sky, but she could not. Nothing happened. It was an unpleasant, creepy feeling to try when you didn't know what you were doing. It was like trying to control the beat of your heart.

She wondered what Boro thought, she tried to see things through his eyes. Lying in her hammock, such was her exercise. Dark eyes dilated just out of the hot sun, in the shade, like an animal waiting for unwary prey.

EIGHTEEN

When Lisa had been in art school, her big brother occasionally would playfully quiz her about art history, it was the kind of elaborate tease Track enjoyed. Lisa took it as a sign of affection, and thus it became a long-running private joke.

He asked her things like, Who is considered to be the greatest painter of horses of all time? What different methods of suicide were employed by Arshile Gorky and Mark Rothko? Sometimes Track might throw in an especially silly one, like, What color is a box of Wheaties? Kellogg's Corn Flakes? Or an unanswerable one: How many Frenchmen can't be wrong?

The game also perhaps obviously demonstrated Track's wish to be in control. He had always liked to teach her things, and Lisa had been an eager, rapt pupil from the time she was very young.

Stubbs turned out to be the greatest painter of horses, and his name itself became a joke for them. Arshile Gorky hung himself. Rothko, clad in long underwear and black socks, took an overdose of barbiturates and then sliced through the veins in both elbows with a razor. A box of Wheaties is orange. Kellogg's Corn Flakes, disregarding the rooster, comes in a box that is white.

So now this whole voodoo business, or evidence of rococo wildness, whatever was going on with his little sister, Track couldn't grasp it, it rubbed in just how far she was beyond his advice and impervious to it, and he didn't like any of it one bit.

He was in Los Angeles, attending to his own affairs, but after a phone call to Brazil he insisted on meeting with the Brazilian detective, who had ended up here after Mexico City, Houston, and Santa Fe. Lisa sounded like she was eating a banana or something, she didn't seem to care much one way or another if Track involved himself, and he found this infuriating, ungrateful as well.

"Somebody ought to check on this guy, see what he's doing, what his plan of attack is at this point."

"Yeah, well, sure, theoretically, but Daddy knows how to manage these things, and he told the guy he was giving him a long leash. *Leash* isn't the right word. . . ."

"If you don't want me to, I'll leave well enough alone. I don't have any great desire to meet him if you think it's unnecessary."

"Just a second, Track. My hands are all sticky." Then, when she came back: "Look, you've already contacted him, right? Then meet with him, see what you think."

Track met Ariel Mendoza at a restaurant close to his hotel, and they had dinner together. Mendoza explained how he had come this far.

"The couch was sold four years ago to a Houston man who owns an antique store and art gallery. He sold it to a man named Lacroix who lives in Santa Fe. Six months ago this guy's house was robbed. All kinds of what you call 'curios,' I think, were stolen. Gold masks, jade figurines, carved mahogany and ironwood pieces, and yes, the jaguar couch." Mendoza thirstily finished his rum and Coke.

"So-o-o," Track said, "how do you know it's here in L.A.?"

"Exactly. Some of the other items turned up when a Señor Osvaldo

Perez was arrested here for receiving stolen goods. His warehouse was, um . . . there was an inventory made."

"No couch?"

"No."

Track said, "Well, what about this Osvaldo Perez? Maybe he's just in the phone book."

Mendoza shook his head. "No." Then, after a moment, he said, "If it is true that he was arrested, it should be possible to find him. But I don't know the system here."

Disappointed, Track thought this over. He was self-conscious at having butted in, and now, having met him, Mendoza seemed competent and bright. Track was afraid he might have appeared to be yet another asshole Yankee big shot, and now all he sought was to dispel this impression, charm Mendoza if he could, and gracefully exit the scene.

"What course of action do you suggest?" he finally said.

Mendoza appeared to consider it, but of course he had reached his conclusion some time ago, it was plain. He was very polite.

"Hire a local investigator. Not from a big agency, but someone who can, for instance, talk to the police. If I go and have to introduce myself, show identification, tell them I'm from Brazil . . . they may become inconveniently interested in the matter. They may refer me to U.S. Customs or the Drug Enforcement Agency. A local investigator won't be so intriguing to them."

Track nodded. He didn't want to look foolish, but he asked what seemed a reasonable question in the circumstance: "How do you find someone who's good?"

"I'll make some calls tomorrow. My acquaintances in Mexico may know someone."

Ariel Mendoza himself was thinking, at this point, that he had really no idea why he was on this particular quest. Clients always lied, lawyers lied, weeping relatives lied. . . . He had never seriously entertained the thought that there might be, say, a lost shipment of cocaine or something of that nature hidden in the antique couch, but maybe he'd been too quick to leave that area of speculation behind. Dr. Nova was a scientist. There might be some new substance nobody'd ever heard of yet.

The problem with this scenario, on the face of it, was that the couch did not seem ever to have been anywhere near Dr. Nova—though who really knew? Not all that long ago, it had been in

Guadalajara and then Mexico City . . . how it passed over the border into Texas was very murky, very hard to pin down.

They always lied.

NINETEEN

There were many reasons not to swim in the river, just as there were reasons not to go for a walk in the jungle—somebody had been bitten by a particularly venomous snake not too long ago. When a snake bites you, it can control how much venom it injects, you can be bitten by a fer-de-lance and not even be poisoned, the snake prefers to use as little of its reservoir of venom as it can manage, only if you really scare it and it feels cornered will it give you enough poison to readily kill. . . . Lisa heard about how one of the corpsevine volunteers had been badly bitten a few months ago, a young Swedish guy, he'd been hospitalized for some time, the decision was nearly made to amputate his leg.

Isabel and Alfredo showed Lisa photos of the site where the vine grew in particular abundance, a clearing where many bones and other remains had been found, old swords and armor, spear points and arrowheads, pieces of jade, even some gold.

"I don't know how much more there'll ever be," her father said after talking about the special properties of the alkaloid they'd extracted. Recent samples seemed diminished in strength. "It might just be one of those anomalies. We may have had a brief chance, never to be repeated, to see into the past. I don't know, maybe if we'd had some Indian volunteers—but the only ones who were talked to had no interest, who can blame them, I'm sure they don't trust us at all."

"How many are going to take it this time?" Isabel asked, sipping coffee. It was 5:30 A.M.

Lisa sat with them, eating slices of mango, wiping her mouth after maybe every other bite.

"Three," Alfredo replied. "Two males, one female. We have enough extract for more . . . but it won't keep for more than twenty-four hours. I'm almost tempted myself—"

"Don't even think about it."

"My own view," he said, "is that after a certain age, there are too many memories of one's own life, the circuits become overloaded if you add something this potentially extreme. No, don't worry, I'm not willing to take that kind of a risk." He smiled, though, as if imagining it for a moment. Lisa, drawn now, imagined it too.

Caitlin walked into view, waved, and continued on her way, meeting Hiroshi, who looked to be vehemently declaiming—in a friendly manner, half teasing, because he liked her. (In Lisa's mind, certainly, they were an item.)

Dogs were barking. A rooster continued to crow once in a while. The air was moist. More coffee. The titrated extract would be administered to the subjects in about an hour; Dr. Nova of course would be there.

Only now did she begin to wonder about the volunteers. Would any of them freak out or die? She was curious—she'd have to go over and see. It would be a case of maybe, officially, she shouldn't be there, but because she was a Nova no one would keep her out, and her father, these days, could not deny her anything . . . he felt inexplicably guilty, she could see it in him, it was awful for him that Boro's spell was beyond his control.

When she came into the lab, she saw that each session was being recorded, by fixed camera, on videotape. Lisa went and stood by Caitlin, who said to her, quietly, "There won't be much to see."

"That's OK. Have they taken it yet?"

"Yes. A few minutes ago."

Lisa nodded, trying to match Caitlin's scientific manner. Her father was in one of the rooms with the young Japanese woman; she didn't speak much English, and Lisa didn't know her name. The other two experimental subjects were male, in their twenties: one a blond American so good-looking he could be a model, who had arrived maybe three days ago—Tim. The other one was a friendly Brazilian—Patricio. He looked the most nervous of the three, in their separate glassed-in rooms. Every effort was made to make them comfortable and relaxed, reassured . . . no harsh lights, no obtrusive blood pressure cuffs or glued-on wires to measure brain waves, as in previous tests these wires had been particularly unpopular, and no interesting data, in any case, was ever gleaned.

It was easy to imagine a science fiction movie, or indeed a documentary with a serene, ultracivilized voice-over.

Patricio, Tim, the Japanese (her name was Toshi, Caitlin informed Lisa, when asked) all held their eyes closed. They did look out of it. At one point Tim bent over to the side and vomited, then drank some water, repeating, "Thank you, thank you, thank you," as Toshi suddenly broke out in expostulations that did not sound Oriental in the least.

After Lisa determined that no one seemed to be in pain, that in fact their eyes were now open, glistening, as if seeing visions, private movies, she felt jealous, like she was missing something, she should be the center of attention rather than one of these. It struck her that this extract might affect her differently than the others, she might see more than they would, understand it better, coming back with unknowable new compositions in her eyes. She went outside. The light now was glaring, ordinary, loud.

She went back to her hammock, restless, irritable, aroused. She had the feeling she was missing out on something important, something necessary, an experience she *needed*, whether it was good or bad. She got back up and walked around.

When Lisa caught sight of Caitlin, still before noon, before lunch, she impulsively went out to her, the midwestern girl shy at the touch—Lisa seized her shoulders, the moment bled like they were lovers, all the possibilities were there, Lisa said to her, "I've got to have some of that shit. It'll go bad by tomorrow, so it's got to be today. My dad said it might not be as strong as it used to be, so this could be the last chance anyone will ever have."

"I can't—"

"Don't tell me that. You've got to get some for me. I *know* it won't hurt me. I need to see what those other fuckers get to see."

The words as such didn't especially matter, they were secondary; what counted was the influence exerted by the eye-to-eye, the magic of the breath, the spirits breathed in by the other, Caitlin's resistance melting . . . Lisa felt triumph, she didn't want to show it but she could *feel* her influence working, dissolving rational objections and rational thought, she was using Caitlin, and the relation felt natural and strong.

"I don't know if I can get it. They put it in the refrigerator."

"Get it. I know you can."

Caitlin started to turn away, and Lisa took her by the arm again, holding her close, just looking at her, their eyes meeting . . . and when Caitlin left Lisa didn't gloat, she felt instead a strange lassitude, an indifference . . . it was taken care of, she knew it. Caitlin would do her best.

Other people came and went. When it was appropriate, Lisa nodded or said hello. When she saw Caitlin emerge from the main building, Lisa didn't wait for a nod or any other signal, cutting back toward her bungalow, it was best to take it in a relaxed atmosphere, and so she'd lie in her hammock, the trip generally put one to sleep.

When they rendezvoused, Caitlin said, "Your dad will kill me . . . God . . . ," but she handed it over, milky liquid in a plastic container, she was trembling. . . .

"What does it taste like?" Lisa asked.

"I don't know. Not too bad, I guess. Nobody really complains."

"Can I wash it down with a Coke?"

Lisa took it, drank it down. It was like "green juice," some health store shit she had tasted once, a combination of about fifteen vegetables not meant by God to be consumed in liquid form. Andrea, her sister, had drunk that and carrot juice, carrot juice all the time. Out to the hammock. Caitlin brought her a Coke.

"You should go have lunch with the others, so they won't connect us," Lisa said. "Will they notice that this much is gone?"

Caitlin shook her head, answering the second question first, and then said, "I'm going to stay with you."

"Cool," Lisa said, leaning back, already becoming contemplative, like she might revisit some important dreams. Caitlin checked her pulse, and Lisa looked right at her but soon didn't seem to know who she was. She was somewhere truly far away. It was frightening. Caitlin couldn't believe she'd given in. How weak could she be? Now Lisa shivered as if she had malaria and suddenly said, clearly, sharply, "No!" with such feeling that Caitlin jerked to her feet, watching her . . . then Lisa flung herself back, moaned for a while, and began muttering to herself in unintelligible Spanish, eyes shut tight now. When she opened them, she didn't look quite like Lisa anymore.

"Oh God," Caitlin said, and cried.

In a little while Lisa groaned anew and pitched herself out of the hammock onto the wooden floor. Slowly, looking around with unseeing, horrified, animal eyes, she crawled on hands and knees. Caitlin tried not to interfere with her, but to keep her from hurting herself. Lisa's balance sometimes seemed as uncertain as an infant's.

When she came to the metal canisters of film—the documentary on ants—she used them as a pillow, lying down on her side, drawing up her knees. She was quiet then.

TWENTY

If you looked like an attorney and acted sure of yourself, with a briefcase and some forms in your hand, the last thing a court clerk wanted to do was mess with you—Max Doppler got the case caption number from the cross index file, pulled the jacket on Perez, Osvaldo J., got his address from the bond receipt . . . then noticed that someone had handwritten *Deceased.*

Great. Just fucking great. It figured that this Brazilian motherfucker was jerking him around, he was just too cute. Doppler tried to look as matter-of-fact as he could, he didn't want anyone to remember him, luckily it wasn't likely these guys noticed much, not at this time of day, when everyone was breaking for lunch.

Max Doppler was forty-two years old, a little soft now, but he still lifted free weights, got on the machines, swam a few laps when he had time. He'd been a football player many, many years ago. After the last time his ex-wife had told him "Not again" about an interesting sports anecdote, he'd made up his mind never to mention any of that stuff to anyone, people either thought you exaggerated or it bored them, even others who'd played. Funny, it was so private, incommunicable, while at the time the experience had seemed like the most public, obvious thing in the world.

Doppler entered the restaurant where he'd told Mendoza they'd meet. He wasn't a particularly good-looking man, but neither was he ugly. He sat across from Mendoza and ordered a salad and some bread. He didn't like to eat in front of others—the last ten years had made him used to eating alone. Mendoza ordered a hamburger. He asked Doppler if he'd gotten the address. He was polite but inscrutable, as before. Doppler couldn't tell if Mendoza knew that Perez was dead. It was always safest to believe the worst. Even so, there was no reason not to tell him and see what he did.

Mendoza seemed to be surprised. "Did it say how?" he asked, and Doppler shook his head. As Mendoza then just sat there, staring off into space, presumably thinking . . . Doppler waited, then passed him the slip of paper on which he'd printed the address. The thought had taken a while to fully arrive, but Doppler'd finally come to it: So what if it's something shady? There might be some good money involved. And Doppler was getting to the point, with his entire existence, where he just didn't give a fuck.

"In the information, it says how old he was?"

Doppler shook his head and waited to see if Mendoza would ask him a follow-up. But Mendoza gave every indication of being able to keep his mouth shut, keep his thoughts to himself.

"Since this guy is dead—I don't know how," Mendoza finally said, "he might've been sick—but since it's a complication, I'll pay you a complication fee, a bonus, to continue. We will go over to find this address."

Doppler said this was OK. Mendoza had eaten only half his hamburger; seeing the big detective glance at it, Mendoza delicately said, "Would you do me the favor and eat this?" and so Doppler got a more satisfactory lunch. He and the Brazilian were getting along. They'd drive out to East L.A.

Doppler was driving, since he knew the territory, but as far as East L.A. was concerned, he didn't really know that much. For a very brief spell (for six months, twelve years ago) he'd done some repossessions, and he'd done some in the barrio. It was a challenge, you definitely went there fully armed, these days if you had a semiautomatic that's what you'd take . . . but this address, the house Perez had lived in, it wasn't so bad. Although sometimes these streets could be very deceptive. The thing to do was look around for bullet holes and broken windows, gang graffiti.

They rang the doorbell and a woman came to the door. Mendoza spoke to her in Spanish, and Doppler couldn't follow too much, though he got the basic drift. Mendoza said he had been out of the country, that he had owed her husband some money (this after first offering his condolences for Osvaldo's untimely death), which he would be glad to give to her . . . but Osvaldo had been holding a piece of furniture for him. When the misunderstanding with the police occurred, had they seized everything, or had some things been left behind? Perhaps in some other location?

Mrs. Perez said the police were doing nothing to look for whoever had murdered her husband. Mendoza again expressed his regrets. She said if there was any property left over, the person to talk to was Miguel. Mendoza gave her what seemed to be two or three hundred dollars, Doppler couldn't tell, not wanting to seem too curious, in the overcast day watching a couple of kids, maybe five-year-olds, walk by, one little girl skipping for a few steps, walking on the sidewalk, teasing the other one, a little boy.

In the car Mendoza explained that they would have to hurry to catch this Miguel, he was a boxer and he should be just about through with his daily workout at the gym. Rosita Perez had given him directions; in any case, Doppler knew where it was.

At the gym, there was sparring going on, other fighters working on heavy bags, speed bags, jumping rope, all sizes of men, most of them Hispanic, most of them slender and fairly small, at least by Doppler's standards, though he wouldn't have wanted one of these tough little bantamweights coming after him with the intent to do bodily harm.

Doppler asked an old man who looked like a janitor if Miguel Casablanca was still here. A young black boy went to look for Casablanca and returned nodding, saying, "He'll be right up," and then in a minute or so the boxer came up the stairs from the locker rooms and showers down below.

He had on a blue windbreaker, with his hands in his pockets, and seemed glum and indifferent until Mendoza spoke for a while. "OK," Miguel said then, after thinking it over, "I'll show you around. Let's go."

Mendoza asked, in English, how Osvaldo Perez had died. Casablanca kind of smiled, as though he couldn't believe they didn't know, and then said, "Man, I don't know anything. All I know is what I heard: Someone stuck a shotgun in his ear while he was sitting there in his car eating a Big Mac, like, eleven o'clock at night. Somebody didn't like him."

"What kind of work did you do for him, for Perez?"

"I helped deliver furniture sometimes."

"I don't care about his other business," Mendoza said. "All I'm looking for is a jaguar-skin couch. It came from Houston, along with some jade and other stuff. The police seized some of those things, but they didn't find the couch. It's from an albino jaguar, and it's very old. If you remember delivering it to someone, there'll be a discovery fee . . . and if you will introduce me, I'd like to negotiate with the new owner. I have no interest in the police."

"What if they don't want to sell? What if it belongs to someone, and money isn't everything to this person? What do you do then?"

"I don't know . . . just talk. I'll have found it, and that's my job."

"Who wants it? Really."

"Some doctor, a scientist." Ariel paused. "I don't know why he wants it, though."

Doppler felt like he was gradually being left out. At first it hadn't seemed like the boxer had cared for the Brazilian detective very much, but now they were developing a rapport. Doppler, to reintroduce his will into the equation, give things a little push, said, "Let's go see the person, Miguel. If you want to make a phone call or something first, why not?"

"This guy, he don't talk on the phone too much. I could show you where he lives, but—you sure you want to do this? He helps me with my training, see, and I don't wanna piss him off."

Doppler had the impatient idea that Casablanca was playing some kind of a game. He tried to communicate this impression to Mendoza wordlessly, and Mendoza stared back at him, aware that he was attempting to communicate something—he might have understood immediately, they might have been in harmony, Doppler just wasn't sure. He pushed it a little more, and Miguel said, "OK. Sure."

As Doppler drove, following Miguel's laconic instructions, he didn't like the boy's attitude. *Boy.* What was he? Twenty-one? Twenty-four? It was as if he had played dumb with them, dumber than he really was, and as if he knew a secret joke. The house they were going to was in Laurel Canyon, so on the way Doppler stopped by his apartment, made them wait for him while he went in and got his gun, a 9 mm automatic. He also brought down a Coke, so it wouldn't be obvious he'd gone up for a gun.

On the twisting road, Doppler asked, "Is this person in films?"

"Not really. He's into everything, man."

There was a gate with a video eye. Miguel got out and announced the visitors' mission into the microphone. He got back in, and the gate swung open. The house was not visible immediately, but soon. This entrance was to the back, at a higher elevation. Several motorcycles, choppers, were parked haphazardly facing a large white Jaguar sedan, which was being washed by a young man wearing dirty jeans and matching denim vest. He appeared to be suffering from some sort of skin disease. He was very pale as well, and Doppler, assuming the worst, wondered that he had sufficient strength to be out here washing the car. He averted his eyes as he and Mendoza followed Casablanca inside.

It wasn't quite a mansion, perhaps, but it was a huge house . . . entering from the back made it somewhat confusing, hard to get a sense of the total layout. Doppler didn't like the feeling he had of intruding into something strange. "Oh," said a young woman with a blue body, coming out of a door and then going back in, as she vanished he realized the blueness was tattoos from head to foot, to the extent that she may have been perfectly nude and he couldn't tell. Around a corner and they were confronted with an Indian, maybe an Aztec, wearing intricate ceremonial garb, mirrors hanging from him. He was a mannikin. That is, he wasn't alive. He did not breathe.

They came into a very large area with a very high ceiling and what must have been hundreds of exotic plants. So that was the smell. A huge, fancy aquarium, red and gold fish swimming by green plants in illuminated azure waters. There stood someone in a dark bird suit, evidently made of feathers, complete with head and beak, the wings as arms, the effect surreal: menacing rather than amusing. There was another life-sized statue of an Indian, probably Aztec, a king or a god in full ceremonial drag. Hardly any furniture. The smell, heavy as incense, was making Doppler light-headed. More unblinking pale young men. Six of them, standing around.

A strange-looking little man of indeterminate age, dressed in an expensive buff-colored suit—but no shirt—came out of the fronds and odd blossoms to say, "Miguel said you two gentlemen . . . you're looking for a couch."

"Upholstered with the skin of an albino jaguar," Mendoza said quietly, with deference.

"I possess such a piece of furniture, but I won't give it to you. I'm saving it, to present it to someone as a gift. She needs it, it is necessary to her."

"You won't sell it, then?"

"Look at me, brother. Do you recognize me?"

"I don't know," Mendoza said, but he seemed mesmerized. Doppler didn't like it. The little man was a dark Indian or Latino, and it looked as if someone had written all over him with medium blue ink, intricate hieroglyphics and messages, an outsized gold ring in each ear.

"I can wait for you out in the car," Doppler said, softly, discreetly touching Mendoza's arm—but at the light touch Ariel Mendoza started, as if he had never seen Doppler before.

"Brother, you have brought him: Do you give him to me? It is right."

Doppler didn't like the sound of this, nor the curiously knowing smile with which the little man looked him over. It was a smile that held within it some affection, yet it frightened Doppler. He turned away from the gathering darkness and began to make his way back out. Colombians for sure. Or Peruvians, Venezuelans, Ecuadorians, Paraguayans. In any case, into some bad shit. If he had felt it wise to go past them all, beyond them there was light, glass doors leading outside . . . but his car was up above. The corridors were darker now than before. It would be disastrous, he felt, to lose his way. He hurried. Fuck it, he might just drive away, leave Mendoza here, even though by so doing he'd forfeit his fee. No, that's ridiculous. There. Yes, it was a red door. Doppler came out into the shifting, undependable lavenderish daylight, constantly altered by messy clouds.

The sickly-looking guy who'd been washing the car stood off by some shrubbery, doing something with a rake. "Hey," Doppler said, but the guy didn't look over or respond. Then, after Doppler had walked to the gate and come back, here came Mendoza and Casablanca.

"Let's go," Mendoza said.

"OK," said Doppler, and then, even though he'd been watching him closely, distrustfully, Casablanca caught him off guard, moving so swiftly, shocking him, one to the belly, one to the head. Doppler fell to his knees. Hands were on his body and then he didn't have his gun anymore.

He looked up and saw Mendoza, but Mendoza wouldn't look at him. Doppler didn't want to say it, but he did: "Please." He got up to his feet, still weakened by the body shot. Becoming aware of movement, he turned to his left and saw the guy coming, taking his time, holding up the rake. Back to his right the other fucking zombies, a couple with knives, all definitely zeroed in on nobody but him. Mendoza and Casablanca stood back, somber or indifferent, and before the first zombie could reach him Doppler turned and ran, the rake just missed him, he plunged through a thorny bush, but there was no place to go. The person in the bird suit hit him with some kind of carved painted stick. There were chickens walking around, a black dog that paid no attention to him, a fountain that sent water into the air, a trembling pretty rainbow against a dirty sky, that's what he saw when he fell. He smelled newly mown grass and felt something wet, there was a lot of it, the world continued spinning round and round.

TWENTY-ONE

Two days after she had taken the alkaloid, Lisa discovered something strange and exciting: The documentary on Amazonian ants had been transfigured by her proximity and her touch. Caitlin said, "You used it as a pillow for hours. The only time you moved was when I tried to dry you, after you'd peed yourself."

Lisa remembered none of this. She did have some vague, impressionistic idea of the images that had taken her over, the ultravivid memories that had stained her mind, but it was only upon seeing the film—an amazing experience, she and Caitlin were there together in the dark, having decided to screen the ant film out of boredom, carrying the old Bell and Howell and the fucked-up screen to Lisa's room—she recognized much of it immediately. Caitlin asked her, "Wasn't this supposed to be about ants?" and Lisa said, "Shut up, shut up, this is my fucking *dream*, this is from the vine."

And indeed it was. If the unique vine grew only in this one perfect ambush-spot where there were uncounted skeletons, preconquest and after, along with broken swords and pieces of armor, arrowheads and lances and even some jewels and gold ornaments, but mostly the signs of repeated massacres . . . it was conceivable that some of the memories from pieces of brain, blended with what she'd been reading of El Dorado, her cinematic view of this material, the characteristic cropping and framing and moving camera, her own memories, paintings she'd seen, or illustrations in art books . . . whatever bizarre alchemy had taken place, all this had somehow fused together, no doubt through a manifestation of hitherto unknown or unconscious powers incited by Boro's magic, there was no other word for it, no concept, it was magic . . . and here was the physical result. A documentary on ants had become a brand-new film–somewhat rough with fade-outs into black, a soundtrack that was often no more than amplified murmurs, weird shadows of half-remembered music, sounding as though it had been recorded backward, muddy, fading out for long stretches at a time (and of course there were no titles or anything like that)—a weird film about conquistadors, Indians, and El Dorado. It "starred" Roy Hardway, and Lisa was in it too, plus a huge cast, fantastic scenes that seemed to be memories of medieval Spain, slaughters and tortures and rapes, Roy there through it all. . . .

The second reel opened with an eerie, bronze-to-copper-to-dull-brick-red-tinted time-lapse scene of Indians in a hut getting smallpox, the disease growing on their flesh, while some bass-heavy, garbled, Gregorian-type chant intoned and decayed.

People were going to have questions about the special effects and the realistic gore—but she couldn't imagine not wanting to show it. It was her product, it came out of *her*. The very notion of not showing it, and her immediate inner rejection of this option, brought home to her how exhibitionistic she was, how exhibitionistic in fact was all of art: the desire to show your insides, the inside of your head, to impose your vision on others, try to make them see through your eyes.

It was in 16 mm; it would have to be blown up to 35. And since she didn't have a negative, there'd have to be an internegative cut. She wouldn't fuck with it much, just some editing, cut out that big black empty section, do some work on the soundtrack, and that would be it. Maybe here and there some subtitles for the speech of the Indians. God, some of this was so alien, like the scenes up in Manoa itself, the city of gold.

PART 3

~

Is this the gift that I wanted to give?
Forgive and forget's what they teach.
Or pass through the deserts and
wastelands once more,
And watch as they drop by the beach.

IAN CURTIS

~ ONE

It was funny how nervous it made Lisa to return to the U.S. It wasn't like she was safe in Brazil, Boro had demonstrated that, but it just made her very uneasy . . . yet, with this strange film she'd been presented with, starring Roy Hardway no less, it seemed the time had definitely come for her to pop up her head.

She was also already late, she'd been supposed to be in St. Petersburg, Florida, a week ago, to visit Jules Brandenberg on the location of *My Evil Twin*. She was to appear in a bit part, really a walk-on, and to show him the draft of the *L.A. Ripper II* script.

Lisa found herself unwilling to leave her father, maybe that was it, the sense of safety his presence provided, however spurious this might be. She had shown him the film—which she'd entitled *Manoa, City of Gold*—and instead of being mad that she'd surreptitiously taken the alkaloid, or overly interested in making her part of the experiment or something, he'd been extremely interested and pleased, delighted with the phenomenon revealed. He was more curious than ever about Boro . . . and Lisa finally told her father how Roy Hardway had died. How Boro had thanked her for bringing him along, as though he were a sacrificial animal.

Or a meal, Dr. Nova hypothesized, something Lisa had never imagined. The point was, he said, ordinary assumptions of psychology did not apply. "He may be fond of you. He hasn't hurt you, and obviously, I think, he could if he wanted to."

And the tattoos might be some kind of symbolic gift, meaning more than mere decoration.

"But don't tempt fate, please," Dr. Nova implored. Lisa said she would not. They talked more about the substance of the film. It was perhaps a map of her dreaming mind, given that the vine had allowed her access to some out-of-her-body, collective memories, filtered then through her imagination, which had been catalyzed by the inflammation of the spell.

Before she left (for Rio and then up to the States), a letter had arrived, from Errol Mwangi.

> Dear Lisa,
>
> I'm sorry for what happened, for my carelessness. I would like to see you sometime again, if that's ever possible.
>
> I am leaving Rio. I will be in Paris, visiting my brother, and then I may return to London for some time.
>
> I am enclosing my brother's address and phone number. He will always know where I may be found.
>
> Errol

Lisa kept the letter in her purse and reread it a few times on the plane, not so much looking for hidden nuances as just holding on to it as a fetish, still having a crush on him, remembering their fuck, the expressions on his face in the nightclub or that day on the beach, the sound of his voice. His dazzling smile.

She felt like Errol Mwangi was too much of a womanizer to be trusted. Maybe Tavinho was a different story. She had so loved him when he had shown up unexpectedly at the ceremony . . . that circumstance had changed all her feelings for him. He had been so sweet, and she hadn't been able to detect any *machao* jealousy in him, which was so cool in a Brazilian male.

Florida worked out better than she could have hoped. Jules didn't seem at all annoyed that she'd arrived late to shoot her scene—a demon for his schedule, he'd simply done a version with local talent, and that took care of that. Lisa hadn't wanted to do it anyway, not at this point.

As soon as she said that she'd been secretly doing a film, and that Roy Hardway was in it, and that everyone had worked for deferred salaries and shares, Jules became intensely interested. He wanted to see the rough cut right away. He didn't care if it was in 16 mm.

Seeing it again, for the seventh or eighth time, Lisa was shy, and it seemed too weird and arty a cinematic experience to appeal to Jules—but she was wrong. He sat silently throughout the entire screening, abandoning himself to it, and then: "I love it," he said.

"Congratulations. I didn't realize you were so close to Roy. People have been extremely curious about him, what happened to him. I think his agent even hired a private eye. Roy looks great."

"This might be his last film," Lisa said.

Jules wanted to know how she had done some of the special effects. The wonderful matte stuff, and those incredible models, and the amputations, the best amputated limbs and severed heads he'd ever seen. Jules was so deferential Lisa hardly knew how to react. Then the thought hit her: This is how men treat other men.

And so Jules offered to help with postproduction, and they arranged a schedule to start having meetings in L.A. for the *Ripper* project. Meanwhile she would try to get *Manoa, City of Gold* into a festival or two; she knew some people, she thought she could at least get it into the Berlin.

TWO

Lisa and Track talked on the phone (he was still in L.A.) while she was in Florida, before she flew to New York, where she would stay at his apartment on the Lower East Side while working on *Manoa*'s sound. He was very unhappy that both Ariel Mendoza and the Los Angeles–based detective (whose name Track had never gotten, and he blamed himself for this oversight) seemed to have disappeared.

"It's disturbing," Track said. "They let me claim Mendoza's stuff when I settled his bill—nothing. No clues. Assuming I would know one if one bit me on the ass."

"But he said he'd traced the couch to L.A.?"

"Yes."

"Then Boro has it," Lisa said. She knew.

"Jesus."

Lisa told Track about the corpsevine and how the film *Manoa, City of Gold* had miraculously come about.

He was fascinated.

"This isn't even something *you* personally dreamed, I mean, all of it? Some of it, if I'm reading you . . . must have, possibly, *bled* into your consciousness from the dead brains, which we assume are somehow synthesized by the vine. . . ."

"That's what Dad thinks."

"What kind of music do you need?" Track and she were close now, they understood each other well.

"Just mostly percussion, I think. The music that's already present is like . . . stuff played backward, or through filters, some of it's like weird samples of orchestras playing on the other side of a hill in a storm."

"And Roy Hardway's in it?"

"Yes," Lisa said. "I'm going to list him as executive producer, even though he's dead. That's typical of executive producers, anyway."

Track laughed. He said he'd see her in a few days, in New York.

THREE

Code wasn't at his old number. It was disconnected. So she called (from Track's apartment) directory assistance and then Alvin Sender. She left a message on Sender's machine, and he called her back almost immediately, as though he might simply be screening his calls. From his manner, someone on Mars listening in on an interplanetary frequency might have imagined that they were good friends, that they'd been good friends all along.

"Where have you been?" he asked. "Everybody's been wondering about you."

"Yeah. I've been in Brazil."

"Somebody said something about you and Roy Hardway . . . and no one's seen him around here."

"He was with me part of the time. We shot a film."

"That's great. Wow."

"Listen, do you know where Code is? His old number doesn't work."

"That's right, you've been out of touch. I'll give you his new one—he's moved in with Lauren Devoto. You know, Vincent Garbo's ex-wife. They're in love."

Lisa didn't like his sarcasm, but it was pretty amazing news. Just what Code had always said he wanted: to be "discovered" by some rich, older, still-beautiful babe. Vincent Garbo had been at one time a successful schlockmeister—producing films of a mediocre tackiness without a cult. His tall, big-breasted, white-blond widow had allegedly become addicted to the knife—that is, cosmetic surgery—so she looked a tad weird. In her forties, she was perfect for what Code had said he wanted out of life. To be taken care of. In luxury. To be a hood ornament, basically.

"Is he still doing music?"

"Sure."

Sender said it with such assurance that she didn't want to ask anything more. She said she had to go.

"Call me anytime," he said, again with this knowing attitude. "If you ever have a temporary cash flow situation, or just want to do something, I can always find you work. Believe me, you're in demand."

She didn't know if Alvin Sender was an agent, a casting director, or some kind of pimp. She was dismayed by the conversation in several ways. She had talked to Christine the other day, and Christine had been friendly on the surface but indifferent, Lisa supposed she deserved it but it had left her feeling bad. Adrian had told her that Christine and Oriole had split up again, that Christine was now living with this guy with whom she was doing a documentary for PBS on animals living in zoos, how they differ from their brothers and sisters in the wild, what adaptations were taking place . . . a subject they could have discussed if Christine had cared to, but Adrian had volunteered more secondhand info than Christine had, she had been sort of unfriendly and vague. So Lisa felt like her two best friends, Christine and Code, had abandoned her. Even if she was the one who had left. She had had to. Emotionally, they were leaving her first. Fuckers.

Motherfuckers.

She went to the movies, by herself, and watched a Selwyn Popcorn double feature: *Thin Skin* and *The Kiss of the Sphinx*. Because she was in a troubled mood, her loneliness, which seemed to have come from out of nowhere, and the pressure of perpetrating this weird, colossal fraud . . . the psychic film . . . it took a while for the ritualistic magic of the film experience to begin to work for her, but early on in *Thin Skin*, sitting there in the dark, eating popcorn, drinking Dr Pepper, the rhythmic images on the screen and the subliminal-to-dynamic soundtrack began to manipulate her, hypnotized her, willingly she received the twenty-four-frames-per-second hieroglyph into the malleable chemistry and electricity of her mind, so that by the end of the second feature she was essentially exhilarated and redeemed.

Walking home (to Track's), some of this feeling was dissipated in the darkness just by the fact that she had to be aware of her surroundings. Two guys looked at her with too much attention. She didn't feel safe. You always had to think about maybe being raped or murdered, attacked as easy and magnetic prey.

The phone rang. It was Code in L.A.

"Lisa, you're finally back in the country. I heard that you got my number this afternoon. Why didn't you call?"

"You're at Lauren Devoto's house, right? In Beverly Hills?"

"Bel Air."

"OK, Bel Air. Where in the house are you calling from?"

"I'm in my room. Oh, you were afraid it might be awkward? Don't worry. Lauren knows all about you. When you come out here again, she's looking forward to meeting you. Really."

"That's wonderful. I don't know when I'll be there; I'm probably going to Europe first."

"Sure, I understand. Film festivals. Make sure, by the way, when you put the credits together, that you list Mr. Boro as coproducer. I think he's done a lot for you."

"Code, what the fuck are you talking about?" Lisa said, just to gain time, because she was shocked.

"You know. I'm the last person you should play cherry with, so give it a rest. He wants to see you. I get the impression there's some unfinished business. You should be happy to know, even though I guess you haven't paid for it, that your vengeance on Lou is complete."

"How did you meet Boro?" Lisa asked, suffused with horror but managing to sound reasonably composed. Code just sounded like Code.

"I hardly know him. I'm just relaying a message. Oh yeah . . . another thing. Check your right ankle tonight. That's all I know."

And he hung up.

On Lisa's right ankle there was now an apparent tattoo . . . of what first looked like barbed wire but then resolved into a kind of crown of thorns, all around the slender ankle in an intricate design.

So the grand total was: fiery cross on right bicep, jaguar on left bicep, dagger-in-heart on left buttock, *L-O-V-E* on right fingers, *H-A-T-E* on left fingers—and now a crown of thorns around her right ankle.

Was it worthwhile trying to analyze what Code had said, that her vengeance on Lou was complete? Did that mean he was dead? She shuddered a bit, though for the most part she was numb. She'd been trying not to think about Lou Greenwood, Lou Adolph, Lou Burke. All that seemed so far away.

Lisa took a bath. The tattoo did not wash off. She felt wounded, exposed—as though Boro could see her, read her mind, no matter what she might decide to do.

Most experiments fail, her father had once told her. You had to keep trying. She rose up, dripping, reaching over for a fluffy towel. Track favored surprisingly luxurious big towels.

The mirror on the back of the door wasn't fogged, so she studied her reflection, mistrustfully searching for any other fresh markings or tattoos. Ritual scarification or piercing might be next. Though maybe not. Boro liked her, Code had said.

Lisa looked at her upper arms, turned to check her naked shoulder blades and back, twisting to see her ass. She looked like a criminal. A prostitute? What did it mean to be a prostitute, anyway? She felt more like a witch.

FOUR

Maybe it was some kind of a demonstration. Lisa tried to avoid it. At the same time, she wanted to get close enough to see. She met a steady stream of people coming the other way, talking . . . it came to seem like there were a lot of lesbians in the disintegrating crowd. Many gay men also. College kids.

Somebody said, "Lisa Nova!" and came over to her, a young woman, and in a moment or two—a definite long *hold* of a moment—Lisa came to recognize Raelyn, the girl from Seattle. Raelyn changed direction and walked with her, and Lisa asked her what was going on.

"There was a bashing down here, and one of the women is in intensive care. She's got a fractured skull. There are witnesses, but the cops haven't done anything." She shrugged. "What are you doing in New York? You look great."

"I was going to ask you the same thing. Are you going this way? I'm staying at my brother's."

"I moved here. I'm going to see if I can get into the NYU film program. You went, let's see—to the School of Visual Arts. Which one do you recommend?"

"NYU," Lisa said, because it was the more obvious answer, the school of Jim Jarmusch and Spike Lee. Raelyn looked confident, her hair cut like an innocent preadolescent boy's. She wore a dark brown corduroy jacket over a man's dress shirt, and light brown baggy slacks. She looked, at first glance, like an effeminate young male, surely the intended effect. She was attractive, in her way.

Lisa said, "Do you want to have dinner with me? I'd like to talk." She liked Raelyn, she wanted to find out if she had any real organizational skills. Raelyn might imagine that this was all a prelude to lesbian sex, but it was not. It was a job interview. She needed to start accumulating people she could trust.

"You never did answer me about why you're in New York."

"Some postproduction on a new film." Lisa felt slightly embarrassed. Raelyn wanted to know all about it.

In a Chinese restaurant later on, Lisa questioned Raelyn about her background, how she'd come to want to work in films. It turned out that she had acted on the stage from the time she had been twelve. In the last couple of years she had been heavily involved in Seattle's lesbian theater scene, from performing in musicals to designing sets and even directing a time or two. Lisa knew the common wisdom that filmmakers generally fell into two categories: actor-oriented and image-oriented. She was, of course, the latter, and tended to see actors as furniture.

Getting out of the cab at Track's apartment building, a black guy was asking her and Raelyn for money, not taking the first turndown as definitive, a tallish, skinny guy in a navy blue pea coat and a watch-cap pulled down over his ears, several days' beard on his face, dirty-looking, asking for a dollar, "Hey, you can spare a dollar, don't give me that shit." Lisa felt a great blankness come over her, she was ready to give the man a dollar if he asked just a little bit more nicely, then as she began to pass him he stepped in front of her, impeding her way to the door. They were very close, and something happened, her hand flashed out in an incredibly swift reflex, for a second she didn't know where she was but felt a profound inner brightness. Raelyn took her by the arm as the man turned away, he ran a few steps, saying things . . . there was blood all over Lisa's hand, though she didn't recall touching a thing. She'd clawed him like a cat, Raelyn said. Certainly there seemed to have been disproportionate damage, given the not-so-long length of her nails. She'd ripped his cheek wide open, Raelyn said. Was she sure she hadn't had something in her hand?

No, nothing, Lisa said, and Raelyn hugged her to comfort her because Lisa seemed shaken, a little spaced.

Upstairs, it was chilly in the apartment, the light dull bluish dark, without color. Lisa gave Raelyn a complicit little smile as Raelyn touched her, and they moved to the bed tentatively, slowly . . . Raelyn thought that Lisa was basically narcissistic and, of course, straight. But curious, and Raelyn was the instrument of adventure for her. That was all right. That was just fine.

"Did you have this planned all along?" she said after a sisterly kiss, her hand now gently exploring Lisa's tender breast, the nipple hard.

"I don't know," Lisa replied, breathing out a long, relaxing breath, closing her eyes. Raelyn didn't ask any more questions. She caressed Lisa's back, her stomach, her buttocks and thighs, lingering over the tattooed area of her left buttock, lifting that buttock, excited by the wildness implicit in Lisa's being marked in such a way . . . touching her expressively, in no hurry, as the other touched her in return without any real intention, coming back again and again to Raelyn's breasts, which she seemed to find interesting, and which were actually bigger than her own. Raelyn assumed, without minding it, that Lisa would be clumsy, as pretty girls seldom had to try very hard to please.

Finally, after waiting as long as she could, Raelyn went down and spread apart Lisa's thighs, licking her with appreciation and a kind of musical sensitivity to effect, feeling the vibrations set off by her strong tongue, tasting her particular, unique taste, registering every little contraction and tremor, as Lisa's hands came down and she ran her fingers through Raelyn's short silky hair.

Lisa was in a dreamy state, close to losing consciousness, her limbs heavy and voluptuous, the flavor of sin and sinfulness that somehow underlay everything only made the pleasure more surreal, the naturalness of two bodies together complicated and transfigured, in her present mood she didn't care if, when she took her turn at Raelyn's cunt, she seemed unsure and inept. It didn't matter if her eyes stayed open or closed, she saw salmon, coral, orange-tinged waving frond-like shapes, rustling and moving against one another in harmony, preconscious but alive, that vision blending into softer forms, illuminated with an inner light, breasts, polyps and buds, swelling or merging, radiant, fending off the blackness beyond, too dark to be blue, the bottom of the sea.

FIVE

When Track arrived the next day, he found his sister alone but still in bed at two o'clock in the afternoon. Raelyn had just left an hour or so before.

"Track!" Lisa exclaimed.

"Yeah. Hi. I'm going to take a shower. I'm fucking tired. Do you want to get some coffee? Who painted *Mares and Foals on a Mountainous Landscape*?"

"Stubbs!" Lisa cried out, delighted, and she laughed.

Later on they went down to the recording studio, and Lisa talked freely, imaginatively, about how she'd like to assemble a team—like Fassbinder had—that could make three or four films a year, dirt cheap. She mentioned various names they both knew.

"What about Boris?" she asked.

"You don't want Boris."

"Why not?"

"You could spring for his rehab, I guess, but you'd probably have to kidnap him off the street."

"Smacked out?"

"You got it."

"What about Julia Hyphen, uh . . . "

"Julia Hyphen-what-the-fuck?" Track said. "She's done some set design for the I Told You So Theater. Maybe she'd be good."

"If we have the sound ready by next week, I can show *Manoa* in Berlin."

"That's right. They liked that other piece of nihilist-slash-Riot Grrl neo–Lizzie Borden art shit, didn't they?"

He meant, affectionately, *Girl, 10, Murders Boys*.

SIX

Selwyn Popcorn had come to Germany on sort of a whim, in order to get out of Hollywood for a while. Postproduction was finally done on his latest film, the sound mix was finished—he had a week in between that and the color timing.

The actual shooting of this last project had been filled with unpleasant turmoil. The script was fundamentally flawed. If you had to think about trying to save it in the editing room, it was almost certainly too late.

Popcorn had allowed himself to be talked into a "package." Not without misgivings, but what overrode those misgivings? Greed. The probably erroneous idea that he could do this film, *Call It Love*, make it more interesting than it might otherwise be, make some money, and be free to do whatever he wanted for the next two or three years.

So he had put himself in the position of directing a "Susan Heller vehicle," a picture in which she manifested exactly the same Susan Heller that had worked before. She would repeat it until she wore it out. She had a powerful agent, and the producer, Larry Planet (Popcorn couldn't really blame him: Larry was a survivor) was completely on her side.

Susan Heller had to have her close-ups and her honest indignation scene, she had to have her designer clothes, she had to break down and cry. She was very proud of these tears. They were her signature, in a sense.

On the set, she had more of an entourage than Popcorn was used to dealing with, it was really the worst he'd ever seen . . . oh, he just needed to get it behind him and go on to the next one.

He needed, as always, to work.

Selwyn Popcorn didn't always keep up with what everyone was doing, but every so often he liked to see a few of the new, off-the-wall films, see what people were talking about, see if he was missing anything, if there was anything out there really new.

He liked Berlin.

If he was going to pick a city in the world in which to die, he might pick Berlin. Maybe this meant that he didn't actually *like* it in any commonly recognizable way. Maybe he hated it. Its architecture, its obvious aura of history, its streets, the people one saw on these streets. Death was here. It was all around.

Popcorn was divorced again, for the fourth time. He had five children scattered all over, but he despaired of himself as a parent. The oldest, Mark, was in Amsterdam, if that information was still valid, and Mark didn't love him, or respect him, or even like him enough to be more than vacantly, coldly civil when they met or talked on the phone. Popcorn's children had no use for him. And he didn't recognize himself in any of them, to tell the truth.

His latest wife had been another actress. He was a fool. Still, that was whom, in his business, he tended to meet.

What was he doing here? A British journalist, or film critic, same difference, an admirer of his work, told Popcorn he wished to write a book about him, that is, about his work. Popcorn was forty-nine, he had made eleven films. Nine of these had made money. Critical opinion had been divided but generally favorable. One of the films that had been rather despised, *The Body Removed,* had done especially well on video, and now opinion seemed to be revising itself.

Popcorn became bored watching these festival films. Tired of being noticed, pointed out, or spoken to, approached.

He went to a museum and no one followed him. Popcorn looked at a painting by Vermeer, *The Glass of Wine.* His favorite painting of all time. He left the Gemaldegalerie and located a gallery with an exhibit of paintings by Gerhard Richter. It was lightly raining outside.

It was a shock to his senses. Here was this girl he'd noticed staring at him in the lobby of a theater earlier. Here she was in the gallery. She had burning dark eyes, extraordinary eyes, brown hair, and she wore a weathered black leather jacket over a dress that seemed more like a short lacy ivory-hued slip. Black tights and Doc Martens.

Yes, he remembered now. She had been with another girl, who had seemed to be her girlfriend. Was she a lesbian? A German?

In English, she said, "Do you like Gerhard Richter?"

"Yes. You?"

"I love his work."

Her very beauty . . . Popcorn's wariness returned. She might be an aspiring actress, or a model.

"You're an American? Are you here for the festival?"

"Yes," she answered, and then, somewhat shyly, "I have a film."

"What is your name?" Then he asked her the title of the movie, and "Do you have a good part?"

"Oh, I'm not an actress. I appear in this, and I was in something else . . . but I'm not an actress. I directed it."

"Really?" Popcorn was faintly interested, but also in a way disappointed. If she'd been an actress, she might have come up to his hotel room. He could deal with actresses. They were well aware of his star-making potential. But Lisa Nova, a young feminist filmmaker, was probably actively seeking to avoid being treated as in any sense a bimbo. Even with those full lips, and the leather jacket . . .

He asked her if she'd like to have coffee with him. She said sure. As they walked down the street together, he asked what her film was about.

"The search for El Dorado. *Manoa* is the Indian name for that, you see. Roy Hardway's in it, and—"

"Oh, Roy. How is he? I'm sort of surprised, actually . . . "

"That he'd be in an independent film? Yes, it's an unusual move for him. But by now he might not be much like people remember him."

"What? Has he become a mystic?"

"Something like that."

When Lisa took off her jacket in the coffee shop, it was the tattoos that entranced Popcorn. Lisa Nova was very pretty, but the tattoos hit at some perverse desire, some machinery he'd never indulged.

Her favorite film of his was *Thin Skin*. Popcorn laughed and said he'd like to see her film. He wondered if she was part Brazilian. He studied her. Had she stalked him? He was afraid of her in a funny way.

SEVEN

Flying from Berlin to Los Angeles, Lisa had to change planes in London, New York, and Chicago. She was exhausted. Sitting in O'Hare, amongst all the glass, it seemed like she'd walked for three miles. And now she had two more hours to wait. She was too tired to enjoy watching the people, to be interested in them.

Lisa asked Raelyn to stay in Europe, represent the film in London, while Lisa returned to Los Angeles for meetings with the rest of the production team for *L.A. Ripper II*. It was time to start casting, etcetera. Only two parts were really etched in stone: the Ripper and the police detective who'd gone after him in the first film.

The rendezvous with Selwyn Popcorn, coming as it did, completely by chance, seemed almost meaningless, in that she had had nothing especially to gain . . . and yet she still contemplated it, even if she didn't believe he'd much liked her film. There'd been some sort of electricity between them, possibly sexual. He was undeniably attractive, though she kept hoping that that wasn't all of it on his part, as she was very conscious of the age difference—he was forty-nine to her twenty-six, the only time she'd done something like that had been with Lou.

She thought of Popcorn's face after he'd seen *Manoa*. He'd asked her about some of the scenes. She tried to recall what she'd said . . . the images from the film kept interfering, overwhelming or at least overshadowing all civilized discourse. It hypnotized her, looking for herself in it, feeling that she could almost, just about, remember having dreamed this scene or that. She had sorted through the flood of images, like Maxwell's demon theoretically sorting molecules according to heat. Yes. Somewhere inside of her, she had viewed all of this material, even if it wasn't all *hers*, and she had chosen, however instinctively, she had sorted, she had directed the dream.

Right now, as she half dozed on another plane, the jet engines soothing her in some kind of modern way, she saw again certain moments that had been vivid to her, sharing the experience in a crowded Berlin theater, a level of exhibitionism and uncalculated . . . uh, exposure . . . the couple of times she appeared on the screen as an actor: first as an Indian girl in the Amazon, her face painted brightly, bisected, half red, the other side black . . . just a brief sideways look at the camera while being raped by Roy Hardway, along with some others being raped by soldiers in a conquered village, faces painted the same, amid corpses and unbelievable amputations and disembowelments, severed heads—and back to medieval Spain, where in the most startling shot she saw herself suddenly as one of the witches accused by the Inquisition, wearing the exaggerated dunce cap they made them wear while on trial, something seemed the matter with her feet, the way she was sitting on the bench, with the others, yet she was brave, she had been tortured, no doubt the *strappado*, and now she would be burned, she saw it in her own face . . . that was a still picture Lisa would never want to study, it had too much painful information. Strangers saw this and hardly noticed, it was "acting" to them, less self-exposure than was shown in her manifestation as the painted Indian girl, lying naked on the ground, panting, frightened, wondering if the conquistadors were done.

The image selected for the poster was the gilded man, the Indian covered in gold dust, before he ceremonially leaped into the cold blue lake against a backdrop of the lost city of Manoa . . . in its perfect geometry and clean white stones. And: Roy Hardway, standing in shallow wavelets, blond beard, shiny armor and red sash, raising and kissing his sword . . . cut back to a procession of white-robed choirboys, doing an intricate dance, slow and solemn . . . and then a penitent scourging himself . . . to royalty in an elaborate Velázquez interior, moving in slow motion, in rich velvet and damask, silver and wine red.

Fast-tracking shots of silent jungle: monkeys in trees, jaguars with faces of yellow and white and black, aquatic plants over still water like a dark green living carpet, fungi, alligators seeming to be fallen logs, endless vines, a baroque profusion of lianas, mosquitoes, snakes, oozing bulbs, sticky, syrup-anointed insect-eating plants, opening like vulvas, then snapping shut around their prey.

In the twilight the Spaniards saw the silvery gleams of movement composing themselves into the strange vocabulary of nightmares: deformed faces, skulking demons, dwarves, creatures half animal and half man . . . these monstrosities blurring into a raucous carnival in Seville, the pre-Lenten revelers wearing grotesque masks, pig faces, impossibly long noses, dancing in the flickering light . . . an insert once more of those condemned by the Inquisition, the distorted music continuing, then a fire against a clear blue sky, red and orange, burning a corpse black, down to the skeleton, the rib cage and skull, the smoke from the body's fat rising black. . . .

As Lisa woke, the last thing she saw was a *tableau vivant,* the Virgin Mary portrayed as a girl of thirteen, according to the Inquisition's directive, a thirteen-year-old girl with long golden hair, only her eyes move as she is enveloped by a paper sun and crowned by silver paper stars; she stands on a crescent moon with its horns touching the earth.

Lisa asked for a Sprite. She didn't want to think about the soldiers shitting, the frenzied massacres, one of which in particular went on for a long fucking time, tense despite hardly being cut, hardly changing point of view, and mostly being in real time . . . or the late scene of Roy painfully vomiting a large quantity of gold and jewels.

The blond stewardess smiled at her. Lisa was very thirsty. When she had finished the Sprite, she got up to wash her face. She kept seeing herself in the dunce cap, unwashed hair and face, mouth open a little stupidly, eyes however alert to the meaning of the sentence passed, a witch condemned to die.

EIGHT

Amazingly, a limo picked her up at LAX. How Jules Brandenberg could have figured out she was coming on this flight, she didn't know. The limousine driver was tall and looked like he knew martial arts, a Steven Seagal wanna-be. He drove her to her apartment. She was thankful he was with her, bringing up her bags. She opened the door, mentioning to him that she hadn't been here in a while. Inside, the vine had disappeared from the piano, and everything looked as if the maid had just been here a few hours ago. It was like nothing strange had ever happened; she couldn't believe it.

The chauffeur left, saying he would be back in the morning. Lisa nodded, walking around, looking at how clean it was, how her plants had been watered—but then, when she took a shower, she still had Boro's tattoos. There was even fresh food in the refrigerator. It was insane. She needed her cat. Casimir. The thought of this distracted her from the other stuff or from trying to analyze the responses to her film in Berlin. She opened a Tecate beer and called Adrian.

"You're back," he said. "Great." He sounded warm and affectionate.

"Adrian, I'm sorry I haven't called for a while. I've been really busy, but—how've you been? Do you need a job?"

"Well, actually . . . I'm doing pretty well, but . . . I think things have sort of fallen through for Christine on that documentary. Don't tell her that I told you, OK?"

"I won't. But really? When I called her from New York, she sounded so gung-ho. . . ."

"She always asks about you, and she's come over to pet Caz a time or two. You're such an adventuress, you know, you leave some people behind. They can't keep up with you. Oh, by the way, I was talking today to a friend in New York who's going over for Cannes . . . and he heard from somebody at *Variety* that some weird film by a little-known filmmaker named Lisa Nova is causing a lot of talk."

"The reviews I heard about," Lisa said, "were like, uh, 'Nova's snuff-film poetics' and 'the nightmare of history, built on a mountain of corpses, formless and chaotic' . . . and then I got on a plane. As far as I know, Idea One *might* be going to distribute, strictly an art-house release . . . well, it's that kind of film, it's all the visuals, there's only about three lines of dialogue in the whole thing."

"It's getting you talked about," Adrian said. "Selwyn Popcorn said something like, 'Lisa Nova may have the most original vision of any young filmmaker I've seen.' Jason—my friend in New York—said he heard that you took some good pictures, you're photogenic . . . he asked me if it's true you stabbed somebody down in Brazil during production of your film. *Did* you?"

"Yeah." Lisa was speechless.

Adrian laughed, at least playing at being further delighted by this new revelation of her spunk. He wanted to know all about it. Lisa had to remind herself that he was a specialist in gossip, writing as he did for *Details, Premiere,* and *Rolling Stone*. Her status with him was now somewhat changed.

"I'm too confused right at the moment to make sense," Lisa said. "I'll tell you about it when I see Caz."

"Do you want me to bring him by? Brad isn't coming home till eight or nine."

"Could you? I need to see him . . . you've got to remember, I just got off the plane less than an hour ago."

"I understand. Don't let me pump you. It's an occupational hazard—I can't help myself. Do you need anything that I can pick up on the way?"

"The refrigerator's stocked with food. All I can think of is that Jules . . . well, he's terribly thoughtful."

"That's what I hear."

While waiting, then, for Adrian, Lisa gathered her thoughts for just a second or two before impulsively calling Christine.

"Lisa! I was just thinking about you. Somebody was talking to me yesterday about Eric Lemongrass, your policeman in *L.A. Ripper*. It sounds like he's an asshole, and I was worried about you. His new movie, that mountain-climbing thing, is turning into a surprise hit, and supposedly he wants more money for everything, naturally, now that he's medium-hot. And he's a jerk about women. So . . . how was Berlin?"

"I didn't think it was that great, but when I talked to Adrian he said I didn't see deeply enough into the nature of reality, I didn't understand anything—so I guess Berlin was pretty good." Lisa felt like somehow she and Christine were back on the same channel. Before she could ask Christine if she wanted (not needed) a job, Christine said, "Now that a studio is actually willing to trust you with a budget and a schedule—can I have a job? This whole zoo-animal PBS thing went all to shit. But I'd really like to see you, to hear about

Brazil and your film. I'm curious as hell. When you called from New York the other week, you caught me at a bad time. Oriole was just coming over, and I was getting ready for some sort of Strindberg deal or something, bitter recriminations on all sides. How is your tattoo situation?"

"I can't remember the last time we talked about them," Lisa said. She had by now realized that Christine was high or slightly drunk, but it didn't matter. The friendly reconnection was there. "Of course you can have a job. What do you want to do?"

"Not production aide, that's all."

"Oh listen, Adrian's here with Caz. I have a meeting tomorrow morning, and it might go through lunch, I don't know—what about having dinner tomorrow night? I can put you on my expense account."

"OK, sure. I'll be here late afternoon."

"All right, see you. Bye."

She let Adrian in with her loudly meowing beautiful Burmese cat. Caz began purring as soon as he saw her, smelled her, heard her voice. Tears came lightly, sentimentally to her eyes. She kissed him and hugged him, petting him as Adrian Gee smiled at her and looked around. He wore a pale lavender shirt and faded, faded soft blue jeans.

"What sort of questions did they ask you at your press conference?" he asked with a certain Hong Kong–style insouciance.

"What happened to Roy. Where's Roy. Is it true that he's become a Buddhist. Are you two secretly married. What made Roy decide to star in such an offbeat film. Where is he. When's he coming back."

"And were the reporters satisfied with your answers?" Adrian often sounded like he knew more than he really did; it was one of his tricks to get people to talk.

So Lisa, gazing at him, said, "No," and did not elaborate, as Casimir with great affection bit her hand, holding it there with his paws. Adrian himself didn't ask her anything about Roy Hardway; he was more delicate than that. He changed the subject to Selwyn Popcorn and his latest film, the one for which Lisa had been set to be assistant to the director until Robert Hand's daughter Alison had been given the job. Popcorn had talked about none of this, though over coffee and a piece of cake (he had a sweet tooth, which might account for the ten pounds or so he was overweight) he had intimated that Susan Heller, though hot now, was not making any friends. It had sounded as if he thought she was dumb.

But now this new shit about Alison, that she'd fucked up and was in rehab . . . while Popcorn was saying Lisa had the most original vision he'd seen . . . what a turnaround! Did Boro deserve very much credit? Regretfully, she supposed that he did. More or less on cue, Adrian began telling her about all the misfortunes that had continued to bedevil Lou and his family, using as his point of segue the fact that Robert Hand had fired Lou from the studio where he'd worked for twenty-three years.

Lou Greenwood, Lou Adolph, Lou Burke had separated from his wife and, after their house burned partially down, had embarked on an ocean voyage—possibly to Samoa or Australia. Veronica, according to rumor, was hard to reason with these days, having given her life to God. That is, she was said to have joined a church that might be described, in California or anywhere else, as a cult. The rumor was she was in New Mexico now.

"The son, Jonathan, may have gone off with some bikers," Adrian said. "I heard he was hanging around with some leather freaks, anyway, out at Zuma Beach. Maybe they killed him and ate him," Adrian said as a joke.

Lisa shuddered but managed a polite laugh. Despite everything that Adrian had told her about Lou's family, she imagined the real story was probably much worse. After Adrian left, she just sat there, communing with her cat.

NINE

In the morning, Lisa discovered that her car was parked down on the street below; she tried her key, and the Trans Am started right up. The battery was fine. It was weird, but she could accept it; when the limousine came she told the driver, apologetically, that she preferred to drive her own car. Sure, he said. He drove away. She was nervous and excited: This was what she had wanted, to be the director of a film at a major studio . . . she felt good. She hadn't yet personally seen anything flattering written about *Manoa,* but assuming Adrian hadn't gone completely insane, those notices would be on the way. Knowing that Selwyn Popcorn had said something nice gave her a certain confidence—confidence in her aura, her momentary heat. Her luck.

What to wear? What sort of look to present? Lisa would have liked to have worn fake clear glass wire-rimmed glasses, to dress more or less sloppy casual, loose clothes and messy short hair . . . but if she was going to use her newly forming image, she might as well have bare arms and show the tattoos right away, get it over with, let her hair keep growing out, go for kind of a rock-and-roll or punk thing. Not all of the young directors aimed at the youth audience had to be out-and-out nerds. For Christ's sake, *L.A. Ripper II* was a horror flick. Splatter. Exploitation, maybe done with style but still judged mostly by numbers of dead bodies, gallons of blood, and exposed naked breasts.

At the gate, sunglasses on, she told the guard her name. It was great. She parked her car. Underneath all this wonderfulness, however, was an uneasiness that would not go away, an uneasiness connected to Boro and Lou. Oh well.

Jules Brandenberg, as producer, was at the meeting, in the tranquil, cool, luxurious room. Also Eric Lemongrass, who played the cop, the homicide detective, extremely tan, having just scored fairly bad reviews but an unexpected moderate hit with *Solo Faces*, his mountain-climbing film. Lisa shook his hand and quietly said hi. Paul Bancroft, the longtime off-Broadway star who played the Ripper, struck her as friendly, reasonable, surprisingly unegotistic, probably gay. The director of photography, Dario Boccioni, had done the first film (and worked with Jules on almost everything he did). The art director was already chosen, Rosa Liszt, so Lisa evidently would not have the option of suggesting Julia Panofsky-Brown, from the School of Visual Arts. As the budget went up, the first-time director's level of control was going down.

Eric Lemongrass complained about the script. Lisa asked what he didn't like. "The ending," he said with some heat. "I think it fragments the audience's response to have the hookers band together and kill the Ripper. They'll feel let down. In a film like this, they want a one-on-one showdown. That's really crucial."

"It's corny," Lisa rejoined.

Lemongrass didn't respond, just giving her the blue-eyed stare he'd been working on. Jules said, "We'll certainly consider your input, Eric."

After the actors left, Lisa and Jules talked about the color scheme and look of the picture for a while, with the cinematographer and the set designer, and the fact that Jules knew these people so much better than Lisa—she'd never met them before—made her feel like quite a lot was being taken out of her hands. She offered ideas she had thought about for a long time, but Dario Boccioni . . . she felt little or no rapport with him. He didn't seem to take her seriously. Could she fire people? She was beginning to wonder. Make the best of it, she thought.

Only when it got around to the casting did she feel like her ideas were avidly heard. She mentioned Mary Siddons, the star of Lisa's *Girl, 10, Murders Boys,* and Jules recognized the name, and said, "Oh you're right, she'll be perfect." When everyone was gone except Lisa and Jules, she said to him, "What do *you* think of changing the ending?"

"I don't know," he said tonelessly, revealing nothing, a model of half-baffled indifference.

After a very long time, he added, discreetly, "You've been out of the country. Have you seen the figures on what Eric's movie has done its first three weeks?"

"I haven't seen any numbers, but I've heard that it's a hit."

Jules nodded. His hair was cut shorter than she remembered, and he seemed even thinner. Lisa didn't find him attractive, and by this time she didn't trust him very far, despite his enthusiasm for *Manoa*.

"Eric's feeling it," Jules said. "He feels larger every day. His agent is very bitter about the money he signed for—he'll probably end up with quite a lot more. The studio thinks it's great that he'll still condescend to do this sort of material. Eric's theory, if I read his mind, and I think I can, is to turn this into as much of an action thriller as possible, expand his role along with his money, and try to make the crossover into being an action star. This could be a nice transitional film for him. But if he's smart, he'll realize it's too late for a major rewrite, and he'll turn in a day's work for a day's pay and then go on to the rest of his career. This just isn't the kind of film for too many car chases and that kind of shit. My bet is he'll do his four weeks. Don't look at me like that. I'm on your side. You'll get used to Dario. You'll see. Things'll fall into place. I was thinking Wesley Crawford for first AD, and you'll love him. He'll do a lot of your dirty work—he's great. Eric's nothing. I know him; he's a piece of meat."

They walked out into the magnificent parking lot. Lisa knew that all this stuff was normal, typical of this factory town. Her ambitions seemed stupid to her right now.

~ TEN

At about two-thirty in the afternoon of this dirty-blond day, Lisa stopped in Venice, going into a restaurant she vaguely remembered having read about in a review; it was cool inside, and she ordered an iced tea, a hamburger, and a small salad, house dressing on the side. She was wearing an emerald green halter that left most of her back bare, a gold bracelet, a watch with a thick leather band, a lucky ring on her little finger (gold with a piece of cloudy jade), sandals, and a short tan skirt. She didn't remember to take off her sunglasses until her iced tea came, she had been clutching her keys while trying to look across the room at some drawings put up in a row.

She felt like a hustler . . . more successful than many, though still a baby by most standards. She sighed, looked at her tattooed fingers, and thought of Tavinho, that quality he had of never seeming to blame her for anything. If she got through this production, maybe she'd go back down to Brazil. She missed her dad, too. It had been reassuring just to know he was around.

A guy came in. The restaurant was just about empty, but she wouldn't even have noticed had he not come over to her table, smiled at her, said, "Lisa Nova? Can I sit down?"

"Sure," she said, neutrally wondering if he was a reporter and if so, why he hadn't called. He was kind of a big, burly dark blond guy wearing tan chinos and an untucked mostly blue Hawaiian shirt.

"Who are you?" Her hamburger arrived, along with the check. She ate a pickle, looking at him, and he put a card down on the table for her.

"That's who I'm working for. My name is Duane Moyer. I've been looking for Roy Hardway for about two months or so, without any luck. It shouldn't be so hard to track down somebody like that, should it? A famous movie star. Everybody knows his face. Excuse me, though, Miss Nova. I didn't mean to interrupt your meal. I'll just be a moment more."

"You're a detective?"

"That's right."

"What do you want from me?"

He smiled again, at her tone. "Why, Mr. Laughton, Roy's agent, would like to talk to you. Is it OK if I call him, tell him you'll come by this afternoon?"

Lisa took another sip of iced tea; picked up the card. Of course she'd heard of him. Nehi Laughton. He also represented Kimberly Chase, the former Miss Universe. He'd been pointed out to her once at a party, back when she had first come out here, way before she'd ever known Lou.

"Sherman Oaks. OK, I'll talk to him."

"Great. Thank you. It's been nice meeting you. I'll tell Mr. Laughton to expect you in, what, say about an hour?"

"Sure." Lisa took her first bite of the hamburger only now, as Duane Moyer left. Shit. The way he'd looked at her. She didn't feel like eating very much more. Fuck. She had them wrap up half the burger and give her an iced tea to go, to drink in the car.

Driving away, she knew Moyer was shadowing her, and it gave her a creepy feeling. He must have followed her to the restaurant from the studio.

The receptionist looked like Kim Basinger, and like she knew it and thought this was swell. Lisa said, "I'm here to see Nehi Laughton."

"I see. Is he expecting you?"

"I think so. I'm Lisa Nova."

Kim Basinger called back—absolute, heavy, expensive silence all around, like one could imagine in the buildings of Texas Nazi oil billionaires who controlled the world—and said, "There's a Lisa Nova here to see you. . . . What? . . . OK, I'll send her in."

Nehi Laughton was in his forties, short, intense, looked like he played tennis, only just beginning to lose a little hair. Those who were dying to meet him might even see him as handsome, with his large nose and thin lips, expensive clothes. He was wearing a very well cut suit, and Lisa admired it for a few moments; when he asked her if she'd like a beverage, she said yeah, she'd like a Coke.

"I've been hearing all kinds of good things about you," he said. "You had this film in the Berlin Film Festival, people are talking about it, and Selwyn Popcorn says you have the most original vision of any young director he's seen. Forgive me if I don't have his exact words, but—as I'm sure you realize—my interest is in Roy. I've known him for twenty-two years, do you know that? When I was at ICM, he was assigned to me—that was before anything was happening for him at all. When I formed my own agency, he was my cornerstone client. We've been good friends. Until a couple months ago, we talked on the phone just about every day. At least once every week. Then, just like that, he goes out one night, and that's the last anyone knows. The police checked into it, but nothing. He fucking disappears. He's not touching his bank account, *nothing*."

Nehi Laughton stood up, having excited himself to the point where he had to prowl around. Lisa drank the Coke that a different, less flashy secretary had brought in. She used the straw.

"I thought he was dead," the superagent went on. "And then, all of a sudden, I'm told about this little film Roy's starring in, in fact he's down as coproducer . . . so please tell me, as his friend: Where is he?"

"Right now? I don't know," Lisa said.

"Where did you see him last?"

"In Brazil."

"What's going on?"

Lisa didn't feel like it was up to her to answer this, so she didn't respond.

Laughton calmed himself and said, "Do you know why he took off like he did? In that manner? Disappearing?"

"He never said anything specific. I think he just got fed up with being, uh, Roy Hardway. I was as surprised as anyone when he turned up in my film."

"Has he been in love with you? I'm trying to understand the nature of your relationship, so forgive me if I pry. But I thought Roy and I were very close."

"I don't want to talk about my personal life," Lisa said, reluctant to say anything more. "I'm sorry, I don't know the answers to all your questions, but . . . Roy is very different now, and . . . we really weren't together much except during the actual making of the film."

"Who financed it?"

"Not Roy. And if by some miracle it makes any money, he knows all he has to do is ask."

"Is there something wrong with him?"

Lisa, feeling like a total liar by now, shook her head.

"Well, can you give me an address where I can write to him? His mother, in North Dakota, has become seriously ill."

"I'm sorry, I don't know where he is." Lisa's composure was frayed by now; she stood up, ready to leave. She thought Nehi Laughton was lying about the sick mother.

In a different voice, colder, flatter, Laughton said, coming up behind her, putting his hand (it was warm) on the nape of her neck, "I know where Roy first saw you. I've seen part of a video you did, and you're very good. What happened that night, when you and Roy went out? You know he never came home from your date."

Lisa pulled away from his hand, turning to say rather impulsively, "Roy hired these strippers he knew, and everybody was doing everyone else. It got to be too much for me. I didn't like those kinds of drugs, so I took off. Roy knew I was going to Brazil, so . . . I don't know, he just showed up later on, when I was doing the film, and he did it . . . I had another boyfriend, and Roy just did his job and drifted away. I got the impression he was either really into some private religion or else doing some new Latin American drugs. He had another whole circle of friends. Guys I was scared of. That's all I know."

It was a lot of wild information to take in, and Lisa acted her part pretty well, believing it as she spoke. It might have been better as a general policy to say nothing, but it hadn't felt tenable. This story seemed like it would be impossible to check out, and it was sort of plausible, given the set of facts Laughton and his detective had. As she drove home Lisa tried to remember all her lies, the sultry wind blowing through her hair.

ELEVEN

Raelyn called from London. She sounded in a good mood and said to call anytime, not to worry about waking her up. Lisa imagined Raelyn hitting the lesbian nightclubs of Europe, a picture that could very well be accurate—Lisa trusted her guess. But she also trusted Raelyn to represent her and *Manoa*.

Petting Caz, as he rolled over onto his back, Lisa thought more seriously than maybe ever before of Roy Hardway, wondering, with real curiosity, what he had been like. Had it been possible that the two of them might have been friends? Maybe he'd been a great fuck, he'd certainly come on that way, but it didn't seem likely, really, that she'd have been able to stay interested in putting up with his shit.

Falling into kind of a trance, Lisa lay on her bed and masturbated, it wasn't exactly intentional, she just touched herself and then wanted to come. She wanted to forget about everything, to de-situate herself in time and space.

The orgasm left her feeling languid and pleasantly lazy. Casimir arranged himself in the crook of her arm and they lay there, almost dozing, in shared animal repose, for an hour or so.

When she finally stirred herself to get dressed, she was determined to wear a certain pair of shoes she associated with fun, going out with Code, sexy and foolish, fashionably glam—back when she first became truly aware of how attractive she could be, it seemed like she had spent a lot of pleasurable time studying herself in a mirror, and Code had taken pictures of her all the time. In her memory this period, in New York, was shiny and diffuse, gleams of reflecting silver beads.

She wanted to wear the shoes, but she didn't want to just wear tights again, so for no good reason she dared herself a little and put on a lacy black garter belt, holding up black stockings . . . and then the black suede twisted-heel pumps. One of her thousand or so black miniskirts, a vampire shirt of rayon tulle and organza, and a black lace-up vest. A little more makeup than usual. Dark red lipstick, bleeding cherries, yeah, that color . . . and her face.

The restaurant was in Santa Monica—Lisa was just the least bit worried that Christine might not show up. But no, Christine was waiting for her. They embraced and went in. Christine was in a T-shirt dress with horizontal pink stripes. She commented on Lisa's hair being longer; she liked it, she said. Being complimented by Christine pleased Lisa, who then felt that the expressed judgment must be true. She had great respect for Christine's knowledge in these things.

They talked about *L.A. Ripper II*, and Lisa explained what Jules had said about Eric Lemongrass. She said she had disliked him on sight, he was really a creep. She asked Christine if she wanted to work on the sound.

"To tell you the truth, I don't know how secure I am," Lisa said as dinner arrived. They were splitting a bottle of wine.

"Well," Christine said, pouring more into both of their glasses, "what would you really like to do?"

She was having a salad of fried lobster, artichoke hearts, and olives, while Lisa had grilled scallops and shrimp with radicchio and red pepper.

"I'd like to do the story of Cassandra," Lisa said. Christine listened, quite interested, as Lisa went over the fairly well known elements. "Troy has fallen, and she prophesied it, but no one would ever believe her . . . and so Troy falls, and as the daughter of King Priam, she is taken as a captive, a slave, by Agamemnon, and they sail back to Greece. There his wife is waiting for him, and Cassandra sees that the wife and her lover will murder Agamemnon, and her too. And there's nothing she can do to escape. When she speaks, they think she's out of her mind. And so . . . you could do different things with it, update it if you wanted to . . . though I kind of like the idea of ancient Greece, play her as a priestess, try to keep the dialogue from getting too Masterpiece Theater, keep it naturalistic and direct."

"You look like a Cassandra," Christine said, and Lisa faintly shook her head.

"I've thought about it, about playing her . . . I don't know. I don't think so. Although, as an image thing, depending on how *Manoa* does . . . it could be something to consider. I don't know."

"I saw your friend Mary Siddons a month or so ago. She's in some band . . . Bloody Murder. They're a mindcrusher band, bonecrusher, skullcrusher . . . earplug time. Her hair's in microbraids, she's really pale, she still looks younger than she ought to . . . what is she, fifteen?"

"Yeah."

"Well, by now she looks about twelve. She still seems like a little brat to me, though I know you guys always got along." Left unspoken, but maybe present in Christine's little smile, was the idea that Lisa and Mary might be, in their willfulness, a bit alike.

"Where were they playing?"

"This place in Redondo. Oriole was trying to see if he could shock me, proving he's hipper than me, same old same old . . . Bloody Murder, I'm sure that's the name of the group."

"I'll tell Jill, the casting director, tomorrow." Lisa didn't sound as interested as she might have a few days ago.

"It seems like I remember," Christine said, musing, toying with her cappuccino, "you having that novel about Cassandra by that German woman . . . you tried to get me to read it, but I never did. Are you thinking of trying to pick up the rights?"

"Well, the story comes from Aeschylus, I think, or Euripides . . . and isn't all that stuff in the public domain? I love the novel, though it's a little more explicitly feminist and men-equal-power women-are-into-mysticism-and-community . . . I don't know," she said, considering it more than she had, "maybe we could use the book." She wanted to, now. She felt the wine.

They went to a bar down the street that Christine knew and had

Spanish coffees. Lisa listened to Christine bring her up to date on Oriole and how the animal documentary had gone wrong. The money hadn't come through. She was back with Oriole again.

It was starting to feel like their friendship was back—after all, it had been Lisa who had run out, for reasons of her own—and they were content to just spend time together, they were comfortable, it didn't matter if they talked or not. She didn't go into the complex situation with Boro, or explain about Roy, or talk about meeting Selwyn Popcorn. She didn't say anything about Raelyn.

Tavinho got a mention. Lisa admitted there was this guy down in Brazil whom she'd seen a few times. Some band across the room was playing jazz. Yes, definitely. Jazz.

When she got home, her head had pretty much cleared: as soon as she unlocked and opened her door she felt something was different, she closed the door and didn't turn on a light. She could see in the dark—there was someone, she could smell him, her first thought was that it was Nehi Laughton's detective, she'd remember his name in a moment, but something about his breathing, his smell, his presence—she sensed it wasn't him. All the same, she needed a gun to keep in her purse. When Roy had shot Boro, it hadn't worked out very well, you could even say it just made him mad, but . . .

"Code?"

"Yes, Lisa. I'm here."

"Why did you come in like this?" Lisa sat down on the couch, still in the relative dark, taking off her shoes. Code sat in the chair across from her. She could see that he'd let his hair grow; it was almost the same length as her own.

"I wanted to see you," he said. "And I would never forget where you hide the extra key."

"OK." Lisa, taking her time, was unlacing the vest. "What was all that shit on the phone?"

"You mean about Boro? I don't know. Lauren deals with him and with this babe who lives at his hacienda, Wanda. Lauren, you see . . . what can I tell you about Lauren?"

"That she's had a lot of plastic surgery?"

"Yeah, well, that's OK. She looks all right, in a futuristic way. But what I was gonna tell you, was . . . Lauren likes to dabble, to know that there's strange shit out there."

"Fuck you, Code." Lisa didn't throw this out with any heat or particular hostility. She took off her vest and unbuttoned the blouse, leaving on the strapless lacy bra. None of this meant that she was remotely considering any kind of sex act with Code.

He laughed and said, "I went to that place where Lou sent you. Why didn't you tell me about it? You had a cash-flow problem, you fixed it painlessly. When I got really poor, I didn't know I had an option like that."

"I was trying to protect you."

"Fuck you, Lisa. Who are you to decide what's good or bad for me? It was good enough for you."

"Is that where you met Lauren?"

"Yeah. She fell in love with my irresistible ass. Can't get enough."

"Congratulations," Lisa said. "A star is born."

"Yeah," Code said, sounding a little puzzled (or hurt) that Lisa was sarcastic. "What do you care? Lauren would love to meet you. She thinks you're great."

"Are you doing music?"

"Yeah, I am. Guitars. Really major guitar action. I'm working with Michael Poe from the Dogs. Remember the Dogs?"

"No. Have you heard Bloody Murder?"

"They're Nazis," Code said. "Fucking asshole Nazis. The only time I ever met little Mary, I thought she was crazy, but that was what you liked about her, wasn't it?"

Lisa didn't answer for a couple of beats, then, after a big sigh, "Yeah. That was part of it."

Quiet.

In about ten minutes or so, Code said, "Can I come sit by you?"

"No. In fact, you should leave. I need to go to sleep. And give me back the key."

Code hesitated only a few seconds before saying, "OK. We're still pals, aren't we, on some level?" He was almost pleading, and sounded weary down to his soul.

"We're pals," Lisa said. "I guess. I don't know."

"You don't like the idea of Lauren Devoto, but it might actually be less fucked up than you think. But Jesus, you and Boro . . . if you owe him money and can't pay him, let me know, maybe Lauren would help. I know she would, if you were nice. Boro's scary, man."

"I know he is," Lisa said. "Thanks."

Code turned on the standing lamp before he left, doing a mock double take at Lisa's state of undress. She still had on her skirt, and with the bra . . . well, it was what you might wear to go dancing at the old Club Lingerie or someplace like that. Funny how different it was when someone wasn't your boyfriend anymore. Code couldn't have left her more cold. Yeah, his hair was longer and bleached blond, plus he had a new earring; he was in the process of evolving a new look. At the door, Lisa kissed him good night on the cheek. Then she went into the bathroom, washed off her makeup, peed, took off her clothes, brushed her teeth, and got into bed with Caz, who stretched out and yawned, asking her a question with an interrogative noise that was not a meow. He had to go check his bowl and eat some cat food, drink some water, before he was ready to return to the bed and go to sleep. Lisa listened to the muffled, lulling surround of the streets, the traffic competing with her slowly lapsing thoughts.

TWELVE

Lisa spent most of Friday with Rosa Liszt, the art director, working on the *Ripper* storyboards. Before Hitchcock, the average movie would usually be constructed of some six hundred or so shots, roughly between five and twelve seconds in length. Alfred Hitchcock would, more or less unobtrusively, use about thirteen hundred, everything storyboarded and well prepared. Working with Rosa, Lisa went through the motions, certainly, more than that, but she didn't feel Rosa liked her or took her seriously, and she in turn did not like Rosa, who struck her as condescending and humorless . . . or at least reservedly ironic where Lisa, if she had felt more relaxed, would have been playful and exuberant. She felt, though, that she should be careful not to appear foolish.

Today Lisa was wearing an untucked apricot-colored blouse, a gray herringbone skirt, a fake Byzantine bracelet . . . Rosa, probably in her late thirties, was dressed in a desexualized manner, by no means casual enough to show any possible disrespect. At lunchtime, Lisa told Amy, Brandenberg's assistant, that she wanted to examine some handguns, if any were available, to check them for the right look. Amy, who was just out of school, USC, said OK.

"And ammunition too," Lisa said, airily, as she went out the door. First thing this morning she'd arranged to have a locksmith change the locks. Now she was on her way to an appointment to have her ears pierced for the fourth time on each side, this time in the upper ear, through the cartilage, the antihelix, at the same time as she would have her split ends trimmed, as she was committed to a somewhat longer hair length than before.

Errands accomplished, the afternoon was spent elaborating on the central plan, namely to make L.A. look "expressionist," as Lisa said, and after a while Rosa seemed to warm to the notion, suggesting that since the city is always seen as dry, "Why not associate this dryness with fire, with flame?"

"Yes," Lisa said. "Because inside everyone here, there is all this barely contained heat, and the Ripper . . . I don't know if I'd want to go so far as to say that when he cuts his victims open he's seeking their wetness, or to plunge his face into a river, a river of blood . . . but every time there is blood spilled, I want to emphasize its wetness, and the Ripper is more sensitive to this, mutely, than these sorts of guys usually seem."

Rosa seemed to maybe approve. In thoughtful silence, Lisa hunted for some of the storyboards in which Paul Bancroft is seen in medium close-up, the camera moving in until his face fills up the frame.

"I want to have him extremely tortured, I want him to have tremendous panic, no trace of enjoyment in his crimes."

It was so important for her to do this film—a union picture, with a studio, as a member of the DGA—and Lisa tended to react against automatic feminist condemnation of movies about violence, she had decided at some point that you could work with the genre and slyly turn it upside-down. But it was important to her that, if she did this, she be allowed to do it her way. So, for instance, if the Ripper was going to kill these young prostitutes, several of them, it was important that they be seen as human beings, with personalities, fucked up but a long way from just being *things* to be slaughtered without any sense of loss. So, then, it was also important that the hookers on the street, a few of them, get their revenge and kill the Ripper, and that it not be left up to the otherwise ineffectual (and contemptuous) police. Eric Lemongrass's character had, in the first movie, shown no empathy for the victims, spending his time off work, for instance, in a strip joint, eating a hamburger and making a joke about how the burger looked more attractive to him than dead hooker number two.

She stopped by the locksmith's shop and got the new keys. Great. She also had—she didn't think Amy had expected her to take it with her, but the assistant wasn't prepared to contradict Lisa until she knew more—a revolver in her purse, a .32, loaded, with the safety on, another ten or twelve bullets in a little box. Maybe she could even be straight about it, say that her life had been threatened and apply for a permit . . . in the meantime, she had this in her purse.

Because, however blithely dismissive she might like to be about it, it made her paranoid, no question, to know that Laughton's detective was very likely trailing her. Not to mention whatever Boro might be up to—she was sure he would be contacting her soon.

When Lisa got home, she found eleven calls on her machine. Too many for her to deal with right away. She'd listen to them later, in an hour or so. She lay on the couch with Caz, drinking a Coke for energy, flicking on the TV with the remote. Lisa watched the news. Before the second commercial, she was becoming sort of curious about who might have called, if any of them could be something good.

The eleven calls turned out to be—

Tone. "Payroll? Is this payroll?"

Then: "This is Paul Bancroft. If you'd like to have coffee or lunch or a drink or something, give me a call. I'd like to talk with you about the script. As far as I can tell, I disagree with Eric's idea for the end. Or if you're booked up, let's just talk on the phone for a few minutes." He gave his number and hung up.

"Hi, I'm Marcia Abrahams, for *Women in Film*. We're doing a piece about New York versus L.A., East Coast versus West Coast sensibilities, that sort of thing. I'd be interested in talking to you—I'm in New York, but I'm coming out to Los Angeles in ten days. If you think you might be able to spare some time, I'd like to meet you."

"Lisa? Christine. Oriole and I are going to a party tomorrow night, and I thought you might want to come along. Call me when you get a chance. Bye."

The next call was from Alvin Sender, "just to say hi," managing to do so in an insinuatuing manner. As always when she heard from him, she was left with a free-floating sense of dread.

Another writer, this time a male, asking if she could call back right away to comment on an item *Confidential Weekly* was going to run.

Adrian: "I was just thinking about you and Caz. I hope you're adjusting again to L.A."

"This is Joey. You remember me, I was living with Zed. I think the one time I met you the bandages were still on—you should see me now, it really worked out great! I don't know if you've known Zed for very long, but if you haven't heard, he's in the hospital. I'm running the business, and I've got some new samples; if you're interested, please call."

Track: "Lisa, listen, I got a letter here for you from Rio de Janeiro; I'm sending it along with a tape. You should seriously check out the new album by S.M.E.R.S.H. It's fantastic. Also 'Inside My Love,' by Absinthe. Good beat, you can dance to it."

Jules Brandenberg: "Lisa, this is Jules, on Friday at four-thirty-five P.M. I'm going to be in Colorado for the weekend, but you can reach me through Amy if anything comes up. I'm going to see Robert Hand for breakfast Monday morning; I'll wander over to the office by nine or ten. See you."

And then, she couldn't mistake his voice, she felt almost an electric shock—"My friend Lisa . . . I want to see you tomorrow, just to say hello. Nothing special. The guy from Rio will come by, to show you where to come. Please, we haven't seen you for so long—wear one of your nice dresses, cheer us up. You have a date, you can leave for it from here. Wait until you see all of my flowers. Until then."

He spoke slowly, and whenever he lapsed into a heavier accent, she was sure this was by choice. Boro could do whatever he wanted; he could sound however he liked.

THIRTEEN

She found out that her membership to the athletic club had lapsed, for nonpayment of dues. She drove over there in the late morning to take care of that and to use the Olympic-sized pool. Her body needed the exertion. It was a mindless way to clear her head. She always felt better after she swam.

As she drove home, adjusting her sunglasses, looking in the rearview mirror, she thought she saw Nehi Laughton's detective, not in a Hawaiian shirt, instead untucked khaki with epaulets, getting into the driver's side of a gray or faded silver Toyota Corolla, presumably to follow her . . . what a boring, lonely job. Lisa didn't care if he stayed on her trail, figuring that she'd wait until it mattered before doing something to throw him off. Still . . . checking the rearview mirror almost constantly, she didn't see a gray car of that type, so maybe she'd been wrong.

Maybe Duane Moyer could have attached a transmitter of some sort to her car. She'd seen it done in movies, of course, so she assumed it could be done in real life.

Tonight Lisa was to go to the party that Christine had mentioned: It was at the house of newlywed stars Taft Flowers and Heather Malone. Lisa didn't know what she was going to wear.

She called Christine when she got home.

"Don't you have that shiny gold dress, you know the one?"

"Yeah."

"Wear that," Christine said. "It's definitely glam. Have you heard of the band Sucker? Taft's little brother is the guitar player. I mean, he's the *lead* guitar player, excuse me."

"I don't know about them. Are they some kind of metal?"

"Glitzo-retro metal-techno, something like that. Oriole likes them."

"Are they going to play there?"

"I think so. So wear the sexy gold dress, OK?"

"Maybe. I'll see. What are you gonna wear?"

Christine was happy to tell her all about it: the dress, the necklace, the earrings. The matching shoes. It was soothing to listen to, and it got Lisa more enthused about dressing up. She needed to wash her hair again, to make sure she'd rinsed out all the chlorine.

She told Christine about the call from *Confidential Weekly* and the one from Marcia Abrahams for *Women in Film*. The supermarket tabloid, Lisa said, would print whatever it wanted; it was better not to be tricked into giving them a quote. This was her weakish theory.

"But aren't you curious? Even if they're just making up lies, it means you're on the map. What do you think it could be?"

"I don't know," Lisa said, unwilling to voice her suspicion. Christine didn't press, but she could tell Lisa was holding something back.

The afternoon passed. Lisa spent a long time—with music blasting—on her makeup and earrings, searching for a certain pair of shoes, a certain bracelet, allowing the music to govern her mood. She put the dress on, took it off. Had something to eat.

At six-thirty someone knocked on her door. She looked through the peephole: It was Ariel Mendoza. The detective. So.

"Just a minute," she said. If Boro wanted to see her, she thought she should cooperate, up to a point. She turned off the stereo and put on her dress. Casimir was meowing. She opened the door and let

Mendoza come in. Should she regard him as an enemy? He was reserved and polite, his manners more restrained than was typical for Latins, yet she sensed that underneath he had a sympathy for her, a liking . . . even as, she understood, he was uncomfortable with women, she couldn't guess what kind of problems he might have had in his life with the issue of sex. He apologized for bothering her; she smiled and said it was OK. She didn't want to deceive herself, but she did see him as a potential ally, to be wooed as such.

"I'm going to a party later on," she said, and then, irrepressibly, "Do you like my dress?"

"Oh, I do. Very much. It's very nice. Here, maybe you can use this." Out of his pocket he handed her a ring.

"Where does it come from?" Lisa asked, examining it closely. The gold seemed very old and soft, with an intricate design, a piece of jade . . . She tried it on her left hand, the fourth finger. It fit.

"It belonged to a princess in Mexico, back before the Aztecs. Since then it's passed through many hands." He shrugged.

Lisa looked at him, trying to read him. She worried that this ring *meant* something, that it had some sort of magic or power attached to it that might enable Boro to play with her some more. She couldn't know. She hesitated, then sat down on the couch and put on her shoes.

"What's the plan?" she asked, feeling dumb.

Ariel explained that she would drive him out to Boro's house, that he would serve as her guide. Afterward she could leave to go on to her party. Lisa agreed to this without asking how he had arrived. She recalled, from the increased weight, that she had the .32 revolver in her purse.

"There might be some kind of beeper, or a device somewhere on my car. A detective has been following me—I'm not making this up, he introduced himself—and it seems like he can keep in contact with me even when I can't see him . . . is this something that's hard to check?"

Ariel frowned, yet he seemed interested. His professional pride was engaged.

"Who employs this detective?" he asked.

"Roy Hardway's agent."

"Yes, I've heard about what happened to Roy Hardway, the movie star." Outside, Ariel found the bug within five minutes. It was in the right rear tire well, affixed with a magnet.

"Let's go," he said. "I'll jump out, at some point and put it on someone else's automobile."

They got in the car. Lisa started it, and they drove off. Lisa beamed at Ariel, who smiled more modestly back—there was a shared sense of mischief, of play. She drove up Olive to Eleventh Street, went over to Flower and Wilshire, there was a lot of traffic, they were bogged down. Ariel opened his door and dashed out, he pretended for the sake of the guy in the next car to have dropped his pen, absurdly having to rescue it. He quickly got back in Lisa's car.

She turned the corner, heading back roughly the way she'd come, through Hollywood to Laurel Canyon Drive. This wasn't where Boro had lived before.

A gate opened for them, closing behind the car as it came in. The house was on the side of a hill. The canyon fell away. Lisa, getting out of the driver's seat, putting her keys away in her purse, felt over-dressed and vulnerable, a bit afraid. Nobody was outside; a door was open to enter the house.

"It's all right," Ariel said.

Motorcycles, and a Jaguar sedan—it looked to Lisa exactly like Roy's. Exactly. *Jesus*. She followed Ariel inside, down a long hallway, turning right and then left, going down two flights of stairs. There were some strangely lifelike statues of Aztec Indians, dressed-up mannequins actually . . . and then a large high-ceilinged room with hundreds of big potted flowers and exotic plants, an extraordinary arboretum, and in the middle a fire was burning in an area of exposed earth, a hole having been chopped through the succeeding floors up to the sky, chopped raggedly, as if with an axe. Boro sat on what looked to be a piece of human furniture: a zombie, in red velvet, on his hands and knees. Other zombies hung around, and in contrast to when Lisa had seen the collection before, now there were several very pale zombie maidens, in sheer white nightgowns, layers of lace. Brides of the vampire.

There were other people, past Boro, lounging around on a luxurious, chocolate brown leather couch. A good-looking young Hispanic male, sitting with his elbows on his knees, his hands holding his face, looking up to see who had come in.

"Miguel Casablanca," Ariel said, "and Wanda."

Wanda was young and sort of pretty, artificially red hair, almost a shade of magenta, heavily tattooed, wearing an uplift bra and a silver-encrusted little jacket, baggy black pants tucked into black boots.

She had a ring in her nose—she stared at Lisa with what seemed to be suspicion and dislike. Boro was eating roasted corn on the cob. A couple of chickens were walking around in the dirt, pecking at it occasionally, and a black dog sat waiting to see if he would be offered any corn.

Boro said, "I'm glad to see you. You look beautiful."

Lisa suddenly felt like shooting him. She came forward and said, "The tattoos make me look like a slut. You marked me."

"They give you power. And . . . being marked has taught you things, things you would never have known. The transmission of *Manoa* could not have occurred without those signs. Here, this is yours." He reached into a bag, looking in, and then tossed her one of the shrunken heads. She jerked away from it, but it struck her on the thigh before falling to earth.

"Ah," Lisa exclaimed, suspecting, then realizing, turning it over with her foot—it was Roy! Ugly, eyes and mouth and nose sewn up, blond hair long, the whole thing a little bigger than a softball . . .

"Put it in your purse. It's yours, the keepsake of your sacrifice. It's clean. It smells of copal. You have a responsibility. Come on, it won't hurt you."

Feeling that by doing so she was making herself a willing accessory, wicked, evil, she reached out and picked it up, stuffed it into her purse.

"Good. Come now. We've been saving Lou so he could see you one last time."

Boro walked with energy toward a corner of the room, on a path through some of the unusual plants: Venus flytraps, others with oily fuchsia flesh and big thorns, ready to spring. Boro opened a door into a dimly lit room. Flickering candles illuminated a weirdly grim scene.

"Oh, no," Lisa moaned, and started to turn, but Ariel turned her back toward the spectacle, murmuring to her, "It's your vengeance. You must look."

Lisa forced herself to open her eyes. The banks of candles revealed a body cut into pieces, the various pieces then nailed or spiked to the wall. Here was Lou's rib cage, off the other bones. Internal organs, each put up separately, intestines looping dark pink around and around. One leg whole, the other separated into thigh and buttock, calf, and then foot, a naked foot next to the head, the eyes of which now opened—somehow, horribly, horribly, it was still alive. The tongue came out to moisten the lips.

"Please . . . just let me die," he said, his voice hoarse and sepulchral, coming from somewhere beyond, echoing—Lisa waved her hand, gesturing in pain, and the candles went out as her hand passed by across the room, the candles went out and in the same motion Lou's head burst into flames, burning so hard and fast it began to melt, as if made out of wax, the mouth moved in agony as the lower jaw collapsed into itself. Lisa was weeping; when she turned away this time, nobody stopped her.

The zombies advanced, activated by the prospect of fresh meat. Lisa turned back to Boro and said, "It was a trick, wasn't it?"

He nodded, pleased that she understood.

"But . . . that's how he ended up. He couldn't be preserved."

"What are they eating, then?"

"Oh, the parts are real. If you hadn't set the head on fire, you would never have known." He looked back to the room. "They need their flesh."

"I didn't mean for you to destroy him like that." She said this, but she wasn't able to say it with total conviction—she had the feeling she'd given him license to do just about anything he wanted to do.

"Don't lie to yourself," Boro said, walking past her. "You can't lie to me, you know, not now. You are mine."

"I'll help you fix up your makeup," Wanda said, and Lisa sniffed but docilely went with her, into a big *en suite* bathroom down another hall.

"Your eye makeup is smeared. Are you OK now? I guess that was a surprise."

"I'm OK."

"Just sit here. I used to do makeup for the stars."

"What is your . . . how did you meet Boro?"

"Don't talk. I met him at a *santéria* shop in East L.A. I was playing around with becoming a witch. Boro's taught me a lot. You're lucky that you look like his old girlfriend, he has a soft spot for you. Close your eyes now for a while. Relax. Boro's given you a lot of power, and it doesn't seem like you've tried to do much with it. You should study . . . there's a ritual, for instance, that Mayan princesses used to do. Boro was talking about you one day, that film, and he said if you did the tongue ritual while under the influence of *ayahuasca*, you could record your visions again, on film, like before. You might not even need *ayahuasca;* almost any good, organic hallucinogenic might do. You'd need to do the ritual, though, and it's hard. It's unbelievably painful," she said, almost as if in some way she desired to dare Lisa into trying it out, just to have the pleasure of her pain.

Lisa opened her eyes finally and gazed into the mirror. She didn't trust Wanda at all. Except maybe to do her eyes. When they came back out to the others, Boro said, "Next time you and I will talk some more, by ourselves." He caressed her bare shoulder, her arm.

"OK," Lisa said, looking around at the others, having regained most of her outward composure by this time. She saw Wanda smile at her, and she frowned, in competition somehow, not knowing the rules. Miguel gazed at her unhappily. She smiled, trying to put him at ease. Another one of the damned.

FOURTEEN

Oriole, in the car, had told Christine about some young actress who had been eating a peach and exclaimed, "Wow, this tastes just like peach Jell-O!"

At the terribly expensive house recently purchased by Taft Flowers and Heather Malone, a house once lived in by Sonny and Cher, Darryl F. Zanuck, and other big stars back into the prehistory before Technicolor, Christine had a couple of quick glasses of champagne after Oriole left her, as always looking for contacts to help his career. Christine wondered if Lisa was really coming, as she'd said.

Meanwhile, next to her, Larry Planet, the producer, was talking to Kimberly Chase, former Miss Universe, about some situation from a script—or at least, since she didn't follow the news, that's what Christine assumed.

"This war's been going on between Sweden and Denmark for a year or two, and it's starting to get really ugly."

Planet took another sip of his drink, dipped another vegetable in aioli. Kimberly had a glazed, professional smile that nevertheless seemed to express real empathy to every eye she met. She wore a sleeveless top made of aluminum rings, an emerald green loincloth-like miniskirt . . . she was taller than Christine, and much taller than Larry Planet, who continued with his story, chewing, swallowing, describing a helicopter that looked like a big sleek red wasp.

Christine, in her early Joseph Stella–style shattered-mirror-print green-black-azalea-pink shirt unbuttoned almost to her tan navel, with black linen pants, mock old-fashioned burgundy lace-ups, blond hair brushed up into a new, forward-looking, somewhat Futurist or Constructivist cut, silver geometric necklace and conspicuous dangling faceted pyramid earring on the left side—Christine saw Christian Manitoba, Trish Featherstone, Peter Ferrari the director, Vienna Free, Pierre Wella Balsam, Joseph Venezuela with one of several wised-up, designer-clad development sluts, agents, studio execs, fashion designers, and restaurateurs, a beautiful blond model she knew only as Freak, wearing some kind of leather harness with metal rings, mostly naked, false eyelashes, next to a New York rock star whose name she thought was Shake.

"He would have had the surgery sooner, but he couldn't bring himself to mess with his portfolio. He's in love with his brother, he worships him, I swear to God."

Moving on, draining this glass of champagne and putting it down, she heard, "The body was found in a citrus grove. Didn't you hear about it?"

Then: "What's more nude than nude?"

Heather Malone smiled at Christine, not knowing her, and turned back to her conversation with Severin Reed.

A film editor named Toshiko, unbuttoned lime green blouse and black bra, said, "Are you still working on that thing with Jim?"

Christine shook her head. The band was starting to play again. It was easy to pick out Taft's little brother. He looked just the same, only shorter, with longer hair. More spoiled.

Deftly picking her way through the crowd, Christine made her way upstairs to the gallery, where it was quieter, you could admire the paintings and shiny metal sculptures picked out by some interior designer, some consultant, certainly not by Heather or Taft.

An experienced sound man Christine knew, Bill something, in glasses, somehow giving the impression of being an undercover Marxist, a son of the proletariat, probably actually enjoying the paintings—yeah, when she showed an interest, he told her something about each one, each artist, James Bishop to Carroll Dunham to Jane Hammond. It was enjoyable, though she didn't know how much she'd remember later on. Bill had a muscle in the big dimple right next to his mouth. When Bill's wife came up looking for him, Christine was sorry to see him go. They were better friends now. No sign of Oriole. No, as she scanned the whole entourage from above, leaning on the railing, she saw him for a few moments, in his drawstring acid-print Bermudas. He was going outside, out onto the terrace, listening avidly to Peter Ferrari.

Ah, and there was Lisa. As promised, wearing the gold dress. It had spaghetti straps and showed a good deal of bosom. Lisa was sexy, in this dress a perfect femme fatale. Why did people obsess over her? Christine studied her, knowing at the same time that it was more than anything physical, more than her body, eyebrows, lips . . . it had something to do with the way she had of not appearing to be aware she was being looked at, a way of holding her body that was unlike, say, the Kimberly Chase or Supermodel of the World electrical Frankensteinian charged-up way of being a body, a form, that knowledge of being seen. Lisa seemed, right now for instance, holding her purse in both hands, shadows of the tight metallic gold sheen changing as she shifted her weight, absorbed in something unseen, yet not in *self*—elsewhere, unaware of herself, it wasn't innocence, but it brought out, inspired . . . a desire to *find* her, bring her back, ground her, make her recognize *you*.

Christine caught her eye when Lisa finally looked up with one of her childlike smiles, and Christine forgave everything. It was bad for women that Lisa and others still made it in the business by using their bodies, fucking a Lou or . . . well, there was probably some reason why Jules Brandenberg had done her such a favor at this point, Christine didn't want to ask.

As she came up the stairs—apparently the good-looking Mexican guy was actually her date—Christine saw again that, yes, Lisa *did* have an erotic investment in having people stare at her, she liked it, she might be more art-damaged and complex about it, more vulnerable, yet she wanted this. . . .

"Christine!"

"You made it, great."

"This is Miguel Casablanca. He's a welterweight boxer, ranked number four by the IBF."

"I'm very glad to meet you," he said, frowning, not looking around. Shy, but not scared to death. A boxer! Jesus. Christine's eyes raced over him. Then back to Lisa, the tattoos on her upper arms.

"I've been thinking about the script for *Cassandra,*" Christine said, not really what she'd been going to say, but then as they talked about it they both got really enthused. They went downstairs, and Lisa got some champagne. Christine tried to help make Casablanca feel at ease. He couldn't have any alcohol, drugs, or rich foods.

Now they ran into Code and Lauren Devoto. Christine, sensing their interest in Lisa, took Miguel, who was somewhat unwilling at first, for a tour of the grounds, perhaps thinking on an ulterior level that they might run into Oriole, this guy would read her mind and knock Oriole down, right on his ass, one effortless swift punch. The hand quicker than the eye.

Back inside, meanwhile, Lisa was sending out unconsciously fetching signals to the close scrutiny given her by *ur*-domme Lauren: palest ice blue eyes and white-blond mane of perfect hair, wearing an impossibly expensive white designer gown, while Code had on wraparound shades, his bleached platinum hair slicked back, the wet look, wearing a rubber scuba diver's top in black with a thin yellow line at the side. Leather Jim Morrison pants, with a low-slung gigantic ornamental Helios the Sun God belt buckle. He looked good.

"You're in *Confidential Weekly,*" Lauren said. "Selwyn Popcorn in Berlin with his young tattooed love goddess. They have his quote about your 'original vision,' and then it says, 'Guess we know what's in *his* line of vision, don't we?' They have a picture of you two together, laughing unselfconsciously, and a still . . . from *L.A. Ripper*. You're nude, but because it's a family paper they've put a black bar over your nipples."

Lisa listened unhappily. Code seemed nervous, fidgety, even without it being possible to see his eyes.

"Selwyn's gonna hate it," Lisa said.

"Why don't you come over to see me one of these evenings? I'd love to get to know you better." And Lauren, cold as a halibut on ice, touched Lisa's throat, lightly, so that Lisa looked up into her face. Satisfied, Lauren smiled, her TV smile, and then turned to have court paid to her by Larry Planet and Jerry Dolphin. Lisa heard someone, maybe not one of them, say, "Imagine if Hitler had had CNN!"

A neo-Bratpacker who'd been in five or six bombs in a row, a dopey smile on his face, wearing cowboy/biker drag with a red kerchief around his neck, was trying to eat everything he could, systematically, it looked dangerously like he'd eat until he puked. Code put his hand on Lisa's arm, they moved away, Lisa saying, "What does she want from me?" in a kind of stunned, very young tone of voice.

"She wants to do things to you," Code said. "I'm supposed to use my influence to get you to come. The tattoos, you know . . . they're provocative. They make people think about seeing you in weird scenes."

"Is that what you have to do? Be in her weird scenes?"

Code shrugged. "Sure. Why not? Why not feel something intense? You might really dig it."

Lisa was speechless, imagining all kinds of gross S&M stuff. Jesus. She knew that on one level Code was doing her a favor by speaking so frankly, but this shit still shook her up. She couldn't tell if he meant to warn her off or if he thought she would actually do it out of a spirit of adventure or something. He mentioned tax-free cash, but she wasn't really listening by now.

In a few minutes they were separated, and Lisa walked in the other direction, looking for Christine and the boxer. As she went out onto the terrace she ran into the megasuperstar Chuck Suede, who noticed her. He was wearing a red jacket like James Dean, white T-shirt, spanking *new* blue jeans, unfaded, with cuffs rolled up above brown penny loafers and white socks. He said, "Excuse me, I don't know you—if no one's told you yet tonight, it works, believe me: You're a beautiful pose."

The smooth hum of the party's apparatus all around them cleared out a little space, a shimmering vacancy. Everyone was aware of anything Chuck Suede did. He was the hottest young star these days. His face was everywhere. Chuck Suede, Chuck Suede.

"Thank you," she said, soothed somewhat by the incandescence of his Higher Cool.

"No Means Yes, Yes Means No. That's how you look in that dress. I love the way your spaghetti strap keeps slipping down. You're unconscious. Are these real?" he said, touching her, putting both hands over the cross and jaguar tattoos.

"Yes."

"Do you want to be photographed with me?"

"Thanks, but I'm looking for some friends of mine."

"Tell me your name. I'm Chuck Suede."

"Lisa Nova."

He walked with her, down past the fountain, his entourage diminishing or knowing enough to hang back, and he nodded. "I've heard of you. You made a film just recently with my old pal Roy Hardway. Nobody knows where he is these days—I worshiped him, I studied him in *Dieability*. He was almost past it, but you've revived him, definitely a new twist, a new flavor for old Roy. Is he coming back? I hope not."

"I don't think so."

"And you know, don't you? You're the one who'd know.

Outstanding. You should try to understand and shape your own myth, if you know what you're doing, and I don't think Roy did."

"You talk a lot."

"Man of action, right," Chuck said, and decisively kissed her, putting his hand irresistibly onto her proffered soft upheld left breast, in the semidarkness there Lisa found the otherness deceptively dissolved. It was like he had to be an imposter because she had such a strong *image* of Chuck Suede. In the theater, on the big screen, a certain physical grace, a natural radiance of gesture, of expression, the music of his voice, perfect, godlike, what else was he but a god, no one would doubt it, yes this was him, his human manifestation, she loved the kiss and wanted to offer herself, he could tell, he stopped kissing her and said, "Seven films. Then up in flames. Five down, two to go. Let's see if my unauthorized biographer finds you. Are you sure you don't wanna be photographed with me?"

"Does Roy Hardway really mean something to you? If I gave you something of his, would you take care of it, treat it with love and respect?"

"I told you: I have worshiped him. I think you understand me."

"Do you have your car here?"

"Yeah, a Lamborghini. Do you wanna shoot up the Pacific Coast Highway? I'll do it. Road to ruin. What do you have for me?"

"It's just for you; I don't want other people to see. If you had a suitcase or something . . . "

"Let's go in here. I know Taft's place pretty well."

Around the other side of a well-trimmed hedge, past the pool into a small building, dark. Chuck turned on the light. There was a billiards table in there, and a large-scale map of the world. Lisa, sure that no one was around, took out of her purse—Roy Hardway's shrunken head.

"It's Roy all right," Chuck said, leaning down to view it just over the edge of the table, emotional, one hand grasping Lisa's wrist.

"A thousand-year-old Indian made Roy a sacrifice," Lisa said. It was sort of good just to be able to say something like this.

"Yeah . . . it's Roy. I see what you mean." He seemed shaken. He looked at her expressively, earnestly. He started to speak, then just stopped, knocked out of his ultracoolness for a sec.

He put the shrunken head in a brown paper bag. "I'll leave right now,out the back way," he said softly, "so that no one will even know I have anything. Goodbye."

Lisa walked back to the party and located Miguel Casablanca and Christine. Miguel was ready to leave. He was in training, he needed his sleep. Sucker was just starting to play another set; it sounded like they'd done some MC^2.

~ FIFTEEN

On Sunday Lisa slept in almost until noon and then lay in bed for another two hours, teasing Caz, inciting him to leap upon and bite her hand, which was concealed under the sheet. His tail whipped back and forth, and she adjusted herself to his sense of time. He could wait for a long time before deciding to pounce; she judged by his eyes whether he was still interested or not, and when he got bored she would try something new.

She didn't want to do anything. Yesterday had exhausted her. She didn't think about the fact that she had kissed Chuck Suede and given him Roy Hardway's shrunken head.

Last night she had called Raelyn in London as soon as she got home, it was three A.M. here and so was some appropriate time in Europe—she asked Raelyn to come to L.A., to work as her assistant on *L.A. Ripper II.* Always, whenever it had come up before, without saying too much, by her expressions, her *tonality,* Raelyn had expressed some reservations about this project, despite the opportunity for Lisa to do a studio feature, to handle a multimillion-dollar budget, get her DGA card—because of the violence-to-women issue, even if in this script the tables are turned and the sex industry workers castrate and kill the murderer, etcetera . . . but Raelyn agreed to come.

On the drive home last night, Lisa had tried to be friendlier to Casablanca, she'd felt bad, like she'd shunned him, treated him like he was retarded. And something about him, the more she was around him, told her that, however different his world, even if being a boxer seemed crazy to her, he had his intelligence within this world, and on the ride home she'd tried to get him to talk to her. They did have in common, after all, that each was Boro's creature, he had some claim on both of their souls.

So as they proceeded through the L.A. night, in a low-key manner Miguel told her about the boxer he most admired, whom he'd admired as a child. Salvador Sanchez, a featherweight, who'd died in an automobile accident after one of his fights.

"I don't fight like him, either, man . . . but when he got into the ring, he put it all out there. He was ready to die. And you could see that."

If Miguel had become sentimental, he wasn't embarrassed, nor did he seem to expect her to sympathize or understand.

"Ariel told me . . . about your rematch with some guy who beat you once, he said it was a big fight for you."

"Yeah. Linton Minniefield," he said slowly, as if seeing it in his mind. Lisa was remembering something very different: the scene at Boro's where Ariel had been speaking to her—the disassembled parts of Lou nailed to the wall. "I hit him with an uppercut." Then, as she parked and he looked around for and spotted Ariel's car, he said, "Look, would you like to see a tape of that fight?"

It was something important to him, and he was being straight with her, she could not sense any games, any hidden agendas, not even sexual ambition, so she said, "Yeah, sure. Drop it by."

"OK, I will. Goodbye."

Today she tried to read. She read a few pages in several different books, putting in bookmarks . . . she called back Joey, and Paul Bancroft, and Marcia Abrahams. She arranged to have lunch with Bancroft at Spoleto's the next day. Joey was going to come by tomorrow evening, briefly, with samples of some wares.

Lisa felt like drinking some champagne, for the taste, the effervescence, the refreshment factor, and to get high a little, and she retroactively wished that she had drunk more at the party, where it had been all over the place. Her taste buds were not acute enough to differentiate, except very crudely, between expensive and cheap champagne. That slightly woozy feeling of exhilaration, with the taste in one's mouth, down one's throat . . . that's what she would have liked.

Wanda had sought to tempt her with the notion of some Aztec princess ritual. To dare her . . . but what was in it for Wanda? That was the real question, Lisa thought.

The next time she went to the bathroom she picked up the ring she had been given at Boro's, which she had taken off last night. She brought it out to examine it for hidden compartments or spring-fired barbs. She drank sparkling apple cider and listened to some classical piano music, not too dramatic or romantic: John Field. She ate a banana—offering it to Casimir, who smelled it and then turned away, he didn't recognize it as food, not for carnivores—and an orange.

A knock on the door. Lisa sort of welcomed the interruption, even though she was wary, thinking it might be Duane Moyer, mad about the wild goose chase with the automobile bug. But she wasn't scared, so she opened the door. It was Sunday afternoon. She was wearing a wine red leotard and jeans.

A skinhead kind of guy stood there, his shaved head just starting to grow out, like a shadow, wearing jeans and Doc Martens, a black leather jacket much more weathered than Lisa's own, this one with ancient silver studs. He had a toothpick in his mouth. He wasn't bad-looking, somehow.

"Lisa Nova?"

"Yes?"

"My name's Jonathan. You knew my father . . . I'd like to ask you some questions about him. Can I come in?"

"You're Jonathan?"

"Yes. I know I've changed, but it's me."

"What made you come to see me? Why me?"

"Come on. We all knew about you and Dad. It was a game for him, to make sure we knew about his little affairs, yet on the surface act like nothing was happening. Are you scared of me because I shaved my head?"

"Uh-huh."

He smiled a civilized smile.

"I'm in disguise. I've been hiding out . . . may I enter, please? You're embarrassing me."

"I'm involved with some strange people," Lisa said, and then let him in and closed the door. She motioned to him to sit down—when he picked the chair, she lay down on the couch, stretching out her legs, her bare feet. Her purse with the gun was under the glass coffee table, under an open Cindy Sherman catalog.

"A few months ago," Jonathan began, "something happened to my family. Within a week, everything changed. All kinds of weird stuff started happening . . . I've been trying to figure out why."

He stared at Lisa. She saw no reason to comment. If she looked sullen or pouty, so be it. For some reason, she felt very little sympathy for this guy. He had on his face the expression of a loser who will never give up.

"My mother's gone crazy, I don't know what's going on with her anymore . . . and my father . . . "

"What about you?" Lisa said, willing herself to remain unmoved, to forget what she'd seen of Lou or some vestige of Lou.

"I contributed, unknowingly, to my mother's problem. I was making this piece of conceptual art. It came to life, trashed my mother's gallery, and blew up. I went to jail for construction of an 'infernal machine' . . . that law's still on the books, I swear. Since then . . . these bikers have been hunting me. Very strange guys. They broke into the apartment and shattered my roommate's legs. He'll never be the same . . . and I know they got him by mistake, they were looking for me."

"What's happened to your father, then?" Lisa asked, feeling very nervy and brazen.

"He's missing. This tattooed girl bought tickets for both of them to take an ocean cruise; she and some Mexican cleaned out his stuff . . . he's never been seen again. I have the feeling that he's dead. I can't explain it. But . . . the tattooed girl just might be the same one my mother was seen with a few times. There's this guy named Boro who has a girlfriend who fits the description. He has something to do with it all . . . he's some kind of a gangster, I think he's South American. Tell me, when you were with my dad, near the end, was he taking any unusual drugs?"

"No. Not that I know of."

"I've heard that he promised you some position, and then couldn't, or wouldn't, come through. That's right around the time when everything started to go to hell."

"I went to Brazil," Lisa said.

"That's right, I heard that. Why did you leave town?"

Lisa's eyes flashed darkly at him. His "learned" dopey naturalism annoyed her—also, she didn't believe that he really cared so much about his family. He seemed unaffectionate, a solipsist. . . .

"My father is in Brazil," she said. "I left L.A. because Lou had fucked me over, and I was disappointed . . . he'd used me, and I didn't like it. I should have seen it coming."

"Promises aren't worth anything here," Jonathan said, like this would be news. "Someone who looks like you, people tell you what you want to hear."

Lisa waited several beats, stopping herself from flaring up. Finally she said, "What do you want?"

"What do I want?" His shaved skull and face made him look—with his dull, glazed, intelligent eyes—like a madman in Charenton, the asylum the Marquis de Sade had ended up in under Napoleon, or like a convict escaped from Devil's Island, a martyr to some cause. He was playing a part. "I want to find out what happened, and why."

"I don't understand," said Lisa. "It doesn't sound like any of it's connected. What do you think you're looking for?"

Jonathan just sat there, faintly smiling, like he knew something. Lisa didn't think he did. She pulled up her knees, hugging them, and from the curiosity now on his face and the direction of his eyes, she could tell he had noticed the tattoos on the backs of her fingers. The fact that he was surprised, that she could see him react a little, oddly pleased her. He couldn't see the others, and he wouldn't.

"What about this guy Boro, the gangster? Did Lou ever say anything about him to you?"

Lisa shook her head.

"Could he have owed him money?"

"I don't know. We didn't talk about money."

It didn't appear that Jonathan believed this.

"I'm going to go see this guy, talk to him."

"Don't do it," Lisa advised.

"Why not? What do you know about him?"

"I used to buy drugs from someone who knew him . . . and they said that he's dangerous, and crazy—he doesn't like white people at all."

"You know more about him than you're telling me." Jonathan said.

"Just that he's dangerous." Lisa was uncomfortable now, and it probably showed.

"Those bikers work for him, don't they?"

This was a distraction, an out. "Yeah," she said, "I heard about something like that. He's a bad guy."

"My mother said that some boys on motorcycles harassed her and Dad on their way home from a party . . . that was when I was in jail, before I got bond. The next thing I heard, she was paying to have a giant moth painted on the side of the house. It all fits together. Sure."

"I don't think so," Lisa said. "Lou would have told me. If I was going to guess anything, I'd guess . . . have you heard about the invitation-only celebrity whorehouse in Bel Air? Lou had connections there," she said, hating herself, aware that he could connect the dots here, but it was all she had left to keep him from getting eaten or stuffed.

Jonathan looked confident, like it had been tough but he'd Philip Marlowed her, he'd gotten a hot lead. He stood up, excited, in his leather pants. She could smell his sweat. Yes, she'd been there, she admitted, forlornly. No, she didn't know the address. A limo had picked her up and brought her home.

He didn't press her too much. Obviously he had some new associations to work on. He left, more or less smirking at her as he said goodbye.

SIXTEEN

Monday morning, when Lisa opened her front door to go to the studio, she found a stack of about fifty *Confidential Weekly*s on her porch, next to what she discovered was a script by someone she didn't know. Great, she was on the cover of the rag, with Popcorn, in a small box down at the side. Slow week for invented dish. Her mouth wasn't open, at least. They liked to catch you eating pizza if they could. She tossed the script in too. She knew she'd never read it. She probably wouldn't even open it.

She was a little bit late to the studio. Rosa Liszt and Dario Boccioni were waiting for her. What had Jules said about having a meeting this morning with Robert Hand? Doing a sequel was an ideal way to break in out here.

They talked about visual concepts, going over the storyboards, seeing where a crane shot seemed like a good idea, until they broke for lunch, when someone came by and asked Lisa if she could drop by Tami Spiegel's office for a minute. There was plenty of time to get to her lunch date with Paul Bancroft, so she said sure.

Sort of a long walk. The assistant showed her in—it was like a cozy art gallery in here. Tami Spiegel herself was short, radiating energy and unscrupulous, cagy power. She was the "right-hand man" to Robert Hand. Lisa didn't think this could be anything good, but she was interested in the art on the walls.

"Is this a Sigmar Polke?" she asked.

Tami was put on the defensive, made a little uncomfortable, but in a few minutes she remembered who she was and what she was here for.

"Everyone loves your work, and everyone loves what you've done with the script," she began. She went on in this insincere vein for a while longer, then began talking about how many people would be involved in the production, the special effects. "You might not be ready for this yet. There's some feeling that you might be much happier doing a more intimate, personal film. This kind of project is more an assembly-line thing, the director is like a foreman, making sure all the bolts get put in the right place."

Lisa didn't say anything. She was on the verge of saying something about Eric Lemongrass, but she refrained. Nothing she could say would make any difference. The decision had already been reached. She tried to make it easy for Tami Spiegel to get it over with. She smiled, which actually seemed to displease Tami, who knew why?—Tami really frowned. Maybe she was afraid Lisa didn't think she had enough weight.

Anyway, Lisa was fired. She thought she'd taken it well, but by the time she was driving down Wilshire, having no idea where she was headed, what her destination was . . . she realized that the transaction had indeed left her in kind of a daze. She felt like crying, suddenly, but tried to control it, behind new sunglasses—the traffic was too thick to cry and drive at the same time.

Oh, she was OK. She'd seen it coming, in a way. She just hadn't admitted it to herself. Jules Brandenberg might even have fought for her this morning with Robert Hand. She wondered if he'd call her or if he was too embarrassed. He'd have to talk to her: He'd put money into *Manoa, City of Gold*.

Sure. She had a picture, even if it didn't yet have a distributor, even if it felt dubious to her, like she'd been used as a medium to transmit some inscrutable message from the past.

She'd missed the lunch with Paul Bancroft. That was all right. He might not have shown up—someone might have called him. Lisa wondered who Eric Lemongrass's agent was. If it was Nehi Laughton . . . no, that wasn't likely. Eric had gotten hot only in the last few weeks; before that, he'd been a mediocrity for *years*.

She pulled into the parking lot of a Burger King. She parked and turned off the engine. Why not? She'd have a chocolate shake, like David Lynch used to. Distracted, once she got inside, amongst all the skateboard kids and Hispanic families and weird street people, she impulsively, when it came her turn, ordered a Whopper to have with the shake. Today Lisa wore a cinnamon-colored long-sleeved silk top, cream cotton pleated trousers, and sandals—she sat down in a plastic booth. The Whopper tasted much better than she expected.

Maybe she was just in the mood. It occurred to her that she missed having a boyfriend; in this case, the concept was somewhat disconnected from sex. (Tavinho was the best possibility, but he was so far away.)

"Can I join you?"

She looked up. It was a rocker-type guy, denim vest and a lot of hair, he must have imagined the hair and a bold manner made him attractive, he was coming on to her—what was she doing in a Burger King, anyway? She said, "I'm just leaving," and stood up and left. The advance worried her. He said something else but she hardly listened, just shaking her head.

From a phone booth in the parking lot she called Christine.

"Hello?"

"Chris, this is Lisa. I got fired."

"Really? Those *fuckers*," Christine said emotionally, making Lisa glad she had called. "It doesn't sound like you're at home."

"No, I'm in a phone booth. Oh shit." The jerk had followed her outside. What did he want? She had no desire to talk to him, to listen to two words. He was blond, with red lips. It would be nice if his nose started bleeding.

It did.

"Christine, I'll talk to you later."

"Are you OK?"

"Yeah."

The blood was streaming down. The guy was dabbing with some napkins, realizing no doubt that he was rendered temporarily uncool. Lisa thought of making him bleed from his ears, but that would be too much. She stayed impassive, sunglasses down, walking past him, managing not to wickedly laugh until safe in her car.

SEVENTEEN

"This one makes you see movies in your head. TVC15. You know, like the song."

Lisa had never heard of this song. Joey, upon seeing an expression of interest, held up another vial of the same pills. Lisa nodded and asked for instructions on dosage, possible side effects . . . it was pronounced *TVC-one-five*. An oldie. A David Bowie song.

The longer one studied Joey, the less resemblance there was to Daryl Hannah in *Splash*, but Joey had a sweet smile nonetheless. There had been a call on Lisa's machine from the head of props, asking about the gun. Lisa paid Joey, and Joey left.

Lisa took the TVC15. It was a day to blot out, to forget about, to leave behind.

An hour later, she was lying on the couch, communing with Caz, when she became aware of someone at the door. It was Casablanca, with the videocassette of his last fight. He seemed shy . . . and yet they had something in common—Boro.

"Watch it with me," Lisa said. "Tell me what you were thinking."

"OK," Miguel agreed. The drug was making Lisa euphoric, and she could easily have become sexually aroused. It didn't seem like it would be a good idea, however, to seduce this boxer, no matter how beautiful his slender body was. The Boro connection made her wary that all might not be as it seemed. His cock might turn into a serpent or something, bite her inside. Meanwhile, it was an interesting fight. Linton "The Undertaker" Minniefield, left-handed, with his bald head and ripped torso, seemed like a very tough character—Miguel had been brave just to be in the ring with this guy, much less mixing it up, trading punches, the announcers kept saying he should jab and move, if he got into a slugging match he'd end up on the deck.

"I don't know why they say that," Miguel commented. "I've always had power. I've put guys down with either hand."

There was an unmistakable little throb of excitement in his voice as he watched himself on the screen. It was the fifth round. The crowd was roaring. It was definitely an action fight.

"Do you know what an uppercut is? Watch for the uppercut when he gets me on the ropes. It looks like he's scoring, but I'm catching most of those on my arms."

"God." She grabbed his arm. "You're not hurt here? Jesus, ow."

"Now," he said, and on the screen his right hand in its red glove hit Minniefield perfectly, and Minniefield fell forward past Casablanca into the ropes. Somehow, at the count of eight, he got to his feet. When he nodded and said he was OK, the ref gave in to the howling bloodlust of the mob and let it continue. There was just over one minute left in the round.

Minniefield tried to hold, to cover up; it seemed almost unnecessarily cruel of Miguel to shake himself free and nail the Undertaker with his right, a straight right, then a left hook and another right—Minniefield fell down again, and they stopped the fight. Miguel, on TV, jumped up into the air.

"He's very tough," he said now, his eyes shining. "You're going to come see me fight on Thursday, aren't you? Whoever wins, he fights the champion. This other guy, Rudy Washington, "The Hammer," he's undefeated. They pick him three to one. It's at the Forum, it's on ESPN. OK? I'll see you there?"

"All right," Lisa said. She had never been to a live fight before. Miguel's excitement was infectious. She was scared for him. He sensed this and felt more confident around her now.

"After I win, we'll go out," he said. "When you're in training, you need all your strength. You never know." He kissed her. She was unresisting. He could have fucked her, but he was afraid it would kill his legs.

When he was gone, she played the piano for a while. Caz sat on her lap, which wasn't the greatest arrangement in the world, but he insisted, he wanted to be touching her at all times, sensing her life.

The phone rang, and she let the machine take it; then, when she heard Christine's voice, she rushed to get to it while Christine was still on the line.

"I'm here," she said.

"Do you want me to come over?" asked Christine. "Oriole's out with his buddy Josh, and I thought—"

"Yeah, come over."

TVC15 wasn't yet manifesting any unusual effects, beyond making her feel languid and . . . "loved." Confident she could deal with the hazards of the world, that everything would work out for the best. When she closed her eyes, she saw some scene in slow motion, the same one again and again. A village in the Alps.

Then Christine was bringing her a glass of iced tea. Christine said, "Why is being a Cassandra seen as bad? She was *right*. Right about the fall of Troy and right about the murder of Agamemnon. But when people say 'being a Cassandra,' they mean someone prophesying doom . . . out of a psychological compulsion."

"I know," Lisa said, utterly tranquil. "She foresaw her own death."

"Can I put your new film in the VCR?" Christine asked. "Or are you sick of it right now?"

"No, it seems different every time. Put it in." She explained about

TVC15, and Christine shook her head. But about halfway through the film she slipped a pill into her mouth. The drug was from Japan, based on the chemical abstract of some plant from the Yucatán. This synthetic version was much milder, though, Joey had said.

"I dreamed this film," Lisa said. "Boro used me . . . I can't explain it right now, but it came through me . . . no actors, no camera, no crew."

"I thought something seemed weird," Christine said. "It looks like you, though . . . like your drawings, and those color photographs you did that one time. And, obviously, some of the paintings you like."

"Or that have made an impression on me, like Bosch. Roy's dead, you know. He was dead before I ever left for Brazil."

Christine, sitting on the rug, seemed willing to believe this all might be true.

"It's so bizarre," she murmured softly.

"I might be able to do it again," said Lisa, lying on her side, nearly asleep.

"How?"

"I don't know yet."

The film was over. They both fell asleep. It was a comfort to Lisa to have Christine sleeping so near.

Asleep, Lisa rose and went to her friend. It wasn't right that she should be on the floor. She took Christine's hand and led her, weightlessly, to the bedroom. They rested, breathing regularly, facing each other, in their underwear, knees drawn up, like an advertisement in *Mademoiselle*.

Then Lisa, in curiosity, feeling secure, went into the front room and pulled back the rug, revealing the suspected trapdoor. Unworried, she pulled it open and descended, going down the ladder into the secret room.

As expected, there were candles burning all over, and there was the long-awaited jaguar couch. Black markings on soft white. A hanged man dangled, swaying almost imperceptibly off in the shadows, but Lisa paid no attention to him. She did not care who he might be.

She lay down on the couch, and it seemed to receive her, she went right through it, into a white stone chamber high up in a pyramid, dazzlingly illuminated by new sunlight, virgin sunlight—she moved slowly, to a different rhythm, she knew exactly what she had to do. She was dressed in elaborate ceremonial regalia of quetzal feathers that shaded from azure into cerise into brightest red, returning to yellow-gold like marigolds, there were marigold petals scattered all over the altar, copal incense was burning, and in a different rhythm, slowly but with no sense of delay, filling each moment like a dance . . . she pierced her tongue, the pain bit her, her mind filled up with it like smoky cloudy swirls, she was proud of how the ritual moved her hands, this force soaked in through the atmosphere, moved her, made her blood beat into the bowl, such beautiful red, there was no red to compare. . . .

From the jaguar couch, her tongue throbbing, she climbed up the ladder without a backward glance, languid and sure, graceful as an animal, in harmony. She closed the trapdoor, arranged the rug, and returned to the bedroom, where Christine, watching her, lying on her side, propped up on an elbow, smiled at her, and Lisa bent over to kiss her, they lay side by side and slept heavily, without remorse.

EIGHTEEN

In the morning they awoke almost simultaneously and, yawning, looked into each other's eyes and knew . . . that they had shared the same dream.

Christine said, tasting her lips, "Your blood is in my mouth." Lisa's tongue was swollen and sore. Had it really been pierced? How fast could it possibly heal?

They raced into the front room, pulled back the Turkish rug . . . to reveal nothing. The trapdoor was gone.

"God!" Lisa exclaimed, letting herself fall down onto the couch in dismay.

Christine walked around, yawning again, sleepy, thinking—she made coffee—and then, when she came back into the room, bursting to ask questions, Lisa stopped her, rather wild-eyed, pointing—and, looking down at her own left ankle, Christine saw, to her amazement, an arrangement of flowers on an entwined vine.

She couldn't believe it. She tried to wash it off. It appeared to be a fresh tattoo.

"How have you handled this shit?" Christine said. "It's all true, isn't it?"

"I'm such an asshole," she said, a while later, drinking coffee. "I couldn't understand what you were going through, I refused to accept it . . . I just thought I would wait, see what happened to you . . . whether you were crazy or not, or what. Can you forgive me?"

"Of course I forgive you. I don't blame you."

"Also, I . . . I've been a little judgmental, like the way it looked when you got the job from Jules Brandenberg. And then I had the nerve to fucking ask *you* for a job!"

Christine seemed quite moved by the revelation of her hypocrisy . . . and she kept looking down at her bare ankle to see if the decoration might magically disappear. They talked about the dream: Christine had not gone down the ladder, but she had looked down, observing Lisa, and seen the mysterious couch.

"I don't know why Boro would mark you," Lisa said. "It might be just—some kind of overflow."

The phone rang, and Lisa answered it there in the kitchen. It sounded like someone was asking her out; the banality of this brought Christine somewhat back to ordinary life, and she realized she was supposed to be in Century City by noon. Working on an independent film, helping with postproduction sound. Foley walking, for *Assbackward*, a sex flick directed by Evelyn Roo. Everything, the smallest atmospheric noise, needed to be dubbed.

"Tonight? Sure. . . . Yeah, that sounds good. . . . No, why don't I come over there, so I'll have my car. . . . Really? OK. . . . Yeah, I'll see you then. . . . Sure."

Lisa hung up and said to Christine, "That was Selwyn Popcorn. We're going to have dinner tonight, at some Italian place he knows. You heard about his divorce? Well, somehow he got to keep the house."

"What's he like?"

Lisa gave Christine a calculating, knowingly ironic (and self-ironic) smile. "He's probably, really, if you think about it . . . a lot like you would expect. He lives inside his head. I'm studying him," she said, more seriously, "and he's studying me."

"Does that bother you?"

"No. It's worth it. He didn't come on to me at all in Berlin. Now I think he wants it."

Together, they laughed. Lisa's tongue hurt, not too badly—it ached. The pain reminded her that it was a muscle, sensitive, subtle, constantly used.

"You know," Christine said, "*Manoa* might really catch on. Roy

Hardway's great in it. I want to see it again—there's so much to see. Just on the level of spectacle, it should have its cult."

"Roy does what Roy does best . . . kills as many people as he can."

NINETEEN

When Selwyn Popcorn saw Lisa Nova drive up and park her somewhat-the-worse-for-wear red sports car in the turnaround, he thought, I should marry her, just for the stimulation and adventure. Another divorce wouldn't hurt me at all.

He was still enough of the old school that the tattoos got to him—they made her look like a whore, and this whiplash feeling excited him, the erotic curiosity it aroused was overwhelming to him right now.

She was, today, in the sunshine, nubile in an extremely short dress, red and orange melting sunbursts on white, bare thighs and calves, dusty cowboy boots with a design, bracelets and long dangly Aztec earrings, sunglasses, puffy lips. She smiled as soon as she saw him, and Popcorn was in love. This was exactly what he wanted, he'd known it as soon as she'd departed from Berlin.

"Do you want to have a drink? You look a trifle . . . harassed."

"Yes, I would like something. You've heard, I'm sure, that they fired me from *Ripper II*?"

Popcorn shook his head, but he was lying. Hearing it had moved him to call.

"Well, Robert Hand's behind it, really," she said. "I don't even care, I think it's for the best. Oh cool, is that champagne?"

"Yes. It's something Phoebe bought a long time ago, as an investment. Do you see? Roy Lichtenstein designed the bottle . . . let's see if it's any good." Popcorn removed the cork with a minimum of fuss and poured them each a glass.

"I love champagne," Lisa said. She drank down about half her glass. "Idea One wants to distribute my film. They're offering to do more for it than they did for the first one, but I'm not very excited. I guess I imagined that if I was working on *Ripper*, Hand would say yeah, let's pick up *Manoa*, promote her like, I don't know . . . "

"You're the new bad girl," Popcorn said.

"Exactly. An image, a hook." She finished off the glass of champagne, looking around in more detail for the first time. It was a luxurious house. "Do you have a swimming pool?" she asked.

"Yes. This way." But first he poured her more champagne. Her eyes were a bit red, like she was tired or sad, but she was young and full of vitality, her body was full of life.

"I've had trouble with Robert Hand myself," Popcorn said, as they strolled out onto the terrace to look down at the turquoise waters of the pool. There wasn't much of a breeze, but the waters lightly rippled and moved. "Have you ever met him? He's brilliant, in his way, but he's a technocrat. All he knows are his focus groups, he's always gathering data . . . and so he ends up only wanting to OK appropriated projects—to borrow a word—kid movies, and special effects. And anything with the short-term star flavor of the month. He's so bedazzled by his irrefutable computer projections that he becomes infantilized by the machinery, it's something I've noticed happens to a lot of technically brilliant men—they become big babies. They stay childish in the bad sense. I don't know if it happens to women."

"Don't look at *me*," Lisa said. "I'm technically inept."

Popcorn was puzzled by this—the models and shots were so wonderful in *Manoa*, and the photography was consciously beautiful to the point of showing off. He felt he had to handle her carefully. If he pressed her at the wrong moment or contradicted her on something trivial, she might react perversely, irrationally . . . she was complicated, she had secrets, problems he could not guess.

"My assistant is arriving tomorrow, from London," Lisa said. "And I don't know where to put her. She's a lesbian, she's idealistic, she loves art . . . but my apartment's too small. Also, I've got a detective following me."

"Why?"

"Oh, Nehi Laughton hired him, just out of spite, I guess. He can't accept that I don't know where Roy is anymore."

"Why don't you stay here for a while?" Selwyn Popcorn said. "There's a maid, a cook, a gardener, my assistant—you've met her—and me. What's your friend's name?"

"Raelyn."

"Have her stay here too."

"Are you serious?"

"Absolutely. I like having people around me, that's why I'm usually so happy on location. I'd almost go so far as to say I enjoy chaos."

"Is there a dog here?"

"No. Why? Do you have a dog?"

"No," Lisa said. "But if I come, I've got to bring my cat. I don't want some Doberman killing him."

"Well, you don't have to worry about that."

He could not, however he tried, completely conceal the sexual component of his interest in her, but that was all right. He was older, he wasn't as attractive or sexy as any number of young men she could have—his best chance was to admit everything, all his vulnerabilities, it was much better to throw himself on her mercy, in effect, than to show false ego . . . that was how he might look a fool. (All of this transaction, or most of it, was beneath the surface of their social intercourse, on the more significant level of looks and nonverbal signals, little shrugs, expressions, and smiles. A raised shoulder, a feline stretch, secret intelligence passed through an occult gaze.)

They went to a trattoria-style restaurant in Santa Monica. It was trendy, but Selwyn knew Antonio, the chef. He would be recognized, and there would be gossip about him and Lisa. This sort of publicity wouldn't do either of them any harm.

They sat in the small loft, under wooden rafters; it was more private. Antonio came out to say hello. Nehi Laughton and his wife, along with yet another vice president in charge of development, Witkiewicz or something—passed by on their way out, as Lisa and Selwyn were eating antipasto. The superagent gave them a kind of friendly wave; Popcorn slightly inclined his head, smiling impersonally, and he was amazed to see the dirty look Lisa gave Laughton, her open mouth twisted, and she was almost ugly for a split second, it really looked like she hated the guy. She should learn to control herself better, Selwyn thought.

Back at his house, there was some vague intention of watching something in his screening room, but she chose an opportune moment to suddenly kiss him, and the only plan left was to climb the stairs and walk down the hall, open the door, and go to bed.

TWENTY

Sex with Selwyn Popcorn had no particular interest for Lisa, considered simply as sex. It was half-assed. (This is the term she would use to describe it to Christine.) A man of forty-nine, he had a little bit of a hard time getting and keeping it up, and so she spent quite some time sucking him, for a few minutes beginning to fear (defensively, but with cruelty) that he'd be Mister Softee, and this affected how she experienced it as he ate her, which he did for a long time, lost in his own movie . . . she was pleased when his erection became dependably hard. She liked him, after all. She liked him a great deal. But her tongue hurt, it felt swollen, and after a good spell of giving him a blowjob, her jaw was threatening to lock up. She just wanted to fuck and get it over with. She concentrated with her eyes shut tight, allowing him to be the audience, the friction wasn't real exciting, it was boring but she liked it . . . sure, she had an orgasm. She let him see her come.

The transaction's residue left her in a bad mood the next morning. He didn't seem to notice, which was cool. He was preoccupied by a looming Santa Barbara test screening of his new film, *Call It Love*. Lisa did want to stay here for a few days, maybe a week. She felt that here she would be safe. His place functioned as a hideout, and she would have to keep him under her spell to some extent.

He reiterated, evidently meaning it, that he'd expect to see her and Raelyn here later on. He kissed her without trying to give her any tongue, and then a limousine came to pick him up, there was some important meeting he had to attend. Lisa said hi to his wan young assistant, Nicole, who in Berlin hadn't seemed to know whether to like her or not. Now she smiled, letting this smile convey that she recognized Lisa and they had an invented retrospective history of mutual friendliness and cordial respect.

Lisa went home to get some clothes and Caz. She checked, nervously, under the rug, but again there was no trapdoor. There was a message on her phone: Christine, calling from Adrian's. And the head of security at the studio, sounding menacing, asking her to immediately return the gun. Maybe she should. Could she lie and say she'd lost it or that it had been stolen from her?

Caz sat on the kitchen table, like an Egyptian cat, posing, content in his being with her and in casually keeping an eye on her as she sat there in her peach-colored underwear and the cowboy boots, reading last month's issue of *Elle*. False eyelashes were back. She didn't believe it. She ate a spoonful of peanut butter, some grapes, a banana, a nectarine. She was tired; maybe drinking some more Lapsang souchong tea would help to clear her brain.

She wondered what the tattoo on Christine meant. It had shocked her, and yet . . . she had been glad. It made Christine understand, at least much better than she had. Maybe it was possible that together they could actually go into a dream . . . and *direct* it, and the vision would be preserved on film. Access to the unconscious, the question of a collective image bank for the whole species, a honeycombed structure with endless rooms and endless access codes . . . it was fascinating. If Christine could help her, she would feel far more able to use the Mayan tongue ritual or whatever it took.

There was a noise. Someone was messing with the front door. It almost sounded like the mailman; or maybe it was the person who'd left the script. Or the police. She went in there, intending to look through the peephole—the door came open; Duane Moyer came in and shut it behind him, throwing the deadbolt.

"What do you think you're doing?" Lisa said. "Get out of here. You fucker, I'll call the police."

She felt at a disadvantage, wearing only semitransparent underwear and cowboy boots. She didn't like the look on Moyer's face. She was scared of him.

"I've been watching you," he said.

"I know. But you're trespassing now. What's wrong with you?"

"It's been driving me crazy . . . I've been sitting in my car, thinking about it, sitting there, hour after hour . . . when the gig ran out on Monday, I had to start doing it all myself."

Lisa thought she understood this, that Nehi Laughton had stopped paying. The implications were unsettling. Duane Moyer wore a lemon yellow and azure Hawaiian shirt and tan jeans, and desert boots. He hadn't shaved for a couple of days, and she had the sense that he hadn't washed. He came closer, stepping just enough in the way that he cut off the escape route to the bedroom, bathroom, kitchen, phone . . . she bumped against the piano and said, "I can pay you. I'll pay you to stop following me, to leave me alone."

"You're not listening. We need to communicate. There's something I want to communicate to you. It's important that you understand."

"Tell me. I'll listen."

His eyes saw her, but they were not eyes she could stand to look into. She was so stupidly vulnerable—but who could have known he was going to get obsessed and go crazy and use a credit card or whatever to get in her door?

"You'll listen to me, huh?" Moyer knew she was afraid, knew she was just trying to keep him talking. He smiled. "I saw that Mexican come over the other night. What was he like? Was he a good fuck?"

"We didn't do that," Lisa said. "He's a boxer; he never has sex before a fight. Look, you better leave. If you leave now, I won't even call the police. You've been in your car too long; you need to go home and get some sleep."

"And that skinhead," Moyer went on. "And your girlfriend. And then the famous fucking director—I want some of it. I've been watching you, I feel like I know you, but we'll know each other much better after this." To her vast alarm, he pulled a coiled length of rope out of his back pocket, still just staring at her, not looking down at his hands as he tested it, stretching, letting most of it unfurl from tense, knuckly, strong hands.

"I want to get to know you," he said, "and I want you to get to know me. I fuck like a nigger"—at which point she made a bound to her right, to go over the couch and out the front door. She was quick and got by him at first, he touched but couldn't hold her, but then he caught her at the door, she screamed and he said, "Shut up or I'll kill you." She fought him and he twisted and threw her down onto the floor, swinging her like somebody tackling a quarterback, landing on top of her on purpose to crush her—the combined impact of hitting the floor and then as she bounced having this big man crash down on her with all his considerable bulk and weight—she was stunned for a while. He tore off her bra and then started trying to loop some of the rope around her left wrist . . . when she screamed again, as loudly as she could, he smacked her with his fist and then couldn't resist hitting her again. She tried to knee him, and he pinned her down, he was much stronger, and he put his knees into her thighs, opening them, holding both of her wrists pinned down above her head with his left hand.

"Don't do it," she begged him, "don't hurt me."

"I don't have to be rough," he said, his breathing slowing little by little. "If you don't fight me, I won't hurt you."

He was going to, though, she thought, but she went limp. He was determined to tie both of her wrists. His knees hurt her thighs a great deal. She couldn't struggle again until he was off her legs.

Luckily, he apparently wanted to rape her in the bedroom. How could he get a hard-on from all this? She was feeling strangely sure that she could do something to him; her body was cold but she was only waiting, absolutely alert, for the right moment to surge. He smelled bad, there were all kinds of strangely intense smells stuck to him. Stale sweat under his arms, now renewed, yesterday's Big Mac, coffee, candy bars, peppermint Life Savers, a trace of urine, of old shit, upholstery from his car, gasoline, french fries . . .

He pulled her to her feet, said, "Be quiet," her wrists were tied together and he meant to probably tie them to the bed frame, a pornographic scene. He thought he had it under control. He pulled on the rope, and she jerked suddenly the other way so hard that the rope flew out of his hands, he came after her and she snarled as they fell on the rug over the trapdoor. She got her teeth into his neck, it was like she had jaguar teeth in a carnivore's strong jaw, she went for the side of his throat and got hold, her fangs found purchase, arms around his head pulling him in closer, he didn't expect it and he was on top but then she rolled lithely over and the big carotid artery tore open, the hot blood splashed out sticky and red, his feet thrashed and she bit him and held on as he fought her with all his might. The blood indifferently, madly burst out of the artery, her jaw seemed to open unnaturally wide, she ripped his neck even more, snorting to breathe, there was so much blood in her mouth and nose it was like she was swimming in it. She felt him weaken, she gasped to get her breath, panting, and then she smelled that he was dead.

TWENTY-ONE

It didn't seem she could get all the blood out of her hair, no matter how long she stayed in the shower. She lingered . . . having a hard time coming back to herself, back to ordinary, more or less focused thought. The water continued to pour over her. She had a bad few moments of panic, thinking there was blood in her hair or that she couldn't tell anymore. This kind of thing was how criminals became deranged.

OK. Lisa turned off the water. Perfunctorily dry, she went into the bedroom, avoiding looking at the front room as she went by. She lay down on the bed. Casimir had come in here, and he meowed, the turmoil had worried him. He needed the touch of her hands and the sound of her voice to be reassured. It soothed Lisa to do this. She thought about how Caz would have acted in the situation if he were big, and she knew there was nothing else she could have done. The jaguar spirit had entered her, she felt. It had been alien, detached, huge, and amused. Yet she *knew* it, somehow. And the great jaguar mother recognized her, it knew her as an animal, through the senses . . . it knew her very well.

Time passed. She got dressed, in terrifically faded soft jeans with ripped-out knees and a red polo-style top on which she figured the blood wouldn't show up as much. No, it did not seem possible to go through channels, to call the police and say, "He tried to rape me so I bit through his throat." The thing to do was . . . she could take the body to Boro. All she had to do was wait until dark.

In the meantime, she had to do the best she could to clean up the mess. Roll him up in the ruined rug. She shut Caz in the bedroom for a while, because she didn't want him coming out and possibly lapping at the blood. She didn't know if he would, but it wasn't something she wanted to see. She got out the mop and went to work. Unfortunately, there was a lot of blood on the couch. She just did the best she could.

It was one-thirty. At three-fifteen she was supposed to pick up Raelyn at LAX. Well, she would just have to do it, take her straight over to Popcorn's, as he'd suggested. She could take some clothes and her cut-for-speed swimsuit and come back here only after it got dark. The problem was that he was so heavy, the stairs down to her car were secluded but she'd be conspicuous, the moving itself would be extremely difficult. Even if she had help, it would be clumsy. And she wasn't entirely sure he would fit into her trunk, certainly not without being folded. But whom could she ask?

Christine would do it, she knew.

Christine said on the phone that she'd had a terrible fight with Oriole over the tattoo. For all his flirtatious promiscuity, he was jealously possessive, and he had deduced from something he'd seen in Lisa's eyes that she and Christine had finally become lovers and that the ankle tattoos were the seal of this bond.

Lisa laughed. "It would be none of his business, anyway."

"I know. Actually, it doesn't matter to me at this point. I wouldn't play his game and try to convince him or make promises . . . I'm sick of him. I mean that. I don't know why I've stayed with him for so long."

In her kitchen, Lisa listened, encouraging her friend to go over the same territory, even if it was repetitious—Christine needed to get it all out. It was soothing to Lisa just to hear her best friend's voice. When she noticed that some time had passed, she remembered that she had to go pick up Raelyn. She asked Christine if she wanted to come along.

"Sure. I'm curious to meet her."

"OK, I'll come and get you. I better leave right away."

"I'll come down to the street."

"Great. See you."

It felt very weird to lock her door, leaving the carnage within, but it made sense to do this stuff, and otherwise she'd just be sitting around with Duane Moyer's corpse. The hanged man? When she had gone down into the secret room, she had hardly paid any attention to him. She remembered her costume far more vividly, the luminescence of the feathers, the jade and gold and turquoise jewelry, the earrings that were dangling mirrors. . . . The hanged man was a card in the tarot deck, she knew that, but she wasn't sure exactly what it meant. Was it Moyer? She didn't think so.

In the car on the freeway, Christine suddenly pointed out that it looked like Lisa had been hit in the mouth. It hadn't really consciously registered, though she'd been putting her tongue to the wounded area again and again.

Hesitating only a moment, Lisa asked, flat out, without preamble, "Can you help me tonight to put a body in the trunk of my car?"

"Yes, of course I will, I'll help you any way you want." And then: "You don't have to explain."

This gesture was quite moving to Lisa, who took off her sunglasses to gaze into her friend's eyes, tears were welling up and they stung—she told her the whole thing.

"I'll go with you," Christine said. "I want to meet Boro . . . if he put this fucking tattoo on me, I should see who he is and what he wants. Maybe we can work out some kind of a deal. I'm not as apt to let things go on being mysterious as you are . . . I want my enigmas resolved."

"You're more rational than I am," Lisa agreed, though it was relative—and although Christine no doubt thought this statement was true and may have even nodded, contemplating it seemed to make her feel sad.

LAX was crowded and jam-packed as usual, Raelyn's plane from Chicago on United was getting later all the time. But the crowd scene cheered Lisa up.

She told Christine that Popcorn was a half-assed fuck.

"But that's OK," she said. "Just like you'd expect, he'd rather watch me naked on film. Total voyeur action. He's subtle about it, sort of. . . ."

Christine laughed. They couldn't talk for a few moments—there must have been an entire Boeingful of Sri Lankans deplaning. As they waited, standing, Lisa said, "I should tell you, so you're not surprised by anything between Raelyn and me . . . "

"You were lovers?"

"How can you tell?"

"I can read you a little. Was it fun?"

"Yeah. The only thing I didn't like . . . was that it was like she was initiating me. Her desire, before we did it, when she wasn't sure I'd go through with it . . . I liked her better like that. She's only twenty-one."

The plane arrived. Raelyn looked more attractive than she had existed in Lisa's memory, more intelligent and more high-strung. Lisa embraced her self-consciously, kissing her cheek. She introduced her to Christine. The two of them seemed to hit it off; Lisa felt a little jealous, falling mostly silent after a while, hiding behind sunglasses and the hassle of driving in the ridiculous traffic.

Lisa's mood improved some when it turned out that Raelyn had clips of all the reviews of *Manoa* right in her bag. Lisa wanted to hear them, even if they were bad. Especially if they were bad. One guy said it looked like a film made by someone who'd never seen one before—and that was bad. He hated it. Another guy said the same thing—and that made it great.

TWENTY-TWO

Wrapped in the rug, Duane Moyer's body wasn't so obvious . . . they let down the backseat and put him in, with considerable difficulty, head in the trunk and feet coming up to stick out between the front seats, the rigor made him seem made out of wood. Headlights illuminated them only at an angle, reflecting, sweeping by—Lisa groaned, "Oh God," and they laughed nervously together, fearful, spooked . . . Lisa was really grateful when Christine offered to drive. Her arms and back were sore from the lifting, and she was bruised in several places from the earlier fight. She had been so attuned to any hint of danger, of cops, every nuance of the atmosphere . . . it had worn her out, she was too tired to stay alert now that the corpse was in the car. Her apartment was still a crime scene, it would have to be cleaned much more thoroughly, but at least she could get rid of the body unless something went wrong. The blood on the floor and walls, seeping into the rug, had been grape-juice-hued turning to black in the evening light.

At the gate of Boro's property Lisa got out, went to the intercom, pressed the button, and waited. It took a while, but she was unwilling to press the call button again. Maybe no one heard it, or it was broken. This stretch of canyon, in the darkness, seemed desolate, the wind blowing scraps of torn paper—all the imposed numbers and nonsense of civilization—and blond, ancient graveyard dust. Finally a voice, probably Ariel's. "Yes?"

"It's Lisa Nova," she said.

There was no reply. She couldn't think of what else to say. The gate clicked and swung in; she got into the passenger seat.

Christine said as they went in, "Do you remember Cassandra's words, when she arrived at Mycenae? 'Hail to thee, gates of death.'"

"Don't do that." Lisa was scared, but Christine laughed. They parked the car behind the Jaguar sedan; zombies emerged from the shadows around them, moving slowly. "They smell him," Lisa said. Now Christine's bravado was disturbed. One of the zombies—Brian?—stepped up close to her, and she violently started, moving back toward Lisa, who told her, "They won't hurt us." Christine's fear soothed her somehow. Ariel emerged, somewhat stealthily, from the back door. She smiled at him; he nodded politely in response. Then he regarded her interrogatively. She introduced Christine and, that done, explained that they had brought along a corpse.

"Let me see," he said, and Lisa opened the trunk. The rug had worked itself off Duane Moyer's face, which was stuck in a rictus of vicious surprise, one side of the throat ripped out below.

"You did this to him?" Ariel asked. "Why? What did he do?"

"Tried to rape me."

"Ah, defending your honor. Ricky! Drew! Bring this man down after us. This way, come," and Lisa and Christine followed him into the house. Christine reached out, and Lisa held her hand. Noticing this, as he turned back to them, Ariel said, "This might be a good thing. Boro is meeting now with a gangster, a black man named Mannix. Some of his friends are here too. Just sit down and relax."

They came down into the huge, high-ceilinged room, lit warmly by torches held by white life-sized plaster statues of a heroically proportioned male. They walked through thirty yards or so of exotic plants to the clearing where Boro held court, a relatively small fire burning in the middle of the dirt.

Mannix had a blue scarf tied on his head, which indicated he was a Crip or had Crip sympathies. He had pumped a lot of iron, obviously; he stood with his legs somewhat apart, his muscular arms folded across his chest. Scowling. His four followers stood behind him, some wearing baseball caps, more or less at ease.

Boro sat on what looked like a pirate's treasure chest, petting his black dog, surrounded by as many as twelve zombies—including, Lisa saw with real dismay, Jonathan . . . his eyes were dead, his skin was bluish like the rest. The bodies were starting to pile up. Jesus. She had warned him. Wanda smiled at her, too knowingly, wearing a white lacy gown like those of the female zombies.

Lisa sat down next to Boro, close enough to pet the black dog. Christine followed; Lisa put her arm around her and pulled her close. Boro rubbed Lisa's shoulders . . . she was here, she was in the moment; then she felt jaded and amnesiac. She yawned.

Moyer's body was laid down, disentangled from the rug.

"Sometimes," Boro said, "your friend of yesterday becomes your enemy of today. My Lisa here," affectionately mussing up her hair, "she is like a jaguar in some ways. She bites your dick, watch out, it's gone."

"OK," Mannix said, "your bitch did a vampire number on the motherfucker. I respect your shit, man. Just tell me when."

Boro was silent, continuing to caress Lisa with a warm, sensitive hand. She didn't mind pretending to belong to him.

"Saturday," Boro said. He nodded; Mannix nodded back.

"Let's kick it," he said to his crew, and they left.

A few moments later Boro asked Lisa, referring to Moyer, "What is this?"

Lisa didn't know what to say. She had the feeling he already knew all about it. Maybe he wasn't as omniscient, though, as she sometimes thought.

"I brought you a sacrifice," she said, and felt Boro's fingers seize her by the hair, not jerking or hurting, but letting her know.

"Who do you think you're fooling with? You did good, you did fine, but don't start exaggerating . . . you cannot lie to me about anything. Don't even try. This isn't fresh; it's not a sacrifice. You want to sacrifice someone, you bring them here alive. You do it here. This thing is just—food." He snapped his fingers, and several of the zombies went to the corpse. "Take him into the other room. Then if you are hungry, you may eat."

They picked up the body, their movements speeding up a little, betraying a certain caginess, making a low growling kind of sound. It was the male zombies who were active, but the women followed behind, also hungry.

"Introduce me to your friend," Boro said.

As usual, Lisa felt like he knew the answer before he asked. Christine's confidence seemed to have quickly returned; she was studying the environment, aware or trying to be aware of everything all around, wanting to take it all in.

"Did you give this to me?" Christine asked, showing him the design on her ankle.

"No, it wasn't me," he said, smiling. "It was Wanda here . . . she's been wanting to meet you. Why don't you two go off and talk about what it can do?"

Somewhat to Lisa's surprise, Christine seemed interested—she followed Wanda off to the right, through the Venus flytraps and suchlike.

"She has a lot of curiosity," Boro said. Then in a moment, he added, "Christine loves you, but she is also jealous of you."

"What do you want from her?"

Boro smiled and stood up; Lisa stood up too. Ariel Mendoza had followed Mannix out, to see him on his way; now he returned. The black dog went to him, and he spoke to it, squatting down to it, as it accepted his ministrations and wagged its tail.

"It is not a question of what I want. It's what does she want for herself. We will see."

They walked toward the room in which Lou—or the ghost of Lou, or a dramatization of "the end of Lou"—had previously appeared. Since Lisa had killed Moyer, making use, it seemed to her, of power derived from what Boro had set in motion . . . power that might be traced, conceivably, back to when Lisa had fizzed urine onto the wax effigy representing Lou . . . she supposed she had a sort of responsibility to see what they did to Duane Moyer's remains. And there was also a mixed desire to gaze upon the worst, to see if she could face it, the allure of evil was definitely there.

Jonathan stared at her, his mouth all bloody, mindlessly eating the big liver, illuminated by a torch off in the corner. He seemed to be looking right into her eyes; she shuddered, but although it was sickening, she found that she could watch. The thought ran through her mind, she was trying it out: It's too intense to be real life, it must be a movie, which she quickly realized ought be reversed. The room was lit interestingly . . . dark gold with glints of red.

Boro said, "They eat the good parts first."

"What about that one, the bald one—when did he come?"

"A few days ago. Why do you ask this, since you know the answer?"

Lisa gestured helplessly as they left the disgusting, squishy feast behind. "I wasn't sure if you knew who he was."

"And so, anytime you might possess a secret, you try to keep it to yourself."

She pretended to be interested in the big aquarium, and after he pointed out a few rare fish to her, she asked him, "Are you ever going to kill me? I want to know."

"Don't be so dramatic," Boro said. "I want you to be my priestess. I would never harm you. But it's possible you might do something to harm yourself. I don't know. You want everything for free."

"You've never said what you want from me," Lisa said. "Do you want money? I have some money, temporarily."

"I don't want your money."

"Well, what then? Do you want me to stand on top of a pyramid and cut out somebody's heart?"

Boro smiled at this, he really smiled at her, and Lisa was moved to say, "Or is it me you want to sacrifice?" She could feel the nakedness of her face.

"You could have a different kind of immortality," he said contemplatively, abstractly, motioning with both hands. "Wouldn't you like to be in the headlines? How about 'Prostitute Found Murdered in Hotel Room'? Or 'Actress Victim of Bizarre Mutilation Murder, Links to Unnamed Stars'? Think what hot items your films would be then. People would study them, looking for a clue . . . there'd be biographers wanting to track down everyone you've ever known. You could be like Sharon Tate or the Black Dahlia. Believe me: Many, many people would worship you, worship your image, memorize your face.

That's what you want, isn't it? You want to be mysterious, you want people to think about you after you're dead. You want to be exposed."

"That's cold, Boro," Lisa said, scared but also feeling he was kidding, not sure. If he was as old as he was supposed to be—and this had occurred to her before—his ideas about women were probably completely fucked up. Virgin or madonna versus whore, with nothing in between.

He laughed. This was fun for him. He liked her, as he had said. Lisa didn't think this would stop him from seeing her killed; aesthetically, it would make it better for him. She was safe right now, this moment, but she wasn't safe.

"What do you want?" she asked.

"What do you think I want?"

"You're just fucking with me."

"I'm not. I'm helping you achieve what you seek. What about *Manoa, City of Gold*?"

"You toy with me. Like these tattoos."

"You don't like them? OK, I can make them fade away, no problem. Remember, though, it's very important they're in exactly the same place. You decide."

Lisa kept her mouth shut. That shit about being found murdered in a hotel room wasn't funny to her. She didn't know what he meant about the tattoos.

She was tired. It was time to find Christine. Her red top felt sweaty and funky; she pushed her hair out of her eyes, and Boro touched her again, rubbing her back for a moment, as if she were an animal he had tamed.

"That way leads out," he said. "Ariel! Ariel will take you. Are you going to go see Casablanca's fight?"

Lisa nodded. "What does he do for you, that you're helping him?" She sounded different, indifferent, and Boro responded without his usual bullshit; Ariel listened too.

"Miguel was supposed to bring an innocent boy. This kid he brings us is a hustler—he sells his ass to Anglos in cars. He's pretty, but he's all done. He ain't going nowhere, you understand what I mean? He's on the pipe. So what do you think of this? Will the magic be strong enough, or did Miguel fuck it up?"

Lisa didn't know, so she didn't reply. She said, "In a sacrifice, does something always have to die?"

Boro sounded weary, impatient with her tone. "Death is all around. Something is born, created, something has to die. You will see," he said, and turned and walked away.

Ariel Mendoza . . . Lisa did not understand what he was getting out of his role. Ten-year-old girls? Usually she sort of liked him, maybe just because he was polite, but at the moment she was inclined to think badly of everyone here . . . therefore she was anxious about Christine and could not help probably frowning at Ariel as he showed her the way through the weird halls, which seemed a maze.

Wanda and Christine were in the upstairs room across from each other, each wearing a blindfold of black cloth, doing a kind of slow, symmetrical dance, one and then the other seeming to slightly take the lead, most of it was with the arms, as one's right arm rose gracefully the other's right arm went up too, then they did an intricate, hyperspeed pattern thing, like kung fu, that was so fast it was shocking they stayed in synch. Christine was stripped down to her lacy white underwear, her mouth moving, almost forming syllables of private, transfigured delight. There was a black band around one upper arm and a necklace with an amulet around her neck. Wanda was completely nude, somehow clothed by her tattoos, bracelets, and rings. No pubic hair. Rings down there too. The lights blinked down almost to dark and came up white with a memory of ultraviolet to blue. There was a large boa constrictor in the room; it flicked its tongue. White birds fluttered in a cage.

Then, simultaneously, Wanda and Christine clapped their hands sharply and, grinning, removed the blindfolds.

Christine told Lisa she was staying for a few days. "Don't look at me like that," she said willfully. "I'm in my right mind. Let's not argue about it, OK? You're in it a fuck of a lot deeper than I'll ever be."

"Here," Wanda offered, writing a number on a piece of torn blue paper. "You can call her every day."

Lisa took Christine aside, said in a low, urgent voice, "Are you fucking crazy? Christine, have you lost your fucking mind? C'mon, let's go. You can always visit if you think it's so interesting. Don't do this."

Christine jerked away angrily and said, "You always want to know everything first. Lisa's the star, everybody else is a sidekick in your movie—well, *not me*, not anymore. I want to find out something for myself. That's it. Now leave me alone."

Lisa didn't know what to do. She hated it. She didn't trust Wanda *at all*. Maybe—this was how magical her thinking had become, she thought to herself—maybe there was some kind of a spell.

At Popcorn's, later, 2 A.M., having collected Caz and some clothes, she sat on the bed (in her own room) while Selwyn, who had been unable to sleep while waiting for her, caressed her thigh like a piece of art he was trying to understand in the land of the blind.

She was sad, and she couldn't tell him why. Everyone who'd come in contact with the situation had gotten in trouble—she didn't want to present Boro with anyone new. All she could say to Popcorn was, "I'm coming to grips with the fact that I'm a bad person . . ." and then, knowing he couldn't understand, she seized on Boro's scenario: "Maybe I'm going to end up murdered in a hotel room, cut in pieces, my head on the vanity in front of the mirror . . . that might be what I'm meant for, sometimes I think I can feel it coming at me like a speeding car."

"No," he said, and for some reason she was soothed. She hadn't wanted to think about it in these terms, but his intelligence reminded her of her dad. In his embrace, the incestuous angle repelled her, which was why she didn't much like kissing him on the mouth.

"Don't take it so seriously," he said in an experienced, philosophical way. She liked hearing it, but he didn't know what he was talking about. Of course not, unfortunately. He thought he did, though, and *pretending* to be comforted sort of comforted her, or came close enough. He sat by her in the dark, silently, not moving, until she was asleep.

TWENTY-THREE

It wasn't hard to figure out that Raelyn was a little more skeptical of Lisa than she had been at first, which was OK. Lisa didn't really require subservience, it was good that Raelyn—thrown into a situation—had done as well as she had, dealing with the Idea One people, when Lisa had given her so little direction. Raelyn, luckily enough, had been unafraid to run up a transatlantic phone bill asking New York lesbian filmmakers for advice, and that had helped a great deal. Lisa was very pleased with her. Things had changed since Lisa had been fired from the Ripper sequel. Now the next likely project was the film about Cassandra . . . though Lisa thought she might experiment, see if she could make it by extraordinary means, like *Manoa* but somewhat more conscious . . . she didn't know if this was possible or not. In any case, it wasn't something she intended to try to explain to Raelyn.

So she was vague and mysterious about an awful lot . . . though she did plan on going to Cannes and hoped Raelyn would come too. What complicated things between them was that Raelyn was still in love with Lisa, it was obvious, and it was also obvious that she (naturally) disapproved of the liaison with Selwyn Popcorn. Though in another sense it was interesting for her to stay at his house. Last night, for instance, he had talked to her and somewhat won her over.

"Someone tried to rape me yesterday," Lisa said, partly to get through to Raelyn past her jealousy, if that's what it was, partly just because it was true, the whole incident weighed heavily, even though she'd done no wrong—Duane Moyer had attacked her and deserved to die.

It was said so flatly, though, that Raelyn didn't know how to respond. She looked at Lisa for a long time, finally gazing away and saying, "If you'd tell me about it . . . I never know where you're coming from, what's really happening. There's always a subtext that I'm missing."

"I tell you what I can, or what I think you need to know. My life's messy."

"I know that," Raelyn said. "I've been a tiny part of the messiness . . . you should realize, though, I should tell you, that even though I've had a crush on you, I've always known you were straight, I mean it's obvious, so . . . I would never purposely add to the messiness. That's all. I can never tell what you're thinking, it seems like you've got about six million things going on at once. Tell me what happened. Who tried to rape you? Where?"

"In my apartment. A cheap detective, who'd been watching me for a week or two."

"What happened?"

"I fought him off," Lisa said. "I was really lucky. I bit him really bad."

"Did he hit you in the mouth?"

"Yeah, he did." Lisa smiled at Raelyn's making a deduction, but also, more powerfully, at the memory of how she'd amazingly ripped his throat with jaguar teeth. "Don't say anything to Selwyn," she added, perhaps unnecessarily, and Raelyn said of course not, barely audible, upset. She seemed very young and insecure.

Lisa leaned back, there by the pool, in her swimsuit, and said, maybe cruelly, "My brother forwarded me this letter from a guy I met down in Brazil. His name's Tavinho Medeiros. He says he might be coming up here, for some seminar at Southern Cal. I'll never forget," she said, smiling, tapping the letter against the glass table, "when he showed up in Bahia, on the beach, after this *umbanda* ceremony went all wrong. Birds started dropping down dead out of the sky. I'm not kidding. The spell went really bad."

"You're pretty superstitious, aren't you?" Raelyn said, and it seemed like she'd discovered a way to work together and be friends—*studying* Lisa, affectionate but slightly detached. That was all right.

In order to get Popcorn in the mood to watch Casablanca fight that evening, late in the afternoon Lisa plugged in the videocassette of his last fight.

"What's this?" Selwyn said, having taken off his tie, looking on with great interest as the zombies carried Duane Moyer into the back room and began tearing him apart, eating the pieces, a handheld-camera-type effect. "Great lighting."

"Oh, it's an experimental student thing," Lisa said, shocked, moving to turn it off.

"Wait. I want to see what happens. It's really gory. Realistic, too. How did you do that?"

"Somebody's brother knew an armless and legless guy, and we built him a fake torso, so that we could rip out his guts. Have you seen enough?" she said.

"Yeah. I get the idea. Have you been into boxing for a long time?"

TWENTY-FOUR

"'Pain looks great on other people. Isn't that what they're for?'" Lisa said, quoting a song lyric to Popcorn, telling him how in New York she used to go to this one theater, Always 6 Kung Fu Hits, with her Walkman on, no subtitles. Animated, she noticed that Rush Fenders was in the crowd, and told Popcorn that Fenders sucked. "All his fight scenes and stunts are edited, so you can never tell what he really does. That's low."

Popcorn liked her when she was this lively. He liked her in the black leather jacket. Christian Manitoba was also here, and the basketball star Dwight Crow. Popcorn had been to a couple of fights many years ago. He didn't want to date himself, so he didn't bring them up. The affair with Lisa was beginning to hurt, which was good, it stimulated him, he was having good ideas for his next film, he conceived of it with her—as viewer—in mind. Little subtleties she might get and be amazed by. But he wanted to marry her, and he was already jealous of all the young men who might cross her path. Like her old boyfriend, Code, the rock-and-roller, who had called her up today. He was living with Lauren Devoto, which explained how he'd gotten the number, apparently he was quite a hustler, at least that's how Lisa seemed to describe him. . . .

The preliminary fights provided some excitement, thrills—Lisa and Popcorn talked to each other throughout, rooting for this guy because of the color of his trunks, against that one because of his attitude and nickname . . . Popcorn was becoming pretty curious how she happened to know this Miguel Casablanca, but it was the kind of question he would deliberately refrain from asking as long as he could.

Now the parties were in the ring for the main event. The bell rang, and the announcer went into his cadenced spiel. Miguel Casablanca was definitely good-looking, and from the way Lisa's eyes were shining, Popcorn wondered if she'd fucked him. He had golden skin, even with his mouthpiece in he was handsome, wearing classic white trunks. He had the crowd on his side, a lot of fellow Mexican-Americans who were really into it. Casablanca looked confident and determined, dancing gracefully on his toes, red gloves taped on under the hot lights. His opponent was a formidable young black man, taller, in black trunks, named Rudy "The Hammer" Washington. The referee was Ernie Perez.

So Casablanca started strong, he looked good, he probably won the first three rounds. But then in the fifth round Washington hit him with a tremendous, perfect right hand. Casablanca went down. He covered up and lasted the round, and fought back terrifically in the sixth.

Lisa was excited, going up and down with the emotional highs and lows of the fight along with the crowd. Popcorn thought she was naive.

In the seventh round Rudy Washington knocked Casablanca down again, early enough so that he had two minutes or so to end it. Miguel was bleeding from cuts over both eyes, wobbling, obviously hurt. When he was backed up against the ropes and his mouthpiece flew out, spinning, you knew it was near the end. There was a dreadful look in Rudy's eyes, like a warrior who was just naturally cruel, a killer . . . and his right hand snapped like a rattlesnake, landing heavily, like he could murder you with one punch.

Casablanca went down and could not get back up. It was a knockout. Washington stuck his gloved hands straight up into the air, exultant. His trainer lifted him for a moment as he flailed at the night, there under the bright lights.

Popcorn put his arm around Lisa's shoulders, drawing her to him, but after just a few moments of shocked sorrow she was curious, she wanted to see, to understand what was going on. There were all kinds of people in the ring.

After the official pronouncement of Rudy Washington's triumph, when the uproar finally seemed to be dying down a little, emotions ebbing, Lisa, shaking her head, said, "Well, Miguel's fucked. I don't know what he's gonna do. He's really fucked."

Popcorn was to remember this comment later on. He would try to replay the look on her face, the tone of her voice.

For, later that night, after they'd had sex, both of them aroused, without question, by the fight—and Lisa by having cried, her temperature was raised, he realized this in the most intimate way as they clung to each other, like Romans full of lust after watching the gladiators, it was natural . . . a phone call came, only a very few people knew the number of his bedroom phone—Larry Planet, who knew about the fight, saying, "Look, I'm sorry to call you so late, but I thought you'd want to know . . . the boxer you went to see, Casablanca?"

"Yeah?" Lisa had gone to her own room not more than ten minutes ago.

"He committed suicide. He shot himself in the head."

"Jesus."

When he broke the news to Lisa, it was like she already knew. At least she didn't seem to be truly surprised, even though she gasped. The doomy look in her eyes had been there since the end of the fight. No tears now.

"Did you know him well?" Popcorn asked at last, puzzled by her reaction, seeing unaffected honesty as his only route.

"In a way I did, but no, not like you mean." She brought her cat up to her face, nuzzling his neck as he shut his eyes and purred. "Selwyn . . . I just want to go to sleep now, with Caz."

Popcorn nodded and left her alone.

"He had nothing left," he heard her say tonelessly as he went out into the hall. The remark had been meant for him to hear but not to fully understand. He saw that they were playing a game.

SECTION 25

The sorrow was physical, like an illness. It was complex, composed of feelings not only about Casablanca but also about herself, and about Duane Moyer in some way, even though he'd basically deserved what he'd gotten. The crimes Miguel had committed in service of his career were abstract to her, she didn't know how much to believe of what Boro had implied, but she had liked Miguel . . . and he had shown such wonderful physical grace and heart there in the ring. She could have been his girlfriend, that dead possibility was something else she sentimentally mourned. She was scared. She was trying to gather her wits; if she was careless now, she might literally die.

She was taking a shower, absently scrubbing herself, when she suddenly realized that the suds on her upper arm were turning blue, the psychic tattoos were indeed fading away, rubbing off. Boro had said something to her. . . that they had to be in the same exact place. She saw this as a problem to be coolly thought through and faced. She dried herself carefully, trying not to rub the towel over any of the areas that had been marked.

Only for a moment did she consider the alternative of just letting them go. If she did that, she would be powerless, and Boro would probably sacrifice her anyway, maybe sooner than planned, out of contempt. Her friends were used to them, she was used to them. She had come to like them. They made manifest her new criminal status—they were now part of her image as the "bad girl" filmmaker, and she knew they turned Popcorn on . . . she'd been given them free, and now she had to pay for them. It all made sense.

The outlines were still plainly visible, but she needed work done *now,* today, no fucking around. By tomorrow they might be gone. Boro was playing with her, here she must play along. He would be laughing, enjoying the thought of her pain. Well, she could stand it. It had to be done.

The trouble was that the tattoo artists in Los Angeles with good reputations were all booked up months in advance. Some asshole in Venice might fuck it up or give her staph.

She called Code. It was early enough in the day that he should still be in bed. He had said he had his own line. She got his machine.

"Code, this is Lisa. It's an emergency, I need your help. Call me back as soon as you can, please."

He came onto the line then, sounding sleepy, half awake. The word *emergency* had gotten his attention. She told him she needed a good tattooist; she needed the tattoos to be done today. Did he know someone? Did Lauren have any connections in this field?

Code laughed, wickedly. "Maybe she does."

"Don't fuck around with me, OK? I'm willing to pay double the going rate. More than that, if I have to. I need to know right away."

"I'll call you back within a half hour, even if nothing's happened yet," he promised, and she knew he meant it, even if he'd probably actually be late.

He called her back in an hour and said, "Do you remember, the other day you said that you wanted to see Bloody Murder, because little Mary Siddons is in the band? Well, why don't we go see them and then drop by here to check out a party Lauren's having for some friends of hers?"

"What's the punch line?"

"The punch line is that a women-only tattooist named Siobhan has agreed, under pressure, to cancel the rest of today's schedule and take you on, as a favor to Lauren. So get ready to be grateful. Siobhan's doing you for free."

Elated, Lisa took down the Santa Monica address. She was ready to go. She asked Raelyn, on the way out, if she wanted to come and keep her company, hold her hand. Raelyn didn't ask any questions, dressed in jeans and a man's white shirt, though she looked a bit baffled. She just said sure. Lisa considered leaving a message for Selwyn, but then decided she could call later on.

The studio was light and airy—Siobhan didn't seem too happy about the imposition, then when she found out the extent of what Lisa wanted done, she at first refused.

"You shouldn't have more than one a day, anyway. You'll have to come back."

"You don't understand," Lisa said. "These were drawn on me by this Amazonian shaman, and they're starting to fade—it's crucial that they be situated exactly where they are right now. So they need to be done *today*."

Siobhan shook her head impatiently. "You won't be able to take this much at one time. It's not a good idea."

"Just fucking *do it*, OK? I understood from Lauren that this was all cool."

Siobhan didn't like it. Even if she thought Lisa and Raelyn were lovers, her initial reaction to Lisa seemed negative. But she and her assistant prepared to go to work. Lisa took off her T-shirt and lay down on her stomach on the black leather table.

The young, shaved-head lesbian assistant dabbed away the blood with cotton balls; the blood came constantly, beading like rubies, welling up . . . the more focused the color, the more intense the pain, because the needle goes over and over the same place.

"Why these particular designs?" Raelyn asked, to which Lisa said, "I don't know."

Siobhan's mood had improved once she had Lisa under the needle. The scab forming was translucent, the same color as the tattoo beneath. At one point the assistant, kind of shyly, offered Lisa a pain pill; she declined. It would be many hours. Lisa suspected she needed to feel it, the initiation rite. Fuck.

Occasionally she exhaled an "uh" or said "ow," but she let herself go so limp, so relaxed that there was no question of her flinching or jerking . . . she couldn't decide if it was better or worse to close her eyes. The pain was like paper cuts, like being given a shot by a nurse, like someone twisting a tiny razor in one's skin. It eased when the needle stopped, but the needle didn't stop much. Siobhan worked patiently on the designs. The assistant also did some work. After a while, when she needed more ink, Siobhan popped in a Bach CD. One thing that *did* help was being able to squeeze Raelyn's hand.

The jaguar. The burning cross. *L-O-V-E. H-A-T-E.* The heart stabbed with a knife. The circle of thorns.

The worst one, by far, was the one on the ass. The needle just went over and over, piercing with a sinister hum, this very tender flesh as Lisa lay naked on her stomach, chin resting on a pillow, unmoving, eyes not really seeing anything but staying open, feeling in kind of a trance. She was glad it was a woman tattooing her, she felt like they were all into it, sisterhood, and Lisa was like a young priestess, she was special. She thought she'd gotten used to the pain, but then the needle would hit an especially sensitive spot, and she'd feel the pain shoot all the way up into her mouth, her teeth, her tongue. But her head was fuzzy, maybe she was high on natural endorphins by now.

Her ass wasn't finished, but to give it a rest Siobhan worked on the ankle for a while. This hurt a lot too, close to the bone.

"You know what I need?" Lisa said to Raelyn.

"What?"

"Some mirror earrings. Little round mirrors, maybe an inch or so in diameter, dangling from thin gold chains."

The unnamed assistant, dabbing blood now from Lisa's buttock, told them where she thought such earrings might be found.

Repetition. On and on. Pain. It was late. Finally Siobhan was satisfied.

"Take it easy tonight," she said gently. "Don't go dancing or do anything else that really makes you sweat. Sweat has salt and uric acid, other toxins. . . ."

"OK," Lisa said, standing up. She was shaky.

The assistant gave Raelyn a printed sheet with instructions about keeping it clean and so forth.

Siobhan smiled. "You wore me out."

Though she felt frail as a newborn kitten, Lisa returned the smile, taking the comment as high praise.

Outside, as they walked slowly to the car, a German shepherd left in a parked Honda Accord commenced barking madly at Lisa, its muzzle sticking through the space where the window had been left open to give the dog air. Lisa looked at it, and the window suddenly went up swiftly, on its own, catching the dog's head, pinning it, making the dog yelp in a high-pitched way. Then the window went back to its former position, as Raelyn looked around.

TWENTY-SIX

Lisa felt better now. She put on her blue swimsuit and went outside to recline by the pool, staying in the darkening shade. The Filipino maid, who seemed to like her, came out and smiled, asking her if she wanted a Coke. Yeah, she did. It was just what she needed to rouse her from what was left of the day's trance. Lying on her side, the now permanently inked left buttock in the air, she took several sips of sustaining Coca-Cola, hoping for quick action from the sugar and caffeine, and called Christine on the cellular phone.

Wanda answered after three rings.

"Hi. She's right here."

It still sounded like it was the real Christine. They exchanged pleasantries and mildly mentioned the fight and Miguel's subsequent suicide. Christine mentioned that Ariel "and some of the guys" had gone by Lisa's apartment and picked up the blood-spattered couch.

"What does Boro do with the rest of his time?" Lisa asked. "Do you know?"

"He's got a room way upstairs . . . he spends a lot of time sleeping. By the way, we're just going to eat in a minute."

"What are you eating?"

"Barbecued chicken, salad, rice."

"Does Adrian know where you are?"

"Sort of. You know, I'm learning some really interesting things. I'm alone now, by the way; Wanda left to start dishing up the food. I know you're a little worried, but I'm OK."

"Tell me: What does Ariel get out of all this?"

"I don't know. I'm not sure. He spends a lot of time upstairs. Supposedly, before Ariel, there was another *capitan* . . . but he went to Peru. A lot of people come and go, I think."

"I want to come see you, Chris, OK? But I don't especially want to see Boro this time."

"Then come early in the morning. Most of the action here is at night. I'm gonna go eat now. Do that, come visit, soon."

Selwyn was dropped off by a limo, tired from a long day of publicists and studio flacks. He joined Lisa, and she had another Coke, this time with Jack Daniel's, while Popcorn took his Jack on the rocks. He didn't ask what she'd done all day. Lisa was glad. She asked him if he wanted to meet her, tomorrow night, at Lauren Devoto's.

"There's a party and it would be nice if you were there. To protect me, whatever."

Selwyn gave her a hard look that she liked, that she found sort of sexy, and in a few moments he told her, "I don't think your friend Code has any fucking conception of how many pretty boys Lauren's seen come and go. She's different. She gives me the creeps."

Lisa liked Selwyn better for this. She told him a version of how she'd met Code, how fashion- and novelty-conscious he had been, how lively, how she'd liked his music and he'd liked her short student films.

"I probably wouldn't have had the ambition to make *Girl, 10* without him. He really helped. Both Christine and I got very depressed, but Code would practically shove me out the door to look for backers . . . and finally it worked. It was also Code's idea that we all come out here from New York."

She left out that if anyone could be said to have sexually awakened her or been present when she had sexually awakened, it was Code. She had undoubtedly had many more and harder orgasms with him than with anyone else in her life. For a while there, without any real kinkiness being involved, she'd pretty much been his sexual slave. She had needed to, in order to find something in herself. He was the first man who'd eaten her to orgasm—stuff like that. Ancient history. Code wasn't the same person now; neither was she. It was amazing they could still be friends, that they didn't get on each other's nerves too much. Maybe Popcorn understood, in a way.

It was seven-thirty. At seven-forty, when they were discussing the possibilities for dinner, the police arrived. The two plainclothes detectives came out to the pool. They apologized for intruding, but there was something they wanted to find out. They wanted to talk to Lisa, they said.

Lisa felt a moment of pure panic, imagining that this was about Duane Moyer, the man she had killed. What else would she think? She took a sip of the water left in her glass by the melting ice, and this helped her regain her composure. If she played dumb . . . that was the only way to go. In her swimsuit, with her tattooed arms, they'd probably see her as some kind of punk bimbo whatever she did.

"Yes?" she said. "What is it?"

The black detective verified her name, her birth date, her mailing address. Then the other one, older, white, said, "I understand that last week you came into possession of a handgun."

Lisa thought. "I looked at some," she said.

"Tell us how this happened, please."

"I wanted to see some examples, because I'd never really had anything to do with guns, I wanted to see the differences . . . for the film. The *Ripper* sequel. I was still under the impression I'd be working on that."

"Did you take one of these handguns off studio property?"

"What's this all about?" Lisa asked. She felt more confident now that it didn't seem to be about Moyer. She remembered the Brazilian police. *These* guys would need a search warrant to go into her room and check her purse. She didn't see the point.

The black detective said, "We're trying to track the chain of evidence on a particular weapon, which might have been used last night in a death. The gun belonged to the studio, and the head of security there says he's been leaving messages on your machine for several days. He accuses you of stealing the gun. A production aide claims that she saw you examine several weapons before putting this particular one, a thirty-two caliber revolver, in your purse before you left—one week ago today."

"Maybe you shouldn't say anything until we talk to an attorney," Popcorn said.

"Last night," the white detective said, smiling humorlessly, "yourself and Mr. Popcorn here—we're assuming that's right, the description fits—the two of you were in the Inglewood Forum as guests of one Miguel Innocenté Casablanca, the boxer in the main event. Casablanca lost the fight, and afterward, down in the locker room, he suddenly produced a handgun and shot himself in the head, in front of seven eyewitnesses. We want to know where he got this gun. It appears to be the same gun that you, Ms. Nova, removed from the studio grounds last week, in violation of clearly posted and stated regulations. When the person brought over the sample guns, they said not to take any of them home."

"Are you going to charge me with something?" Lisa asked, a faint smile on her lips, almost daring them to try.

The white detective shrugged. "Do you have any knowledge of how Miguel Casablanca came to possess this particular weapon?"

"I don't," Lisa said.

"You didn't give it to him?" the black one asked.

"No."

"Do you think he stole it from you?"

She saw that she'd already said too much. She should have listened to Popcorn.

"What was the nature of your relationship with Casablanca?"

"I'm not going to answer anything more," she said, taking her index finger away from her lips.

"Unlawful possession of a firearm," the white one said as they left. "That's one," he said, as though there were several more. Like this was a game.

"He was just trying to scare you," Popcorn said when they were gone. He added, as they went inside, Lisa shivering for a moment, that Larry Planet's brother was a lawyer. He probably didn't do criminal, but he'd know someone who did and was good.

"You're bleeding," Popcorn said with alarm.

The jaguar tattoo.

TWENTY-SEVEN

The dark circles under her eyes were too plainly visible, Lisa had to do something about them—she dabbed on matte concealer until she was satisfied with the effect. That looked better, she thought, studying herself dispassionately in the mirror.

She remembered learning somewhere along the way, perhaps in reference to the work of some abstract expressionist, the concept of looking at a picture and getting into it beyond the image, beyond the brush strokes, beyond the color, beyond the paint—and she could understand this, how the canvas could affect you irrespective of anything retinal, you looked at it and it passed through you, you retained its essence, beyond anything that was merely there before you . . . and she had thought that women could look at men this way, experience them without fixating on the mere surface, one might say its "flatness" . . . but when men tried to see women, invariably the surface qualities served as a barrier to full apprehension, it was very rare when this was not in effect. And so, as a woman, one had to be prepared for this, realistic, one was presented as a more desirable or less desirable commodity in this world, if you pretended not to be aware of this you were simply presenting yourself in yet another, well-traveled way . . . Baudelaire or somebody's first rule of dandyism, and thus fashion, was that the look had failed if it appeared overly premeditated . . . it should seem unselfconscious, uncalculated, thrown together . . . there was no way to begin to untangle all the strands of irony present in any sort of postmodern pose, however one looked or whatever one wore.

One thing about the tattoos was that they were undeniable, they brought the situation to a kind of constant crisis, reborn with everyone she met. Were they for her, because she liked them on her body for themselves, or were they for others to view, to shock them, make them angry or provocatively turned on? This was also scary, but this problem existed with them, it was not really altered because she had her own private reasons for needing them, the presentation of her body continued nevertheless.

Today the tattoo sites felt much better, though still tender. Lisa, prepared for a long evening, dressed herself in a zip-front black patent-vinyl underwire bra minidress, bare arms and bare legs . . . Code had said on the phone this afternoon that he wanted to take her to the clubs on his new motorcycle. Pleading cowardice, she told him no, she'd drive.

The visit from the police had unnerved her, partly because she saw in it Boro's hand. She had the impression that there was no way Casablanca could have taken the revolver from her purse (and how could he have known of its existence?) when he had visited her to drop off the videocassette of his fight . . . and, furthermore, she had had the gun with her when she and Christine had delivered Moyer's body Wednesday, she couldn't be absolutely positive because there had been a lot going on, a lot of details demanding her attention, but she knew that at the time she had certainly *thought* she had it. She might have put down her purse in the big room with all the plants when they had first arrived. So if it had been taken from her then, it might have been given subsequently to Casablanca, by Boro or Ariel, in order to involve her . . . and though this version did presuppose that Boro had anticipated Casablanca's shooting himself after his loss, this was hardly beyond belief . . . and it would serve as one more little thread, if Boro meant to sacrifice her in a hotel room, in a flamboyant unsolved murder with a lot of clues and connections impossible to get to the bottom of once she was dead.

But he might be just teasing her, knowing she might think this, or—and here it started getting ominous again—not caring if she did think this or not. How many suspects would there be if she was killed? How many different men would have their photos in the best-selling book pseudoexamining the hideous crime?

Early this afternoon, while Lisa was putting Neosporin on the tattoos, Raelyn had come into her room, bouncy and confident, showing her some mirror earrings like Lisa had asked for, seductive and playful, asking Lisa, "What will you do for these? How badly do you want them?"

When Lisa, in her underwear, didn't offer anything, the joke still seemed successful from Raelyn's point of view, she laughed, she was so cocky that she must have gone to bed with someone, she practically smelled of it.

Raelyn had given her the earrings, and Lisa had them on now. She had a vague feeling—maybe because of the larger mirrors hanging off the Aztec figure at Boro's—that wearing these would contribute to her power, but she didn't know how. Maybe when Lisa saw her later, Christine would know some new things . . . if she was still OK.

Her neck was too bare, too vulnerable and exposed. She put on two necklaces, one a gold chain with a pendant of milky jade, the other a twisty leather thong. She put on the ring she had been given before, the antique ring she had been reluctant to wear.

Code showed up with a Band-Aid on his nose, over the bridge. Some unidentified person had dropped him off; he rang at the gate. Selwyn was nowhere to be seen . . . he had been a little funny ever since the police came yesterday, and since he'd seen the jaguar bleed. They hadn't slept together last night. She hadn't wanted to, but he hadn't asked or come by. When she'd asked him if he had any pain pills, he'd acted sort of moral about it—that is, he'd asked what she needed them for—whereupon she'd said, tired, with some annoyance, it didn't matter, never mind. He'd brought her two Percodan a bit later. She'd taken one, thinking it might put her right to sleep, but it had not. Popcorn hadn't hung around.

Code seemed sort of sullen, his platinum hair wildly moussed, wearing a paint-spattered T-shirt (yellow, rose, green, a trace of blue) under an antique psychedelic velvet coat, plum-colored, with little gold fleurs-de-lys all over it, mismatched bronze and copper buttons that must have been sewn on as the originals came off and were lost. As he told her the coat's history, after she'd commented on it, he brightened up. It had once belonged to Stevie Winwood, way back when he was in Blind Faith, twenty-some years before the Coke or beer commercials or whatever it was he did. Lisa had never heard of Blind Faith, a "supergroup" formed by members of Traffic and Cream when those bands had broken up. Code loved telling her stuff she didn't know. Guys. He was wearing gray corduroy pants. She didn't ask him about the paint on the T-shirt but couldn't help noting the Band-Aid on his nose.

The story became complex, and she lost track. They proceeded through traffic toward Venice, where Bloody Murder was opening for Godvomit at some dismal little hole.

It was dark out, but not really, because of the white lights on the street. They went into the club. Neither of them was expecting the music to be any good. So what. Everybody here wanted to be Charlie Manson, or Richard Ramirez, the Night Stalker, or that was the pose. Lots of shaved heads, both sexes, lots of fat girls with stockings and garter belts, skirts too short to cover the white flesh above the black band . . . Lisa stopped noticing details. Fundamentally it was the same scene it had been for many years. More ritualistic behavior—undoubtedly there were some changes, fashion marches on, maybe Code was noticing, his antennae out, maybe there was some little current he could glean, but Lisa just wanted to get through Bloody Murder's set, see Mary, and get out.

It's hard to judge a noise band, seeing them live. The acoustics of the space, accident (happily embraced), the traditional showcasing of contempt for the audience, etcetera. Mary Siddons, her hair in microbraids, looking terribly thin, with swastika earrings, played bass. Another woman, older, blond with a large ring in her nose, was the lead vocalist. There were three guitarists and a drum machine.

After a set, Code and Lisa were allowed backstage, the bouncer here looked fierce (crew cut and a death's-head earring, a Godvomit T-shirt) but when Lisa said she knew Mary he yielded to her at once, tongue-tied and shy.

Mary herself, sweaty, with red eye shadow, acted as if she'd seen Lisa last week. She introduced her boyfriend, Rod, a guitarist, a glowering hulk in a black tank top and a semimilitary haircut.

"I knew you were out there," Mary said. "I sensed your presence."

"Yeah," Lisa said. "Do you want an acting job?"

Mary shrugged and looked at Rod. "I don't know," she said. "Doing what?"

"In *The L.A. Ripper* sequel . . . the casting director's got your name. I was supposed to direct it, but I got fired."

"They won't want me, then, will they?"

"They might."

"OK, maybe I'll go over there."

"Don't wear swastikas," Lisa said, and Rod put in, "Why not?"

"It doesn't necessarily mean anything," Mary said. "It's just a design. It's called the twisted cross, or the flyfoot—"

"Hindus use it all the time," said Rod, who had one tattooed on his wrist.

"Do what you want," Lisa said, looking at Mary, not particularly liking her right now.

"I'll call you, OK?" Mary said, and Lisa said OK and wrote Popcorn's number on the back of the casting director's card. She didn't want to receive a call from Mary asking for money, a call she could imagine all too vividly; yet even if Mary was unattractive to her in her present circumstances, with a Nazi boyfriend, embracing evil . . . even so, Lisa felt a certain responsibility for her, an unwilling state almost of love, because in *Girl, 10, Murders Boys* Lisa had used her, or she had found in Mary an embodiment of destructive psychic forces that were tempting but which Lisa ordinarily held in check. There was a connection between them, a sisterliness.

Code drove them to Lauren Devoto's. He took Lisa up to a room with video monitors that could zoom in anywhere in any of the many crowded rooms.

Popcorn was at the video controls, with Lauren at his shoulder, dressed in red, and Alvin Sender was also there, studying the console's images as some sort of perverse sexual theater loomed. Lisa had never before observed Lauren looking so attractive, if hard, scary, the tight red patent-leather tunic accentuating her large, overfirm, beyond-perfect breasts. There was something funny about her, Lisa didn't know quite what it was.

Lisa said hi to everyone. Popcorn didn't respond, fascinated, like a spaceship captain, roving the sixteen cameras all around.

"Stairway to Heaven," Sender said, nodding toward Popcorn, and Lisa understood. Selwyn was no doubt terrifically high. She sat next to Selwyn, putting her hand on his back, massaging him, trying to establish contact, but he was happy, concentrating—maybe imagining he was directing the action in the different chambers, lit by different colors of light, which gradually changed, red to electric pink to turquoise to gold and orange and then back to red, linger on red.

Lauren and Code left the room, saying they'd be back. When they were gone, Alvin Sender waited a while before saying, "Quite a scene, isn't it?"

Lisa shrugged. So what if people were doing S&M? She didn't like Sender and didn't care if he knew it. All she knew was that he was connected with the video business somehow . . . the video that had supposedly been made of her that time. She hated to think of it.

"Why aren't you down there?" Lisa finally asked. "What do you get out of all this?"

Sender smiled and sort of squirmed. He was not unintelligent, but probably evil.

"I would never let myself be photographed like that," he said. "When you let yourself become an image . . . it becomes more than just a representation. It takes breath, it becomes an emanation . . . and you lose your otherness, your capacity to be natural. That's what happens to stars who are overphotographed—they turn into icons, religious images painted on a piece of wood. Or images painted on a piece of film. The more intimate the pose that is publicized, the more reproductions, the less of your *self* you have left." He paused, staring at her. "With some people—I don't think this is true with you, but some people—it's not much of a loss. What do I get out of all this? I supply the talent, I provide the opportunity."

"You're a pimp." Lisa didn't say it with much emotion, little or no indignation; Sender looked up at the ceiling and said, "I'm an agent. I provide talent. My clients want to work. I'm on a different level, in a different kind of space from 'pimp.' I do so many other kinds of business . . . like your video, for instance. You've become quite an underground star."

She didn't want to hear this. She couldn't imagine exactly what was on this video, and she didn't want to know. There was a strong chance also that Sender was exaggerating, to torment her—this supposed video might not even exist. How long could it be? What did it show?

Popcorn was starting to slow down, no longer flipping switches and hitting buttons and guiding toggles with the same inspiration as before. He turned to Lisa and said, "This has been like Hieronymous Bosch, and El Greco, and James Ensor—all these feverish bodies . . . I think I've seen enough. Do you want to go?"

She did. It was nice that he now seemed so rational, it was a relief. They went down the hall, the stairs, and out. The cool, dark night air refreshed her, and she suddenly thought: Fuck this "underground star" business. It was just a lie, Sender was lying to freak her out. She didn't like his civilized smile, the knowing expression that might be from viewing and reviewing the same orgasm ninety-six times.

"Ouch." She reacted with alarm when, in the car, Selwyn unzipped her dress down to her stomach, his right hand meaning to feel her left breast, not to fondle it so much as to examine it tactilely, as though he didn't know what one felt like anymore. It didn't really hurt. But it wasn't welcome either.

She sat there passively for about a minute, feeling like maybe she should just surrender . . . considering total surrender, trying to get in that frame of mind, experimentally . . . as now Popcorn leaned over and bit at her nipple, tonguing it, his tongue tracing a circle around it until the nipple was sensitized, erect.

Then he pulled back, sighed . . . she zipped up the patent-vinyl dress and started the red sports car, quickly leaving the Devoto estate.

"I want some french fries," Popcorn said. "Stop someplace and let's get some french fries."

There were bright lights and automobiles all over. In Hollywood, Lisa chose an all-night diner she and Code used to go to. When she parked the car Popcorn woke up, or opened his eyes. She couldn't tell how fucked up from Stairway to Heaven he might be.

Inside, he ordered fries and a Coke and started examining the napkin dispenser very closely, presumably because it was polished shiny silver, with reflections of the whole room. Lisa had ordered a chocolate milk shake. She resisted telling Popcorn that he reminded her of a crow. But crows were her favorite birds.

"Your earrings," he said. Yes, they were mirrors. He reached across the table to touch them; she experienced a moment of real fear that he might tear one out of an earlobe.

It was very crowded in here. Lisa had taken off her jacket because it was warm. Popcorn ate his french fries, with catsup, and looked around at the other denizens of the cafe.

When he was done, he said he wanted a cigarette. He didn't ask her to get him one, but she decided to do it for him, she got up and walked over to these spiked-hair or mohawked motherfuckers.

"Can I borrow a cigarette?"

"Yeah," said the guy who seemed the dominant male. He lit it for her as one of the girls, chubby, dyed black hair, smirked but did not meet Lisa's eyes.

The lit cigarette was held out, and then, when Lisa went to take it, it was jerked back. But the second time he gave it to her with a smile. She inhaled seriously and then exhaled, watching the swirly, pale blue smoke. Popcorn showed no sign of remembering he had wanted to smoke. It was almost dawn.

No, it was already dawn. The sun was making itself known, at a distance, two planets away. Pinkish, gray light against brown. Silver and dead blue. Totally sky.

TWENTY-EIGHT

The next day Lisa was picked up and taken down to the police station. Homicide detectives Bluestone and Brown. She got the impression that, being Sunday, it was their usual day off. Bluestone, the older, white one, now that he was convinced she was "wrong," seemed almost sympathetic in a funny way, like he was sincerely interested in the workings of her mind. She found herself wanting him to like her, but it was impossible.

The apartment she had lived in had blown up in the middle of the night. That was where the explosion had centered; much of the rest of the building had burned, but no one had been seriously hurt. Remains of a body had been found amongst the rubble and ashes. Bones, mostly, and a skull on the other side of the smoldering ruins.

"Do you know someone named Duane Moyer?" asked Detective Brown.

"I've met someone who said that was his name. This person told me he was a detective, hired by Nehi Laughton, the agent, to follow me around."

"Why did Laughton want him to do this? Do you know?"

Lisa hesitated, then said, "He used to be Roy Hardway's agent. Roy left L.A. sort of suddenly, made the film with me in Brazil, and Laughton hasn't heard from him. He wants his ten, fifteen percent."

"Roy Hardway," Bluestone said, writing it down. "Miguel Casablanca." He stopped. "Did you ever know an Osvaldo J. Perez?"

"No. I've never heard of him."

"He used to be Casablanca's employer, until someone threw down on him with a twelve-gauge shotgun, both barrels. Did Casablanca ever talk about this to you?"

"No. I barely knew him."

"How do you think he got that gun?"

She shook her head.

"Why would somebody blow up your apartment?"

"I don't know. It's weird."

"You don't seem very worried," Bluestone said. "If someone blew up my home, I'd be concerned that someone meant me harm. What about it? Are you afraid of anyone? Any jilted boyfriends, anything like that?"

"No. I don't think so. Do you think that body is Moyer?"

"It might be."

"Maybe he blew himself up," Lisa said.

"In your apartment? Why would be do that?"

"Maybe it was an accident. Maybe he was trying to kill me and something went wrong. I don't know, I've been at Popcorn's."

"Have you seen Moyer? Have you had the feeling he was out there watching you?"

"Not really. No, I haven't. I guess I figured that after I talked to Laughton, he'd call Moyer off. It was stupid, anyway. And agents usually don't like to throw money away. Unless they've gone crazy."

"You think Nehi Laughton's crazy?"

"I don't know. Somebody must be, I guess."

After a few moments Detective Brown said, "You can account for your time last night, I take it."

Out with Code to see the band Bloody Murder, a visit backstage, then to a party at Lauren Devoto's. Home with Popcorn, stopping at a diner on the way.

TWENTY-NINE

Popcorn asked her about the police in a reasonable manner, and it was only later, when he came to her room, that Lisa realized how angry this stuff was making him. It wasn't the fuck or the manner of it—though, for the first time, he pinned her knees down, pressing down, bending her supple body so that her feet were up in the air near her face as his unusually stiff penis stabbed into her vagina, making her involuntarily emit a low percussive "uh" at the end of each rhythmic pelvic thrust—but when, about halfway through, he stopped for a while, tantalizing her with his stillness, pulling back and then pushing slowly, as she was breathing hard, she was suddenly aware of the fragrance of Jack Daniel's on his breath and in the oil of his distant skin as he spoke, a monologue to fill the interlude, he knew he had her attention but not in this way, still she heard him and understood, he said, "I *know* you're not telling me anything about what's going on, you have your secrets, you can't help it, *right*. I don't care, the only time you're on the level is when you're staring at the ceiling, I don't mind, I don't care if it's these drugs or whatever, Brazilian gangsters, I'm very *fond* of you, even if you're just using me for your own reasons, that's OK. I don't have to *know* if you don't want me to, I'll do whatever you want. The police can show up for dinner every other day and as long as it's *OK* with you, it's cool. I'm cool too, as long as you're OK."

The velocity of the fuck returned to an athletic level she didn't think he could sustain; for no reason she said "ow" as a signal just before she came, gripping him so tightly both inside and with her arms around his neck that he was sentimentally moved.

"Oh, I love you, I love you," he said as he sawed away another hundred times so that he might ejaculate where he was. She endured this, and could have fucked some more. She had gotten used to his cock in there; she gave a little groan of discomfort when he pulled it out and rolled off to one side. He had been saving up, she thought.

Boro had had her building blown up, she felt sure. Moyer's actual fleshy head was no doubt in the process of being shrunk: his skull and his bones (and maybe his wallet) had been thrown in to excite the cops. Boro was building a case, and she felt trapped. She had called the number, and no one answered, no Christine. It might have been unplugged. Was this a ploy to lure her in? Her breathing slowed, she was limp and relaxed, spent, as the perspiration dried on her skin.

Knowing nothing, Popcorn kissed her shoulder, squeezed her hand. She managed a faraway, soft smile.

After seemingly dreamless, dark sleep, morning came quickly. Popcorn had an erection against the back of her thigh, and she turned over and jerked him off a little, then sportively placed her mouth over the head of the organ . . . she was giving him a blowjob, in her mind as a prelude to a morning fuck, but his pleasure was evidently so exquisite, he liked it so much, that she kept at it, his hand held her there, pressing on the nape of her neck. When she was ready to leave he pushed her back, he wanted her to keep sucking him, and she went back to it, but she could feel through the throb in the end of his cock, a kind of gathering heaviness, that he might come. The hand on her neck seemed more powerful to her now; she breathed through her nose. She glanced up toward his face; his eyes were tightly closed. She didn't spoil it for him, keeping her mouth tight, her jaw—and he really held her there, she felt the contractions through her tongue and the roof of her mouth as he came, he kept her head there in such a way that the hot spurts of semen laced the back of her throat, she choked and swallowed, she felt coerced into swallowing it all. It tasted like the memory of bitter licorice crossed with snot.

This left him in a wonderful mood.

After showering, brushing her teeth, Lisa saw that he was having a big breakfast in his room: pancakes and coffee and orange juice, slices of ham. All she wanted was coffee and a croissant. Journalists were coming over to interview him, *Premiere* in the morning, *American Film* in the afternoon.

What she needed was to alter her physical state by some vigorous swimming. Raelyn came in to see her, and Lisa asked her about Cannes. Despite whatever misgivings she might have had, her eyes flicking away and then coming back, Raelyn said sure, she'd come along.

The blowjob had been educational. At breakfast, with studied casualness, Popcorn had said he'd marry her if she wanted, he just put the idea out . . . in a different situation, Lisa could see how this would make sense. Her jaw was sore, her lips felt bruised. Some men saw a blowjob as complete only when you swallowed. Aesthetically, this made it beautiful to them.

THIRTY

At lunch Lisa had a salad of leeks and fennel dotted with roasted garlic, while Jules Brandenberg had grilled yellowtail with wild hijiki. She was very glad that he had called her up.

"I like your necklace," he said, relaxing more and more as he realized that no, she wasn't mad at him, she didn't blame him for her having been fired. He seemed nervous and drank more wine with his meal than she expected.

"I've become excellent friends with this chimpanzee I'm working with," he said—seeing that she didn't follow, he revealed that he'd been shooting a commercial for MasterCard.

"I'd like to do commercials," Lisa said. "Fox Quigley comes out of commercials, doesn't he?" referring to the guy who'd taken over on *Ripper II*, and Jules acknowledged this was true.

He asked her if she knew of any good art to buy, flattering her about her art-world background; she liked hearing this, and told him about Andrea Goodweather, a woman in New York she'd gone to school with, giving him the name of the gallery at which Andrea should very soon be having her show.

"I'd really like to get in on the ground floor of somebody," Jules said, as if he'd been missing this all his life.

Lisa felt a little pauperish, wearing just another print minidress, black tights—she really mourned all the clothes she had lost in her apartment explosion, the gold dress she had kissed Chuck Suede in, for one . . . she had driven by the wreckage on the way over to the restaurant. There had really been nothing left, just pipes and burned pieces of wood, the hulk of the piano lying one floor down, on its side . . . a chicken-wire fence separating the ruins from the street.

The day was bleached out by the sun. There were mountains you could see today that you hadn't been able to see yesterday.

"You had some good drugs once, didn't you?" Jules said, and she had to nod. He was spacy.

Plainclothes police were following her around. Right now someone was sitting down the street, across from the restaurant, in an overly anonymous small Plymouth. The police always had to drive Detroit iron, it was a rule.

"I'm in a slump," Jules said. "People are pushing me around."

"I'm not doing too well either," said Lisa. "I've got a lot of stuff hanging over my head."

"Well, one thing . . . you're going to Cannes, aren't you? Don't just send one of your friends. I probably said this to you before, but . . . for you, the art-film kind of thing you want to do, given the way distribution is, your image, and the idea of your personality . . . you need that. Popcorn doesn't really need it. He can more or less stand back, trimming his nails, giving interviews about yellow filters and light meters, it doesn't matter, he already has his mystique. In your case, the more you're photographed, the more people see of you, the better."

Lisa thought about it. About how much certain women artists—artists whom she admired—had been helped by what they looked like, the visual image helping to get them attention . . . for instance, in the case of Eva Hesse, photogenic, who'd died in 1970 at the age of thirty-four. Maybe the attention gained in this way was shallow, mere publicity and nothing more. The cult of personality might lead one—surprise!—to the actual work.

Is this what I want? Lisa asked herself. Is this the only way it can be done? Also, it occurred to her, the dark side of such possible mythmaking was Boro's tabloid spectacular of her as sacrificial whore. The whore transformed into a madonna by ritual murder, the bloodiness of childbirth visited in reverse.

Jules talked more about how close he now was with this chimp, whose name was Merlin. Lisa, thinking of Caz, agreed there was a lot to be learned from the animal bond. Somehow at this moment the jaguar presence came back to her, just a taste, and she looked around for a mirror.

That night she and Selwyn Popcorn went out to dinner with Nicholas Davies and Dana Ricks, the actors. They were very cordial and refined. Selwyn recaptured some of Lisa's affection and talked about his likely next project, a biopic of Upton Sinclair. The story of how he was almost elected governor of California in 1934. One of the craziest elections anytime, anywhere.

Listening to Selwyn tell the story animatedly, Lisa saw where the passion might join the cool reflective student of composition and camera angles, the calculating pro, and she liked him more. And she'd never known about Upton Sinclair.

Dana Ricks wanted dessert. Nicholas Davies laughed about something, decided to have a dark chocolate truffle, and said, looking into Lisa's eyes, using his great nuanced voice, "We're going to Vegas this weekend, to see Madonna. It's supposed to be quite a show."

Lisa ate a truffle too. She loved dark chocolate. She gave half of it to Selwyn, who had it with his cappuccino. She could have put out the candles on all the tables, but she did not. Yet it might have been worth doing. Pierre Wella Balsam was here, with a model, and the new rising executive woman of the moment, Roxanne Phelps, with her date. Sudden darkness might have been good for them all.

THIRTY-ONE

Adrian was curious about where Christine was, and Lisa felt that he thought she was being too vague, that she knew more than she would tell. Which was correct. He was too tactful to say it, but he thought she was irresponsible. And Lisa felt she owed him something (a lot) for taking care of Caz while she was in Brazil.

Lisa had tried the number several times, but no one was answering anymore. It seemed likely it was unplugged. She knew she should go see what was happening, but she was scared. The way things were going, she was afraid Boro really did mean to kill her, and she didn't see how she could resist.

Adrian told her that a Latin male had come looking for her, having gone to her apartment and seen that it was blown up. Adrian hadn't talked to him, he hadn't been home. Brad had dealt with him, and because of the explosion he'd been very wary, he wouldn't tell the guy anything. Brad had been unhappy that the fellow had somehow made the connection and come to their address.

"What was his name?" Lisa asked on the phone in Popcorn's big living room, classical music (that, and jazz, was all Selwyn had) punctuating the silences in the luxurious decor.

"I don't know. Just a second. *Brad!*" and, when Brad evidently came back in, Adrian asked him if the guy had told him his name.

"Ask him if it was Tavinho," Lisa said, excited by the possibility, but Brad said, "I just wanted him to go away."

"What did he look like?"

Adrian was sort of interested, even though he had obviously decided to distance himself, to quietly disapprove. But Brad wouldn't say very much. He didn't want to have anything to do with Lisa's crazy life, she could hear him say.

She was really having doubts about herself and about doing films. She wondered if her reasons for doing them, or wanting to do them, were all wrong. The need for recognition, praise, acceptance . . . this seemed so childish to her, so narcissistic or something, the need to be confirmed from outside . . . she felt so inadequate, she needed to find something stable and peaceful inside of herself and it was never there. For *Girl, 10, Murders Boys* she had used Christine to help fake some stability, while very basic and conceptual aims were still unclear.

It had seemed so natural, going from painting through photography to film. Compared to all of the others, cinema was the newest, most popular art. But then, doing an independent film hadn't been enough. The hypermodern, inevitable course was to go to Hollywood, to dive into the world of legend and cliché. What else was there? Fuck.

Lisa was actually perversely pleased to have Bluestone come over once again. Let him arrest her, it was OK, it would take matters out of her hands.

"Come in," Lisa said, though her laughter did not reassure Rosa, the maid, who'd let Bluestone into the front hall. Who knew what kind of a relationship people in the Philippines had to the police there, how frightened they might be? Lisa sat down on the couch, crossing her ankles, a loose semi-lotus, bare feet, as Caz meowed and jumped lightly into the newly created open space, surrounded by her legs, a space he seemed to regard as created just for him.

"What have I done now?" she asked, with what was undoubtedly an inappropriate semblance of a what-the-fuck attitude.

Bluestone smiled without showing his teeth. Maybe he thought he had her at his mercy, or would soon. He was tanned, not handsome. He didn't look like he'd win a fight with any tough young gangsters, but then there was a sense about him that no one would fight dirtier or with less hesitation. He turned down the volume of his walkie-talkie, there on his hip.

"You've said you know Nehi Laughton. Have you ever met his wife?"

"I saw him with a woman in a restaurant, a week or so ago. As far as I know, that could have been his wife. Why?"

"She was beaten up yesterday evening in a parking lot in Westwood. Some bikers, it sounds like. There were a couple of witnesses, saw the whole thing."

"What do you mean, they beat her up?"

"Do you care?"

"I don't know her." Lisa was remembering now that he was the enemy, he wanted to fuck her up. Sitting on the edge of his seat, flipping through the pages of Popcorn's expensive art book, looking at the color reproductions of Richard Diebenkorn's abstract *Ocean Park* series, blue, sometimes yellow, sometimes white paint thinly applied, suggesting memories of beach and sun and sea.

"Nehi Laughton thinks you had it done." This said quietly, ironically, again with the wide but thin-lipped smile.

The bad part was that Lisa reacted, she tried to look dumb and indifferent but she felt something register—because she immediately thought of Boro, he would have done it just to have another suspect . . . although . . .

"I don't understand," Lisa said. "I don't understand this shit about my apartment blowing up and Duane Moyer's bones, and I don't get this part at all, I really don't. Something weird is going on, and I don't think it has anything to do with me. Laughton and Moyer—I think they must have had something else going on. Maybe Roy Hardway's back in town, hideously disfigured, something like that. Some strange factor no one knows anything about yet."

Bluestone continued looking at the pictures, seemingly absorbed. Then he said, "'Hideously disfigured.' I like that. Sort of a *Phantom of the Opera*–type thing, right? You're pretty good."

Lisa knew not to say a word. He hadn't asked her where she'd been at the time of the attack, but she was reasonably sure they'd been following her, making note of who she saw and where she went.

Bluestone took out a pack of spearmint gum, unwrapped a stick, and folded it into his mouth. He mutely offered her one, and she wanted to take it, out of natural friendliness, but after hesitating she shook her head.

He looked at his watch and said, "Oops, I'm running late. I'll keep your Roy Hardway theory in mind, let you know how it comes out."

It was hot outside. Although she felt like just lying down, hiding, sucking her thumb, Lisa changed into her swimsuit and went out and jumped into the pool. It was a way both of not thinking and of clearing her mind for making serious plans.

Then she sat by the pool and had a Coke.

THIRTY-TWO

Having plainclothes police shadow you was quite a bit like starring in a movie: She was self-consciously aware of being seen at every moment, it gave significance even to minor, random acts.

She went into a store and bought Hershey's syrup, Snickers bars, peanut butter, butterscotch chips, two bags of shredded coconut, Oreos, cheese popcorn, the magazines *Spin, Elle, Vogue, Mademoiselle, Newsweek, Time,* and *Rolling Stone*. She ate a Snickers, slowly, as other shoppers brought out bags of groceries to the parking lot.

The guy following her was in a bronze Ford Taurus. If he began vomiting, if he vomited up the contents of his stomach—she could sort of smell the take-out window Quarter Pounder, and in this context it made her a little sick—he wouldn't be able to follow her for a while. He would lose her. It was against the law, she thought, for the local police to plant electronic devices without dire cause.

She saw the guy hunch over, and she drove away, letting the last bite of the Snickers melt in her mouth.

By the time she reached Boro's gate, it was maybe seven-thirty in the evening. The gate swung open as she slowed, as if it knew who she was. A flock of red birds flew up from the other side of the house.

As she left her car no one seemed to be outside. The spooky vibes made her go slowly and deliberately, looking around so she could not be taken by surprise. She had no weapon, nothing to protect herself with. If Boro wanted her, it wouldn't matter, but if Jonathan or one of the other zombies came after her for some reason, maybe just from the scent of flesh, it would have been nice to try shooting them in the head.

The door was open. She went inside. The dimly lit hall increased her sense of foreboding, at a distance she could hear some music, like an industrial dance band played through an air conditioner. Instead of going down, as before, she went up.

Up here there was a sound like a hundred wind chimes, a rushing, something high-pitched behind it all—Lisa went right to that door, up another half flight, at the end of this hall.

Yes, this was the room where Christine was. Lisa entered the room and shut the door behind her, and then did nothing, immobilized by the weirdness. The room—which was pretty big—was radiant with pinkish, goldish, flesh-colored, then back to pale white light. Hundreds of glass wind chimes hung from the high ceiling around a central skylight, which seemed to somehow create the shifting, eerie light.

There was a mass of vines—both real and fake—and small pieces of white pseudomarble statuary, almost all of them broken, of varying size, angels and Corinthian columns and indistinguishable pieces, more or less in rubble. . . .

Two fairly intact white angels stood as if at attendance upon a pool of what appeared to be diluted, gleaming milk . . . in which Christine floated, on her back. She was not naked, but her white dress, or angel's robe, was in disarray, soaked, baring one breast. Her eyes were shut, mouth open, definitely breathing—she seemed plumper and paler, her blond hair dark gold in the milky fluid . . . the noise of the chimes, or the music (there was music in here somewhere), was very loud, drowning out thought.

Lisa cautiously approached the pool. The vines slithered a bit, trying to grab at her ankles. She put a hand on one of the standing plaster angels, to steady herself, and said, "Christine?"

Nothing happened for a few moments. Then there was a stirring in the milky water, in the area of Christine's ankles—there must have been oil on it, to make it so reflective—and the coils of a very large glittery snake broke the surface, just as Christine looked over, opening her eyes—all white, frighteningly, wet milky white, with hints of red.

Wanda came in, dressed up like a headwaiter, her carmine hair slicked down and parted the middle.

"She's a moon goddess," Wanda said. "She's accumulating knowledge and gravity . . . she'll be an oracle when the process is complete."

"How long has she been like this?" Lisa asked in a thin voice.

"She comes out to eat, to grow fat." Wanda motioned over to some cushions and a low table stocked with baklava and other sweets, cookies, and cakes. "And to sleep, and dream."

Wanda spoke in a somewhat theatrical voice, tinged with mockery, and Lisa hated her—this all seemed like a cruel joke. She waited and didn't ask any more questions, walking around and examining the room. Wanda tagged after her, anticipating the questions that never came.

"The neurochemistry of her brain will be permanently altered," Wanda said. "But she needs to become much fatter."

"I want to see Boro," Lisa said. Wanda tried not to let it be seen, but she was pleased, Lisa could tell. The trick had worked. Lisa wanted to rescue her friend, to get them to release her from the spell. She already felt like she'd waited too many days.

The atmosphere was very different up in Boro's austere, quiet room. One of the Aztec wooden figures, all dressed up, stood outside the open door, as if on guard. Was this one alive?

"My dear Lisa," Boro said, standing up from his cot inside, "I've just been thinking about you."

"Yeah, I can tell. You blew up my apartment with that detective's bones in there . . . and you had somebody beat up Nehi Laughton's wife."

"What a tangled web we weave," he said with satisfaction, yawning a bit, as if he had not been awake very long.

"Let Christine go. Whatever you and Wanda are doing to her . . . stop it. Please. Let her go."

"Why should I? What will you do for me?"

"What do you want me to do?"

His crinkled, intricately inked brown face cracked open in a smile, and he laughed once, harshly, testing her, always testing her. In his room, Lisa could see a director's chair with some clothes on it—a picture of the Mona Lisa on the canvas of the back of the chair.

"What do I want you to do? I want so much, I have such high expectations . . . how old are you? You're twenty-six. That's two times thirteen. A perfect number. You don't know this stuff."

"I don't know about the numbers," Lisa admitted, but not really seeing how she could have gained such knowledge, not in the normal course of her life.

"I tell you what. How about we playact? You in the hotel room. We do it for fun. Then we're all done, I forget about it."

"What do you mean?"

"Explain," he said to Wanda, making a gesture. "In an hour or so, she can come down to the stage." And Boro left them, taking his time.

"Boro wants you to be an actress . . . all you'll have to do is lie there. It'll be a painting come to life. Like the headlines, except nothing will be real. Your lurid murder."

"My murder? Right. I don't believe this."

"Nobody will touch you. Do you think he would waste it, waste the theatrical possibilities, the publicity, by killing you like this? He could kill you anytime if that's what he wanted to see. This will be very beautiful, a composition, and then you can go home with Christine. She'll be OK."

"Shit. Like I can believe anything you tell me."

"Christine is all right. You'll see. She *wanted* to do this."

"What exactly am I going to have to do?"

"Just lie there. You might want to take something, 'cause Boro has kind of a different conception of time. He might want to look at the tableau for a long time."

The word *tableau* wasn't so rarefied as all that, but in general Lisa was coming to believe that Wanda was more intelligent than she'd thought, and this made her inclined to cooperate, to let things happen according to the obviously prearranged plan.

"I have something with me, in my purse," Lisa said, and commenced digging through it. They went back to the moon goddess room, now silent—Christine was out of the milky pond, reclining on the cushions, eating, with her eyes shut, her jaw moving very slowly, a piece of cake. She was dry, in a flesh-colored silk slip. Her hair was cut shorter than it had been before she had come here.

Lisa hugged her, kissed her cheek. Christine smiled but did not seem to know who she was. Her blue eyes now looked normal (if filmy), but she still seemed in a deep trance, far away.

In her purse, Lisa located the little packet of pills. TVC15, Heaven 17, Stairway to Heaven—all of those were too strong. Joy Division was supposed to make you feel content and somewhat numb.

Somewhere between a tranquilizer and a pain-pill. Lisa broke one in half and swallowed it with her saliva. She held out a Snickers for her friend, and Christine took it from her, biting into it with the wrapper still on. Stubbornly, she didn't want to let go of it so that the wrapper could be removed. Lisa had to pry it out of her fist. Wanda left them together.

It was dark outside now, but it was still light in this room. The shifting light was much dimmer . . . the wind chimes, above, continued to clink, but that was the only sound. If there was a real or mechanical serpent in the pond of milk, it did not stir.

The atmosphere was soothing. Very slowly, like a retarded, single-minded child, Christine ate the sweets, letting the crumbs fall as they may. A few tears fell out of Lisa's hot eyes, but then after a while it all seemed OK. She was neutral. Subdued.

It seemed like a lot longer than an hour passed. Peace. Christine seemed to have fallen asleep. Lisa was apprehensive, scared, but fatalistic. Joy Division.

Ariel came to get her. He was dressed in an expensive pinstriped suit.

"Come with me."

Down, down, down through the big room with the plants and aquariums, down a stairway to the basement. To the left was a dark passage; they went to the right, going down a narrow hall lit by green fluorescent tubes, the walls seeming to want to meet at the top, throwing off one's sense of perspective a bit.

After several turns, they came into a dressing room, with a vanity, a mirror . . . ordinary electric light, in which Lisa recognized makeup that must have been taken from her apartment, and, in an open suitcase, some items of clothing. . . .

"Undress," Ariel said without affection. He bent over and picked up a newspaper, the *Los Angeles Times*, only when he showed the front page to her she saw it was a dummy paper; in an instant she knew this, yet she was shocked.

Actress Found Murdered in Hotel Room: "bizarre sex scene . . . mutilation . . . ties to stars . . . "

She couldn't read it.

Ariel left the dressing room when Wanda came in. Wanda said, "You need to put some makeup on. Sit down there, and I'll help you. All you have to do is relax."

Wanda assisted her, coaxing a bit, until Lisa had stripped down to her underwear. She sat obediently as Wanda applied makeup to her face, deep red lipstick, blush, saying once more that she'd done makeup on some films and for some bands.

A lacy black garter belt, snapping onto sheer black nylons, the darker band around the tops always a slightly discordant feature to Lisa's eye.

"He wants me to look like a prostitute."

"You shouldn't say that. These are your clothes. Sure, he wants you to be a prostitute. He wants you to look like what he's seen in the movies or in whorehouses . . . pornography. Off with your underpants. Don't pretend to be shy. 'Nothing can defile the sacred.' That's what Boro has said. This is a performance piece."

"Is anybody going to take pictures?"

"Why? Do you want some souvenirs? Some documentation?" Wanda laughed.

It was an outfit from Victoria's Secret. Or Frederick's of Hollywood. Porn. Code had been crazy about this sort of thing. The tattoos, however, exaggerated the whorish effect. Red stiletto heels, with a double ankle strap, stiletto heels she could barely walk in at all, garter belt and stockings, a matching strapless pushup bra that left her nipples bare. Long, dangly gold earrings with imitation red jewels. A similar necklace. That was all. She was essentially nude.

"Wait a second," Wanda said, patting her hand. When she came back, a few moments later, music began to play. Funky, seventies-style, stupid jazz. It was evocative of *something*, Lisa felt. So innocent, in some way, yet sleazy and corrupt. With strings.

"What do I do?"

"Just lie down on the bed. Arrange yourself like you've just been fucked. Do whatever you like."

Shivering a little, but then shameless, seeing it as a part to play, Lisa walked out onto the set. The stiletto heels hurt, and she could only take small, mincing steps. She sought to be expressionless, but her dark eyes were alive.

Beyond the lights and a red velvet rope was an audience, which amazed her for a second, until she saw that they were all zombies, zombies sitting impassively on rows of folding chairs. She didn't see Boro, she didn't see Ariel—the lights glittered in her eyes. She lay down on the unmade brass bed. She noticed her lost violet and black minidress hung over a chair.

It was a hotel-room set, with jury-rigged walls, a red neon blinking sign off to the left, out the phony window. There was a clock on the wall, unmoving: 3:35. On a table was a half-empty bottle of Ron Rico rum, two glasses, and half a squeezed lime. Next to the bed, on the nightstand, was a tiny pile of pure white powder, so white it glinted pink and blue, less likely heroin than medicinal-quality cocaine.

And then Lisa just lay there. The sheets were fresh, lavender, smelling of Chanel. She looked up at the ceiling, which was a basement ceiling, except that right over the bed—over her—there was a big mirror. So she gazed at herself, dispassionately. She rolled over. Stared at her sex for a while. Then forgot. She watched herself breathe.

The Joy Division made it easy to lie still. A lassitude came over her. She could shut out the music for long periods of time, and it changed, but it was always there. She wondered if she was being filmed. If she was going to be raped or killed.

She wasn't really frightened, not of something like that. She sighed, and watched herself sigh. Did Boro still fuck? She didn't think so, but it was impossible to be sure. Could the zombies see her very well? Was this all that was going to happen? She shifted her hips, stretching her black nylon-clad legs out—just to stretch—then pulling up her knees a little bit.

Something changed. She was startled, and raised herself up on her elbow, watching, with deep suspicion, as a tall, black zombie in a suit, a zombie she was sure she'd never seen before, appeared by the table, setting down a small rectangular object, like a radio.

His suit was somehow old-fashioned, and there were anomalous touches: a faux-pearl necklace around his neck, glossy pink lipstick on his lips, rouge on his cheeks. Yet he was very masculine, tough-looking, and so tall.

He pressed a button on the tape recorder he'd set down, and a man's voice—deep, but seemingly Caucasian, almost like a professional broadcaster or an irrepressibly hammy actor, began saying, out of the lo-fi speaker, "I love you. I hate you. I love you. I hate you," repeating these words, expressively, over and over, a litany that began to make Lisa fall into a trance. She could feel it happening, she was going to be asleep in a moment. She fought it, it seemed darkly monstrous, as her body went utterly relaxed she protested, "No, no . . . "

"I love you. I hate you. I love you. I hate you."

She didn't become completely unconscious, but she couldn't tell what was going on. She was dreaming, but in her dream she kept telling herself to return to earth, she saw herself reflected in the mirror above the bed in the hotel.

I love you. I hate you.

When she came back, she was horribly afraid. She couldn't feel any pain, but everything seemed very *different* . . . she was afraid to open her eyes.

Some of the lights were down. The music was gone. She could feel some sort of wetness, some . . . she looked.

There was blood—or stage blood, but it stank—all over, far in excess of what she could imagine as realistic. When she moved just slightly, her eyes traveled up to the mirror.

It appeared that she had been disemboweled. There were bloody intestines coming out of her left side, extending out in a warm pile down to her knees. Some internal organs, dark and shiny: a slippery liver, a kidney, something else, she didn't know what it was. Her vulva was *drenched* with drying purplish-black blood, her pubic hair slicked down . . . and there was brown shit on her buttocks, as if she had soiled herself, gross, blood also all over her lower face, around her mouth, sticky, across her throat.

All over the bed, and over the blood everywhere in the room, yellow marigold blossoms were strewn.

Nothing hurt, though. Except, strangely enough, her nipples, which felt as if they'd been bitten rather cruelly. If this blood was all fake, the humiliating thing here was the presence of shit. It didn't seem like it was hers. But how could she be sure? Ugh.

She started to raise herself up, finding that she was very weak for a moment, her head swam like she might faint. She groaned and pushed herself to the other side of the bed, away from the dark brown pile of excrement. She sat on the edge of the bed, ass dirty, queasy, thinking she might vomit, then stood. She immediately wished that she'd taken off the spiked-heel shoes. But the zombies began applauding her, standing up, batting their hands together while their faces and eyes remained quite affectless and blank.

The tall black zombie with the pearl necklace stood just offstage, with Boro, and with a person in a dark bird suit, the wings serving as arms.

Boro stepped forward, and she went to him, unable to control her horror, tears raining down her face. She was filthy, her legs were so weak, she felt like she could hardly walk.

"How do you like Tomorrowland?" he said. "You want to be Cassandra—now you've seen, you've lived your own death. Tomorrowland!"

Out of this, Wanda suddenly took her hand in a moment, saying, "There's a shower over here," and led her there, over the cement floor. A toilet—she suddenly felt very sick, she threw up. Candy bars and some carbonated beverages. Oh, she had been murdered, yes: a shadow death, a death in mirrors. She got those fucking shoes off and went into the cubicle, stripping the other things off under cold water, it didn't matter, she washed off the makeup and came out naked—Wanda handed her a big black fluffy towel. Lisa felt irredeemably soiled and, now more than ever, truly afraid of Boro—that gory snuff-movie scene might really be what he wanted from her. Edgar Allen Poe had said that there was nothing so poetically affecting as the death of a beautiful young maiden, this was the highest subject art could attempt to treat. Around the areola of her right nipple there was some red-purple bruising, a sign to her she'd been bitten, bitten hard.

Back in the dressing room, she put on her jeans and blouse and sandals, as quickly as she could. Like a pro. Her hair was still very damp.

Boro and Wanda came in on her, and Lisa said, trying in vain to sound confident, "Now . . . we go and get Christine."

"Oh no, I'm sorry," Boro said. "This was a rehearsal. You've seen your own immortal death. Christine will be much better off in communion with the moon."

"You fucker," Lisa said, helplessly.

"You belong to me, I love you. In the real scene, it will be more spectacular . . . your head cut off, your tits."

Lisa ran. She ran down the corridor with the green fluorescent lights, up the stairs, then, running through the maze of Venus flytraps, she saw Jonathan, some fuzz of dark hair having grown on his pale scalp—he seemed to *know* her, he was in her way and he was stalking her, he was between her and the next door.

She picked up a plant and threw it at his head. It didn't faze him. All she could hope to do was fake him out. All zombies seemed somewhat slow.

Simply, she went way over to the left, then, when he was attracted that way, ran swiftly around and past him to the right.

Despite what Boro had said, maybe she could take Christine. In any case, her purse and keys were up there.

She ran up the stairs, athletically—but Christine was not there. Oh fuck. Where could they have put her? Her purse and keys, right by the cushions. So it was OK with them that she leave. It was in their plan.

But why leave? Inadvertently, or intending something else that she had not picked up on, Boro had given her some minor powers. She didn't know what she could do, or how it worked when she pulled something off, yet . . . there were certain things she could do. She decided to search up here for Christine. It was distinctly possible she could unlock these doors.

The first door she opened: nothing but raspberry and electric blue horizontal stripes of moving light.

The second: It seemed the same scenario she'd been in down in the basement—she closed the door immediately. But the woman on the bed hadn't looked like her. Maybe it was a mannequin. It didn't look quite real. Could she be hallucinating?

Third door: She looked out through a reddish, rocky cave to a desolate landscape and a different sky—interesting, but she had no time.

The fourth door: It opened to an empty room, completely bare, with a door on the other side, near the corner, near a mirror. Lisa went in. She opened the door in the corner, to another empty room, without furniture. Then . . . she looked in the mirror, on her right, watching the door in its mirror image, and opened it again, like that, watching it open only in the mirror. She stepped inside.

The jaguar couch was there, and the room was almost dark. The couch undulated, quivered, like it was alive. Lisa kicked off her sandals and threw herself euphorically into the couch's embrace.

In the clearing, beaten-down green grasses, Lisa's bare feet were tougher, she was browner than ever before. She did not have the power of speech, but she could communicate with the mother jaguar very well. In her simple white shift, joyous, she threw her arms around its massive neck and kissed its head, inhaling its musky smell. It let out a friendly growl and then purred.

The jungle was brighter than it had been in Brazil, the colors were sharper—there also seemed to be all kinds of blossoms and plants she'd never seen. The jaguar, a beautiful jaguar, white with black markings, just a tinge of orange-gold at the tips of the ears and the end of the tail, rolled on her back, biting at some flowers, panting, then fixing Lisa with her regal gaze as orange and red butterflies flew by out of the twelve-toned leaves of green. Lisa rolled around with the mother jaguar, both of them laughing, lolling, playful as newborn babes.

Many hours seemed to pass. They shared a luscious baby pig, a boar, which tasted like it had already been smoked. Flamingly colorful birds flew overhead, keeping well out of reach. Lisa lay dozing, safe, her head resting on the breathing side of her adopted, true mother, and she was ecstatically content.

As evening came, it was understood, without words, that the time for instruction was at hand. Watching a kind of movie, Lisa observed Boro—a young, handsome, taller Boro—mutilated, placed in a wooden cage. She saw herself—or the young Nastassja Kinski—as the princess, overseeing the severing of penis, tongue, hands, and feet. Lisa couldn't watch it all. She turned to find those large jaguar eyes on her, filled with a kind of philosophical sorrow, an acceptance of cruelty as an inevitable fact.

Boro lived. He survived. Shrunken, with new members sewn on. They nursed him back to health. He thrived. The practice of sorcery eased his constant pain, the pain of his missing parts.

She saw him with a machete, cutting off the head of a chicken. She saw this again, and knew.

Embracing the jaguar, eyes closed, mouth open in a silent cry, she wanted to stay, she was happy, this was all she ever wanted . . . but the embrace dissolved, she went through it . . . and found herself lying on the couch, in a room lit by one guttering red candle on the floor.

It took some time to come all the way back, to form an intentional thought. What a strangeness, to see that the simple, coarse cotton gown had been replaced by . . . oh, the affectation of ridiculously torn blue jeans, a muslin blouse . . . she had to move. She put on her sandals and, without looking back, departed the room, a casual motion of her left hand extinguishing the candle's flame.

Out in the hall again, she remembered Christine. She went back to visit the pond of milk. The wind chimes were going fiercely again, the music a sort of ghostly battle between cherubim and seraphim, a high children's choir at a distance, maybe electronically altered—she stared upward, at the now open skylight, sensing somehow that Chris was up there, maybe levitating . . . but she couldn't find her.

"I'll be back," she said, to give herself courage, and went out the door.

Whereupon she was immediately grabbed by Jonathan,

immensely strong hands seizing her by the shoulders and flinging her, so that she went tumbling into the dead-end portion of the hall. Getting up on her hands and knees, feeling roughed up, she was terrified. Jonathan had her cornered, and there seemed to be something in his eyes that knew she'd fucked up his family. He also seemed a little swifter on his feet than she expected him to be. "You . . . *bitch*," he got out in a low voice, the first time she'd heard one of them talk.

"Get back!" Lisa said, trying to sound authoritative. Jonathan reached forward—again, faster than he should have—and ripped her blouse down the middle, with the same hand coming right up to grab her by the throat.

She got out an awful, choked-off sound, and then he started to squeeze, she couldn't breathe. She struggled, hitting, kicking, trying to fling her body's weight all to one side and then the other, wishing desperately she knew some kung fu, but nothing was happening—

"Jonathan, stop! Jonathan! Omo-poke-*eye*-cha! Omo-poke-*eye*-cha!"

Lisa found herself dropped onto the floor. All she was trying to do was catch her breath. It was Ariel who had saved her. Jonathan stood frozen, glowering. He wanted to kill her. As Lisa got up, swallowing, rubbing her neck, she didn't know if he could have finished her off or not. There were tears in her eyes, but they were not emotional tears. They were physical.

"Are you all right?" Ariel asked.

She nodded. She couldn't speak.

"Do you want to go home now? If you do, I'll walk you to your car."

She said hoarsely, "My blouse."

"Yes, that's bad, you can't go home like that. You're about Wanda's size, aren't you? Come."

Lisa cleared her throat again and said, "What about him?"

"Go downstairs with the others, Jonathan. Get out of here."

"How do you kill them?" she asked when he was out of range.

"Shoot them in the head. Hit them in the head with an axe."

It was as she had thought. Just like in *Night of the Living Dead*.

A room she hadn't tried. Wanda was not there. A television, clothes all over—a very messy room. In the closet, Lisa picked out a leopard-patterned top with spaghetti straps. She took off the torn blouse and put this one on. Ariel watched her, frankly looking at her breasts.

"You think less of me," Lisa said, gazing into his eyes. "I'm not a whore."

"I like whores," he said easily. "It is my weakness. I have evil desires, evil thoughts."

They started walking out, down the now quiet dimly lit halls.

"I am worse than you know," he added after a while. As he opened the red door for her, standing aside, he said, "I didn't like what they did with you tonight."

As they came to her car, Lisa asked, "Will Christine be all right?"

In the darkness, the stale wind, he shrugged. "More of the same. She was jealous of you. She wanted powers of her own. But . . . I heard Wanda say it takes a month to do what she wants to do."

Lisa started her car. She turned it around and drove out of the estate. Ariel had made his own deal. If it came down to it, she thought he'd watch her die if that was what Boro wanted to see. Tomorrowland. Was that really what she had been through? A preenactment of what was to come?

Popcorn had waited up for her. Lisa saw the look on his face, and "I love you, I hate you" started going through her mind.

"I'm really tired," she said, but he was full of lust, full of love. "Don't," Lisa said in a spoiled, irritated voice.

"What happened to your neck?"

"I've got a scratch."

"Are you drunk?"

"No," Lisa said. She lifted up her hips to take off her pants. Then her underwear, and she laughed.

"Do you want me to leave you alone?" he asked.

"No, you can stay if you want. Do you think you could get me something to eat?"

"Like what? What do you want?"

"I don't know. Some bread and cheese. Whatever you would get for yourself."

Lisa was intentionally being a bitch, sort of to see how much he would take. If he noticed her voice was unusually hoarse, he didn't comment on it. It was funny to see him wait on her, bringing her in a plate with slices of apples, two kinds of cheese, etcetera . . . anything he brought her would have seemed stupid right now, she knew. She pitied him, she had turned on him to such an extent.

He waited, lying there next to her, as she ate a little bit. When she said she wanted a Coke, he went and got her a Coke. He had probably never waited on anyone like this in his life. She just wanted a sip or two of the Coke.

Then she turned off the light. He waited, she could hear his breathing . . . as he slowly moved his hand over her thigh, finally getting up enough nerve to try her cunt. She let him. Whatever he imagined she'd been up to this evening, he still wanted to fuck her! It didn't matter! No, it made it better for him, in a way.

He crept down there, parted her thighs in the dark, spread them apart, and commenced eating her, doing his best. She relaxed and dreamed dreams utterly disconnected from Selwyn Popcorn's tongue.

Then he sought to fuck her, but he couldn't get his hard-on together. He tried to stuff it in. He sighed, big time, and rolled onto his back. His hand went behind her neck, hoping to gently urge her down there, to put it in her mouth, but she didn't want to, she didn't respond. He sighed again, realizing that this was going nowhere, and it was nobody's fault but his own.

Lisa fell easily to sleep, exhausted, her dreams a disturbing review of what she had been through and seen. She needed the rest. She had no idea what time it was when Popcorn left her room.

THIRTY-THREE

Who would be the suspects if she was killed in the manner of the *tableau vivant?* Nehi Laughton, for sure, since he seemed to be overwrought. Selwyn Popcorn, possibly, depending on his alibi. Perhaps Code. And maybe the ghost of Roy Hardway. Also Jonathan and Lou. And, hypothetically, strangers who might have seen the video, if in fact it did exist. Connections and mysterious disappearances . . . it would be a confused case to try to solve.

It had shaken her, this Tomorrowland thing. It had been much worse than she had ever anticipated—she had thought she could breeze through it, playact, remain blasé . . . but she was deeply bothered, scared to her soul.

The only solution was to kill Boro first.

If it could be done.

Cut off his head like a chicken. She needed a machete and, once more, a handgun of some sort, to protect her from the Jonathans she might encounter in that house.

Tomorrowland. She kept seeing that first, unbelievable reflection in the overhead mirror above the bed. How sickening. The endpoint of pornography, of fetishism . . . to open her up. It became very impersonal, Lisa thought, she could see how serial killers remained unmoved by the slaughter, the blood, because they fetishized. . . .

The important point for her was: Boro had lied. He might have been joking there at the end, very blackly, about how the photo op was incomplete, he might just have been trying to shock, to horrify, but it had been the wrong moment, and besides, he had proven unreliable in regard to Christine. He had said he would let her take Christine out of there. It hadn't happened. The fuck.

So he had to be destroyed.

At Regime, on Melrose Avenue, lonely, absurd, Lisa considered her financial situation. She felt a desperate need to shop, to buy new clothes whether she'd ever get to wear them or not. She had several thousand in the bank, more to come from Idea One. She put down plastic for a plum-colored slip dress and Danskin black cotton fishnet tights. Shopping. Nothing mattered. She was fucked, so why not? It was a distraction.

She ducked in someplace to have a quick lunch. And then, out the window, it couldn't be—

In the company of two young women and another young man, it looked like Tavinho strolling by. Lisa ran out to see, to catch up if it was really—yes, she could tell by the way he walked.

"Tavinho!" she called, and he turned, he saw her . . . and the first thing he did, distinctly, was frown. Maybe Brad had really been an asshole to him. It didn't matter. If this thin blond girl was his girlfriend, that didn't matter either.

In a moment, though, he smiled at her, and she knew, in total innocence, that things would be fine. She threw her arms around him, greeting him without inhibition, like in Brazil.

Actually, Tavinho had nearly decided to forget about Lisa Nova once and for all. Her affections were not reliable, to say the least. She was a temptress. There was no sign that she would ever love him as he loved her.

When he had the opportunity to come to L.A. to attend a seminar, he wrote, because he knew Lisa's home base was here. There was no reply. It was a little maddening to come to Los Angeles and not know if she was even here. She might be in Europe. Or have moved. He had both her phone number and address, but he called several times and only got her machine. Although it was in some way pleasing simply to hear her recorded voice, Tavinho did not want to leave his cousin's number and then never hear from her, that was too painful, to be a part of her Latin American adventure that could not survive the cold light of the States. He despaired. Borrowing his cousin's automobile, he drove by her address on Sunday afternoon, only to see that it had burned down. Behind yellow tape, police technicians combed through the debris.

Stunned, afraid she was hurt, Tavinho asked one of them what had happened to the person who lived there. Nobody wanted to tell him anything. Back at his cousin's, excited, alarmed, needing to take some action, Tavinho called Lisa's brother in New York. He told Track about the explosion, and in turn Track told him to try this Adrian Gee. But the fellow at Gee's was unhelpful and unfriendly.

Tavinho said to his companions, "I'll meet you in the restaurant," and lingered with Lisa; once she kissed him with her tongue in his mouth, some of the initial distance seemed to dissolve. She was nervous, she kept touching him, as if afraid he would melt into thin air.

"I need to see you," she said. "I've been thinking about you all the time."

"Your friends keep telling me to go back to Rio," he said, underplaying whatever resentment he might have felt. Seeing her honest bewilderment, hearing the expressiveness of her "Really?" Tavinho said, "It doesn't matter. Here we are."

"We have to go somewhere," Lisa said. "We have to be together." She meant, and he knew this, that they had to fuck.

The logistics were awkward.

"Where I'm staying," Lisa said, thinking aloud, "I don't think . . . it wouldn't be right to have you come over, I mean to come into my room. I'll do it, but . . . there are so many people there. I'm staying with Selwyn Popcorn." Her eyes said what this meant.

They were on the sidewalk, with people walking by them, teenagers and old ladies and stylish women, a transvestite.

"I've always loved you," Tavinho said. "You've known that from the start."

It thrilled her to hear it; she smiled, deliciously, eyes lighting up, forgetting that she had been "killed" in Tomorrowland.

She said she loved Tavinho, he wouldn't believe how much.

"Where are you staying? Give me the phone number, the address."

They had to borrow a piece of paper and a ballpoint pen from inside a shoe store.

"I'm at my cousin Paulo's . . . but it's not the best place for privacy, I warn you."

"Tonight some people are coming over to Selwyn's for dinner: Manning Spendlove, for instance . . ." She saw he didn't know the name. "What about if I come over a little later? Will that be all right? If you want to, we can go somewhere else."

"I don't want you to embarrass him unnecessarily," Tavinho said, "or . . . make your position difficult there, if you're dependent."

"He won't question me. I'll be there by . . . nine-thirty, as close to that as I can."

They kissed again, and parted for the moment.

THIRTY-FOUR

That evening Popcorn did not appreciate it when he realized she was going to leave, that she intended to slip away.

"This is really pretty bad," he said, having followed her up to her room, his guests left downstairs.

"I'm sorry," she said, helplessly embarrassed.

"It's all right," he said then, changing his mind, maybe seeing himself in a bad role. "I told you that you could use my place as a hideout, and you did. It's all right with me, really. Maybe at some point, when and if you think I can handle it, you'll tell me what's going on. You could tell me, you know. If there's any way to help you, I'd try."

Lisa felt bad. Not that bad, because she felt she'd paid her way in terms of access to her body, but in his own fucked-up way Selwyn Popcorn still wished her well.

It was a long drive. She did some things to throw off any potential tail, but she realized that maybe no one was watching. It didn't feel like it right now.

The address wasn't so hard to find, but it was farther east than she'd imagined, and she felt nervous. She got out and, locking her car, noticed all the candy and magazines in the small backseat.

Tavinho awaited her. Paulo and his girlfriend, Barbara, had gone to a movie. After one fuck, a short rest, then an exquisite, timeless one that went from tender, minute sensation to slick but frictive stormy intercourse, draining them both, Lisa, lying in Tavinho's arms, could not help but compare these orgasms with the ones that she had recently been able, on occasion, to close her eyes and have with Popcorn . . . it was like those other ones had never touched this part of her, like she was a fruit with juice inside, and she'd been waiting for this slowly rising reservoir of hot juice to be released. Every muscle in her body felt relaxed now.

Paulo and his girlfriend came home and went to bed—they had classes in the morning, so they set the alarm, they talked, Tavinho went out to say something to his cousin while Lisa just remained in the bedroom, lightly covering herself with the sheet.

When Tavinho said to her, having brought them something to drink, "I have this feeling that you're in trouble. Why don't you talk to me about it?" maybe he was remembering the failed exorcism in Bahia, putting it together with the blown-up apartment, maybe it was something in her manner . . . anyway, she told him everything she could. It took a long time but he was extremely interested, he listened there in the dark as she talked about Boro, the spell, the pain of being tattooed and why she had done it, the miracle of *Manoa*, Christine, Duane Moyer . . . when something was not clear, Tavinho said, "Wait, just a moment," and asked her to clarify. She was aware that a lot of it didn't cast her in a very good light, and she told these parts coldly and severely, judging herself . . . until at last it seemed that Tavinho knew what was going on, the full weirdness and horror of it. He gently kissed her cheek as she shed tears while describing the Tomorrowland scene.

"Nobody tied me up and made me do it. Nobody put a gun to my head. They just . . . suckered me."

"Tell me more about the part with the jaguar. You said you thought you knew how Boro might be killed. I didn't stop you . . . but how is that?"

"Like a chicken," Lisa said. "I've got to do it with a machete—chop off his head." Her voice became a bit excited; she moved her legs in the bed.

"*You* have to do it?" Tavinho asked.

"Yes. My hand. Anyone else, he'd just laugh. But through me . . . the mother jaguar will help me do it."

"I will help you, too. I can maybe keep the others from interfering with you. There are a lot of variables, you realize. Like: What will

Ariel do? The way you describe him . . . his attitude is ambiguous. You sense that he likes you, but—"

"But I also think he might find pleasure in watching me die. Yes," she said, seeing it, sorrowful. "I think he would." Then, after a few moments, she said, "I've even had the feeling . . . that Boro *wants* me to kill him, like a suicide, I don't know."

"Maybe he's lived too long."

It didn't matter if Boro wanted it or not, Lisa thought. She couldn't worry about his psychology at this point.

She wondered if, by sleeping here, she was fraying the Popcorn thing just about beyond repair. Or no, she could repair it, with a blowjob on her knees, but she wouldn't do it. Tavinho seemed willing to die for her, to risk his life. She didn't think she was worthy of such love.

THIRTY-FIVE

The next day they tried some simple experiments with her powers, to see what she could do. The process amused them—and they were still full of elation, from having found each other—but they kept straight faces, it was interesting . . . and Lisa, naturally enough, wanted to demonstrate that she could be believed. Tavinho had listened to her fantastic story, ready to accept it all; some show of magic here would prove she was not crazy, that the rest of it was also true.

At breakfast, without touching them, Lisa rolled some oranges around the table—the smell of the orange peel penetrating deeply into her nostrils—but she could not lift them, could not levitate even one into the air.

"Sometimes I just *know* I can do something, and I don't think about it, and it works. If I think of something I want to do, usually thinking about it means I won't be able to do it . . . and if I try, if I concentrate, I get a terrible headache . . . so I don't ever push it."

Tavinho asked her, in an analytical manner, to tell him everything she had done that she could recall, every separate instance. She understood that he was looking for common factors, some kind of a law.

At the Burger King she had given the guy a nosebleed. She had caused the electric window to go up, trapping the head of the barking dog. She had clawed the face of the guy asking her for a dollar in New York. The plainclothes policeman tailing her, she had caused him to vomit uncontrollably in the front seat of his car. What else? Ripping Moyer's throat open.

"Can you unlock your car?"

Lisa tried. Yes, she could. This was satisfying. On the way back inside, she picked up a thicker-than-usual rubber band, and a minute later, not knowing what to do with it, she put it on her right wrist. You never know what might be good luck.

Tavinho seemed to be thinking about all of these new phenomena; she liked the way his face looked when it had problems to solve. It was peaceful, sort of concerned, but basically cheerful, even if he did not smile.

When he spoke to her as she was eating an orange, it was not what she expected to hear.

"Do you remember the first *Alien* movie?"

"Yeah."

"Well, when Ripley activates the launch sequence in the escape shuttle, the message that appears on the screen is the same one that appears in the hovercraft police car near the beginning of *Blade Runner.* It's 'ENVIRON CTR PURGE 24556 DR 5."' Tavinho smiled. "That just stuck in my head."

Lisa sort of tackled him, and they play-wrestled onto the couch. Her laughter infected him, and Tavinho laughed like she'd never heard him laugh before.

"Ripley," Lisa repeated, the name cracking her up. It was a joke to her—the idea that she should model herself on Ripley, that that was who she'd have to be like.

THIRTY-SIX

Early that afternoon she returned to Popcorn's, alone. Tavinho was going to seek some necessary equipment, stuff he thought he could easily score in East L.A. They planned on getting together later tonight. Lisa didn't know what would be going on. It made her faintly sick to think of facing Popcorn right now. She was nervous.

She proceeded very cautiously, but he was not home. Nicole, Popcorn's assistant, and Raelyn were there, out by the pool, Nicole in a one-piece red swimsuit, Raelyn in cutoffs and a tank top, fine gold-to-light-brown hair on her legs. It appeared that Nicole had been reading something to Raelyn out of a book. The way they gazed at Lisa, she had to smile. It was plain they knew she had been gone all night, and further, they—Nicole certainly—knew something about how Selwyn had taken it, what had gone on after Lisa had left.

Lisa changed into her dark blue swimsuit. She would sit with them, talk for a few minutes, and then swim. Nicole didn't really like her, she knew. However, she certainly trusted Raelyn.

"Where's Selwyn?"

Nicole laughed. "You're amazing," she said, shaking her head.

"What's your problem?" Lisa rejoined after a glance at Raelyn, who offered no help with her eyes.

"I'm not being critical," Nicole said, still laughing a little. "I think it's great. You're reckless as shit, and maybe that'll catch up with you, but just in the short term, I enjoy seeing you do your number on him."

Lisa was actually a little shocked by Nicole's disloyalty to Popcorn. Her general semblance of shyness and lack of color hid her true emotions well. Still, her implied judgment of Lisa wasn't one Lisa liked.

"I shouldn't tell you this," said Nicole, "but he has this notebook he writes in all the time, a lot of the time he just doodles, but what he does is go back through it and circle in red the notes he wants to save, and I enter them into the computer every couple of weeks. He likes to write in longhand. Anyway, I saw this page where he'd written down all his former wives' names, making a list, and, like he was fooling around, he tried out your name: Lisa Popcorn, Lisa Nova Popcorn . . . I shouldn't tell you, but if you want it, if that's in your plans, there it is."

Lisa felt bad. "Jesus." Her elbows resting on her drawn-up knees, she ran her fingers through her hair, then put one hand over her mouth.

"He's introduced you to a lot of fucking people," Nicole said, sounding oddly wistful, even forlorn.

Lisa reached over to Raelyn's bottle of strawberry pop and took a sip. It was warm and awfully sweet. Nicole was wicked to tell her what Selwyn privately wrote down. And just because he wrote it, that didn't mean that was what he wanted in the light of day. She felt sorry for him nonetheless.

She liked him, after all.

Maybe if she tried to be absolutely honest with him about their relationship, maybe . . . no, he'd still hate her. She would try, though, maybe.

Standing, stretching, she yawned, wondering what Tavinho was doing, missing him, he had a sureness about him she was lacking, she sensed he knew how to get things done. She dove into the glistening pool.

There were a lot of things she hadn't told Tavinho about. Raelyn was one of them. Another was the uncomfortable, corrupting sense she had of being somehow complicit with Boro, of cooperating with him overmuch. Wanting to. The whole thing of *Manoa, City of Gold* . . . she had very mixed feelings there, a bad conscience. It was like she had cheated on an exam. And Boro, obviously, was the one who had passed her the answer sheet. It was his film as much as it was hers.

She'd left out details all over the map. Like how much she *did* like meeting people in the company of Popcorn, the snob appeal . . . she liked that a lot. And there had been no reason to mention Chuck Suede or Roy Hardway's shrunken head.

The story of Miguel Casablanca had come out, though, and she had admitted her attraction to him. It remained a mystery how, exactly, he had obtained the stolen gun.

"He shot himself in the head to avoid being made into a zombie," Lisa had said. It made perfect sense. Any other manner of suicide, or most of them, would have left his dead body at risk.

As she finished her swim, staying in the water while her breathing slowed, it occurred to her that the ideal solution, in a parallel universe, if she were more demonic, would be to marry Selwyn and hardly ever fuck him, enjoying the social functions as his trophy, his trinket, while having Tavinho as her lover on the side. The audacity of the concept made her smile at herself. Was it rotten of her just to consider this, to think it over for a while?

No, if she married anyone it would be Tavinho. The idea actually excited her, to think of their individualities blending deep in her belly, becoming pregnant, having their child. That had never sounded remotely attractive before. It had been frightening, almost monstrous. Your body swelling, changing, only to ultrapainfully let loose this wailing creature, with all its immediate demands.

That part still didn't sound too great.

Tavinho, holding her this morning, had talked to her about outer space, how he had become interested in astronomy at the age of nine, when he had been given a telescope for his birthday, something to keep him occupied because his mother had died. Becoming an astrophysicist, however, was hard to do, on a world-class level, down in Brazil. He had come up now for this seminar at USC; next week he had an interview for a position at the Goddard Space Flight Center, in Maryland. The concepts were just appealing to him. He liked the idea of liquid nitrogen oceans on one of Saturn's moons, or of doing computer modeling of galaxy interactions, exotic particles that compose the two varieties of dark matter: hot dark matter and cold dark matter.

Lisa followed hardly anything of what he said, even though her father was a scientist . . . she let the poetry of it, and the interest in Tavinho's voice, wash over her. Some of the wonder came through, and it made her feel sentimental about what she regarded as his innocence, his admirable (here) naivete.

Uniformed LAPD came to pick her up and take her down to be questioned. They didn't tell her anything, and she thought she should just keep her mouth shut. They had waited while she got dressed; she had put makeup on, keeping them at bay until she'd fixed her eyes, lipstick, put on her *faux* Russian Orthodox necklace . . .

Now she waited. It was 4:45 P.M. They had left her waiting in a fucked-up interrogation room that had probably been reasonably new and modern in, like, 1975; since then it had seen hard use. She waited and wondered whether she should give that lawyer a call right away, she'd retained him on Popcorn's advice a week ago through Larry Planet's brother. She'd talked to him once. His name was Watson Random. She hadn't seen him yet, but her impression was that he was an extremely smart black man. He'd been a little impatient with her on the phone, trying to get a straight answer out of her, but she believed Larry Planet's brother's claim that he was good.

It was intimidating, being here at the station; all kinds of people walked by and glanced at you through the open door, sizing you up. Wondering what sort of a criminal you were. Bland, extraordinarily cynical looks from policemen and policewomen, it rattled her a little, waiting, surely the intent. No matter how nice you looked, there lurked in the air the implied threat—the power—to at any time take you and strip you, make you put on a rough-cut blue gown and confine you in a tiny cell on a row of cells full of vicious women unable to exist in peace out on the street.

Detective Bluestone came in, his jacket off, shirtsleeves half rolled up. She could smell the cinnamon gum in his mouth.

"Duane Moyer's Toyota Corolla was parked down the street from your apartment for nearly a week before the explosion. He ate in the car, even peed in a bottle in the car. He had a pair of binoculars. So the implication is that he was watching you . . . this even after Nehi Laughton fired him. Did you see him, were you aware of this?"

"No, I wasn't."

"He took three rolls of photographs. We've had them developed. Almost all are of you, coming and going, a few apparently of your guests. Miguel Casablanca, for instance."

"So?"

"A lot of shots of you with your sunglasses on, getting into your car."

Lisa had no comment on this.

Looking down at a folder he'd opened, Bluestone said, "You know, some pretty dramatic cellular changes take place when someone dies . . . in a way, you're not really dead till about twenty-four hours have passed." He closed the folder and looked Lisa in the face. "The forensic pathologist says that Moyer was already dead when the apartment blew up. That he'd been dead for something around three days."

Lisa frowned, not liking this at all.

"There's something else. The pathologist thinks there's something strange about how all the flesh was gone from the bones. More tissue should have been attached, however fried."

"I don't know anything about any of this," Lisa said. "I want my lawyer, now."

"You can have an attorney join you at any time," he said, but she knew he didn't want it, because Watson Random would advise her not to say a word.

"Are you going to charge me with anything?" Lisa asked.

"Did you kill Moyer?"

"No."

"You didn't answer that very well," he said, with a fast, hard smile, and it was true, her response had been too direct, she had unaccountably "blinked," there'd been an infinitesimal but unmistakable hesitation before she'd been able to get it out. She'd blown it, and they both knew it. It was funny too, because although she had in fact killed him, she didn't feel guilty. He'd attacked her, and she'd won. But this shit was hard. The thing with the bones was irrational, it confused her, probably Bluestone could see this. He knew that she had some guilty knowledge, but he didn't know how much. The fact that she had lost the tail the other night probably annoyed them; if she lost it again, as she would have to, well . . . but she would need to, in order to visit Boro and try to end all this, and rescue Christine.

Knowing that Tavinho was on her side consoled her—she smiled to herself and let her mind work more concisely, like the daughter of Dr. Nova . . . trying to be sound.

It hit her where the big danger was: that they would search for blood inside her car. Given the thorough methods they had now, it seemed unlikely to her that Moyer hadn't bled through the rug wrapped around him, at least some.

But at this point, why would they imagine that his body had ever left her apartment? That was weirder, inexplicable in ordinary terms. The most direct, simple line was probably almost always the best.

She saw that she had to stay with Popcorn for a while, as camouflage. They wouldn't want to involve him in a scandal unnecessarily, and she had moved in with him only a day or so before their projected murder date. Everything indicated, then, from their point of view, that Popcorn was involved. This was a company town; if Bluestone and his superiors fucked up over the death of a sleazeball like Moyer in what might be an unprovable case, their careers would be ruined.

Bluestone and Brown came back in and gave her mean looks, but Lisa was confident now, and when Bluestone said she could go, she said she wanted a ride home in an unmarked car.

"If it's possible," she then amended, feeling embarrassed by her demand. It wasn't in her nature to be arrogant like that.

"Wait fifteen minutes, and I'll drive you," Bluestone said, after exchanging glances with Brown. Lisa wondered if there was a fatal flaw in her logic. She was scared.

All the way to Popcorn's they conversed pleasantly, desultorily, never touching on anything to do with the investigation. Good cop, bad cop. Bluestone, sensing early on that, even if he was tough, she liked him, thought he was the good one. More or less. At least in comparison to Brown, who hated her guts.

Before she got out of the car, Lisa said, addressing the subtext of the ride, "I only met him once, and I didn't like him, he gave me a creepy feeling . . . I wasn't sorry to hear he was dead. Especially now that you tell me he was spying on me when he wasn't even working for Laughton anymore. Isn't that what you said? I don't know how he got killed, I don't know who blew up my apartment, I don't know what he was doing in there, you say that he was already dead . . . it's weird stuff, but I don't feel like it has anything to do with me."

By now she was out of his car, leaning back in, holding the door open. Bluestone said, "Maybe you're right. We'll let you know when we find out anything new."

She thanked him for the ride. It was seven o'clock. He zoomed away, and she walked into the big house, saying hi to Maria Luisa, one of the maids.

THIRTY-SEVEN

Did it matter that Popcorn had expressed to her, before dinner and afterward, the hope that she would continue to stay there, that he wasn't interested in being possessive, he had been through all that before? Lisa had recognized what Selwyn was doing, no problem. Did it matter what they'd had for dinner? If she died tonight, the coroner doing the autopsy would identify the various elements of the half-digested meal and write them on his form. Lisa wouldn't care, she'd be gone—absent, missing, someplace else, nowhere. Did it matter how she and Tavinho had eluded any possible tail?

The electronic eye opened the gate for them at a wave of her hand. Boro's estate was dark, and Lisa was so scared now she felt like she might get sick. Tavinho, sensing this, touched her tense shoulder, giving her a reassuring look she could feel more than see. It was close to midnight, and Lisa was tired, frazzled—it had taken a long time, and many inconclusive phone calls, for them to connect. Paulo had grown weary of her questioning voice. No, Tavinho had not come home. Nor had he called. Finally, at eleven-thirty, Tavinho had called Lisa and said he had everything; purchasing the gun had turned out to be hard.

He had seen no reason to wait. "Let's get it over with, do it tonight. We'll get more nervous if we wait, we'll lose our resolve. Let's go."

"OK, OK," Lisa had said, and here they were. She parked her car on the grass, away from the path of the Jaguar sedan. She wondered again if it was Roy's. She somehow assumed it was which gave her the creeps. Tavinho wore a dark blue T-shirt, blue jeans; Lisa wore black, a disposable outfit of black cotton tights and leotard, her mirror earrings, flexible black ankle-high lace-ups that she could run in, and a black minidress that was ancient, she wouldn't miss it if it got ruined.

There was no light on outside, but Lisa knew where the door was. Inside, it was not pitch black, thank God. Down around the corner, there was some kind of red nightlight. Eerie, but at least they could find their way. Actually, if it came to it, Lisa had every confidence she could see in the dark, but in here, with the possibilities—all bad—it was better if there was some light.

She held the machete, which had black electrical tape wrapped around the handle, concealed in a drawstring canvas bag. She was serious. Tavinho had the gun, a policeman's .38. He didn't have as many bullets for it as he would have liked, he had said. So they'd have to be fast on their feet.

Their first task was to rescue Christine. The house was so quiet it made them reluctant to let themselves make a sound.

"Up here," Lisa whispered, and Tavinho nodded. Because she knew the layout, he had to allow her to lead the way. His eyes were shining, dark—never had he seemed so foreign to her, and yet he was familiar, she trusted him, she loved him. She would not have been able to try this on her own, she now believed. She wouldn't have been able to stand the fear. It would have seemed suicidal to come in here like this.

Perhaps it still was, but she had someone to share the folly with, and this made it bearable. They exchanged glances, and Lisa opened Christine's door.

A dim, lugubrious, bluish silver light, sometimes an afterblink of pink. Ariel Mendoza sat on a plain wooden chair, facing them, a shotgun open across his knees. Tavinho pointed the .38 at him, but Ariel merely shook his head with a little smile and dumped the red shells out of the shotgun's barrel onto the floor.

"I won't do it," he said. "You don't need to shoot me, Lisa. I knew you'd come."

"What are you doing?" she asked, unsure.

He stood up and stretched out his arms, yawned. "I'm leaving. I'm going back to Brazil. My visa's expired," he said, and smiled again.

"Why?" Lisa asked, frowning at him.

"It's over. I can't do it anymore. He could make me pull both triggers on you and your boyfriend, and what would I be after that? I was just waiting to see if you'd really come. I can't help you—I wish I could."

He went out the door. They turned their attention to the pond, in which floated, once more, the pale, unconscious Christine. The skylight was open to the crescent moon. When Lisa reached into the milk—it had a plant smell, like some sort of sap—the coils of the serpent stirred, splashing, frightening her . . . Tavinho came over, through the ivy; together they reached and pulled Christine by the arms, she was floating, oh fuck she was *attached,* there was a glistening tentacle or cable stuck in one shoulder blade, like a deep-sea diver's oxygen line, another up between her thighs, into her vagina. Christine's eyes fluttered and she groaned.

"We've got to cut her free," Tavinho said, and Lisa agreed. She shuddered. Tavinho had a smaller knife, one with a jagged blade. He went after the one on her back as Lisa, getting wet, held Christine halfway out of the pond. He sawed at the sucker as it bled and quivered . . . the blood might have been Christine's.

"Look!" Tavinho said as the bleeding tentacle suddenly let go, leaving a raw wound on Christine's back, which slowly began to fill with blood. "It doesn't like to be hurt," he said. "Take the machete."

The water was moving, but there were targets. Lisa struck hard at a coil and the large knife stuck in the firm flesh, the machete was almost wrenched out of her hands, the water roiling and turning pink—she whacked at the tentacle between Christine's legs, and it abandoned the sex organ, making a squishy noise, as Tavinho pulled Christine's mostly limp body all the way out of the pond. Christine's eyes opened, and she screamed.

"Christine," Lisa said, as they tried to steady the moaning erstwhile moon goddess on her bare feet.

"I've been dreaming the most incredible dreams," Christine said, looking at Lisa in full intelligence for a moment, licking her lips, looking at Tavinho in curiosity, damp blond hair stuck to her skull, clad in a soaked white goddess-type gown, now stained with blood at the crotch.

"How do you feel?" Lisa asked Christine.

"I don't know. Weird." She stumbled, swooning a bit, but then seemed to regain herself as they reached the door; it didn't seem like she knew what had been happening to her.

In the hall they didn't see anyone, Tavinho had the gun ready, but in the dim red light there was no one.

"Come on," Lisa said to Christine as the latter suddenly fell to her knees, weeping helplessly, shaking her head, inconsolable.

At the first turn, Christine again making progress (the notion was to get her out, lock her in the car, then come back to do business with Boro), they found that they were cut off. Tavinho was afraid, Lisa saw, but he adjusted: Four zombies, maybe more beyond that, were coming slowly, up from the only way known that led outside.

"Let me try something," Lisa said, and skipped forward, holding the machete—she tried the phrase or word Ariel had used to call Jonathan off her that time. "Omo-poke-*eye*-cha! Omo-poke-*eye*-cha!"

It seemed to get their attention. But then, from the other direction, Wanda called out, with malice, "Get them! Eat! Kill!" Her near-violet hair sticking up like a frozen flame, wearing only a little red tutu, a red leather choker around her neck, all her tattoos, Wanda made beckoning motions with her fingers in the midst of more zombies from that end, and as soon as Christine turned and saw Wanda, she whimpered and broke away—Tavinho wasn't actually touching her, he was preoccupied with the gun, watching Lisa and the advancing zombies—and Christine ran back up the gleaming crimson hall, disappearing. Maybe she would continue past that awful room, up toward other doors. Right now that looked like the only reasonable way to head.

Suddenly a zombie had Lisa from behind—she'd turned her back to them to watch Christine run. Lisa cried out and tried to hit it with the machete—its teeth scraped the back of her neck just as, really deafeningly, Tavinho blew away half its brain. He carefully shot another one who had hold of Lisa's leg, clawlike fingers ripping the material of her tights . . . finally she extricated herself, and they started up the red hall, just dodging the converging zombies from Wanda's side.

"You're dead meat, Lisa," Wanda called. "The room's already rented. You want it, so why don't you relax? Tomorrowland," she jeered.

"Fuck you," Lisa replied, turning back, feeling ineffectual for the moment. They went around the corner, checked Christine's room, but she wasn't there, unless she was hiding or submerged in the pond. Tavinho and Lisa went up the hall, turning another corner . . . there were Polaroids of Lisa taped to the walls, hundreds of them, many from the setup in the hotel-room set. Except worse. Like Lisa had really been murdered.

Lisa hesitated, slowing Tavinho as they neared the open door to what she remembered as Boro's room. They heard a scream up around the last bend, past Boro's room. It was Christine. Boro came out then, with Jonathan, blocking them.

Jonathan moved more quickly than the other zombies—he had hold of Tavinho's wrist before the Brazilian could shoot him. They grappled. The gun went off into the zombie's body without effect. Jonathan threw Tavinho against the wall, and Boro moved out with a carved sacrificial knife, looking for his chance, saying to Lisa, "I never wanted to hurt you. You let me down."

Taking the initiative, overcoming a terrible inertia that felt like a spell, Lisa slashed Boro's left arm with the machete, surprising him—he bled some clear fluid, like tears.

Christine came back around the corner, the zombie maidens coming after her, she was bleeding, stumbling . . . Boro moved over there and, for Lisa's benefit, drove the dagger in between Christine's breasts, twisting it, digging it in as if to—right there, as she fell—extract her heart.

Blood all over . . . Lisa cut Boro as hard as she could, cutting off some upraised fingers; he turned and looked into the round mirror of one of the earrings, it was perfect, she caught him forcefully, a little under the chin, nearly severing his head.

Jonathan knocked her over, clawing at her neck, the machete came up into his groin, but it didn't seem to help, the zombie maidens were close now . . . Tavinho finally recovered enough, crawling, to pick up the gun and put more bullets in, he missed twice before getting Jonathan in the back of the head. He got to his feet . . . Jonathan, half the top of his head gone, was still trying to get at Lisa—there were zombies coming from both directions, there was no place to go. Tavinho took out two or three more of them. He and Lisa ducked into Boro's room, and before closing the door Lisa flicked her fingernails and set all the photos on fire. As soon as they had locked the door zombies began trying to break it down.

"I'm almost out of bullets," Tavinho said, reloading for the last time. A zombie fist broke through the wood of the door, letting in the ruby red light from the hall.

Lisa spun herself around like a top, three times, and a door opened, a door you could never have seen. She didn't know what she could do until she did it. They went into this next room. If they went out from here into the hall, they should be behind most of the zombies who had come up.

Where was Wanda, though? Opening the door a thin, thin crack, she saw Wanda right there. Lisa looked at Tavinho, asking him, mutely, if he was ready to make a run. He smiled gamely.

It turned into a melee at once. Lisa slashed at Wanda's face with the machete, awkwardly, in a hurry, but it caught and pulled the whole lower half of the face off, leaving the hideous red upper jaw, the rest of it must have been some kind of a mask, flesh grown on . . . Lisa involuntarily shrieked at the sight.

Tavinho shot Wanda in the cheek, making a mess, and two more zombies in the head. They got past them, and then the dark bird man came around the corner and stabbed Tavinho in the abdomen; Lisa went for him with the machete, and he seemed to dissolve into feathers, floating all around. Wanda was on her knees, tearing away the rest of the mask, the hair and flesh around the eyes, all in one piece. Tavinho, collecting himself, appalled at the transformation, aimed carefully and shot Wanda once more through the head. In the forehead. That seemed to be enough.

They went downward in the red-lit halls. Tavinho finished off one more zombie that surprised them. Tavinho was hurt but he could walk, it was painful, he shook his head and said, "That was the last bullet. That's it."

An Aztec warrior stood with a machine gun; they could not go past him. He was seemingly one of the wooden figures she'd seen before, though now come to life, heavily muscled, like a weight lifter. He gestured with the weapon, and Lisa dropped the useless machete. There was a door to the left. She opened it. This was what the warrior wanted. Lisa and Tavinho went in.

It was the hotel-room set, with yellow marigold blossoms scattered over everything. The black zombie with the pearl necklace stood by the table, turning to look impassively at them as they came in.

Lisa lay dead . . . her mostly naked corpse lay on the bed, decapitated, annihilated in other ways.

"It's wax," Lisa said. "He's done something like this before." She was horrified, but she was trying to be brave for Tavinho. Impulsively she twisted off her Aztec ring and surreptitiously tossed it at the big mirror. There was no clink.

"I'm not that bad," Tavinho said, knowing she was wondering. "It's a deep laceration, nothing more."

"Stay here, then," Lisa said as Boro came in through the door. His neck hardly seemed scratched; she had thought she'd nearly cut off his head. She smiled at him, sort of a come-hither look, and he was intoxicated or mad enough to approach her as she backed up to the big mirror.

"You're very weary," Boro said. "The room is rented, we need to wash you, prepare you . . . the numbers come together tomorrow night."

"How much will it hurt?"

"I tell you this: You won't want it to end. You'll be immortal, I promise you."

"Calm me, then, touch me. The last time you touched me, I was calm."

He neared her. She was acting, using a seductive tone of voice that also registered all that she'd been through. It was not unnatural. It sounded like she had given up, like she wanted peace and rest. Tavinho was leaning against the dresser, wounded. Boro looked at him, then back at Lisa, smiling, and she reached out and grabbed his wrist, pulling him as hard as she could. He fought like a maniac, realizing what she wanted to do.

"Help me, push him!" and Tavinho did it, Lisa pulled Boro with her, they fell together right through the mirror into the clearing. The mother jaguar leaped on Boro at once, she tore him apart, this time it was the end. She batted around the severed head a little, and Lisa kicked it back to her in play. No eyes, no tongue. Lisa used a small sharpened obsidian blade. Castrated him, cut out his heart. The mother jaguar ate the heart with pleasure, her tail whipping back and forth. Lisa raised her arms, and birds descended to pick the flesh from the skull. Wild dogs ate the penis and the meat from the rest of the bones; the white jaguar let them be. Lisa lay down next to the great cat, nuzzling her, as she continued to chew and tear.

Hours later, Lisa reluctantly dove into the pool of clear water, tumbling out dry from the mirror. On this side no more than two or three minutes had passed. The wax images burst into flames. The tall black zombie did not move, so they ignored him, more or less.

She embraced Tavinho. He said he was OK. He was in awe of her a bit—she kissed him and said, "Oh, Tavinho. Can we get out?"

"I don't know. Let's see if that Aztec is still there. If I had one more bullet, I'd put him down."

The Aztec warrior had taken off. Several zombies were in the vicinity, however. Lisa tried "Omo-poke-*eye*-cha" again, and this time it worked, it kept them back.

They didn't know what else to do, so, dangerously, Lisa and Tavinho walked in amongst the zombies, through them, through the maidens, brushing against them on the way out. Lisa suspected that Tavinho was hurt worse than he'd said. *Machismo.* She loved him. They made it out the door and into the night air. He was having a little trouble now. She got the car door open, and he made it onto the seat.

"Tavinho, hang on," she said, and then there came several loud pops; one of them shattered the right side of the windshield, Tavinho's head jerked and in the dark she saw blood flowing down from high above his ear. At the same time she felt a deep, nasty sting at the top of her shoulder, and one hand was horribly numb. She started crying but had to function, to hurry, she lifted Tavinho's leg into the car and closed the door on him. It was the fucking bird man, no, the Aztec, she could see them together moving down through the bushes, down the hillside, in the company of the black dog. There was nothing she could do. She got behind the wheel and started the car.

The gate was wide open, the Jaguar sedan stopped there . . . it looked like Ariel Mendoza hadn't made it off the grounds. Injured or dead behind the wheel.

"You'll be OK, Tavinho, don't worry, we'll be at the hospital any minute, they've got good doctors here, they won't let you die." She was crying so much it was hard to keep the car on the road, she was driving as fast as she knew how, faster, barely making some of these curves, tires squealing, all the lights and other cars and black night and sky blended together into a death trip that went on forever and wouldn't end just because she pulled up at the ambulance entrance and the medical personnel took Tavinho away to watch him die.

Lisa had cried herself out. She grew cold, numb, removed, as complications began to ensue. No bullets had struck her, only glass, but they needed to put some stitches in her left hand. She had a number of other long scratches and bruises; she welcomed the aching pain. She would also welcome anesthesia. The police were coming, she knew. She would send them to the house. Let them find whatever they would find.

THIRTY-EIGHT

After quite a bit of inconclusive questioning, which Lisa had the feeling was being videotaped, the detectives she was dealing with decided to take her back to the scene of the crime. Lisa had gotten her black leather jacket out of the backseat of her car before the police had arrived at the hospital, and now this looked like a wise decision, as it had turned oddly cold and was actually drizzling, brownish silvery slate gray, ugly rain, dirty, it was somewhere near 8:30 A.M.

They pulled in past the yellow police ribbon, and right away she was asked to identify the body behind the wheel of the Jaguar. Lisa gasped, bringing her bandaged left hand up to her mouth. She hadn't realized earlier, in the dark—gasoline had been poured on Ariel's body, and it was partially burned, along with most of the front seat . . . he looked horrible. One unburned hand dangled out the open window, new rain beading on the skin.

She explained that he was a private investigator from Brazil. The female police detective, Gomez, frowned for about the three thousandth time, making notes as the other member of the team, wised-up clever jock Detective Lancaster, coughed and again seemed to pay no attention at all. There were a lot of ordinary uniformed policemen around, as well as a horde of various techs, police photographers and the like.

Detective Bluestone greeted her as they came into Boro's house.

"Well, it finally hit the fan. What a surprise. *You* made it, though, didn't you? Just about everyone else here seems a little the worse for wear."

Lisa had been extremely vague about what had happened, just variations on "Somebody started shooting, and I was trying to get out." She hadn't wanted to start talking about zombies or anything else too weird. She had, however, said that she and Tavinho had come to rescue her friend Christine. These people were gangsters, and they had Christine on drugs. Lisa had mentioned Mannix, and Detectives Gomez and Lancaster had become extremely interested. They recognized the name.

"What kind of drugs?"

"I don't know. New ones. Joy Division, I think."

Now as they walked through the house in daylight, windows

open, she saw many fewer bodies than she'd expected to see. All of the zombies—those that had fallen with bullets in their heads, those that had been left standing—seemed to be gone.

Except for Jonathan. She identified him as the son of Lou Greenwood, Lou Adolph, Lou Burke. And then Wanda, her head completely blown off now, the shotgun lying there self-evidently . . . Christine, her chest gaping open, a disturbing little half smile on her face, like it hadn't hurt. Lisa hadn't thought about her much, absorbed in the loss of Tavinho, but now tears rolled down her cheeks.

In the room where the Tomorrowland set was, where she'd burned the lumps of wax, the black man still stood there, pearl necklace around his neck, pink lipstick, rouge, wearing a respectable suit. Was he a zombie or merely catatonic? A uniformed policeman studied him, hand on the butt of his gun.

"Do you know this guy?" Bluestone asked.

She shook her head. What was wrong with him? Was he alive?

With the eraser end of a pencil, Lancaster pushed the play button on the little tape recorder. Nothing. Lisa was relieved. She decided she could mention Boro—there'd be no trace of him, and others (Mannix, for instance) knew his name. He could be another suspect.

She saw herself in the mirror and stared. Her clothes were more extravagantly torn than she'd known. Where had the zombies gone? She felt like her mind was blown, her emotions burned away to shiny, ugly black tar.

They took her back to the station in a police car, past television reporters at the crime scene, then more at the police station. The decision had been made at some level not to let go of Lisa; she was all they really had unless the catatonic guy started to talk. Watson Random was on his way to try to get her released, but meanwhile they booked her as a material witness, charged her with the theft of the .32 that Casablanca had shot himself with (though they didn't ask her about this). They were fucking with her, trying to intimidate her . . . she had to pose for mug shots, she was fingerprinted, stripped, and subjected to an internal examination, she saw the matron putting on the latex glove and said, "This isn't necessary, this is bullshit." She was exhausted and naked, listening to them catalog her "tats." They could do this with impunity, but it was just sadism, power—well sometimes the exercise of power arouses resistance. She'd been cooperative within what she saw as the realm of the possible. They asked her to pee in a container for a drug screen, and she remembered she'd taken the Joy Division a few days ago; obediently she put on the ugly blue one-piece county garment and the clear plastic slip-on jelly sandals, she was led into an interrogation room . . . no doubt the plan was to work on her when she was feeling as vulnerable as they could make her, and so they would pretend she was a suspect for a day or so while they dog-piled on her.

Lancaster and Gomez questioned her. They acted like she was a common criminal, a bad-check artist or a thief, some small-timer who'd gotten in over her head. Gomez asked when she had first met Boro. How had they been introduced? Lisa said it was through Lou. What were the circumstances? Lisa said she didn't remember. When would this have been? She didn't know.

Anita Gomez looked at Lisa as if she couldn't comprehend her bad attitude, as though Lisa ought to like her and trust her because they were both women. Gomez had a nasally accented voice revealing mediocre intelligence, and she kept on asking boring questions, going back now to begin at the beginning, where Lisa had been born, how many in her family—this could go on for hours, Lisa realized, and build up until her innocent past became a large pressure to talk in similar detail about the parts she didn't want to talk about. She could see it coming, maybe it was stupid to get openly hostile, but she was exhausted and grief-stricken, she hated them. She said, "I don't want to talk about my childhood to you motherfuckers. I'm one of the victims in this, my boyfriend was killed, and you're treating me like shit."

"We've got a mass murder here, and it seems like you're holding back, you're being selective about what you choose to tell," Lancaster said.

"No, I'm not," Lisa said boldly, another lie. She clutched her Styrofoam cup of coffee, wishing it was still warm. She was frightened, but so used to being frightened she didn't care—at some point they would have to let her sleep. That was all she wanted. Oblivion. Respite from physical grief and guilt and shame.

Lancaster shook his head in disgust. He muttered something, and tears stung Lisa's eyes again. She had thought she was dry. Someone brought in a map of the grounds, with the bodies marked. They wanted her to describe the occasion of each one.

Jonathan: shot by Tavinho.

Christine: stabbed by Boro.

Wanda: shot by Tavinho.

Ariel Mendoza: she didn't know.

Tavinho: probably the unknown person in Aztec garb.

What had happened to Boro? She didn't know. He'd run away inside the house.

Who was the tall black guy? She didn't know.

What was the real story on Duane Moyer? How had he died? She didn't know.

Would she take a polygraph? No.

Whom had she killed? No one.

Were there other people there? Ones that the police didn't know about? Maybe. It was dark inside. The only light was red, and a lot of the time she and Tavinho had been running.

What about Jonathan's father, Lou? She had heard he went on a cruise.

PART 4

~

The ideal film, it seems to me, is when it's as though the projector were behind the beholder's eyes, and he throws onto the screen that which he wants to see.

JOHN HUSTON

~ ONE

Publicitywise, it was almost as if Tomorrowland had come true. The case went from local television feeds to network news, and CNN was all over it from the start. A semicharacteristic, fairly flattering head-and-shoulders shot of Lisa Nova (taken in Berlin, at the film festival, by one of the freelancers who took photos of everyone, because you never know) accompanied most stories on the case, and usually, thanks to Watson Random's energetic work as spin doctor, she was portrayed not too unfavorably—as, for instance, "the only survivor of the bizarre voodoo drug murders"—and the visuals shown during an update usually featured Watson Random prominently, tall and black with a booming baritone voice, not so much handsome as forceful-looking, with quite a stare, either next to Lisa or on the courthouse steps, cut from there to the yellow-tape-marked crime scene . . . each day for a while there was a new development, from the discovery of an undisclosed number of shrunken heads, to the press (not the police) breaking the story of Lisa's arrest in Rio, somebody in Miami coming up with video of her in handcuffs, a sullen look on her face, arms exposed so it was the first time her tattoos were clearly revealed.

Much was made of possible romantic links to the dead boxer Miguel Casablanca, to Roy Hardway, and to Selwyn Popcorn—though the studio's publicists were doing all they could do to downplay this last liaison, and the studio had acted immediately to help Popcorn get her out of his house ("She needed a place to stay, her apartment was destroyed; I just put her up for a couple of days"). Before Lisa was even out of jail, Robert Hand had spoken to Larry Planet and Popcorn, and Tami Spiegel had found a house to put her in. Popcorn was shortly to leave for New York anyway, but he (even though he knew Lisa probably would never know of his role, the symbolics here were very bad—she'd think he was an asshole, disloyal, but there was so much money involved in *Call It Love*) insisted that she be situated in a nice house with a pool, rent-free for a few months. A payoff. A settlement. Raelyn was privy to just a bit of this, getting Selwyn's side (he made her promise to convey to Lisa his love, whatever he meant by that), talking also to Larry Planet—for some amount of cover, the house, which was in Topanga Canyon, was put in Raelyn's name. A double limo switch was needed to get Lisa temporarily free of the press, but this house had high walls around the grounds, and Tami Spiegel said that if security became a problem (she didn't think it would) to let her know. Larry Planet said that if Tami Spiegel was any trouble, to call him instead.

The existence of the shrunken heads made for quite a sensation, the more so as they couldn't be identified without skulls or teeth. Plus there was found (in separate locations) the head and body of a young blond woman, aged approximately nineteen. Nude. The tall black man in custody remained catatonic; the police ran his picture, hoping for an ID. They said that Balthasar d'Oro, aka "Boro," the prime suspect, believed to be a Venezuelan (wherever they got this), was still at large. No photograph of him was yet known.

When it came out that Lou Greenwood, Lou Adolph, Lou Burke had never gone on his cruise, Watson Random (via CNN) asked why they hadn't been looking for him from the start.

"My client was in a state of shock, but she told them what she could. Instead of acting immediately on this information, they delayed, browbeating Miss Nova, letting precious time expire while they grilled her on such things as an old relationship having nothing to do with this matter. If Mr. d'Oro has gotten out of the country, you may well ask yourself if it was because of this senseless delay."

Random was telegenic, and he liked to be on TV. Lisa had told him quite a lot of the truth. She needed to trust somebody, she needed somebody on her side. So Random knew that Lou and Roy Hardway were dead, and Boro too.

"You *think* they're dead, you mean, right? It's, like, hearsay. You haven't seen their bodies."

"Yeah, I think they're dead."

"OK. There's no reason to talk to the court about hearsay unless we're really against the wall. I don't see that happening either, unless there's something new. How are you doing at your new house?"

"Oh, it's nice."

"How are you feeling? They sent Tavinho back to his parents today—are you OK about that? You know, I have two sons and a little girl, but three years ago we lost a boy to meningitis . . . I'm trying to say that grief is a natural, physical thing. Unfortunately, it's part of life. If you start feeling it take over, say something to me. You're under a lot of pressure now, people talking about you, making up somebody to fit their fantasies . . . it's a lurid case."

"I'll be OK," Lisa said. "It's just weird seeing myself on TV every night." She shifted her weight in the posh leather chair. That wasn't really what she had wanted to say. She liked Watson Random's office, and his staff, and Random had been extraordinarily thoughtful since she had become big news (and big bucks). That was all right. She understood.

~ TWO

There was a beat-up lemon tree and a dying palm outside her window, and tonight, her mind wandering before the news came on, Veronica, Lou's widow, permitted herself to recall the jacarandas that had been just outside her window at home, the violet blossoms and sweet smell . . . she had the VCR set to record *The Real Story*, which would join, on the tape, a basically nothing *Nightline* and a pretty sleazy *Behind the Scenes,* the latter emphasizing the possibilities of Lisa Nova's sluttishness, her likely complicity in any evildoing. The producers had been moved to show the longest excerpt yet of Lisa's Rio de Janeiro arrest tape and her part in *The L.A. Ripper,* freeze-framing just before she got a knife driven into her belly (the first of many wounds to come).

Veronica took a sip of diet Coke diluted by melted ice. Should she wait and take a pill nearer to bedtime, or take one now and chill? Why put off till tomorrow what you can do today?

The Real Story educationally showed stock footage of the Jivaro, in the Amazon, demonstrating how one went about shrinking a head.

Then they broadcast a clip of Dr. Nova accepting an award for the "Nova molecule," pointing out that he was now working in the Amazon—making this sound pretty sinister: "the scientist's daughter . . ." Finally they showed a clip from Lisa's first film, *Girl, 10, Murders Boys*.

Oh, but this was new. Lisa Nova's former boyfriend, Code Parker, smiling, ring in his nose, peroxide hair blowing in the wind, saying, "She was always interested in the dark side of things. She likes to push things, to see how far she can go. What you might call all-American kinkiness." A big grin on his face.

Just at this moment, Veronica's boyfriend, her former trainer, Steve Zen, came in through the front door, letting the screen door slam. He was lately a male stripper. Tonight he had had a party, a private gig. From the look on his face, it had gone very well. Veronica couldn't remember if it had been all girls or all boys. His shirt was already unbuttoned; he stepped out of his Bermuda shorts. He'd toweled off, but there was still a fair amount of oil glistening on his shaven torso.

"I'm high as a motherfucker," he announced. "Will you do me? I gotta come down. I'm skronked."

"Sure," Veronica said, taking a syringe out of the backgammon box. The cheap living room was really sort of an intense mess, if that's what you wanted to see.

"Watch," Veronica said, her own eyes never leaving the TV set, even as she began to melt the pill, "there she is."

Footage of Lisa, head down, sunglasses on, ducking into a black limo, wearing black herself. The righteous announcer called her "the mysterious Lisa Nova," and they showed her in slow motion, grainy color, sullen, jaguar tattoo right there in the Rio night. Then into a commercial for Susan Heller's new film. Popcorn had directed that, Veronica knew. *Call It Love*. Then the screen filled with a tight shot of a woman's wet, soapy belly, her navel. Camay soap.

THREE

What was left of her life? Was it what she saw about herself on TV? Lisa couldn't figure it out. She couldn't concentrate. A couple times she thought of subjects she wanted to read about and sent Raelyn to find books about them, and then she had a hard time reading, though she tried.

It was hot, and this place didn't have air-conditioning, it had ceiling fans. The swimming pool wasn't very big, but she supposed she couldn't complain. Caz was scared of the ceiling fans at first, but he got used to them.

She felt bad about Tavinho. She would always love him. Every moment they'd spent together was holy, or she wanted that to be true. What had happened to Christine was more difficult to sort out. Christine had kind of done it to herself.

It was hard, moreover, for Lisa to believe that Boro was really dead. She supposed she had thought he was God. He *had been* God. Now everything was confused. Or rather, she didn't understand anything. Not enough. The universe was in chaos.

She couldn't get very excited about this pool. While Raelyn was gone, off renting videos or buying food, Lisa swam naked, but it just seemed like she was constantly doing her Olympic-style turns, beautifully, she liked her form, but she wanted a longer pool and a diving board. If she'd had a diving board, she might not have started thinking about, well, looking in mirrors.

Sadness was getting boring, no question. Sadness and hate. There were all kinds of people who deserved vengeance from her, but she'd sworn off that, she wouldn't even think about it, she tried not to think about them, and if accidentally she did, she tried on some level to wish them long and happy lives. Or the fate of being eaten by sharks. What the fuck.

She needed some equipment. Some 35 mm color raw stock, a Panavision camera (which could be rented), a crystal-sync Nagra, batteries, one-quarter-inch Scotch recording tape, three mags, a 35 mm Steenbeck console with a digital frame counter, and a guillotine splicer, some splicing tape, etcetera . . . Raelyn had said she liked to edit, that was what she did best. Lisa didn't tell her exactly what she had in mind. She had an experiment planned.

They ate some Indian food, masala and saffron rice and hot strange pickles, thick sweet bread with yogurt in it (Lisa guessed) called naan, and watched some films, including Jackie Chan's Hong Kong martial arts action movies *Armour of God* and *Project A*.

The movies were funny, and Lisa and Raelyn were entertained.

FOUR

Dave Bluestone drove by a sign that said Reality Wrecking, past old men walking slowly in Panama hats in front of buildings that were fuchsia, turquoise, and lime green. There was an elaborate message in an unfamiliar alphabet, newly printed, black on white, perhaps in Tamil, or Azerbaijani. Everyone came to L.A. People from hot climates liked it better than New York, and people from cold climates imagined that they would like to finally be warm. He and Phil Lancaster got out, stretched a bit, walked up to the entrance of the sprawling house. They didn't have enough information to really put the squeeze on. Maybe next time.

Bluestone knew the city as an infrastructure of freeways: He was always highly aware of exactly where he was, of how far he would ultimately have to drive to get home. He went from dry to green, from poor neighborhoods to security-patrolled areas of unbelievable wealth. If he thought about the sociology of it at all, it was mostly in order to tease his partner, Profit Brown, who thought about it a lot. Profit (whose gravity of manner discouraged flippant remarks about his first name, though many criminals and criminal associates were irrepressible) had originally thought he was going to be a sociologist, and then a high-school sociology teacher, and although he'd ended up a cop, he still occasionally talked about going back to get a teaching certificate and leaving the force. He'd say that he would rather reduce people to socioeconomic statistics than constantly, every time, meet them at their worst. He'd say, "I don't want to get jaded and see the whole world as potential perps . . . or victims who actively aid and abet their own fate." It was their running joke that while Bluestone was irredeemably cynical and thought the worst of everyone he met, almost always to be proven right, the funny thing was that it was Profit Brown who tended, in his personal judgments, to be the more severe. He'd decide somebody was bad and that was it, he just wouldn't like the person, and some of the time this would show. Usually it didn't matter, but sometimes it wasn't a good tactic . . . still, he didn't always make up his mind right off the bat.

In the present case, Brown had early on lost faith in any possibility for Lisa Nova's redemption; in his eyes she was an evil, lying bitch, and he and Bluestone had recognized that Brown would be more effective dealing with other suspects or peripheral characters in the case. Like Mannix, who told him some surprising things. Brown also interviewed Casablanca's mother, and Hollywood figures who would give him time because he was serious, and black. He talked to Robert Hand and Tami Spiegel and Jules Brandenberg about why and how Lisa had been fired, and he and Bluestone caught Selwyn Popcorn before the director got out of town.

It wasn't that Bluestone thought Lisa Nova was innocent—clearly she wasn't that. But if someone murdered her now, or if evidence came up to put her in Tehachapi for however many years, Profit Brown would feel gratified in a way, proven right about her, while Bluestone would in some small way be saddened that it always turned out like this. She might be self-destructive, but she was also full of life.

Detectives Phil Lancaster and Anita Gomez were busy trying to coordinate the technical aspects, to nail down the scene. Boro's house was completely trashed; in an area of such high property values it was kind of amazing, this disrespect for real estate . . . the whole structure would probably have to be torn down. How had Boro been able to rent such a place? Well, it had been through a company that was a paper subsidiary of something owned by Lauren Devoto, and Alvin Sender's name was on the lease.

Phil loved this connection, he was proud of it, so Bluestone had let Lancaster accompany him to interview both of them, he thought he might as well. Bluestone had already talked to Lisa's ex-boyfriend, Code, and to Lou's wife, Veronica, who was living in reduced circumstances. Why? It wasn't yet clear. And Bluestone had interviewed people who knew Christine, like her boyfriend, Oriole, and the gay friend, Adrian, and the fellow named Jim with whom she'd almost done some wildlife show for PBS. Earlier Bluestone had also talked to Nehi Laughton, to Raelyn (now twice), and to Popcorn's assistant, Nicole.

Predictably, Lauren Devoto completely stonewalled on the property aspects; she didn't know anything about it, that's all she would say. A cold one. Acted like they were gratuitously wasting her time. She managed to be icy and rude while maintaining perfect decorum.

They drove to Alvin Sender's office, hoping to catch him by surprise. But he was out of town, gone to Jamaica. The Mexican woman in his office said she knew nothing, that she only answered the phone, and that most of the time people left messages on his voice mail. She didn't have a very cooperative attitude, and seemed unafraid. Shit. Another long drive for nothing. Ordinarily Bluestone was careful to call ahead, but Lancaster had been eager, excited about his lead—it was a good one—and Sender was a shady figure. Lancaster had figured that Sender might turn out to know more about this business than anyone else, if they could ever get him to talk.

Back to the station, listening to the female dispatcher's voice. Lancaster called Jamaica, to no avail.

Profit Brown said to Bluestone, "Why don't you come in here? Check out what Mannix has to say about Lisa and Christine."

Mannix described the only time he'd met them. "They killed this guy for Boro. They cut his motherfucking throat."

"Did you see this?"

"I saw the body, man. They carried him in."

"Who carried him in?"

"Fucking zombies carried him in."

"Wait—where were Lisa and Christine?"

"I told you. They come in and sit down, like, at the man's feet. Boro starts giving the good-looking bitch a neck massage. Zombies bring in the dead white dude. Boro says, 'My friend today, my enemy tomorrow,' some shit like that. A warning, see?"

"Did either of them say anything like, 'Yeah, I killed him'? You know, something specific."

"No," Mannix said, answering Brown. "It might all have been a lie. 'Cept the motherfucker was all bled out."

"What did he look like?"

"I don't know. Dead. White dude."

"Is this him?" showing him a picture of Moyer, two years ago, when he'd been booked (though never charged) for assault.

"Might be. He had on one of those jive-ass wack Hawaiian shirts, pineapples or something."

"What kind of a deal did you have with Boro, that he was showing you dead bodies and giving you warnings like that?"

"I told you: I barely knew the motherfucker."

"Do you know *him*?" Brown said, putting down a full face and profile, in color, of the unidentified African-American male, still catatonic at this time.

Mannix studied the pictures, then shook his head.

"We found some skulls down under the house, buried in some dirt," Profit said, revealing news that Dave Bluestone hadn't yet heard. "Any idea who they might be?"

"I heard about the shrunken head shit," Mannix said, as if this was just too vile. "No, Boro never mentioned nothing like that . . . but he was such a freak, nothing would surprise my ass."

They let him go. The only one he would ever have talked this much to was Profit Brown. They now knew more than before about Duane Moyer's demise, but still not very much.

"What's this about the skulls?"

"More madness," Profit said. "Three skulls, not enough to match up with all the shrunken heads . . . oh, but there's a possible ID on the blond female. And it's not going to help cool things down. One of the lab techs recognized her from some porno mag he's seen . . . and it turns out she's been missing for a few months, we had the photographer in, and he said yeah, it might be her. Candy St. Claire. He had a Xerox of her driver's license, along with the release. Scared as shit."

"They're supposed to be eighteen, aren't they? I haven't worked vice in a long time, but that must be the same."

"Supposedly she's a local kid, so maybe there'll actually be dental X rays out there someplace."

"Have we got them for Lou what's-his-name, the producer, and Roy Hardway?" Bluestone asked after draining his paper cup of decaf coffee, heavily creamed. "I'm suspicious as hell of people who just drop out of sight. You know what I mean."

"Yeah, I do," said Profit, and he smiled before saying, "And you realize, both these missing males were good friends of Lisa Nova."

"Well," Bluestone rejoined, "they both probably also knew Lauren Devoto, the way things are going, and maybe this scumbag Alvin Sender. I think Sender's the man we need to push hard on when he gets back."

"Where'd you say he is?"

"Jamaica. Loading up on ganja for his friends."

"Your girl Nova knows most everything we need, if we could squeeze it out of her," Profit said, not without a certain repressed fury.

"You think she was out there fucking chickens and all the rest of it? Boiling heads to shrink them down?"

"I think she knows about it," Profit said, and Bluestone had to agree.

"The part I don't understand—one part, anyway—is what has happened to these bikers we've heard about. Usually people on motorcycles are more outgoing . . . but nobody seems to know anything about these guys."

"Mannix just called them zombies," Profit said. "Maybe they're strung out on one of those new drugs. Lisa Nova had traces of some unusual chemicals in her urine. . . ."

"Maybe Alvin Sender will know," Bluestone said. "We need to get something on him and make a deal."

"We've got theft, and unlawful possession, on Nova. What Mannix describes . . . it sounds like she either killed Duane or was an accessory to snuffing him out."

"It's not even circumstantial."

"It's *something*. Maybe she'll crack."

"I wonder how that shit went down in Brazil. Until she managed to bribe her way out. It might have some bearing on what happened to Duane." Bluestone did wonder. He was curious. He had seen the video of her under arrest in Rio de Janeiro.

"Indeed," Profit said with a nasty smile. "I don't know why we're pussyfooting—we've got her as accessory on the people Tavinho Medeiros shot down. As far as I'm concerned, that makes a lot of sense."

"Pass the potato salad. You're crazy."

"Our big mistake was believing even a single word she said there at the beginning. If we had just started with the facts we had, the bodies at the scene . . . but we let her model of the scenario control how we approached it. If she'd been in a coma for a week, we'd have a completely different case."

Profit was just talking, Bluestone thought. Going off on a jag. Making Alvin Sender sweat seemed a reasonable plan, so until that happened, Bluestone would collect all of this other information, and wait. Some of it was starting to cohere.

"Why don't we go see Javier, Roy's houseboy? No pussyfooting," Dave said, and Profit laughed. The word was their new private joke.

FIVE

Naturally, on TV they made quite a sensation out of the confirmed identifications on the unearthed skulls. Lisa and Raelyn watched, Lisa controlling the remote. Now everyone finally knew that Lou was dead, along with Max Doppler, private detective, and Candy St. Claire, porn star. This morning Lisa and Watson Random had met at the police station, by invitation, and Lisa had said no, she didn't know anything about these apparent murders, the only person here she'd ever known was Lou. She hadn't seen or talked to him for several weeks before she'd left town for Brazil.

Detective Brown said, "You're sure you didn't know this Candy St. Claire? Never met her?" He tossed a garish pink magazine down on the table. *Dildo Babes.*

"I don't think I recognize her," Lisa said coolly, gauging the deliberate insult in Brown's manner of presenting the pornography.

"Are you sure?" he said. "Think hard. You might have gone to a party together, something like that."

"Lieutenant," Random said, looking to Bluestone, "she's said she doesn't recognize her. Is there anything more?"

"I'm curious about this private detective, Max Doppler," Bluestone said. "After all, there's precedent. Duane Moyer was hired to follow you, to check you out, and we have some idea by now of what happened to him. So when we find the remains of another detective, the question naturally arises: Was he also, at one time, following you?"

Lisa and Watson huddled. She actually thought she knew who Doppler was–the local guy hired by Ariel Mendoza before Mendoza changed sides . . . posthuddle, since (as Random said) she'd never heard a name, so it was only an informed guess, sheer speculation, she said only, "I don't know him, I don't know anything about him." She felt slightly guilty, though strictly speaking this was the truth. Then she couldn't resist adding, since *Dildo Babes* was still in front of her, "Do you have any more magazines for me?"

Bluestone smiled, and put the pornography away. "Leaving Doppler for now, why don't you tell us again about your relationship with Roy Hardway? How did you meet him? He just suddenly called you up?"

"That's right."

"Why?"

"He saw me at a party or something. I don't remember exactly."

Brown said, "Javier, his devoted houseman, insists that Roy went out with you and never returned. You've said you don't know anything about that. Someone's told us you and Roy went to a motel, had a party with some other young women. What motel was that?"

It was the story she'd given to Nehi Laughton. He'd blabbed.

"I don't know. I got really drunk."

"Maybe Candy St. Claire was there."

"I've already said I don't recognize her."

Bluestone nodded and asked a few more kind of bored questions about where the motel might have been. Was it on Sunset? Well, if she had to make a guess? She wouldn't, she said.

Now home watching TV, she flicked from a commercial for Prell shampoo to more coverage of the press conference where the newly uncovered victims had been revealed.

Q: Do you expect to find more?

A: We're digging up the grounds.

Q: What about the rumor that Roy Hardway's back in the U.S., that he's had plastic surgery?

A: No comment.

"You know," Lisa said to Raelyn, "I never fucked Roy. I'm being linked with him, and with Miguel Casablanca, and I never fucked either one."

Raelyn tried to assume an expression of sympathetic understanding. The night before, Lisa had totally lost it, thrown a tantrum, broken some glasses and a lamp, after seeing for the third or fourth time Code's "all-American kinkiness" remark. She was under tremendous pressure. Eric Lemongrass, on a talk show, had smiled and acted coy, showing his dimples, not coming out and saying it but clearly implying that Lisa had come on to him, that he'd turned her down. The tabloids proclaimed Lisa and Christine to have been lovers, to have attended a "bisexual black mass" together in New York. The voodoo-and-black magic angle was, from this point of view, why Lisa had gone to Brazil.

Penthouse was going to run nude stills taken on the set of *The L.A. Ripper.* She supposed they were of her in the dressing room, or walking around. Windfall profit for some voyeuristic gaffer or key grip. *Rolling Stone* wanted to talk to her. *People* was running a story on the unsolved case, running a black and white photo of Lisa's face on the cover in a little box.

Idea One was rushing *Manoa, City of Gold* into stateside distribution and pairing it as a double feature in some places with *Girl, 10, Murders Boys*. Lisa wasn't impressed. The newer film had been reviewed twice by the *Village Voice,* the paper that for many years had set her standards for all kinds of things. It was still important to her. Lucinda Max hated *Manoa* and went back in time to hate *Girl, 10;* she was someone, Lisa knew, whom the Roy Hardway connection was sure to annoy. The other writer, Emerson Gill, who was young and black and gay, liked *Manoa* as a "symphony of colors" and "an impressionistic visual tone poem" of medieval times. He mentioned the earlier film only briefly, calling it "a chilling study of a young female psychopath, shot in the same style as her emotional apprehension of her life." Lucinda Max, by contrast—and hers was the name with more weight—called the first film "typical morbid art-school tedium" and the second "unrelieved garish pain. Really, it's pornography with production values. I wanted very badly to walk out. I kept thinking, Is this a joke?" The review caused Lisa some anguish that strangers would read it and think badly of her, that they wouldn't think there was another side to all this stuff.

She and Raelyn hadn't slept together in the Topanga Canyon house. There was tension between them. Some nights Lisa tossed and turned, and her bedroom was right next to Raelyn's, but she was afraid of what would happen if she invited Raelyn in. Once they started again, they'd be at it all the time. She didn't know why this so troubled her, but it did. It was better, even if harder in a way, to be austere. Lisa couldn't actually connect the dots on why she shouldn't do it, but sometimes when they laughed together during the day, or when Raelyn reassured her about something, telling her earnestly that everything would be OK, telling her how talented she was, the friendship between them was so simple and pure, and Lisa trusted her totally in a way she might not have if Raelyn had been her sexual partner, because those things always came to an end. Look at Code, talking about her like that, so shamelessly. Big smile on his face. Loving it. What a motherfucker.

Sometimes they lay next to each other on the couch, sort of entangled, watching TV, and they embraced, and Raelyn sometimes rubbed her shoulders and back (Lisa had only once returned the favor). That was enough.

Raelyn, on the other hand, although resigned to the situation, believing she understood Lisa's position to some extent . . . still, she fantasized about her—tonight she borrowed Lisa's car and drove to a bar, kind of a long drive, but out here everything was.

The bouncer carded Raelyn; she looked that young. Well, she was barely twenty-one. Dressed neutrally: tailored black pants, cream-colored silk shirt, big silver bracelet. Sort of a young intellectual look, a bit innocent, maybe.

A lesbian Elvis impersonator was doing her act, which most everyone enjoyed. Raelyn went into the bathroom and watched a killer femme in a short-short skirt apply her lipstick, staring into the mirror. The femme smiled at a leather dyke who came in, greeting her by name.

Back in the bar, Raelyn was surprised when a tall young dyke with a blond crew cut, wearing sunglasses indoors, asked her if she could buy her a drink. Usually Raelyn made the advance.

"Do you want to dance?"

"Sure."

Rae didn't know her name, but she was looser than many butches, a better dancer . . . they had one more drink, or one sip each, before they decided to leave. They went to the other woman's home. Her name was Danica.

"How do you like it, big boy?" she said a while later, and Raelyn blushed intensely, she could hardly stand being rolled over this way. But her ass moved uncontrollably, and she was so wet, there was certainly no going back now.

"Make it pretty for me, baby. That's a nice little boy. All the way."

SIX

Breakfast at the Hollywood Canteen, on Seward, with Larry Planet, who asked Lisa not to judge Selwyn too harshly for bugging out. Larry had pronounced male pattern baldness, but was younger than he looked at first glance. He seemed very intelligent to Lisa, and very worldly wise, someone who knew how the game was played.

Lisa shrugged, or didn't respond. She had written Popcorn off, he was fucked, but since Popcorn was one of the people taking care of the house in Topanga Canyon, she wasn't about to start saying things she couldn't take back. It was true, she hadn't let Popcorn in on things, she hadn't confided in him. And his movie had been just about to open; if it had gotten derailed due to him, the studio would've held it against him. A lot of money was going into promoting *Call It Love*—and it had opened big, the Susan Heller cult was in full sway, even a certain dress she wore in it was becoming the fashion (of course, this too had been planned). Lisa blamed Popcorn anyway and now felt competitive with him, even if he was unbelievably far ahead, it was hopeless, she had already lost but she didn't care. Maybe in ten years he'd take seriously what she did. She knew it was misdirected—trying to get Daddy's attention, as her therapist had said when Lisa was thirteen—but she didn't care. Bad motives could fuel you as well as good ones could.

She was conscious that a few people were noticing her, recognizing her, giving her second and third looks. Larry Planet noticed it too. He smiled, as if this was what he had expected, what he had planned. Still, he seemed benign.

Lisa wore a long-sleeved red shirt and her totally ripped fucked-up jeans over red cotton tights. Rae hadn't come home with the car until five o'clock. It had been just about dead empty of gas.

Lisa ate sliced fruit arranged beautifully on her plate: mango, papaya, pineapple, kiwi. Larry picked at an omelet and seemed to particularly like his toast and jam. The coffee was great here.

Larry asked her what her plans were, and she told him how she'd been thinking about doing a film about Cassandra, but this was out of the question now since Christine's death.

"But I'm going to mess around, spend my own money . . . I'm going to be working on something very soon."

"Like what?"

She shook her head. Biting into toast made her see wheat fields somewhere. "I won't talk about it until I have something," she said.

"Well, you kept *Manoa* a secret . . . and maybe there are outside factors, sure, but it's getting attention and doing well."

"In New York," she said, somewhat dismissively. "I can't imagine people getting off on it down South or in the Midwest."

"We'll see," Larry said with a little smile, as if he thought she was playing at false modesty. She was all ready to say something about how she hated celebrity art, that kind of motivation for people to go see something, but something knowing in his expression held her back. He was two moves ahead of her, perhaps.

"I have a message for you," he said, and gave her a little slip of paper. "I know you've got a service, but for some reason this person convinced one of my secretaries you'd know who this is and want the call."

The note said, *Charles Head. Let's talk again soon.* Then in maybe thirty seconds Lisa had figured out a possibility: Chuck Suede.

On the way out, some guy backed up in front of her, taking photographs, and she didn't know what to do. "Come on, leave me alone" didn't seem to have any effect. If she changed direction, he did too, smiling in a creepy way, showing his teeth. She wasn't a fellow human being, she was prey. He was determined to keep getting her, to stay in her path. Maybe he was actually trying to bait her, to get her to swing at him with her purse. She couldn't do anything to him, she felt paralyzed.

Paparazzi. He'd make some money from this, but it was like there was more in it for him than that. Her notoriety made her, in this instance, again, despised. She finally managed to get in her car and drive away, unable to stop herself from giving him the finger as he began cannily shooting another roll of film. He wasn't human to her, though he probably had a wife and kids. And a screenplay.

She drove off to the athletic club, where she swam without incident, and then she went to visit Joey and Zed in Cucamonga to buy some necessary hallucinogens.

SEVEN

Profit favored nabbing Sender at the airport, but he listened to Dave, who said, "Why alarm him? Besides, let's see how he lives."

So that was the plan. They'd interview him for a while at his home, then take him downtown.

Alvin Sender had been in Jamaica as the executive producer of some special on swimwear, sponsored by five or six different designers, with twelve models—each different segment with a different swimwear line. Tommy Boy's new action prints. Their space-age silvers and golds. Estelle's floral patterns, or classic black and white. Like that. The resultant program would be sold, perhaps to ESPN. A topless or seminude version would be offered via an 800 number at the end of the show.

One of the models came home with Sender. While they were unpacking, they were visited by Bluestone and Brown. The event seemed to completely blow Sender's cool, while the girl, if anything, became even more blasé.

"Go in the other room, Cindy, OK? Wait for me there. If that's all right with you guys?"

"Just a minute," Brown said. "Cindy, you got a California driver's license?"

"Listen," Sender said, "she's with the Sable Agency in New York."

"You got a passport? Find it."

Brown followed her into the other room. He almost always felt hostility toward these young white bimbo-model-actress-hooker types, and it didn't give him any satisfaction to think how many of them he'd seen dead in the morgue, their faces rolled down the front of the skull while the coroner's assistant removed the inconsequential, bitchy, wet pink brain. Cindy, typically, had contempt for him. He was an ordinary-looking forty-five-year-old black man with a mustache and a receding hairline, a second wife and three kids from the first marriage living with another dad, the younger two having changed their name to Pendergraph. Brown hadn't had sex with his current wife in at least six months. All she wanted to do was go to church, to church socials and picnics, and, as much as possible, drag him along. Right now, at this moment, disconnected from this young bitch, he didn't care about her—the thought of his life, his inevitable mortality, all the things he'd missed . . . it made him sad. Then he forgot, turning his attention back to this fucked-up case.

He checked Cindy's passport, making a note of her hyphenated last name. The only address she'd give him was in care of the modeling agency in New York. He didn't think he had sufficient cause to search her luggage, looking for drugs.

Back in the living room, Bluestone ran a bluff on Sender.

He said, "We know you knew Candy St. Claire, so don't waste time trying to deny it. Now, tell me: Did you introduce her to Boro, or did Lauren Devoto?"

"He met her when he came over one day. She was lying out by the pool. Naked. He knelt down by her and started talking, I couldn't hear what was said. I went inside to turn the stereo down, and when I came back out she said, 'Yeah, sure.' And that was it. I think that was the only time she came over here."

Brown had inconspicuously come back into the room. Bluestone gave him a look that said, Don't break the mood.

Dave said, "Why was Boro visiting you?"

"It was something about a piece of furniture he thought I had. A couch. Upholstered with albino jaguar skin. I told him I knew nothing about it. I dealt in antiques and artworks, paintings and sculptures, but that was, like, ten years ago. I still invest in art, but only in stuff that I personally like. I told him to try the Horizon Gallery, they dealt a lot of things from Mexico and Latin America . . . since

Madonna drove up the price on Frida Kahlo, that's all been hot for a long time now. Yes, I know—the Horizon Gallery was the one run by Veronica, uh, you know . . . I just read about Lou in the *Times,* but you might remember that their son destroyed the gallery in some kind of weird publicity stunt. . . ."

"The same one who's dead."

"Right. But this was a couple months or so before that. I don't know if Boro went to see Veronica or not. That was the only time I ever saw him in my life."

"Who told him you might have this couch?"

"I have no idea. Really. I didn't ask. He's not the kind of person you question about details like that."

"What about Candy? How many more times did you see her?"

"Maybe twice. Just at the office. She got auditions for a couple of films. I wasn't really interested in her. I told her to get a boob job and come back in a few months. And to eat a healthier diet. All she wanted to eat was tortilla chips and Twinkies, Whoppers and fries."

"Were you her agent?"

"No. I'm not an agent. I'm a facilitator. I put people together, sometimes."

"Who was giving her these auditions?"

"I think it was Javitz Coolbaugh. He makes these ridiculously cheap exploitation films, they're supposed to be funny, vampires and chain saws and naked girls. Sometimes he does a hardcore version, though the hardcore market is shit. I have nothing to do with that kind of thing."

"Did you send Candy to meet Lauren Devoto?"

"Look, I saw Candy at one of Lauren's parties. I don't know anything about how she got there."

"What was she doing?"

"She liked to give head. She prided herself on how good she was."

"Just to men, or women too?" This from Brown.

"I don't know about women. I'm sure she would have put on a show if that was on the menu. She started out real young, thirteen or so, as a groupie, and the favorite thing those guys like to see is two girls going down on each other. That's entertainment in the back of the tour bus, when there's nothing to do."

"So Boro said something to her, she said, 'Yeah, sure,' and you don't know anything about the two of them beyond that?"

"Right," Sender answered, tan and fit, somehow more refined and intelligent-seeming than he needed to be. Bluestone thought this might be enough for a first shot. They could always come back and pick him up. He hesitated, then said, "Do you know Lisa Nova?"

"Mm, very slightly. We've met two or three times, at different places."

"Where?"

"Once at Code Parker's, when he had that place in Hollywood. And once at Lauren Devoto's, upstairs. There was a party downstairs. We could see it on the monitors. Selwyn Popcorn was there. I think that's all."

Bluestone ran through a few more names connected with the case. Yes, Sender had known Lou. Not very well, but enough to say hi.

"What about Roy Hardway?"

"Yes, I know Roy."

Something was making him nervous. Sender had told so much so readily, it had seemed like he was scared, but maybe that underestimated him, Bluestone thought.

"Where do you think Boro is?" Bluestone asked.

"My guess is that he's down in Yucatán or Guatemala and that he'll never be found. That's just my intuition. I don't think he'd hang around here."

Profit asked, after a few seconds had passed, "Why did Roy leave town the way he did? Supposedly he had this date with Lisa Nova, and they met some whores at a motel, and that's all anyone knows until he turned up in this film down in Brazil. Could he have flipped out and be back here in town?"

Sender said, shaking his head, "I've never understood what happened to Roy."

The detectives glanced at each other, shrugged, and then left on that note.

~ EIGHT

Lisa set the wooden kitchen chair backward in front of the three-paneled standing mirror in the room she thought of as her studio, because all of the filmmaking equipment was in here. She had taken the TVC15 an hour ago, then went for a swim, knowing from previous experience it would take a while to come on.

Now she sat in front of the three-sided mirror in her swimsuit, leaning on the back of the wooden chair. Bare feet on the wooden floor. She took a deep breath. Raelyn was gone to Redondo Beach or somewhere. It was a sunny, clear day. Lisa wore the mirror earrings. She recalled the pain of being tattooed and wondered if standing that pain then would make it any easier to withstand this ordeal. She thought vaguely about what she'd dreamed last night, trying to call it to mind.

She lost track of time. There were—it felt like she was asleep—there were fascinating things to look at in the mirrors. If she tried to really memorize them, they faded or blinked away; the trick was to just let it happen, flow into focus and out . . . a different sense of time. She was seeing what had happened in these mirrors, mostly women studying themselves, turning . . . this kind of thing was accessible to her, she saw it, it was there.

Deeply entranced now, she overcame the inertia of the heavy air, the molecules taking on color and weight and sheen, iridescent shimmers everywhere, even in the skin of the chair. She was interested in the pores of her own skin, she looked at her arm and then down at her tensed thigh, a half hour could go by or a single minute stretch out to some impossible lifetime of a dust mote, a subatomic particle smashing into a flamy gold interior sea. She licked her lips. What beautiful lips she had. Lisa wondered at herself.

It would be best if she did it quickly. She arranged the bowl in the most likely place. In the mirror, just glancing up, she caught a swift flash of the princess in her feathered garment, imagination or memory, but it gave Lisa strength. She had decided that without a forceps, she would have a hard time preventing the muscle from its natural urge to retract.

Left hand holding the Pennington forceps, she clamped her tongue and held it, pulled it a bit out, over the top curve of the wood. The stingray spine, with tape wrapped around it to effect a handle . . . she touched it to the pink, sensitive tongue flesh, watching in the mirror—then she really stabbed it, and she almost dropped the forceps, her eyes shut, tears welled out of her eyes uncontrollably, the pain was unbelievable, primitive, much worse than she could bear—but she did it, she was strong and she fucking jammed it, like the creation of the world, lava flowing and mountains falling and coming back up, burning rivers and creatures crawling from the swamp onto land, the soft ones eaten and ripped, the soft pretty ones torn apart, she pierced her tongue with the razorlike jagged spine, she made sure it was all the way through. Something big loomed in the mirror and she sensed it was the jaguar though she didn't see her, she waited before extracting the spine and then immediately groaned, she couldn't stand it, she stood up and staggered back, eyes closed . . . as the camera, on its own, began to run. It was quiet, but she knew that it was on. This calmed her a bit, though the hallucinogen made it hard to think, to understand.

She had taped over the eyepiece and left the lens cap on, so there was no possibility of any . . . the fucking blood in the bowl began to smoke, it fizzed, red smoke billowed up as Lisa felt an incredible wave of happiness and heightened pain. Her tortured tongue was huge, beating red-orange with every heartbeat, beating, filling her head. Everyone was her ancestor, she knew. Everyone in the ground and in the air. She would have cried out, but she was mute. Lisa screamed inside her mind. Animal wisdom, animal *now*, the jaguar shaman loves the captured flying bird of bleeding thought. The tattoos tingled like they possessed an electric charge. She could have danced on broken glass.

NINE

Kicking her feet and whimpering, Veronica was having a nightmare that evil children were coming up the alley to break in and rape her and kill her; she couldn't tell which window or door they were going to come in—she couldn't remember where the door was in the dark, and she was freaking out. . . . When she finally woke up and turned on the light, she saw that the door was in a completely different place than the configuration in her dream, and she wondered what that noise had been, it had sounded so real . . . probably a cat.

Steve Zen slept on his back and occasionally snored, the sleep of the beautiful, the dumb. He took more drugs than she would ever dare, but then he also took a lot of vitamins and protein supplements; he used to take steroids when he was into body sculpting to try to be Mr. Universe or whatever Arnold Schwarzenegger had been, but he said his sex organ had started to shrink and he'd feared it might be permanent, so he'd stopped the steroids and went on a program to exercise it all he could to stretch it back to its former bulk.

This corresponded to Veronica's needs in that, ever since a certain time, she'd needed a lot of sexual stimulation. Steve liked to at least eat her even when he was worn out from work.

Wanda, who had worked as a topless dancer, stripper, live-sex-show star, live nude dancer—always in demand, getting top dollar because of her shamelessness and, more than that, her total body tattoos—had taught Veronica self-hypnosis, and it worked. Veronica was able to get in touch with the power within and become a universe unto herself. She could block out everything else. She had been told that Lisa Nova had had a curse put on Lou and their family; it should have been obvious to her, but someone had had to tell her this, she had been that naive and inexperienced at her age.

Veronica went to the refrigerator, completely indifferent to the roaches that came out and patrolled the kitchen at night, and she opened the refrigerator door so that the light came on, she leaned on it . . . and then drank some of Steve's almond-flavored protein shake. She needed all the energy she could get. Her stomach felt queasy. Her asshole hurt, just one sharp twinge. She went to the backgammon box and found the Percodan bottle. Someone else's prescription, someone who had scratched and clawed at the label to keep from leaving their name. Steve had scored this off a john. It was sort of too bad to take a Percodan just to go back to sleep, but she didn't want any more bad dreams. That was too creepy. She didn't need that. Not when the curse remained. What a fucking thing to have done. How evil. She shuddered and lay down next to Steve, who said, in his sleep, distinctly, "It's all Greek, man. It's all Greek."

TEN

Raelyn came home to find that Lisa had written her a note: *Can't talk. Bit my tongue.* The author of this was on the couch, watching TV, sucking on pieces of ice.

On the way back from her new lover's, Rae had stopped in at the law offices of Watson Random—all the crank mail and love letters and fan mail were being routed there. The law clerk, Shelley, said that they were still getting twenty-some weird calls a day. A lot of this attempted communication had some religious angle, from old ladies praying to save Lisa's soul to satanists or pseudosatanists congratulating her on having evidently made a sale. There was also, naturally, a lot of sex stuff: nasty threats of rape with a Coke bottle, proposals of marriage from San Quentin, photos, Xeroxes of material—it was Raelyn's job to screen all this stuff, and she liked doing it. It was interesting, and since the weird feelings weren't directed toward her, she could view it mostly without alarm. Anything too specifically threatening was to be turned over to the police.

The whole process—seeing the fantasies people had, aimed at Lisa—made Rae feel very protective, as if Lisa were a fragile flower. She never showed her anything unless it was obviously funny . . . most of it was not. *Whore of Babylon, prepare to fry in Everlasting Hell,* or *Dear Cunt,* or *Thou shalt not suffer a witch to live.*

Headlines in the tabloids were things like "How Many Did She Kill?" and "Is Starlet Really a Killer Voodoo Queen?" As long as it was in the form of a question, it wasn't actionable. The answer could be none, or no. The less information actually offered in these stories, the better they worked. Next to a photo of Lisa, the interrogative headline read "Kill-Crazed Witch?"

"Are you OK?" Raelyn asked. "Can I see?"

Having her attention, Lisa slowly stuck out her wounded, swollen tongue. Raelyn thought it looked more like it had been stabbed than bitten, and gave Lisa a hard look, which Lisa seemed to register, to answer in a way, without telling her a damned thing. But Raelyn loved her. She had made a bargain—to accept Lisa with mysteries intact.

Rae had made gazpacho earlier, which was good, because now it was cold. They ate it. Lisa had another note for her: *The film is exposed, so please download the mags. It needs to go to the lab tomorrow, OK? Print everything.* By means of gesture, Lisa gave her to understand that she would tell her more when she could talk. It didn't make any sense to Raelyn, because when she looked in the studio, there was tape over the eyepiece and the lens cap was on. When they got the processed film back, what could it possibly show?

Well, she didn't think Lisa was crazy. So they'd see.

Lisa wrote a note: *Ice cream?* Rae smiled at her as if Lisa were a child. Yes, there was ice cream.

Then, with the remote, Lisa boosted the volume a little. The tall catatonic black man had escaped. He had been unresponsive, they hadn't known what to make of him, so he'd been turned over for psychiatric evaluation—and he had suddenly come to life and injured two guards on his way out.

"Uh-oh," Rae said, speaking for both of them. "Are you afraid of this guy?" she asked, and Lisa shrugged, shook her head. She didn't know, she wasn't sure.

When the cops—Detectives Lancaster and Gomez—came by, Lisa and Rae were just finishing their ice cream. Raelyn was torn between feeling hostile to them, like they were persecuting Lisa, and glad, like they *ought* to come by to warn her in person about the guy who'd escaped.

To show them that she really couldn't talk, Lisa tried. Raelyn had told them about the tongue injury, but they were skeptical; it seemed demeaning for Lisa to make those semiretarded sounds . . . Lancaster in particular had an attitude, from Raelyn's perspective. He thought he was good-looking, and of course he made it clear that he recognized Rae was a dyke. He was curious about what was going on, if they were sleeping together . . . he didn't come out and say things, but he had a way of making idle comments, walking around as if he owned the place.

"Nice room," he said, looking in Lisa's bedroom, turning on the light.

Gomez, by contrast, seemed all right in her way, as if she saw that her partner was a jerk but was powerless to intervene or cramp his style. She tried to look sympathetic, but she was an ambitious cop. Rae wouldn't trust her an inch.

Finally they left.

Lisa and Raelyn watched television in silence for a long time, the former continuing her regime of sucking on ice.

"It hurts pretty bad, huh?"

Lisa didn't nod, but she meant yes.

ELEVEN

In another two days Lisa could talk again, without too much difficulty, and she did in fact explain to Raelyn the magical basis of her art. She had to trust someone, and Rae was willing to believe what she saw without asking pointless questions. They settled into a routine.

Each day Lisa gazed into the mirror and went into a trance, and they shot three mags of film. Then, after Lisa had recovered a bit, they edited what had come back the day before, or at least categorized and cataloged the material viewed. There was dream stuff, fast little scenes coming from daily life, from memories—often from Lisa's point of view, but also sometimes in third person, with Lisa herself seen as she did this or that . . . and these scenes were in color; so far none had come through in black and white. Other, more mysterious scenes, possibly culled from the histories of the mirrors, were sometimes more restricted in viewpoint, frustrating in that one couldn't necessarily see what one wanted to see. Lisa could induce this sort of experience by merely closing her eyes and concentrating, then opening them and staring into her own dark pupils in the mirror until a different reflection began to appear; if she looked away, it was lost. Only once or twice did she try to catch these glimpses into the past on film, but if the camera was running, the transference worked, quite as though she had developed into an appendage of the machine.

What was hard was trying to control what she saw, to shape it, to direct the visions that would appear. This did seem to be possible, however, to some extent. This was what she wanted to experiment with, as well as with gazing into older, antique mirrors. As many different old mirrors as she could.

Should she keep notes, like her father undoubtedly would? She wasn't sure, but she thought not. She wasn't trying to amass evidence or prove anything. Rather, it was still so new, she just wanted to explore. Processing all this film was expensive, but the one positive bit of fallout from the publicity was that, for the moment at least, people wanted to invest in her, and it didn't seem to matter what sort of product she might turn out. They didn't care.

Lisa called the "Charles Head" number and, as she had suspected she might, connected with Chuck Suede.

"Why don't you come over?" she said. She had something in mind.

"Yeah, I'd like to see you. Quietly."

"Right." Her tongue was still sore enough that she tried to talk as little as she could. She spoke more slowly, more formally . . . she gave him the address. It was already eleven o'clock at night. He said he'd be there soon.

Each morning Lisa swam, and she swam again before dinner. She mourned Tavinho, but real sadness or grief for him only hit her at unpredictable moments; already all that felt sealed far away in the past. In a sense this seemed heartless, and she felt guilty, but the new faculty she possessed was so interesting, so exciting, it blotted out everything else.

The most interesting thing she was able to voyeuristically spy on in the mirror was what seemed to be an affair, perhaps back in the fifties, it might even have been the late forties—Lisa couldn't date the fashions too exactly. The woman's name was Mona, and she lived in a very different bungalow than this, someplace where you could hear the ocean . . . the light seemed to be California light. Lisa, watching—and almost none of this was captured on film, she'd watched for several hours, sort of tuning in and tuning out—observed that Mona spent a good deal of time checking herself out before the mirror. She was a kept woman. Her lover, an older guy, just forty or so, though, was married, and they talked a lot about his wife—when they weren't fucking, enthusiastically, in the bed. Mona really vocalized. "Oh Richard, Richard, oh God, oh God . . ." At first it was embarrassing, but Lisa was too curious to look away. Actually, she had never before been in a position to so closely observe two people having sex like this, in real time. It was illuminating. When Richard and Mona weren't considering the character of his wife, Elaine—who evidently had some degree of control over the money in the family, since when Mona asked Richard for money, he sometimes complained about how tight Elaine had become—they talked about plans for an ideal future. Richard was confident he'd have money, and they fantasized about going to Europe, New York, taking a cruise.

"I've always wanted to go on a ship," Mona said. They were both smoking cigarettes, drinking bourbon, lying in bed. Lisa could practically smell the sweat.

None of this was captured on film. It didn't matter. Lisa was interested in the possibilities. She wanted to know more. Maybe Richard and Mona would end up planning to murder Elaine . . . she hoped so. The thought quickened her pulse. Maybe this was evil, but . . . she wouldn't mind a plot.

Raelyn knew that Chuck Suede was coming over; she went into her room to read a novel while listening to her Walkman. She smiled, fairly benignly, before closing her door.

When Chuck arrived, Lisa offered him a drink. He looked good. His hair was darker now than it had been when he'd been into that total James Dean thing. Now maybe he was trying for a young Montgomery Clift. But he still had James Dean dimples when he smiled.

"When I said that I'd visit you 'quietly,' I meant without anybody seeing me, without publicity," he said, sitting near her on the couch.

"That's what I thought you meant."

"Well, it's hard for me to control myself, control my instincts—I've been doing this for twelve years. Since I was fourteen." He shook his head.

After a drink of Jack Daniel's, the heat of it down her throat, the low-level intoxication, made Lisa say, "Still, even if you're sneaking in tonight, it wouldn't be bad for you if it got out. Another little dark facet to your image, like it's a diamond, shiny bright."

He gave her an expression that wasn't really a smile, but it showed his dimples, he was amused, and he said, "That's not why I came over here, though. I like that, 'another dark facet'—it's true, in a way I wouldn't mind that—but I've been wanting to talk to you about . . . what to do with old Roy. His shrunken head, man. It seems like it's gotten pretty hot. I can keep a secret, but I'm going on location in a few weeks, and I'd sort of like to . . . bury it or burn it or something. Put it to rest. You know about these things, I'm guessing."

"Bring it over here next time you come," she said. "Put it in your bowling ball bag."

"How did you know?" Chuck said, raising his eyebrows. "How did you know that's where it's been? My sure-strike bowling ball's been out of its natural habitat for weeks. I'm letting down my team."

Lisa found this idea—and that of him being a serious bowler, which he was inventing—very funny, and they laughed together, playfully, like they were kids.

"If you want to use me for publicity," she said, "go ahead. But don't think you're doing me a favor—they'll just make me out to be more of a witch, or a slut."

"Yeah, you're right," he said in a measured way, dreamy-eyed, sincere or not. "Maybe I can do something else for you."

"Maybe you can," Lisa said, pushing her hair out of her eyes, waiting . . . then he leaned over and they kissed. She told him her tongue was sore, and so he was careful, delicate and gentle. Even so, there was pain in it for her. Lisa abandoned herself to Chuck Suede's embrace, his mouth, his hands. He caressed her and caressed her, her thighs, her stomach, taking a long time to unbutton and open her dress. He seemed to be very interested just in the feel of her skin. They kissed, and it was so expressive . . . there was no need to speak, to say anything, words were beside the point.

"Why don't we, uh, go in my room?"

"Yeah, sounds good."

She unbuttoned his shirt, kissed his chest, lingering, biting his nipples to see if he liked that. In her bed, without transition, they were naked, getting to know each other in the dark. Chuck could go from the play of an eight-year-old to hushed consecration in an instant, and she could too, she felt less socialized with him, it seemed less of a social encounter to be played by those rules . . . the layer of self-consciousness that, for instance, had certainly always been there when she'd been fucking Selwyn Popcorn. If she couldn't succeed in forgetting the social game she got nowhere, she had wanted to forget who she was and who Popcorn was, there was only intermittent, fleeting connection beyond these social selves. It was different with Chuck Suede. She didn't know if it was him, or if she was just in a peculiarly receptive mood. In the dark she didn't know where her body ended and his began.

She could have been dead. Tomorrowland—and she woke up having an orgasm in her coffin in her grave, a beautiful corpse, melting into the thick, thick air, the air lifting her up like she dwelt on the bottom of the sea. The life in the shook-up solution of shadowy minerals and salts, drifting, floating shapes, not yet ready to form and walk on land. Beating black.

You could forget everything like this. You could forget everything. You could go to sleep and not know who you were, who you were supposed to be.

~ TWELVE

Chuck was so lovable, Lisa couldn't help but suspect him a bit—although she was by no means immune to his lovability, no. She knew, though, that he was friends with Taft Flowers, and she could easily imagine him telling Taft how he had fucked Lisa Nova, saying, in a lovable, boyish way, "She's a great piece of ass," something like that, or that he went over to see if he could get some pussy, and he wouldn't mean anything by it, he was too lovable. The canniness he had about his position in the world as a megasuperstar didn't rule out innocence, he could afford to keep himself innocent, there were many things he probably would never have to see or know, which was why it was an open question how well he'd age . . . except, given that he was intense, he'd probably always be intense. Lisa loved him, but somewhat impersonally, sure, not like Tavinho—she knew what it was to be desired, but she had also known the other side, she had felt undesired, awkward, and fat. She knew what it was to go to a private-school dance at thirteen and be a wallflower, to be asked to dance only once. She didn't think Chuck Suede knew about things like that.

So, in the morning, she set about seeing if she could exploit him. Raelyn took some lovely Polaroids of them having breakfast together. Lisa and Chuck agreed on the best two. These were for Chuck to hold on to or leak as he saw fit.

He said, "Have you ever heard of Darby Crash?" His mouth was full of scone.

"No."

"See. Proves my point."

"Yeah. What?"

"Darby Crash was the lead singer of this band called the Germs, in 1978 or something. They were, like, America's answer to the Sex Pistols. Darby had this plan: He'd make one album, and be in one movie, and then he'd kill himself. The magnificent gesture."

"Yeah?" Lisa scratched her right breast.

"Well, you know, that's what he did. The Germs cut their album, which everybody liked, and Darby was pretty much the star of *The Decline of Western Civilization*, by Penelope Spheeris. You see that?"

Lisa shook her head. "I fell asleep during *Part Two: The Metal Years*." She waited for Chuck to go on.

He made a face.

"So, at the peak of his stardom, Darby Crash killed himself. It was big news. Only, the next day, John Lennon got shot."

"Oh."

"Right. He was a fool."

They went into the studio with Raelyn. Chuck seemed interested in Raelyn. Or at least, in a mild way, he put out some lovability rays. They showed him some footage on the console.

"I can look into mirrors," Lisa said, "and see things that have happened, the history in the mirror. I can sometimes put memories, or dreams, directly onto film."

"You don't have to convince me," Chuck said after a few moments. "Why shouldn't I believe you? Roy Hardway was never down in Brazil."

"No, it was all done after he was dead."

"OK. What do you want to do with me?"

Lisa told him about watching Richard and Mona in the mirror. It had suggested something to her.

She said, "I'd like to use that situation, but play off it. I'm Mona; you're Richard. It's, like, 1954. I want you to kill your wife. We fuck and bicker, and bicker and fuck—not too explicit, not too much nudity, I think too much skin distracts—and in the end you kill me because I've threatened you, and you want to stay with your rich wife."

"You're talking about shooting real footage, then, I take it—"

"A combination," she said. "I'd see what I could come up with . . . but yeah, we'd shoot a lot of it right here, with Raelyn."

"Off the books," Chuck said. "Let's sign a simple paper: fifty-fifty. You take care of expenses and Raelyn out of your half. I'll buy some film and shit, I'll pay some cash down at the lab. But we'll cut and sync as we go, right? I can give you two weeks, but after that . . . "

"That's fine."

"We improvise," he said. This was the part he loved. "It'll be sort of like *Last Tango in Paris*, won't it?"

"Yeah," Lisa said. "Two people in a room, basically. The other way to do something like that is *My Dinner with Andre*, but this is better, it's more like something I might do."

More stuff—some of it highly surreal—from Lisa's inner eye. They discussed Richard and Mona. Raelyn suggested they buy more Jack Daniel's and start smoking cigarettes.

"That's good," Chuck said. "I like to smoke." He laughed. Method all the way.

THIRTEEN

Rachel Farb leaped at it when Alvin Sender called her and asked if she'd like to collaborate with Lisa Nova's ex-boyfriend, Code, on a tell-all quickie biography of the voodoo priestess, the kill-crazed down-and-darkest femme fatale . . . It was totally cool! What a break! This book would be *huge*.

Rachel was not pretty, but with a kind of bent big nose and twisted smile, short haircut, hair dyed very dark purplish red, a stud in her left nostril, multiply pierced ears, and a taut, slender body, she was attractive, relatively speaking, in some punk sort of way. Alvin Sender knew her because she'd ground out a series of S&M porno novels, literally masturbating as she wrote them, "no plot to get in the way of the story," and she'd attempted to go on from there with the inevitable screenplays, but there was always something fucked up or too obviously ripped off about them, anyway she'd also done some secretarial work for Sender a couple of times. She'd also done some music journalism, on a very low-paying level, so maybe Sender figured this would give her something in common with Code, that she'd be familiar with his now defunct band.

Code was still living at Lauren Devoto's mansion, and the situation there seemed completely different from what Rachel expected. All she had ever heard was that Lauren was a dominatrix, that she liked to do things to young men and women both, that she paid hustlers large sums to be pierced or whatever, marked with her sign.

Evidently Code had flipped her. Lauren waited on them in a sexy French maid's costume, a red ball gag in her mouth, wearing light little chains, walking on impossibly high spiked fetish heels. It was weird.

There were no servants working here, Code explained, because Lauren's financial situation was not so wonderful as it had once been.

"Investment by astrology can go only so far," he said as they walked around, getting acquainted, smoking cigarettes and checking out many rooms emptied of furniture, all recently sold off. Code gave her this drug to take called Kick, and it made Rachel Farb feel outgoing and confident, a little itchy and thirsty. She felt talkative, she told Code her life story in about five minutes and then felt like elaborating, telling it all over again, but she zoomed in on what they needed to do and said, "Let's start taping, OK?"

Code smiled with nervous lips—she wondered how long he'd been high—and said sure. He had dyed black hair, cut short and spiky and messy, maybe some blue in there, earrings in each ear, wearing a charcoal gray shirt and baggy sand-colored brushed cotton trousers, wing tips, and he was drinking orange soda pop and walking around in circles the whole time he talked.

"Just a minute." Then he came back in with Lauren and hogtied her, using the ropes and rubber straps with great facility. Soon Lauren couldn't move, or at least move much. This was what Lauren wanted, Rachel Farb decided. Code gave Rachel an ironic, tired smile, an indecipherable shrug, and when he nodded, she pressed the red *record* button.

"I met Lisa Nova in New York, when she was in art school . . . before film school. She and I and her friend, Christine, used to get together occasionally for a *menage à trois*. Lisa loved to fuck, she loved to give head. She loved the taste of sperm. I think she had some voodoo theory about getting power from it—she and Christine were into all that stuff, they knew some Haitians and some old woman from Guadeloupe . . . it was, like, Lisa's dark side."

The insouciant smile made Rachel Farb understand they were doing fiction. She was restless, her body felt restless. She was turned on by Code's corrupt fuck-it-all philosophy of life, and his looks, all that.

"What happened here in Hollywood when she didn't make it?" Rachel asked after a while. They had finished yet another tape, and it was dark out. They had gone through the tactical liaison with Lou.

"Lisa financed that film she made in Brazil with tax-free money she made through prostitution. She was what you'd call, um, a high-class call girl. That's how Roy Hardway met her. He saw this video of her and fell in love with what he saw."

Rachel Farb was laughing. She'd had more Kick, and they were also drinking Bombay gin and tonic. Now that it was dark, it seemed more humid out. The door was open to the extensive terrace, but there was no breeze. Lauren was tied up on the couch in a position that incidentally revealed that she was a transsexual, a pre-op transsexual. Old Vincent Garbo had been married to a chick with a dick. This seemed unremarkable just now.

Code sat next to Rachel on the bed and rubbed her back. Then, without even kissing her yet, he helped her pull her olive-green t-shirt off over her head. She had dog tags, real ones collected from pawn shops, Vietnam vets. Nice little tufts of hair under her arms.

After sex they became hungry and took Lauren's black Mercedes to go get some food. When Rachel asked about Lauren—"Should we just leave her like that?"—Code said, "Sure. I'm so sick of that fucking bitch, you cannot imagine. Have you ever fistfucked anyone?"

"No. Why?"

"That's the ultimate for her. Do you wanna do it next time, maybe tomorrow night? It would be good research for you. We build up to it, down in the dungeon, downstairs."

"I'll think it over. Is it messy?"

"I don't know. What's *messy* anymore?" Code said, pensive as hell.

They went to McDonald's because of the take-out window, and Rachel said, as they ate, "If Lisa was this prostitute and that's how she met Roy Hardway and all that . . . who else did she do?"

"Oh, you want other names, like famous clientele?"

"Right."

"Let's think about that one for a while. Who would be good?"

Then, a little later, when Rachel realized there actually *was* a video of Lisa, she wanted to know if it was available, if she could see it.

"It's expensive," Code said. "It's become this incredible collector's item."

"Who sells it?"

"Who do you think? Your friend Sender."

"Oh."

Back on tape, unable to sleep: "You know Boro?"

"I met him twice," Code said. "He liked Lisa because she reminded him of Nastassja Kinski, or at least that's one story I heard."

"Really? I don't see it that much."

"I know. There's one movie, though . . . called *Harem*, where Nastassja gets kidnapped by this Arab sheik and taken away. Not too many video stores have it, because it wasn't very popular. I don't think it was ever theatrically released. Nastassja was still young, it was before she married that Egyptian millionaire and started having kids. . . . There's this one scene at the end, in a hotel room, where she takes off her top and gives Ben Kingsley—uh, Gandhi—this kind of 'Well, here it is' smoldering pouty look. That look is so totally Lisa."

"Yeah?"

"I've seen it a million times."

It was 7:30 A.M. by now, and Rachel needed a shower or something. She drank more gin, and shivered. It was cold out, kind of. She felt cold.

~ FOURTEEN

When Richard was away, Mona lolled around, drank, listened to music, had trouble sleeping, didn't know what to eat, hating to cook anything for just one and then throw away the rest. She cried sometimes, just out of nowhere, or when the afternoon passed and he did not come. Of course it was ridiculous to expect him to come every day, that was unrealistic, but still, every day, unless she specifically knew he wasn't coming, at about eleven o'clock or so she began to make herself up and lay out her prettiest clothes. It was for him, only for him. Afternoons were the only possible times for their trysts.

And then, more and more, after she had so longed for him, when he came to see her, the slaking of their mutual lust was not enough. She worked on him, to kill Elaine, and at first he was all for it, they fucked more wantonly with murder hovering over the bed. But he delayed, he picked holes in the plan, he seemed to lose his nerve. Elaine was ten years older, not especially blessed with good looks; it wasn't fair. Mona came to hate her more and more, and she built up a whole class-warfare justification for the planned crime. She said, "I'll do it if you won't, I'll kill that rich bitch in a second!" Richard slapped her, and then was sorry. She went down on him, her arms fiercely around his hips. She reminded him that this was something Elaine would never do. Elaine would not even kiss it, he had admitted once, and now, smoking a cigarette, Richard wished he'd kept his mouth shut.

"What if we don't get away with it? What if something goes wrong?" he said, in some anguish. "Then we've had it, we've thrown away our lives. If I'm going to risk my whole life like that—risk *dying*, being *executed* . . . I want to be goddamned sure."

"I can't go on like this," Mona said. "It's not so bad for you, you have your whole other life, you see people all the time, but I'm here like a prisoner, just waiting, waiting for you . . . and most of the time you don't come. When I really need you, when I'm so lonely . . . I can't call you, I'm just stuck. If I didn't love you, it would be different, I'd go meet a shoe salesman, bring him back here . . . just to talk to someone, to have someone to hold me during the night."

"You'd do that? You'd cheat on me?"

"I said if I didn't love you. But I do."

"And I love you," Richard said. "Every moment I'm in that house with Elaine, I'm thinking of you."

"Then why don't you just walk out, and we'll go away? I wouldn't care if we were poor. We'd be together."

Richard laughed briefly, scornfully, maybe more at himself than her, and shook his head.

"I need money," he said. "I'm not going back to taking orders from jerks."

"Let's kill her, then," Mona said. "We can figure out a way it'll look like an accident, and no one will ever know."

"Doesn't it bother you, just a little?" Richard asked, his head coming up from her breast. "The idea of taking a life? I'm worried that if I do that, if I kill someone, it'll drive me crazy, it'll haunt me the rest of my life. I worry that I won't be able to think about anything else. Everything will be poisoned; my conscience won't leave me alone. Aren't you afraid of something like that? If we love each other, maybe there's nothing more sure to destroy that love. You'll always have something on me, and I'll always have something on you. We might come to hate each other worse than we ever hated Elaine."

"It doesn't have to be like that," Mona said, after taking a drink. She wore lacy black underwear. One strap of the bra was down. When she turned a certain way, a tattoo could be seen on one cheek of her ass. There were no marks anywhere else. "You're too high-strung," she said. "You think about it too much. It's better to just *act,* do it, and then you forget. You're sensitive, I love that in you, but sometimes you have to be a Borgia, you know? You don't let anyone stand in your way. You just *act*. You do what needs to be done."

Richard, almost crying, yes, he was crying, shook his head, embracing her, his face visible over her shoulder. Maybe he was just drunk. He had a glass of golden bourbon in his hand. His mouth was open like he wanted to say something, like he was trying to speak, but nothing came out.

FIFTEEN

Veronica didn't know why she was having the memories she was having. They weren't hers. She was afraid she was going crazy, or that she'd been crazy for a while now. She remembered hiring the Mexicans to paint the giant moth on the side of the house, a project that was doomed to incompletion, events conspired against her, it would have been a powerful sign to keep evil away. Naturally, what with the curse that had befallen the family, her countermagic had to be foiled. The world was evil, and evil's representatives must win.

She had spent a month in New Mexico, with this odd group of people, they believed a spaceship was going to come and take them away, help them escape (not completely unreasonably, Veronica thought), before coming back to a burned-down house, no Lou, and then getting together with Steve Zen. Other things followed from that.

But she was crazy. She'd seen a short Guatemalan man with tattoos on his face come into her gallery and ask her for something. What had he wanted? She couldn't remember it right. It was different every time.

He had a two-headed penis, like a hammerhead shark, agile and long, wrapping around her neck. Or he spat on the floor, and within the gob of spit was the whole world. He said he wanted to buy a jaguar from her, a stuffed jaguar, and she said, "We're not taxidermists." He said, "You don't understand. The jaguar is white. It is a white woman with the spirit of a cat. You can tell me where this jaguar dwells." She said, "Get out of here and don't come back." He had said—was she imagining this now? it was all mixed up—he had said, "I'll send your son." Then Jonathan's art-project facsimile of a normal, naked white male had blown his mother's gallery into the sky.

She had called Steve Zen when she got back from New Mexico, and things had gone on from there. Steve knew some weird people. She had found out some things.

She was now waiting for a sign. The television was always on: "How Many Did She Kill?" Veronica reflectively clicked the remote.

Nobody knew where all Lou's money had gone. Veronica had the uncomfortable feeling that she was responsible for part of this shortfall, but she didn't want to think about it for a while.

She had wanted her fortune told, she'd wanted some things explained to her, and none of that was free. Everything had a price.

Veronica took a Heaven 17. It gave you a glittering yet soft-lined high. She cut out pictures, carefully, newspaper clippings and headlines, but mostly she liked photographs, she taped them to the mirror until it was all covered up, all you could see was the slut. She drew on this person with an ink pen, tattooing her face with swirls and curlicues, she drew with a thick crimson Marks-A-Lot, suggestive of blood (why not?), and sometimes she idly wrote words, cartoon-type voice balloons out of the person's mouth, and then it was hard to think of what to have her say. *Hi, I'm Lisa, I like to eat shit.* That was OK. Veronica burned fat red candles and arranged a couple of dildos, turned on this one that moved (batteries) in an obscene manner all by itself. One dildo was clear glass. She took another Heaven 17, and it soothed her, it melted her bones in a remarkable way. Her mind cleared. She hadn't gone crazy. She brushed her ash blond hair, walked around in her underwear, as lithe and boneless and full of poison as a walking serpent in disguise. Serpent goddess on this foul plain.

Veronica waited for Steve. When he came home, they laughed together about something. Steve was dressed up like a cowboy. He showed her his fast draw.

"Sometimes I'm the cowboy," he said, "sometimes I'm the Indian. Depends on the script," and Veronica, energized, laughing, tackled him onto the messy bed.

Did he still think he'd connected with a rich widow, that when the legal shit went through his future was set? Did he care?

"Let's do something," he said. "No, wait."

SIXTEEN

An image of a mirrored dressing room, soft focus, reflections multiplying, back and forth, forever, now out of focus, close-up on the face, a face that is now dry, but Mona's mascara has run, she is thinking, a bare shoulder, a strap, dissolve to an ice cube in a glass of bourbon, unmoving, the glass on a stand next to the bed, lose focus to diamondlike shards of light, a groan, someone is crawling on the hardwood floor, the grain of the polished wood, the spilled liquid flowing slowly, like mercury, toward a single pearl. Under the bed we find more, a pearl necklace must have broken, the window is open but from this angle nothing is visible, just bright light, not even the blue of the sky. The silent, slowly moving ceiling fan, going out of focus, like some kind of wings.

Then, in the afternoon light, a taut landscape that gradually becomes skin. A bead of sweat, leaving a track. Up from that to the extreme close-up of soft male lips, beyond which are the tongue and teeth, seen when the mouth opens to say something, or comes forward, merging into the darkness of the kiss.

In moving your head from one side of the room to the other, you briefly close your eyes. You do it automatically. Once you know the distance between two objects, you blink instinctively. You cut.

Black and white photographs of Richard's face, in a variety of expressions. Mona sorts through them, sitting at her vanity, several necklaces (including a string of pearls) lying in a jumble near her hands. Focus on her hands. Dark red nail polish. In one photo he is wearing a dark sport jacket and white shirt, and he appears to have been caught unawares, a lost look on his face, as he brings the cigarette up to his mouth. He is distracted, perhaps afraid. The photograph may have been taken in a bar. Clothes that are 1950s-style. She makes an almost silent exclamation, like a child playing a dreamy game with her dolls. Her hands are shaking a bit. She takes a sip from a glass. She brings the cigarette up to her lips and inhales. Just now, as she exhales pale smoke, she looks into her own eyes. The familiarity changes to something less assured, the gaze seems to tremble and lose confidence; she looks away, leaving the photos in disorder next to and partially covered by the jewelry and one small bottle of perfume.

A plane flying low overhead, out the window, at the same time that a bird chirps and a radio plays, low, some indistinguishable announcer's words, during a close survey of messed-up sheets. A foot sticks out. After some time it moves, and we see more of the ankle and the calf.

She eats, slowly, a piece of bread, with butter and red jam. Picks it up with one hand, looking at it before presenting it to her mouth. Her hair is messy, looks uncombed. No makeup. She sits at the wooden kitchen table, in a beige or flesh-tinted, slightly shiny slip in Venetian-blind horizontal stripes of light and shade. Pan in a blur over to an ant, which approaches a smear of jam, almost transparent, on the table some distance away from the plate. She makes a series of noises setting down her cup on its saucer, unable, evidently, at the moment of contact, to feel she has set it down right.

Split screen: Richard is smiling, then turning away from some people, hesitating before getting into his car. A Packard. The ant's mandibles descend to the sweet. Both are in brilliant, brilliant light. The ant is in sunshine, just barely out of a stripe of shade.

SEVENTEEN

It was just about ten-thirty in the evening when Alvin Sender thought he heard a noise outside. He opened the glass door, standing there shirtless and barefoot, wearing mellow blue velvet jeans, listening, scratching the hairs on his tanned chest. He heard something like a hissing, no, a whispering. Could it be Boro? Sender was frightened. But he'd never had any problems with Boro. Lauren had said he was out of the country, anyway.

"What is it?" snuggly fifteen-year-old runaway-turned-model Amber asked him, yawning, from the futon. Loaded on a combination of MC5 and Asti Spumante, up all last night on the Net, coming down now, drowsy, in T-shirt and black bikini bottom, golden hair, freckles, not really interested . . .

"Nothing, I think," he said, stepping back in, hesitant, the TV on without sound, lights low and pinkish violet, the place immaculate because the maid had come today.

Not really knowing why, he slipped on his soft turquoise rayon-silk velvet jacket, rumpled, with wide lapels, and red patent leather loafers—maybe if he went outside barefoot he'd step on a thorn. Could that have been—whispering, calling his name—someone who didn't wish to be seen? What did that mean? If it was a customer, then who? Why not simply call?

He stepped outside, smelling the flowers. It was dark, the sky purplish, no stars or visible moon.

"Hello?" he tried experimentally, and heard or sensed a movement, not much, but then he cried out, involuntarily, in shock, knowing nothing really, as the axe split open his head. He cried out, knowing that something tremendously significant had occurred. A great light shone into his skull and flooded down his face. He fell sideways, staggering, falling back into the beckoning safety within. Screaming, not his. He knew everything now, understanding, he saw impossibly swift Technicolor visions, mouth open as if packed with black earth. It was impossible to tell what he knew. The axe stuck there, bisecting his brain, as Amber expeditiously ran out the front door.

EIGHTEEN

They had called Larry Planet, and he had provided them with instant technical assistance. And so for several days Kenny the sound man and Mark the lighting guy, Danny the cameraman and Scott the assistant camera guy (who also operated the boom) had been present to help. Then, after they left, Lisa and Raelyn edited the previous day's stuff. Raelyn, from her experience in theater, helped with makeup and such. The skin tones for the body makeup covering Lisa's upper-arm tattoos had to be exactly right. Camera angles and lighting would help. Plus work in the lab.

Tonight Larry had come over and hung around with Chuck, watching a baseball game. Larry had brought take-out Mexican from some expensive restaurant in Santa Monica. After a couple hours more of editing and splicing, Lisa and Rae, exhausted, came in to have a couple of beers and watch the end of the game. It went into extra innings. Lisa lay with her head on Chuck's shoulder. Edgar G. Ulmer used to shoot films in six days. He shot *Detour* in six days. Jean-Luc Godard protested when some of his French brethren, in the early sixties, devoted an issue of their magazine to acclaiming Ulmer. Godard thought that they were lowering their standards, that this craze for Hollywood *noir* was getting out of hand.

Because he was so "method," Chuck usually went home for the night, returning at noon the next day. There were two problems in Lisa's mind right now. One was the final fuck scene. The other was, how should she die? A knife was always good, because it was personal, it was intimate, and you get the visual excitement of the color red. They'd wrestle and struggle; Mona was almost as strong as Richard. OK.

The fuck scene . . . well, after watching the real Mona, Lisa wanted to emulate her, but the idea of faking such an orgasm was embarrassing, faking it in front of the crew. Mostly the shot would be her face and Richard's: Richard watching her come. This acting shit. It almost seemed like it would be better just to fuck and take her chances like that. Chuck would be up for it, she knew. No, it was ridiculous.

She ate some more popcorn, drank some more cold Beck's beer. If they had to, they could do all kinds of retakes. The title, at this point, was *Glamorpuss*.

One thing that would cost a little money was the score. Chuck wanted an old-fashioned full orchestra; if it was melodrama, then go all the way, right? People talked about tragedy, but most everything ended up melodrama anyway. *Hamlet* was melodrama. So was *King Lear*.

Lisa's cat was on her lap. Caz liked her hand best, but he also really seemed to enjoy being petted by Chuck and Raelyn. He was promiscuous.

The Dodgers won the game. Chuck and Larry went away. Leaving the beer bottles out, Lisa and Rae, in just fifteen minutes or so, headed to their respective rooms. It was after midnight. Lisa was really yawning, beat. She fell asleep wearing only a marigold yellow cotton T-shirt, the ceiling fan sluggishly circulating the warm and humid air.

NINETEEN

The cops burst in, only Lisa didn't realize at first who it was—there may have been an element of playacting in this, of dramatization—she had been dreaming, deeply, presumably about some of what she had seen in the company of the jaguar . . . anyway, she fought them, struggling wildly, perhaps in the midst of it even managing, as her arms were being restrained, managing some version of a kung fu kick, striking with her heel the head of Detective Gomez and knocking her down, right out of sight.

"You fucking bitch," Lancaster said, and Lisa tried to spit in his face but was jerked off her feet by the handcuffs and pinned down on the polished wood floor. This bumped her head and hurt her knees. She panted and groaned.

Lancaster had woken her up by loudly smacking—spanking—her bare buttock with his hand.

"I always knew you had more," she now thought he had said; he must have meant tattoos. Then she'd gone wild. A big blond uniformed cop had grabbed her; he'd been way too strong. He was still kneeling by her, his hand on her shoulder blade, holding her down. She remembered that she had nothing on below the waist. She let out a big sigh and lay calm and still.

"What the fuck is going on?" she asked, in a semireasonable voice that came out more choked up than she would have wished.

"Why don't you shut up until we get downtown?" Lancaster said, walking over, his shoes right next to her face. "You're not helping yourself, adding resisting arrest to murder with an axe. Gomez here'll need to have stitches."

Did he really give a shit about Gomez? Lisa didn't think so. She thought he was pleased. As the police rummaged through the house she gave up trying to guess what they were doing, what they might get into or wreck.

"Can I get dressed?" she asked the blond cop, and he didn't reply. A few minutes later he said to someone across the room, "Why don't you see if you can find her pants?"

They allowed her to stand up, handcuffed, the Aryan cop rather absurdly holding on to her by the arm as another uniformed cop, a blond female, held the jeans so Lisa could step into the legs. It was humiliating. She knew Lancaster was watching, staring at her pubic hair and such. She wouldn't look at him. Her hair was somewhat in her face anyway—she looked down at the floor, avoiding faces and eyes, as they took her out the broken-in front door, out past the bright lights of the press . . . fuckers yelling at her, saying her name, as if there was much to say at a moment like this. Maybe they were just trying to get her to look up.

Sitting handcuffed in the backseat, Lisa realized that if they put the brakes on suddenly, she'd crash face first into the Plexiglas barrier without the usual guarding reflex of the hands. So she braced herself, bare feet up, knees flexed. It gave her something to do. A few stray tears fell, she couldn't help it, she wasn't that tough, she shook her head and said to herself, "Why? When will this shit come to an end?" She cried for Tavinho again, hating to let them see her break down, those clear blue übermensch eyes studying her in the rearview mirror. There was nothing she could wipe her face on . . . if she'd had the use of her hands, she could have pulled up some of the T-shirt material, but that option was lost.

At the police station, news cameras again. She kept her head down, though she stumbled on the top step, she stubbed her toe.

"Ouch. Come on, slow down."

They slowed just a little bit; in the light of the hall, she saw that her right big toe was bleeding a small amount of bright red blood.

In the big, modern area, with the computers, something like a newspaper office but more unfriendly, they sat her down, waiting for whatever. Detective Lancaster was probably still outside, schmoozing with the press.

Standing nearest to her was the female officer who'd helped her into her jeans. Extremely poker-faced, tan, with her blond hair in a ponytail, gun there on her hip.

"Would you wipe my face, please? Would that be OK?"

The woman looked around—Lisa thought of her as being named Debbie—and then replied. "Do you want a tissue? We can't undo your hands, you know." When Lisa looked dismayed, if resigned,

Debbie said, "Here, I'll do it for you." And she did, even cleaning up the prisoner's runny nose.

"Thank you. I really appreciate it."

"You're welcome," Debbie said formally, and that was that.

Lancaster came in, and with a movement of his head indicated that he wanted Lisa walked into an interrogation room.

"Why don't you undo my handcuffs? They're too tight, they're hurting me."

"You assaulted an officer," he said superciliously, almost smiling a little.

"You broke into my bedroom when I was asleep, I didn't know what the fuck was going on. I still don't. I want access to a phone."

"Did anyone read her her rights?" asked another man in a suit, older, someone Lisa had seen here before but didn't know.

Lisa spoke to him, even though he didn't look particularly nice, saying, "They didn't read me my rights, they didn't say they were police, they've never explained any of this to me. They just broke in and started beating the shit out of me in my own bed. Call my attorney, Watson Random."

"We know who he is," Lancaster said. "And the videotape of the scene will show we knocked on the door and called out who we were before we went in."

"I was *asleep*!"

The older guy went out of the room. It was just Lisa and Detective Lancaster. She then did something she knew she might regret, but emotion took over, having to look at him, and she said, "If I have to go through getting booked and fingerfucked by a matron again, just because of you . . . I'm gonna fucking kill you," and she wasn't sure what she was doing, she looked from his face down to his belly, his crotch, she felt something loosen, and his face changed . . . the tan material of his pants darkened at the groin and down his thigh, he pissed himself, and from his eyes it looked like he dimly saw some connection, it shook him, he dropped his Styrofoam cup of coffee and, trying to control himself, in a very strained voice, got out, "It's a felony to threaten an officer of the—excuse me . . ." and he walked funny out of the room.

Was there urine on the floor? Yes, but next to the spilled coffee you couldn't really tell, even if he left a trail.

Detective Brown came in and said Bluestone would be arriving anytime now.

"I'm not talking to you guys. Nobody's told me a thing. What's going on? Lancaster and Gomez just broke in and jumped me in my bed, like a gangbang."

"Well, you remember Alvin Sender?"

"Sure," Lisa said.

"Tonight he caught a hatchet in the head. Naturally we're curious where you might have been."

"Larry Planet and Chuck Suede were over, watching the baseball game. Ask Raelyn."

"We will." Brown considered her answer, looked down, looked at her again. Then he came around to unlock the cuffs. He put the phone down in front of her and said, "Make your call."

Bluestone showed up, and Brown went out to talk to him in the hall. Watson Random was on his way. The two questions seemed to be, for now, When had Sender been killed? And what time had the baseball game ended? In any case, if Planet and Suede had really spent the evening at the Topanga Canyon house, it was a vastly different circumstance than if it had been just Lisa and her friend Raelyn. What about the tall black guy, who'd escaped from custody not too many days back?

A janitor—an old white man—came in to mop up the spill. In a few minutes Bluestone walked in and said, after sitting down across from her, "You really didn't hear them say they were police?"

She shook her head.

"Who won the ball game?"

"Dodgers. In the twelfth. The Mets' guy couldn't throw the ball over the plate."

"Yeah. I watched it too. Until I got the call." He appeared to be thinking it over, rolling a Life Saver around in his mouth. "What happened to Lancaster in here with you?"

She shrugged. A gesture: I don't know.

"He says he suddenly got the flu really bad."

Bluestone looked at her as if he knew something or suspected something—but this was the way he looked a good deal of the time. It was a mannerism, a ploy.

"He abused me," Lisa said. "I don't think he can get away with treating me like that. I'll see what Watson thinks." Then she added, out of spite, "He acts like he's on drugs." She was sort of trying this out, to see if it got a reaction.

Bluestone didn't say anything, though, and now Brown came in with coffee, followed by Debbie with a box of donuts.

"Somebody's checking the mileage," Brown said, "but it doesn't seem likely if you really saw the end of the game. Larry Planet confirms it over the phone. He'll give us a statement tomorrow morning. Clark's still trying to get hold of Chuck Suede."

Lisa kept her mouth shut. She had the impression that neither of them much liked Lancaster, but she didn't want to spoil things by threatening to sue. They'd close ranks then for sure.

Detective Brown said, after a bite of glazed donut, holding up the rest, gesturing with it, "So tell us: Did you kill him? Did you hit him in the head with an axe?"

There was some kind of obscure cop humor going on here between the two men. Lisa said, without annoyance, "No. I didn't do it."

"You hear that? She didn't do it," Brown said, looking over at his friend, who nodded without surprise and indicated with a slight head movement that Lisa should take a donut from the cardboard box, so she did.

After a while Lancaster appeared in the doorway; it looked like there had been water all over the front of his clothes, on his shirt and tie and even in his hair, obviously he'd splashed himself and washed himself as best he could. But he seemed rattled, he didn't linger, it didn't seem like the other two detectives wanted him, so he just said, "I'm going to my desk. I've got some things to check out on the computer."

It was satisfying to see an enemy so shaken. Lisa remained deadpan.

In a few moments Brown said, shaking his head, "Well, it looks like the best thing to do is blame it on the black man. James Doe." He sighed and wiped his mouth with a napkin, wiping his fingers as well.

Bluestone said, "Looks like the tall black guy or some assailant unknown. That is, if it's true, like everyone's assuming, that Boro's gone south."

"Blame it on the black man," Brown said again, making a kind of mournful, deep joke. Then he spoke to Lisa directly, asking, "Are you in danger?"—like she would know.

As a matter of fact, she had been seriously considering this question, on one level or another, since the moment it had become clear what happened to Sender. Whom did she suspect? The tall black guy, "James Doe," zombie or not, and the other zombies still at large—she didn't see them as doing something out in the open like this. She thought they'd hole up somewhere and not be too dangerous unless disturbed, or unless—she didn't know—they needed something to eat.

The people in costume comprised the evil unknown. The guy in the bird suit and the Aztec warrior.

"I don't know who it is," Lisa said, glancing into both men's eyes, demonstrating sincerity, admitting she was afraid. Showing a certain desire to please.

"What about the black man?" asked Brown, intently.

"I have this *feeling,*" Lisa said, "that he isn't a big threat to me, that he's just gonna go away, they just used him as a prop . . . but I don't know what he wants. Maybe he was supposed to be the one who killed me in the Black Dahlia thing."

"What Black Dahlia thing?" asked Bluestone, and she realized she'd gone too far. But she felt like talking now . . . it was a relief.

"Boro wanted to stage this kind of Black Dahlia murder, with me as the victim, the star . . . he was playing with me, and I was never sure if he meant it or if he was just trying to get me to act a certain way."

"Tell us more," Brown said. "He told you all this, and you kept going out there? Or what?"

"I, uh, acted it out for him one night. He said it would get it out of his system, to see it, you know, as a *tableau vivant*. It was really dumb, but he told me I could take back Christine, so I went along. It was too gross, and too intense, and I got sick."

"What do you mean," injected Bluestone, "you 'went along'? The Black Dahlia was cut in two." This idea seemed to make him mad.

"I dressed up," Lisa said reluctantly, "and lay down on this bed, in a set, like a hotel room . . . and then I passed out for a little while, after the tall black guy played this tape, and when I woke up I was covered in blood and shit. They all applauded, and I went into the bathroom and threw up. And then he didn't let me take Christine. He called the scene Tomorrowland and said that was how I was going to end up. I ran away and went looking for Christine anyway, but I couldn't find her."

It went on, and at one point, when they touched on Boro again, Lisa blurted out that it was her opinion he was dead. She said she had no evidence, that this was just her belief.

Watson Random arrived, and he and Lisa talked for a while, alone. Then Watson talked with Brown, and Lisa was allowed to leave.

Raelyn was waiting to go, all indignant, but Lisa's own feelings had been soothed by the trick she'd played on Lancaster, and by the fact that nobody was saying anything any longer about resisting arrest or assaulting Gomez, and she thought this was quite a concession on their part. She felt weird that she'd talked so much. A little mournful, too, though not exactly because Alvin Sender'd been killed.

~ TWENTY

Lauren said, "It isn't as bad as it looks."

She and the detective sat on the only two chairs left in the large living room, two wooden chairs, incongruous, the only pieces of furniture to be seen. No carpeting, either. There was a vacancy surrounding them, and the windows seemed far away. Lauren wore a black bustier top, a champagne-colored little jacket and skirt . . . she had the look of an aging sex symbol, heavy makeup on her face, exquisitely composed, blond hair tumbling in uncountable ringlets, a certain confidence peculiar to Hollywood in Detective Brown's experience, he a somewhat roly-poly black man dealing with these celluloid folk. No woman twenty years old, or thirty, would wear so much makeup, but it mimicked beautiful youth, it came close to a kind of beauty—it probably created a perfect illusion when seen the right distance away. He could smell her expensive perfume. Her throat . . . her throat was a slightly different shade of flesh-pink, and it had too many muscles or tendons that moved when she spoke, or simply thought—this throat gave her away.

"I didn't say it looked bad," Brown said—thank God the air-conditioning reached them here, quite efficiently, for outside it was nearly a hundred degrees.

"I'm going to go for an ultramodern, even futuristic look," Lauren began. "I have this Italian interior decorator all ready to go . . . I needed to clear out all these antiques, sell them or put them in storage. Besides, having some of the rooms empty gives you a better idea of the space."

Profit Brown looked around. Bluestone was off somewhere else talking to Code, who'd greeted them shirtless, with three days' growth of beard, looking like a male model or an actor, offering them ice-cold beers.

"I didn't say a word about the lack of furniture. All I'm thinking about . . . well, excuse me for saying it, but you don't seem too busted up with grief over your friend Alvin Sender getting killed."

"Business associate, Detective Brown. And barely that. He was into a lot of disreputable things. I'm sure he had a million enemies. I'm not really surprised he met a violent end."

Brown just looked around again. "Amber . . . the girl he was with last night . . . the one who ran away when she saw him with an axe sticking out of his head . . . she says he had some videos, you know, of this Lisa Nova."

"What about it?"

"Nothing, I guess. I just wondered if you knew who might have wanted them, those videos, 'cause we didn't find any there at the scene."

Lauren appeared to think about this. Brown wondered if she was high, and if so, on what. She had a hard to read smile.

She said, "Well, the first person that comes to mind is someone I'm sure you've already thought of."

"Don't assume we've thought of anything. Tell me, who comes to mind? We overlook the obvious all the time."

"Well, then . . . Lisa Nova herself, of course."

"Yeah, I suppose she might want to get hold of them, if they're like some people say. Have you ever seen this video yourself?"

"No. I've only heard about it. Rumors."

"There's a lot of rumors about that girl."

Meanwhile, in the control room, Code couldn't sit still, but he was amiably, even fondly dispensing his views to Detective Bluestone while Detective Gomez was outside on the grounds with Rachel Farb. (Gomez's partner, Lancaster, was out sick.)

Code said, "So many people—just about anybody in the entertainment industry, ha, which means most of America in some metaphysical, hypothetical, in-their-dreams type of sense—would *kill* to get this kind of publicity. They would, quite literally, kill, they'd sacrifice a stranger at the crossroads on a moonlit night, they'd do it and it wouldn't be enough, you know? Lisa is the chosen one, you can't buy or plan or ever anticipate this kind of luck—maybe she did exactly that, what I was saying, maybe she sacrificed an innocent, made a pact with the devil like Robert Johnson the blues player or Frank Sinatra or some such . . . and now she's gotta wait until the devil comes to claim her soul."

"You were close to her. Would she do something like that? Does she have that kind of lust for fame?" Bluestone asked, trying to play into Code's mood, flatter him somewhat, as he sensed a part of Code wanted to be admired for his brains, his understanding of the world, his canniness, judged not as a hustler but as something more.

"Where you been?" Code said, his answer, smiling. "Who did she know? Who did she get next to, in fact? The mystery man, the one nobody knows. Boro. I met Boro twice. I made a call for him once, to Lisa when she was in New York. He said to me, 'I *own* her.' What do you think he meant by that? She's got everything the way she wants now, even if she can hardly go outside because the paparazzi nag her like dogs after a big leopard in a tree. But she loves all that, man. All that attention. She's a fame junkie. The whole world's watching her now."

"She told me she thought Boro was dead."

"He might be. Then who killed Alvin Sender? I don't know. That might be peripheral, a sideshow, a joke. Ask yourself this, just as a character question: What was Lisa doing with Selwyn Popcorn? What was she doing with Roy Hardway? She's not innocent in all this. She's impure."

"That's what my partner keeps telling me," said Bluestone in a rare moment wherein he felt like confiding something in return, because he knew Code would appreciate it, and he did, it was between the two of them—at the same time as there was also, somehow, an unspoken affection for Lisa, or if not straightforward affection, then a mutual acknowledgment of her spell, her charm. . . .

"I'm doing a tell-all with Rachel Farb," Code said, looking into Bluestone's face. "My contribution to the Lisa Nova cult. Tell me: Do you think I'm scum?"

"I don't know enough about you to judge you," the homicide detective replied. "For instance, I don't necessarily see very deeply into what you're doing right here, in this house."

"Uh-huh," Code said, maybe a bit offended, or simply embarrassed, scratching his nipple and frowning, finishing off a beer gone warm. "I completely understand what you're saying," he said, but the momentary communion had slipped away.

Bluestone and Brown sent Detective Gomez to make some phone calls, tasking her with tracking down definitively Lou's daughter, Celia, who had not come west for her father's funeral: why not? She was supposed to be in North Carolina, where she was going to school, but no one had talked to her yet. Or was she in Israel? Nobody knew. Find her. She's a loose end. Think how meaningful it might be if it turns out she's secretly here in L.A.

Bluestone and Brown drove over to where Lou's house was, they were in the neighborhood—that fire had never been satisfactorily explained. The house hadn't burned all the way down. The wall on which Veronica had hired the Mexicans to paint the giant death's-head moth still stood. It was hot as hell, but they got out of the car and walked out to take a closer look.

"She owned that art gallery, didn't she?" Profit Brown asked rhetorically, not caring if Bluestone answered or not. "And her son was some kind of artist, or at least he'd been an art student, he was a wanna-be . . . a fuck-off."

"Yeah, so?"

"I don't know," Brown said, coat off, red tie loosened, kicking some pieces of doll's bodies or something that had been half rescued from the flames and then discarded. He was thinking.

"Let's go see the widow," Bluestone said.

They stopped to pick up Sno-Kones on the way. Jesus, it was hot. Especially when you were stuck in traffic, gas fumes levitating up like wobbly mini-mirages; wearing sunglasses didn't seem to affect one bit the overwhelming desertlike brightness shining off the concrete.

Veronica was sitting on the front porch, in the shade, wearing sunglasses and a little black dress, her ash blond hair pulled back in a messy ponytail, her skin so white, so pale, translucent . . . with bruises on her legs.

"I'm still in mourning," she said, and removed the sunglasses when Bluestone removed his. "I heard about Alvin Sender," she said. "Do you have a suspect, or are you just revisiting everyone who has any possible connection to the larger unsolved case?"

"Jesus," Profit Brown said. "You got an attitude today." He sounded like he was developing one himself.

Some Latin kids were playing, young enough so they seemed to require no props, just running from one place to another, talking in sped-up, excited voices, sometimes shrieking with laughter, the little girls screaming just to scream.

"Listen," Veronica went on, "Lou and I were all right. He had an affair. I forgave him. Maybe he had others through the years—a man in his position has a lot of opportunities—but for the most part they meant about as much to him as masturbating to *Playboy* magazine. I think Lisa Nova got him somehow involved with this Venezuelan gangster Boro, and I don't know what happened after that. My son Jonathan . . . was an artist, and I'm afraid he tended to think of his whole life as performance art, like somebody was following him around, filming it; he would turn around now and then to make deadpan remarks. He wanted to find out what happened to his father, and he got in over his head. I don't even necessarily think Nova had anything to do with any of it beyond bringing Lou and Jonathan to Boro's attention. I've never met her, but I don't have the impression she's exactly capable of masterminding a complicated plot."

"Hard to say," Profit Brown said, sweating profusely, wiping his face with a clean sky blue handkerchief.

"My husband was a fine man," Veronica continued, still somewhat inexplicably antagonistic, "and I know he'd want people to remember him for the great movies he produced, like *Monkey on My Back* or *Stone the Sinner,* with Dirk Young." She seemed to forget what she was going to say next; she paused, almost stammered, then wouldn't go on.

When it was clear she'd finished, Bluestone said, changing the subject completely, almost as if he'd heard or understood nothing, "Where is Steve Zen today?"

"He's inside, sleeping. I don't want to disturb him; he didn't sleep well last night in the heat."

"Are you aware of his record?"

"I know there were some misunderstandings."

"You could call them that, I guess. He was a trainer and masseuse, but he kept getting these complaints that he became overly familiar. There were a couple of rape charges that for one reason or another never went to trial. Plus one conviction for prostitution, possession of a controlled substance, assault—"

"You're not going to tear him down to me," Veronica said with asperity, putting her sunglasses back on. "He and I get along, we're good for each other, but I wouldn't expect you to understand or even try."

"Can we come inside for a moment? Not to wake Steve up, I promise, but to use your telephone?"

"I'm sorry, no. It's a mess."

"We won't even look," Bluestone said. "It's just something I forgot to tell Detective Gomez down at the station."

"No. You can't come in. It's just too messy. I'd be embarrassed. There's a pay phone around the corner at the Korean grocery."

"Everyone's got secrets, don't they?" Profit said back in the car, and Dave Bluestone agreed.

"I wonder if Steve was really in there sleeping or not."

Profit Brown shrugged. "She was telling us stories, that's for damn sure. 'My husband was a fine man.' Shit."

When they'd interviewed Steve Zen before, he'd been excessively friendly. He said he'd always wanted to be a cop himself. He was a type they'd often seen: sleazeballs who thought it was a big joke to butter up the police. Like they were tricking you. People never realized how many hundreds of times you saw the same fucking acts.

The detectives were tired; they felt disillusioned and out of their depth. Everybody was lying, everybody was telling some part of the truth. Poor Gomez was still working, staying late, a tiny Band-Aid on her eyebrow covering the spot where she'd had three stitches put in after being kicked by Lisa Nova during Phil Lancaster's ill-considered roust.

TWENTY-ONE

Richard sometimes affectionately called Mona "Glamorpuss," sort of kidding, but it pleased her; she liked the way his regard could make her feel. When they fucked, perhaps she exaggerated her histrionics with some corner of her consciousness, wanting to make him feel powerful—as well as, effectively, to spur him on—but it all worked, the sex charge was very strong. If everything else went wrong, they could always rediscover their love by going to bed.

It took a while, after the fuck, for things to go sour again. They smoked cigarettes and drank bourbon. Looked up at the ceiling fan.

Some bebop jazz was playing somewhere, from the neighborhood. Wardell Gray on the sax. "Twisted." His signature tune.

Richard and Mona were both completely naked, except for her pearl necklace and earrings. She lay on her stomach, head up, resting on her elbows, forearms down, Richard's left hand idly, slowly fondling her buttocks, her thighs. He was on his back, looking up, knowing her by touch, like the blind.

Finally she said, "You're not going to do it, are you?"

"Do what?" although he knew.

She didn't speak to him. Her face gradually changed as she thought about her situation . . . maybe she overdramatized it, but she started crying, no sobs, just tears, her hair was unkempt with fuck-sweat, and now she just let the tears roll down her cheeks.

"Glamorpuss," he said affectionately, touching her head, trying to defuse her, to reach her sentimentally.

"I just can't go on like this anymore," she said. "If we can't be together, I'd rather be dead. I mean it. You don't understand how unhappy I get when you're not here. It's like the house is haunted or something . . . all the bad demons whisper to me in the middle of the night, and I wake up and turn on the light, I'm afraid to go back to sleep . . . I can't stand it. I'm so alone."

"I'm here for you," Richard said. "I just don't want to murder someone. Things aren't perfect, but . . . I don't think they ever are. This way we have money, I can buy you things, keep this house, and if you can be patient, if you can only wait a little while . . . she's not that healthy, her stomach hurts her all the time, something's really wrong. . . ."

"I can't wait," said Mona, intoxicating herself, shaking her head back and forth, getting up, standing up, walking over to the dresser, sniffling. "It'll *never* happen, those rich bitches never get out of the way. I was born unlucky, and I've come to this . . . I love you but I can't have you, lately you've been coming by less and less, I can't go on like this, I'm sick of it, I hate it!"

Having worked herself up, she tore the pearl necklace off her throat, pearls rolling around on the hardwood floor, and she opened the top drawer of the dresser and said, turning so he could see what she had, "I'm gonna cut my wrist, and you won't be able to stop the bleeding. I want you to hold me while I die. Just do it! No phony stories!" and as he scrambled to stop her, concerned, his face going from anger at her ploy to real worry, she held the knife away from him, and, turning her body away, she cut her wrist a little, it bled, he grabbed at her, saying, "Stop this, please Mona, I love you," and he didn't want to hurt her, she was stronger, she was wild, he couldn't hold her, she groaned and twisted the knife-holding hand away, now saying, in a terrible voice, screaming, "I hate you! Leave me alone! Let me go!" and then she turned on him, slashing at him, the tip grazing his neck as he tried to catch her arm, maybe she was horrified by what she had done, but she relaxed her arm just as he caught up to it, prepared for the wild strength she'd been demonstrating, he grabbed her wrist just as she stopped the knife's arc and it all went wrong, it was as if she stabbed herself with his hand holding her wrist, the blade went in just to the side of her left breast, in the middle of her chest, it stopped her, she looked at him, sorry for him, she said "Richard" in a soft voice, and he held her as she collapsed, he touched the hilt of the knife but it was buried deep and snug, he cried out "No!" but then tried to comfort her, he wept but tried to compose himself for her sake, her eyes still saw him as he caressed her cheek, brushing the hair out of her face. He said, "Mona, Mona, baby, I love you, don't go," and she died, the knife stuck there, between her breasts. When Richard at last made another effort to pull it out, he succeeded, and, as the wound was unplugged, there now flowed, over her ribs and onto the floor, over her stomach, a quantity of rich wine-colored blood. Mona's eyes were open, somewhat astonished, her lips parted . . . for Richard's kiss, which he now gave. He held her, rocking, talking gently, soothingly, as if she were just asleep. Two figures, alone.

TWENTY-TWO

Her new girlfriend, Danica, had come to pick up Rae the night before, to go to the mountains for the weekend. So Chuck had spent the night with Lisa, and they fucked, and talked, and slept, and in the morning he made smoothies for them, he said he had a smoothie every day.

Lisa swam, and they talked some more, and called Larry Planet. They wanted to shoot one more scene: Richard in jail. Richard told the police the simple truth, not trying to excuse himself, but of course they wanted to take what they had, they didn't want to see any complications. He'd stabbed her, it was manslaughter or worse. Richard's wife, Elaine, came to visit him, and she was better-looking than one might have expected, though definitely older than he was, and she said, "I knew you had someone like her, and it was all right. But you couldn't control her, could you?" No, Richard admitted, a certain almost-nobility now with him since he'd stopped lying or hiding anything. A man who had nothing to hide, nothing to lose. "I loved her," he said, breaking the last tie with Elaine, you could see it, she still might even have stuck with him if he hadn't said this, insulting her by throwing it in her face. Elaine said, "You never learned, glamorpuss; you make a bargain, you have to give some things up. You can't just have everything at once." Richard let her get the last word.

They'd need a jailhouse set and some other actors. Larry Planet asked if they had anybody in mind. Chuck said, "What about Angela Bennington for Elaine? Tell her it's small but memorable. She can do it in a day."

"Good," Larry said, "I like her. The audience won't totally hate her, though they'll see Richard's point."

Chuck drove Lisa downtown to buy her some antique mirrors. They had to really speed to get away from this one female stringer, who was trying to follow them in her Saab.

People recognized them, and Lisa tried to study Chuck's cool way of dealing with the constant attention, just having everyone aware of you, watching you—it made her feel slightly paranoid and exposed. All that crazy witch stuff on TV. She didn't feel very safe. On the other hand, there was a feeling of belonging to the aristocracy of fame. Ordinary people were just background. Anything a "civilian" did or said was graceless, dumb; anything she and Chuck said or did had a rightness to it, a gracefulness . . . oh, Lisa was confused.

Three teenage girls stood there on the sidewalk as Chuck put another mirror in the backseat. The boldest one said, "This is incredible. Chuck Suede and Lisa Nova. Would you guys . . . um, would you mind signing something for me? This is incredible. You both look great!"

The first autographs Lisa had ever signed. She paid attention as Chuck made sure he asked each girl's name and smiled at each one. What would happen if you tried to go to a regular supermarket, buy personal items like tampons and deodorant? You'd be trapped.

Back in Topanga Canyon, the same woman was waiting for them, camcorder poised. The security guy Larry had insisted on hiring let them in; the guards came from Pinkerton's and worked eight-hour shifts, so that someone was always hanging around the grounds. The guy last night had, no doubt, through the open window, listened intently as they'd fucked. Listened as they peed and flushed the toilet.

Lisa went to the bathroom, disturbed by these reflections. When she came out, she found that Chuck had turned on the TV, the

Dodgers were on. To him it was a low-key but pleasurable way to spend a Saturday afternoon. Lisa thought sports were mostly boring, with exceptions now and then. He was drinking a cold beer. She smiled at him, and he asked her if she wanted to have dinner with Taft Flowers and Heather Malone. She took a sip of his beer and asked, "Where at?"

"I don't know. I was gonna call him. But I know they'd like to meet you. Taft and I have been good friends for a long time."

Lisa remembered: The two had been in *Ride the Snake* when they'd been fourteen. It had made them teenage stars. She said sure, and went to take the mirrors into the studio. *Glamorpuss* had been shot almost entirely in her bedroom—in her bed, in fact. It was amazing how into the role she'd gotten. Really, it was spooky. Though the real Mona hadn't died like that, as far as she knew.

Chuck would get a cowriting credit, since they'd improvised so much, and they were also coproducers. Larry Planet was executive producer, and maybe with his clout she'd get into the DGA. She could hear Chuck laughing, talking on the phone to Taft.

There had been a lot of trouble on the set of *L.A. Ripper II*. Fox Quigley hadn't gotten along with Eric Lemongrass either, and there'd been all kinds of shooting problems, accidents and illnesses and so on . . . but then, when Lemongrass fell—not doing a stunt, no way, just walking down some stairs—and broke his ankle, he'd blamed it on Lisa, probably just to get some attention; anyway, he'd told someone at *Behind the Scenes* that she'd probably put a curse on the production out of spite. The narrator of this *Behind the Scenes* segment was one of those British tabloid scumbags with a cut-rate accent . . . and so of course he had enumerated the different men Lisa had been involved with, saying "the latest to *fall under her spell* is Chuck Suede." He'd thrown in Roy Hardway and Miguel Casablanca, and Jules Brandenberg, none of whom she had fucked. With Jules that one time, that was "heavy petting," she'd told Raelyn, and they'd laughed.

This film, *Glamorpuss* . . . well, it was old-school, but Lisa felt like it was another gift from someplace, she'd *had* to do it, it had just happened, she was unbelievably lucky to be able to do such a project with an "element" like Chuck, and he was great. It was funny, because she'd never meant to be an actress, she'd never thought she could act. As a matter of fact, she'd never had much interest in actors in general; in film school they'd joked and called them furniture, and now here she was . . . she wondered what Christine would have thought. She was naked in it, but so was Chuck, it would have been impossible to do it fully clothed. The whole idea of exploitation, of exploiting oneself . . . she was more comfortable thinking about exhibitionism, the desire to show oneself, to find some truth in that. . . .

Although this was a performance that might (Larry Planet said it would) generate a lot of offers, she didn't think she'd appear in anyone else's film. There were so many other possibilities she wanted to explore. *Glamorpuss* was an anomaly—as was *Manoa, City of Gold*—but at least this one was fairly conscious; if people liked it, Lisa could feel good about accepting some praise. She was much more confident about what she might be able to do. It would be interesting to hear (and she probably would, through Larry, eventually) what Selwyn Popcorn thought of this new film.

It was one-thirty. She made sandwiches, and she and Chuck ate them while they watched the developments in the game. He explained to her some stuff about certain players as they came up to bat that made it more interesting to her.

When they were getting close to evening, Chuck revealed that it was a bigger dinner party than he'd earlier thought, and she should dress appropriately, to "knock them out."

"What if Nehi Laughton's there?" Lisa asked. "He thinks I had people beat up his wife."

"Don't worry about him. I'll keep an eye out. He doesn't want to piss me off." Chuck sounded sure of this, and Lisa believed he knew what he was talking about.

"I don't have anything to wear. I really don't."

"We'll figure something out. Let me help you find something."

They went into the closet, going from one hanger to the next.

TWENTY-THREE

Another week passed, more or less peacefully. Nothing happened crimewise, as far as Lisa knew. Nothing connected with her. She did, however, allow Watson Random to file a lawsuit against the police department, related to Lancaster's slapping her on the ass in her bed. If they didn't fuck with her anymore, she intended to withdraw it, she didn't want to be bothered, but Watson said doing this would make it less likely that something similar would happen again.

Her legal fees were really huge by this time, but the money coming in and going out didn't seem real, so it was hard to care.

The press seemed to have gotten sick of her, or rather, simply bored because nothing new was happening, and it wasn't cost-effective to have someone camped out when she so rarely stirred. She'd adjusted to the siege mentality . . . now it was only a few desperate freelancers who lay in wait.

Lisa had put a stud through her tongue. It didn't hurt, but it reminded her of the ritual pain. The metal felt weird, and Chuck, when he saw it, was quietly amazed. She'd bought it in a leather shop, hating to go in but feeling she needed something to put in there to preserve the piercing, keep the hole in her tongue from closing up. Her taste buds had not been affected, or at least it didn't seem like it. Sweet, salty, bitter, sour. They were all there.

She and Chuck disposed of Roy Hardway's shrunken head in a respectful manner one day; somehow Lisa knew instinctively what to do. They simply set it out in the sun.

As they watched, on their knees, the head seemed to turn into a gold mask, really shining, stitches gone . . . and then the gold turned into wax, glowing with a bit of red, and they heard a sigh, and it slowly melted away, it kept melting on the grass until there was nothing left.

Chuck went away to the location of his next movie, to be directed by James Anka, whose first film, *Inevitable*, had won the Golden Palm at Cannes. Lisa was sorry to see Chuck go, she was almost in love with him. It was hard to tell what he felt about her. Absence, separation would probably make it clear to what extent each might need or want the other around.

Glamorpuss was pretty much cut; all it needed was some soundtrack work. There was apparently a rumor going around that Lisa and Chuck had fucked on camera; Larry Planet said that this kind of thing would only increase interest and curiosity. . . . The last scene, Richard in jail, had been shot without difficulty. Lisa thought Chuck was awfully good. Great, really.

When she called Track to see if he would do the music, he said sure. The idea of doing a straight melodramatic soundtrack, like Miklos Rosza, appealed to him as an exercise in style.

The next day, he called her back and said he'd just got a phone call from someone named Martinho Vidal down in Brazil.

Track said, "Vidal says that Dad is sick, and that he's on his way to France for some special treatment, it's some rare tropical disease."

"Is it life-threatening?" Lisa asked, stunned, scared.

"No, no, in fact he specifically said his life isn't in danger, that there's a treatment, that he should be OK."

"Maybe I'll call Isabel," Lisa mused, sort of hurt that her father had not let her know. But then, probably he didn't want to worry her. That was how he would view it.

"I think she went with him to France. Vidal said they'd be in touch. 'The worst is over,' he said. Really."

"He didn't like me."

"Who?"

"Martinho Vidal."

"Oh, you can't be sure of that," Track said, though he didn't sound very sure.

"Are you going to go to France?" she asked, and Track hesitated, she could hear him hesitating; he answered her question with one of his own.

"Are you?"

"Yes. I will."

In one of the new mirrors, gazing to distract herself, to kill an afternoon, she watched a delicate Japanese child trying on this dress and then that. Unsmiling, staring as if she knew that Lisa was watching, uncanny, coming back in a kimono, slowly, ever so slowly belting it up. She was perhaps twelve. It was hard for Lisa to guess. A pink party dress with a white collar, worn with white tights. A white dress with a lace collar, exquisite against the golden skin. Now, after looking to the side, as though hearing her hated mother, the girl stuck out her tongue. And then she finally, fleetingly smiled, just for herself.

Lisa was left exhausted, with a strange kind of intoxication; she had to go lie down for a while. Her head swam, she was dizzy. She fell asleep for an hour until she suddenly heard Raelyn open the door of the refrigerator and take something out. Caz padded in from outside, already purring in anticipation of being petted and caressed. Something was slightly funny with Lisa's vision, but when she opened her eyes again, it had passed.

TWENTY-FOUR

Saturday night was always busy, although Joey tried to encourage customers to think ahead; if it was possible, she liked to make her rounds during the week. But Saturday night, almost all night, her pager went off again and again and again.

It was very good money. She and Zed had split up, and Zed had decided to live with his mother in Paso Robles for a while . . . he had problems, he no longer felt equipped to deal with the world.

Whereas Joey, since the unveiling, was in her glory, she felt so beautiful, the surgery had been so successful, and these days she stayed high, blissfully, almost all the time. Her life was now so organized that she had a solid baseline of static pleasures, as Epicurean philosophy recommended (Joey'd once attended, briefly, Dartmouth, though she hadn't learned anything much about pleasure back there), with frequent episodes of kinetic, wild pleasure—that is, of the sexual and hardcore exhibitionistic variety—with any of three devoted male admirers, all of whom treated her like a beautiful princess, they adored her . . . and one of them, the rock star Dash Pilgrim, Joey sort of loved in return. She didn't think of him as just a john.

She had become good friends with another transsexual, Lauren Devoto, who had never quite opted to take the plunge, that is, go under the knife. Lauren advised her to stick with an older man, someone rich, who would take care of her . . . a connoisseur who could appreciate the "best of both worlds," the beautiful she-male, the chick with a dick. Lauren, of course, had pulled off the seemingly impossible and been legally married, and very few knew her real story, her triumph . . . Joey had sold her drugs for two years before Lauren had seen fit to fully confide. Joey had kept her mouth shut and showed proper deference, and eventually Lauren had wanted to share.

The silicone augmentations to the breasts, ass, and thighs, the hormones, electrolysis to remove unwanted hair, makeup secrets—there was a lot to talk about, so when not together they spent a lot of time on the phone.

These new chemicals were so wonderful. If you really knew what you were doing, and had quality-control checks and a plan, there was no reason to experience anxiety or dread, and a whole new range of brilliant emotions became available; naturally you had to be careful, but . . . Joey was a good ambassador, and Lauren was one of her best customers. She liked to try each new flavor the boys in the lab came up with, once it had been given its trial to watch for bugs.

Joey felt this was the wave of the future, and she hardly even dealt in traditional substances like cocaine. She specialized, and a lot of these new formulas were not even illegal . . . some had no known bad side effects unless you were an asshole going out of your way to fuck yourself up.

It was 5:30 A.M. Sunday morning and Joey had been up all night, hitting the clubs, going to private parties, called to the homes of movie stars and studio executives, rock stars, supermodels . . . then she was betrayed. And it wasn't exactly a secret who betrayed her: the conceptual artist Mark Ferdinand. He didn't even say he was sorry! Nothing! He introduced her to this guy outside his home in Silverlake, it looked OK, and then Joey was busted: "You're under arrest. You have the right to remain silent," all that.

On the way to the station, Joey thought of what Zed had taught her, and one thing was for sure: Mark Ferdinand would have to pay, and pay big time. She knew some rough people. Maybe the next time he went to Milan, chasing baby models who didn't know if they were going to make it or not—he was the kind of jerk who preyed on them, he had money and knew the ropes over there—Joey thought: I'll have both his elbows broken. Then he won't be able to feed himself or wipe his own ass.

Now to the task at hand. She was calm, she hadn't wept, the problem was going to be convincing these shitheads—narcotics detectives Wheeler and Chung—to make the phone call, they weren't going to want to give up their bust. They were dumbasses.

She would never, it was inconceivable, give up any of the chemists. Second, she could never spend any time in the L.A. county jail. Were they kidding? These were *real* breasts, a *real* ass, and she did not intend to be auctioned off as a sex slave.

So she began.

"I swear to God, they'll want to talk to me. They will *thank* you forever for calling them in."

"Do you have any idea, sweetcheeks, how many assholes call in every day with so-called critical leads? You don't know how badly you're boring us with this shit. Quit fucking around."

"Listen, just get this straight: *I know who wore the bird suit.* Tell

Bluestone or Brown. I—hypothetically, in another life—might have, you know, sold stuff to *Lisa Nova, Boro, Lauren Devoto, Veronica, Steve Zen,* and *Code*."

"Oh fuck," Godfrey Chung said, throwing his fresh butterhorn against the wall, bouncing it like a bank shot into the wastepaper basket.

Tom Wheeler, his partner, took this to mean that Chung believed her, and that even though it was Sunday morning they'd better call in the homicide dicks.

Joseph Allen O'Brien. Hard to believe that she was a man. Just to punish her a little, make her sweat, they made her wait in the holding pen with all the motherfuckers taken in overnight. Chung told the sergeant to keep an eye out, stay ready with the Mace.

Profit Brown's pager went off in church. Then he called Bluestone, who was still apparently lying around with his wife in bed. *Interruptus*.

Some formalities had to be gone through. Like Bluestone and Brown could promise Joey the moon, but it meant nothing unless someone from the DA's office agreed there would be no prosecution—and the assistant DA on call, a young monotone-voiced woman, was not being cooperative at all. Joey's lawyer, Patrick Seagull, had shown up, and maybe this woman had a hard-on against him, so to speak, whatever . . . negotiations were not going well. Joey wanted total immunity: "I want out of here today and nothing relating to this can ever be filed. In return I'll tell you all kinds of things, I'll answer everything you ask and more."

Finally, since they were into the afternoon by now, Profit Brown did something he ordinarily would never do, but this was just too maddening . . . he called at home a senior assistant DA, another black man, someone he'd worked with before. As soon as the guy understood the situation, he said, "Put her on the line. Go get her and put the stupid bitch on the line."

The assistant DA on call was very angry—Brown knew he'd made an enemy, no question, and her father was a judge, the only reason she'd ever gotten hired—but this was what had to be done. He'd live with it. Her father was an extraordinary idiot, an arbitrary judge, and little Renee here showed every sign of living up to the family tradition.

Joey was served lunch, they had takeout delivered, and at last she could smile. She freely gave it all up.

"Veronica located a piece of furniture for Boro, way back, and then she used to go out there to see Wanda and get her fortune told. She hated Lou. I don't know all the stuff she saw, but I know she used to dress up in a bird suit, nobody could even tell if it was a woman or a man. And Steve Zen got dolled up in Aztec drag, in body paint, because Boro wanted somebody who'd lifted weights, someone with a big chest. Alvin Sender was the connection there."

"Who has the videos? Do you know what I'm talking about?" Bluestone asked.

Joey laughed and accepted a light for her cigarette.

"Veronica and Steve, most likely. Veronica has called up Lauren a couple times in the past few days and hinted that she'd sell them if the price is right. But Lauren's been tied up. You should be careful if you visit Veronica—she and Steve have some weapons in that bungalow. Steve worked as a freelance enforcer, hired muscle—Sender used him once to beat up some guy. Veronica . . . she has all these pictures of Lisa she's cut out and taped up on the wall. I think she tries to put spells on her, using things Wanda taught her . . . I think she's hallucinating quite a bit. At least, that's one kind of drug she seems to go through pretty fast. She's tripping out," Joey said, and snickered, smoked her cigarette, yawned. Little freckles across the bridge of her nose.

TWENTY-FIVE

On Sunday afternoon Code called. Lisa answered after two rings. Raelyn was gone somewhere.

Lisa said hello, and Code immediately started leaning on her, saying, "You've got to come get me. Nobody's here right now, but I've got to leave. Just take me out to LAX."

"Where are you going?"

"New York. Look, just do me the favor. You're the only one I trust. It's gotten really bad. I have to get out."

"Code? Why can't someone else take you? Why me? We haven't even talked for, like, *months*."

"Just come, OK? Please don't fuck with me."

"If you're trying to get me over there for some sex thing, I'll kill you. I swear to God."

"Lisa, Jesus . . . you once said you'd stick by me no matter what. Well, right now is 'what.' I'm in over my head. Just come and get me and take me to the airport, OK? I need you to do this for me."

"All right. I'll come as fast as I can. You'll be ready to go?"

"Yes. It's the servants' day off, so nobody will be around. I'll be waiting."

Lisa felt like saying, I don't even know you anymore, but that seemed too cruel. She was tired. She had swum earlier, but otherwise it was a lazy, motiveless day. Overcast and humid. Something in Code's voice had bugged her, but she didn't see what she could do. She got dressed and at the last moment decided to leave a note for Raelyn.

TWENTY-SIX

Nobody answered their knock, the doorbell, taps on the window, calls of "Veronica!" "Steve!"—nothing. Bluestone and Brown looked at each other, looked around at the neighborhood, trying to ascertain if they'd attracted particular attention. It didn't seem like it. People were yelling around here all the time.

They could smell burning charcoal briquets.

"Man, I love that smell," Profit Brown said.

"Me too," Bluestone agreed. "I even love the smell of the starter fluid."

A vast laziness descended on them. They didn't know what to do. It was possible, it wasn't to be overlooked, that Steve and Veronica might be inside, just not answering, stubbornly waiting for them to go away. It wouldn't be the first time.

The day was cloudy, but hot. Somebody was playing salsa music loudly just down the street. All that crazy percussion, that love for trumpets—Profit Brown found himself musing about how gang tattoos looked on brown skin.

"Why don't you call her, how about that? Veronica said there's a phone at the Korean grocery."

"Call Lisa?" Bluestone asked.

"Yeah. You have a better, uh, rapport with the suspect than I do."

"I'll call this number too. And Devoto. Let's call everybody we know."

"Yeah, do that. I'll stay here."

"OK," and Dave Bluestone was gone around the corner just like that. In a minute Brown could hear the phone ring inside the house, but he didn't hear anyone stir. In another few minutes Bluestone was back, with two cold Cokes.

"Nobody's home," he said.

They drank their cold beverages thirstily. They wondered where Lisa was. Who knew? It was a Sunday afternoon. Maybe if they called up *Behind the Scenes*, some sleazy producer there would know where everybody was. Lisa was now romantically linked with Chuck Suede. The detectives didn't know what that was all about.

"Are you curious, Dave?" Brown asked, and Bluestone knew he meant why don't we go in, take a look. It was the only thing that might relieve their tension for a moment or two.

TWENTY-SEVEN

As she drove, Lisa had the volume up high on the car stereo, it was soothing, but she was hardly listening . . . her mind wandered, ideas came to her . . . like maybe spending a few months quietly, anonymously, in Europe, visiting her father in France and then renting an apartment, maybe in Budapest or Prague . . . maybe Rome. Not Berlin. When she'd been there for the film festival, she'd jaywalked—like she would anywhere, traffic permitting—and some purple-mohawked post-neo-punk had rebuked her in an intimidating fashion, he'd actually scared her . . . and yet the whole thing had been absurd. A joke.

Brazil again? Rio? Not now that Tavinho was dead. Where else down there . . . maybe Buenos Aires would be nice. She didn't know. She was sure, however, that she would leave Los Angeles for a while. She'd leave the United States. Somebody was following her, even now, some tabloid reporter, she'd seen him hanging around off and on for weeks. If she could control her powers better, she would do something to him, just some relatively harmless mischief, make his car break down . . . such jackals deserved all the petty misfortunes she could cause.

Pulling into the open gateway of the Devoto place, going up the long driveway to the turnaround in front of the house, Lisa felt a certain uneasiness mingled with dispassionate irritation at Code. Why had he ever come out here? How could he have been able to make himself spend so much time with that woman? He must have really despaired of the future, hated himself even, under it all.

Could you make a comeback once you'd hit that all-time low? She hoped so, but she didn't know. Code might be just fucked.

She pulled up to the front entrance, by the stone steps, and sat there, the Trans Am in neutral, waiting for some sign of life. She didn't know if she'd shaken the tail or not. Code had said he would be ready. Goddamn him. She honked the horn.

Not a sound.

OK. Fuck. Honked again. Turned off the ignition and, taking her time, hesitant, got out of the car. Shit.

Lisa was wearing a short slip dress, pale rose pink, almost beigeish, slightly iridescent, a silver chain around her neck with a triangular sacred Zoroastrian seal hanging down, something like that, sunglasses, midankle biker boots—there had been some thought in her mind, as she had dressed, since Code was an ex-boyfriend, of showing him what he had been missing.

When she'd come here before, with Selwyn Popcorn, the night of that party, there had been so many people . . . it was a little eerie now to have the place deserted. She went up to the front door. It was just barely ajar; you wouldn't notice until you were up close. Lisa opened it wide.

"Code?"

Maybe he had come down, gone outside, then realized he'd forgotten some tape or something just as crucial, and run back upstairs.

"Code?" she asked again, stepping in, taking off her sunglasses, now also with her keys in her hand. This place was huge. Blondish hardwood floors. So bare. What was going on? Lisa spun around at a noise partially behind her, but it was nothing. . . .

There was some—there was something—up ahead, to her right.

"Lisa . . ." It was Code. Now Lisa saw him. Code stood on a chair in the middle of an immense empty room with a noose around his neck—a noose on a new rope attached to a beam high overhead. Wrists cuffed behind him? She wasn't sure.

On the wall, spray-painted in big, thick blood-red letters: *I did it.*

"Lisa, I'm sorry," he said—and then a woman dressed all in black—of course Lisa had seen her but she hadn't really registered, it was Veronica, Lou's widow—kicked the chair out from under Code, and his legs splayed out, it wasn't a joke. The noise he made.

There was someone behind Lisa. She turned just as a handsome, tanned, muscular guy, in a shining white T-shirt and blue jeans, sleeves torn off to show his swollen biceps, grabbed her, giving her no chance, smiling at her, hands hard on her arms, his fingers hurt her . . . he pulled her, half pushed her, out of the scene, away from the evidently hanging-to-death Code.

Was this real?

Veronica was in a black shiny plastic catsuit, like Catwoman or Diana Rigg in *The Avengers*.

"Let go of me, you fuck," Lisa said, dropping her sunglasses and her keys. He kicked them away from her as she started to bend over.

"My name is Steve," he said with a curve to his mouth, showing by his smile his contempt for her, his relish of the role he played.

Veronica had a gun in her hand and was pointing it somewhat casually at Lisa, indicating she should continue. Code passed out of sight, legs kicking out.

"What are you *doing*?" Lisa asked, hating the fear that came up into her voice. It showed that she immediately thought or semi-intuited that they'd killed Alvin Sender, etcetera. . . .

"Don't play dumb," Veronica said. "You fucked Lou, and when he couldn't pay your little whore's ass in the way you'd planned, you put a curse on our whole family."

Lisa had nothing to say in her defense. She couldn't struggle for the moment. She was in shock. Maybe she deserved this. . . .

They proceeded down a short hall to an elevator. Steve pushed her in, and Veronica followed, punched *B*. The elevator moved, descended.

"But . . . why Code?" Lisa got out.

"It's a setup, baby," Steve said, his face close to hers. "You saw it. 'I did it.' He confessed."

"And then committed suicide out of remorse. We'll take off the Velcro cuffs, and his wrists will be unmarked. He killed you and then himself. No loose ends," Veronica said, her eyes spacy but clear, unreadable, intelligent and somewhat excited, wet and cruel. She looked attractive in the catsuit, her hair and makeup done with care. Had she had a facelift? She didn't look that old.

They came out of the elevator into a darkish space. There were various doors down here, to the left and right. The ones to the right seemed to be bathrooms . . . or storerooms of some sort . . . it was the area to the left they were going to enter, and Lisa recalled watching S&M and other sex games going on, seen on the screens of Lauren Devoto's household monitors, Popcorn had been playing with the switches, stoned . . . they'd never come down here.

"You remember Tomorrowland? Well, this will be slightly different, but it'll still get you that kind of coverage, it'll be the crime of the century, considering who you are by now," Veronica continued, opening the middle door. "Oh, did you know Code was cooperating with a writer, dictating a tell-all?" she said as Steve pushed Lisa, hard, into the room, which was lit with creepy emerald green light . . . the light colored everything, it made everything glow green.

Lisa collided with someone sitting in a chair, but the flesh was so cold, now the person began slipping, waxy-stiff, sideways to the floor. Short dark hair, eyes open, a bullet hole in her forehead. . . .

"Meet your biographer," Veronica said, as Steve laughed with her, and Lisa made a noise—fear, she couldn't help it, in the green sourceless light she turned back to them and said, "Veronica, I'm sorry for everything that happened, you've got to believe me. I—I didn't ask for all that shit to come down. Boro just did whatever he wanted to do. Look at me, look at the *tattoos*! He put them on me, he decorated me like his pet!"

"You're *not* sorry! Don't lie to me!" and Veronica rapped Lisa with the hard barrel of the gun, instantly bloodying her nose. Veronica had on black gloves. "Wanda told me all about it, and I saw you with Boro. I saw how you two were. You're not sorry for any of it."

Lisa wiped at her bleeding nose with her bare hand, tears from the shock of fresh pain in her eyes. She was powerless. She backed up; the green room had things in it, but she didn't even see them, she didn't know what they were.

"Don't hurt me," she said, a moment of cowardice, weakness, and this probably encouraged them: Fear was the designed response.

Backing up, Lisa opened the door to the next room—red light poured in, it overwhelmed the green, Lisa turned and went in, there was gymnastic equipment, or no, it was meant for sadomasochism, and someone was hanging upside down.

It was Lauren Devoto, in a corset, wrists handcuffed behind her back, dark shadows, stockings . . . everything in this room was either *red* or darkest brownish red to black . . . oh, she had a penis . . . still erect, in a series of black cock-rings . . . electrodes attached to her nipples, a smell of ozone, singed flesh, she was dead, upside down, grotesque . . . in jewel-like, glowing red.

Lisa ran to the next door, and Steve ran too, he caught her, he had a knife or a razor, he cut her on the shoulder blade, twice, diagonally, ripping the thin dress, then coming up close, hugging her for an instant, she could feel his strength, how weak she was in his arms—he cut her throat, just a little, a shallow, tiny, playful laceration, to terrorize her . . . and it did.

The next room was blue, luminescent blue, and it was full of dummies. Mannequins, all naked and vacant and blank, bluish, were in her way, and Lisa fought through them desperately.

The mannequins were like a forest of plaster. They were heavy, inanimate, she had to knock them over to make her way, as one fell it tangled with another and started complications, Lisa was tripped but instantly scrambled back up, it was as if she could feel new sharp cuts on her back, phantom razor slashes in the cool blue, an otherworldly blue like on another planet, these hard neutral-faced bald female dummies mocking her, they were alive, their posed hands clawed at her as she pushed through. She knew Steve and Veronica were controlling all this, it was a scenario they'd planned, but there was nothing else she could do, they had her where they wanted her.

She was so afraid the next door wouldn't open, but it did, into perfect blackness. She hesitated for just a moment, maybe there was some horrible trap she'd run into like a driven animal, but they were coming, they were saying, "Li-sa . . . Tomorrowland . . . "

So she went into the darkness, but turned right and stayed next to the wall, which was covered with vast thick drapes, she moved quickly, trying to feel for obstructions ahead of her, but there was nothing . . . she couldn't see *anything*, anything at all. . . .

She kept going, feeling her way, hearing only her breathing, slowing it, trying to be collected, to think. What could she do? How could she get out?

Suddenly, just like that, lights were flicked on, normal yellowish, bright lighting—and then the drapes pulled back, one two three four . . . to reveal a room of mirrored walls, mirrored ceiling, tiled floor in an intricate pattern of Islamic blue and purest white and black.

Lisa turned to the mirrors, so quickly hoping for strength, for her powers to manifest themselves, hoping for something . . . and maybe Veronica read her, she had her suspicions, because Lisa had no sooner seen herself, bleeding, wet red from her neck and some from her nose staining her all down the front, her eyes dilating, glimpsing beyond that all of the teeming repetitive sex acts, the nudity in these mirrors, trying to summon something beyond that, sensing rather than seeing that something was way back there, so far—than Veronica began shooting her gun, and Lisa screamed as the mirrors shattered, Veronica shot each one, and they all burst out into shards as Lisa went down holding her ears, down to one knee, eyes closed, until all the reflections were gone but for those in random unstable crooked panes shining here and there.

"You thought you could do something with the mirrors, didn't you?" Veronica said as Lisa scanned the room, looking for anything, a weapon, a door . . .

Then, in a few moments, Lisa looked back over at Veronica. She had hopes that all the bullets might have been fired from the gun. And Steve wasn't yet here.

"No," Veronica said, smiling, reading her gaze. "These new ones hold quite a few. Get ready for Tomorrowland. It's going to hurt. But don't worry. There's a secret exit out of here, and we'll tip the press as soon as we get away. You'll be the most famous whore of all time."

"Just kill me, then," Lisa said. "Don't torture me." Where was Steve?

Veronica shook her head. "It has to be done a certain way," she said. "Just shooting you wouldn't be nearly as good. You'll see."

And then Lisa did see. Steve came in, entering from the blue chamber—which flickered sometimes, in some way—and he had put on a clear plastic raincoat, hood pulled up, and goggles, and rubber gloves. He had put on big rubber boots. Ready for wet work.

Steve had a chainsaw in his hands. He glanced at Veronica, nodded, and pulled the cord. Lisa screamed, she couldn't help it now, and all her cries were drowned out by the chainsaw revving up. She fled to the farthest corner, she saw her face reflected in a little shard of mirror and knew utter terror, there was no way out, she was trapped.

The *pain*, the unspeakable pain of it, those teeth ripping into your tender flesh, merciless, atrocious . . . it was so much worse than a simple bullet in the head. She would be mutilated, cut apart. She looked at the inhuman goggles approaching, the insane saw, and, cornered, gave way to absolute horror. She screamed.

TWENTY-EIGHT

They were concerned when they saw the shrine to Lisa that Veronica had constructed. They also found a quantity of videos in the closet, in a black plastic trash bag, which might well be the ones missing from the murdered Alvin Sender's home. This too was cause for concern.

When they called Lisa Nova's number again, the machine answered, but when Bluestone spoke this time, saying it was important, Lisa's assistant, Raelyn, picked it up, and said that Lisa had left her a note saying she'd gone to the Devoto estate to pick up Code.

When they arrived at Devoto's, they saw Lisa's car parked in the turnaround. The front door was open. They discovered the body of Code, a hanged man swaying in the breeze, *I did it* in red paint on the wall.

"Did *what*?" Profit Brown said. Bluestone remembered the control room, the console with the monitors of every room and much of the outside estate.

As soon as they saw the brightly lit room with Lisa in it, Veronica with a gun, they ran to the elevator.

Down in the basement, past the two corpses, through the colored rooms, hearing a chainsaw . . . Lisa was screaming . . . Bluestone got through the blue room filled with mannequins first.

Immediately, without fucking around, he shot Steve high in the back, and then, as the heavily muscled killer turned, Dave shot him in the chest, the neck, the face, the rounds rising as the gun kicked and Steve began to slowly collapse, falling on his chainsaw, blood and flesh flying off in gobs from his thigh, the saw making a choking, busy sound, eventually getting stuck.

Veronica resolutely shot Bluestone once in the chest and then was quickly turning to take care of Lisa when Profit Brown's hollow-point bullet took off a good portion of her head. Was she dead yet? Well, she was now.

"Help me," Brown said, and Lisa controlled herself amid the carnage. Brown packed the wound with Bluestone's own ripped shirt; shaking and trembling, Lisa put all her swimmer's strength into assisting the black detective as he carried Detective Bluestone, who had what was called a sucking chest wound . . . they took the elevator up to ground level and got the half-conscious policeman out to Brown's car.

"Pressure!" Brown said fiercely. "Hold it on there!" and he was off, gas pedal to the floor out through the gates, calling on his radio to get the trauma team ready, officer shot, ETA five minutes. A hundred miles an hour, siren wailing, Lisa hanging on to Bluestone for dear life around the curves. She really didn't want him to die. Not like Tavinho and Code. No.

TWENTY-NINE

A few days later Lisa went to visit Bluestone at the hospital. She brought flowers. She felt very shy. Bluestone's wife, Kate, was friendly enough in a neutral, observant way, rather as if she thought Lisa was an untrustworthy vixen; somehow Lisa could neither really blame her for this perceived attitude nor, she guessed, do much to alter it.

Kate Bluestone was blond, probably tinted her hair a bit to keep away the gray, attractive in a big-bodied Dutch or German way, and the two college-age children, one girl, one boy, were serious, intelligent, fairly good-looking . . . Lisa admired them and felt out of place, ridiculous, with her magic and tattoos.

Bluestone himself—expected to live but still in Intensive Care—seemed reasonably pleased to see her, though it might well be that he would remember little of this doped-up time.

The press, the TV, the tabloids . . . all had greatly relished this whole business. The chainsaw was an irresistible detail. Profit Brown told Lisa that Jennell Fonvergne, a blond TV reporter, was Phil Lancaster's girlfriend, and Lancaster had gone to the Devoto mansion to mop up, along with the fire department, so it could be presumed he had told Fonvergne all he knew.

Lisa had five stitches in her throat and a few on her back. Her nose wasn't broken—it was fine. She felt the hangover, though, from all the terror she had been through. It hadn't "broken" her, but she felt different . . . it was going to take a while to calm all the way back down. But she was OK.

She didn't know what to feel. It was so hard to think. Code's death bothered her a great deal, and Christine's had come back to her, Tavinho . . . everybody she'd loved, or so many, were now dead. Being a survivor was shit. It had all started with her, as Veronica said. She couldn't concentrate, she couldn't do anything.

Chuck Suede had flown down and spent two days with her, screwing up the schedule of his in-progress production, but it was great of him; she'd needed someone to hold her while she cried.

Chuck, and Raelyn, and Casimir.

When she swam one day, a helicopter filmed her coming out of the pool; since she wasn't nude, they zoomed in on her face.

Adrian Gee called her, and that was nice. She talked to Track, and to her father, who was in Aix.

But she was having a hard time. She was a murderess. She had effectively murdered Lou, and Wendy Right, and Duane Moyer. She had blood all over her.

What was she now? She was damned, and she wasn't a victim, she'd done it to herself. To blame Boro was an untenable excuse. She had *desired* havoc, mayhem, violence; inside she had been curious, she'd wanted the sky to come down.

So it had.

THIRTY

Track brought along a shotgun, and he said he knew how to use it. They drove out into the desert, near Barstow, a long motherfucking drive. Following Mannix, of all people, but his presence only made the shaky story seem even shakier, fishier, more absurd.

Lisa drove. They were going to fetch Mary Siddons, who was strung out on heroin. It was she who had called and said Boro was alive. He wanted $10,000. Then he was leaving, for good. Otherwise . . . the tape had come on: "I love you, I hate you."

How could it be? Lisa couldn't explain it or understand it, but then Mary said, "He says to tell you he never went through the mirror. That was a fakeout. He says he's not going to kill you, he could have done that anytime. Bring the money, and he'll go back to the land of his ancestors. Come *on*, Lisa, I'm fucked up. I need to get straight. I'm sick. Mannix will show you the way."

So Lisa got the money, and Mannix showed up, a smile on his face, surprisingly dapper and polite, no bandanna on his head, in a used Renault. Track, who had arrived yesterday, was grim and suspicious. He and Lisa had had a little argument about what she was about to do . . . but in the end Track had yielded. However, he insisted on coming along, and she was glad.

Mannix pulled in at a little roadside café, and when they got out he told them this was the last place to get a Coke. He wanted a hamburger, he said. Lisa was hungry too, so the three of them went inside and took a red upholstered booth. Because of the presence of a jukebox, they fell to talking about music. This place mainly featured Elvis

Presley, Jerry Lee Lewis, Patsy Cline, and early Charlie Rich. Track put in a couple of quarters to demonstrate that there were no sounds on earth he could not dig.

It seemed like Mannix's whole gangsta facade was a role he played, Lisa thought. She wondered what powers he might possess. There was no telling, if Boro was still functioning as before.

She ordered a date milk shake and loved it. Mannix had a cheeseburger, a Coke, and fries. The old white waitress might have been prejudiced, or at least not used to seeing many black people out here in the Mojave. Track ate a chili dog and was somewhat sorry. Too much Tabasco, or maybe too long in the pot. He got a date milk shake, following Lisa's advice, to take with him on the rest of the drive, drinking it like Maalox, to cover up the burn.

Up into the barren hills. Following Mannix in his Renault. After several switchbacks they took a little side road, in dust, away from what looked like the beginnings of a small settlement.

"Uh-oh," Lisa said, seeing all the choppers parked around the ramshackle house.

"The zombies are all dead," Mannix said, having parked, walking over to Lisa's rolled-down window. "Me and this white dude rented a truck, loaded 'em up, then went down to Long Beach and took out a fishing boat for the day. One by one, we popped 'em in the head and dumped 'em over the side. Boro had this thing, he wanted a burial at sea. Some of them used to race catamarans, some kind of shit like that."

"So they're at rest now," Lisa remarked, not totally ironically.

"That was the plan," Mannix said, and again it was hard to tell what he was getting out of all this or if he saw it as just an elaborate goof. Lisa got out of the car. So did Track, slamming his door, checking the shotgun so Mannix would be sure to see. The latter only smiled and shook his head.

They went up to the house. Mannix went first and knocked. Mary Siddons opened the door, sniffling and trembling in a dirty olive green sleeveless minidress. Her arms were bare, little purple-and-yellow bruises all over them, her skin so pale, so white.

"Gimme the stuff, OK? I can't wait."

"Damn, I knew there was something I forgot," Mannix said, acting it out.

"Motherfucker, that's really low, that's low . . . Jesus, I'm climbing the fucking walls."

"Mary," Lisa said, and Mary embraced her, crying, her head on

Lisa's shoulder. Lisa caressed her dirty hair, patted her back, and gradually, in a few moments, Mary seemed to calm down. Her nose had stopped running, the trembling heebie-jeebies of withdrawal melted away.

"What'd you do?" she said softly. "It's like you put some methadone in my corn flakes, if I had some corn flakes . . . how did you do that?"

"I'm not sure."

"She is a witch," said the tall black man, the one who had previously been mute and, later, catatonic. Profit Brown had once jokingly called him "James Doe." He came out of the shadows, eyes locked on Lisa's face.

Track reacted with the shotgun, pointing it, but Mannix motioned for him to put it down, saying, "This is my new brother. Jamal . . . formerly known as Boro."

"I jumped into the vacant body," Jamal said, "when you were pulling me through the mirror. I'm different now."

"Boro?" Lisa asked, awestruck.

"That's who I am, but I've changed. It's taken me a while to begin to understand. An awful lot of the old Boro is gone, chewed up by your mother, the cat. Did you bring the money?"

"What do you need it for?"

"Mannix and I are going to go to the source of the Nile." The tall man smiled. "We're going to go the hard way, as a test, but still, we need some funds. The powers I helped you find . . . you still have a lot to explore. And you never did actually pay me for your vengeance on Lou."

He was maybe six foot nine.

"I know. But you would never come right out and set a price. You kept on fucking with my mind."

"Maybe I did, but it was for the best. Please don't blame me for Veronica; she did those things on her own. That was private, between you and her. I'm sorry about your Brazilian boyfriend. Things got out of hand, and Veronica had that gun . . . I'm different now, very different. I hope you can forgive me for anything unnecessary that I did. I was wrong sometimes, careless. Loose."

Lisa liked this black man's voice. She was fearful of being too credulous—she knew Track thought she would believe anything—but if this was Boro, why not take him at his word? She enjoyed the idea of Boro—Jamal—and Mannix seeking out the source of the Nile.

She said, "The money's in the car. Let's go get it."

The wind was blowing blondish dust over the rocks. The pale blue sky above them was so high and huge. Didn't Mary have anything else? Apparently not. Just what she was wearing. She seemed quite pacified for now. Track said something to her, quietly, that Lisa didn't hear.

Jamal stood there, majestic in the bright sunlight, next to Mannix. Lisa gave Jamal the paper bag of small bills. It seemed like a solemn ceremony, somehow. She smiled shyly, uncertain of what to feel.

It had always been impossible for her to guess what Boro really wanted, and now it was just as bad, trying to have any idea what was going on inside Jamal. Would he keep turning up?

Track and Mary, taking their time, got into the car. Mary'd be a handful, though she was just a kid. In five days Lisa would be in France, seeing her dad. Would he have anything important to tell her? Probably not. But maybe. You never knew.

Lisa put her sunglasses back on. OK. She'd figure it all out later on.

Readers Group Guide:
BRAND NEW CHERRY FLAVOR

The questions included below are to enhance your enjoyment of **BRAND NEW CHERRY FLAVOR** by Todd Grimson, either as an aid in group discussion for book clubs, among friends, or to further your individual inquiry into this multifaceted novel. Unlike much of the literature in the contemporary urban supernatural fantasy genre, **BRAND NEW CHERRY FLAVOR** has elements of many other forms of literature from noir to surrealism to satire, and employs a complex layering of imagery and symbolic references that will provide food for thought for readers and discussion groups for years to come!

1) In describing this novel, author Todd Grimson has said that it is set "five minutes in the future." What do you think he means by this? How does this add or detract from the narrative? Are there are other works of fiction or movies that you can think of in these "near future" terms?

2) ***Publishers Weekly***, in its review of **BRAND NEW CHERRY FLAVOR,** described the novel as "perfectly poised on the edge between humor and horror." In what ways is Grimson able to sustain this balance? In what ways is the novel humorous? Are there particular scenes and/or characters you can identify as being particularly humorous? Is there a corollary between the two responses to humor and horror?

3) Though written in the 1990's, easily a decade or more before the advent of the current popularity of zombies/vampires/werewolves in literature, **BRAND NEW CHERRY FLAVOR** features not only zombies, but cannibalism, necrophilia, and other paranormal activity now considered mainstream. How do Grimson's zombies and necromancers function differently from the current breed popular in such novels as "World War Z" or the HBO series, "The Walking Dead?"

4) Similarly, the heroine of **BRAND NEW CHERRY FLAVOR** bears certain resemblances to another popular female avenger, Lisbeth Salander of Steig Larssen's series "The Millennial Trilogy," albeit Lisa Nova's appearance predates Salander by fifteen years. In what ways is Lisa Nova similar to Lisbeth Salander, and how is she different?

5) Throughout the novel, Grimson has interspersed many references to film and filmmaking. For example on p. 50; "She clicked out a video cassette and put in another, a French horror film she'd heard of but never seen, ***Les Yeux Sans Visage*** (Eyes Without a Face), directed by Georges Franju, 1959. How many of these references are you able to catch?

6) On the subject of movies, given that the novel is set largely in Hollywood and in the filmmaking world, you could say that **BRAND NEW CHERRY FLAVOR** is very filmlike in its structure and plot-development, and also in the very way that the scenes are described, what Grimson has described as "cinematic realism." Does this technique work for you, and how does it affect the overall "tone" of the book?

7) Grimson has also described **BRAND NEW CHERRY FLAVOR** as a phantasmagorical novel, one based on his dreams, yet with a novel structure (ie. longform) that dreams generally don't possess. In this way he sees a corollary between dreams and film. Do you think he succeeds in creating a "dreamscape" novel? Are there particular passages in the book that you can point to that exemplify this quality?

8) Despite the satirical and horror genre elements to **BRAND NEW CHERRY FLAVOR**, there is also a very realistic and "human" element to the story as exemplified by Lisa Nova's struggles with her own extraordinary powers, but also within minor characters as well. In what ways is Grimson able to portray the human element against the backdrop of "the horror, the horror?" What about the character of Boro for instance? Is this struggle apparent to you in any other character?

9) Most readers of **BRAND NEW CHERRY FLAVOR** are not contending with a paranormal talent/ability in their own lives. But if you did find yourself so affected, how would your reactions mirror those of Lisa? How different? And if you could choose your own talent, what would it be?

10) Todd Grimson has said that, ever since he was a child, he has been fascinated by names, and how they define a person in real life and in fiction. Think of "Selwyn Popcorn," "Chuck Suede," "Ariel Mendoza," "Roy Hardaway," "Boro," "Track," or even the heroine's name, "Lisa Nova." What names of characters do you like best, and how do they "embody" that character?

BONUS QUESTION: Grimson has said that he was influenced greatly by the *Nightmare on Elm Street* films and others in the slasher genre. In fact, he claims to have had all his victims die in similarly ghoulish ways as the victims in these movies. Can you identify the ten different ways in which people are killed within the novel, and their filmic counterparts?

Visit the author's site at **www.toddgrimson.com** to discover the answer.

Q& A with Author Todd Grimson

(Based on An Interview with Mark Christensen)

What were your key inspirations?

Early (Thomas) Pynchon (I don't like anything after GRAVITY'S RAINBOW), some (Don) DeLillo, less well-known writers such as Witold Gombrowicz (COSMOS), Hermann Broch (THE SLEEPWALKERS), Cesare Pavese (THE DEVIL IN THE HILLS). Ryu Murakami (ALMOST TRANSPARENT BLUE), William Burroughs (THE SOFT MACHINE is my favorite of his), Philip K. Dick. Charles Portis. And then a ton of films. Some of the Dario Argento and NIGHTMARE ON ELM STREET movies – but of course all of this material becomes violently warped when it comes through the milieux I've known and what I dream.

What were the most difficult things about writing BNCF?

I had a lot of fun working on it– I actually take pleasure in doing research, and there was a lot of research needed for this project, delving into such areas as fashion, film history, and the lifestory of Nastassja Kinski (which meant I became long-distance pals with Jim MacLennan, a writer in London who was somewhat obsessed with her — he also then edited a magazine dealing with low-budget horror films like *Nekromantik* and *Re-Animator*); Mayan history and myth (seeking some background for the vivid dreams I had starring and / or acting as Boro); behind-the-scenes workings of Hollywood… in all of these areas, enormous quantities I never used or touched, such as more than one book on the 1923 murder of director William Desmond Taylor, but also watching endless horror films – especially all those by Dario Argento, over and over, which though not exactly tight or good in the manner of Hitchcock, have a lyricism connecting with the dream-logic sometimes on display in the *Nightmare On Elm Street* films, which explicitly invoke dream-logic as such – the only time Freddy appears is when you're asleep. *Nightmares I, III* and *IV* have sequences invoking more sheer surrealism than anything Hollywood horror usually does. Falling into mirrors, for instance, came from there.

Was there a primal inspiration for *Cherry Flavor*--or did it come to you, so to speak, in sections?

I had always been interested in Nastassja Kinski – partly because of her father, and her connection with Roman Polanski, which was semi-disgusting the more I discovered about his sexual practices. And Klaus Kinski was a maniac. But in the novel I generally left the real-life Nastassja alone. My character Lisa Nova was in my conception somewhat defined by her film *Girl, 10, Murders Boys,* based on the true story of Mary Bell. Before I started the novel I had written a long – 50-some pages – story, embodying pretty much the beginning of the novel, but which much more explicitly featured Lisa Nova working one night at a techno Hollywood brothel employing lookalikes. The story was entitled *Lisa Says Yes to a Variety of Things.* After all kinds of adventures it ended with Lisa castrating someone and escaping from the grounds of the estate driving a white Jaguar, meanwhile high on designer drugs. The story was too pornographic to be published. It made some editors seriously angry at me. One said if this was the future he didn't want to live there. I thought I was probably tapping into something cool……though it crossed my mind I might get sued. By Nastassja. When I connected this beginning with my intense, dreams about Boro the book started to write itself. I also had all kinds of thoughts about postmodernism and Cindy Sherman and her *Untitled Film Stills* and other pictures which I was deeply studying at the same time, thoughts about how females present themselves in roles defined by the cinema (and so on).

I've spent nearly half my life around Los Angeles and consider BRAND NEW CHERRY FLAVOR equal to Nathanael West's DAY OF THE LOCUST **as a portrait of LA. Yet, while you've lived a lot of places, Los Angeles isn't one of them. In fact, you've never even been here. How'd you draw such an inspired and accurate picture on such a large scale?**

I wrote about the Los Angeles in my mind. Movies helped flesh this out, of course, but I also read a great book about the architecture of LA, as well as Kevin Starr's various volumes comprising a history of the city. I was fascinated by the names... like Pomona, or Santa Monica, Laurel Canyon, and I tried to get some sense of how these different locales related to each other. The names held some romance for me. I studied my Thomas Guide. (This was also a period when I was first getting used to the idea of being more or less crippled by MS, plus I was poor, and I knew I would have needed my own car... plus, I was used to watching films all night while working on my book while listening to music and looking at art books, leaving them lying open so I can glance at the images now and then). Sometimes I would watch *Suspiria* or *Cat People* over and over, all night, going to sleep at 6am. The years working nightshift in the ER had changed my relation to day and night forever – and I still do most of my writing in the still of the night, when everyone around me is asleep. I thought this might be the last book I would ever write.

Is, for lack of a better term, reporting important to your unique brand of story telling?

I think I'm a good listener, and I don't seem morally judgmental, so through the years all kinds of people have confided in me. People generally like to talk about themselves... Working in the Emergency Room for years taught me – or greatly aided my education about – how the world really works. It took a year there until, uh, I sort of lost my cherry... and really started to get it, beyond cheap "wised-up" cynicism anyone can affect. I knew about violence from the inside, as well as the outside...but I don't really want to talk about that. Maybe in some respects such intimate knowledge is literally "unspeakable" or incommunicable...but then as a writer you try to communicate it anyway. You know how it works –and how it doesn't work. You recognize immediately when you read something false.

What novel do you feel BRAND NEW CHERRY FLAVOR most resembles?

If any novel was in the back of my mind, strangely enough it might have been *Gravity's Rainbow,* though I find most of Pynchon terribly flawed. I still think he most likely died in 1973. The"softer" comeback novels are the product of a ghostwriter who studied the superficial aspects of his style... But *V., The Crying Of Lot 49, Gravity's Rainbow* – all were often quite cruel. They express a real hostility to the common reader. Just so, William Burroughs, though he's much more limited and repetitive. I have a framed photo of Burroughs, taken in Mexico City, when he was thirty years old, right around the time he shot his wife Joan Vollmer in the head.

A Brief Biography of Todd Grimson

Todd Grimson was born in 1952 in Seattle and moved to Portland, Oregon at an early age. At the age of 22, having gone through all kinds of dead-end employment, Grimson took a civil service exam and ended up working at the VA Hospital in its surgical intensive care unit, which he found highly educational. He went on to work nightshift in the emergency room at Emanuel Hospital, where most local victims of violent crime were seen—an intense experience informing his first novel, "Within Normal Limits," which he wrote under the mentorship of Paul Bowles, whom he had met and studied with during a summer writing workshop in Tangier, Morocco. Published in the prestigious "Vintage Contemporaries" series as a trade paperback original, "Within Normal Limits" earned Grimson critical acclaim and was the winner of the Oregon Book Award in 1988.

It was shortly before the publication of this first novel that Grimson was first diagnosed with multiple sclerosis (MS), an incurable, degenerative disease. However, his symptoms went away and did not reappear until the summer of 1991. Stricken suddenly, housebound and incapacitated, Grimson found himself having vivid and surreal dreams, which later became the source and literally a part of the novel, "Brand New Cherry Flavor," which blends this phantasmagorical dreamscape with the innovation of "cinematic realism." Critically acclaimed both in the US and in the UK, this novel was followed by "Stainless" (to be reprinted by Schaffner Press, Feb. 2012), an urban noir vampire novel set in late 1990's L.A.

In recent years, Grimson has been writing and publishing short fiction online under the nom de plume "I. Fontana," appearing in such literary reviews as *BOMB, Bikini Girl, Juked, New Dead Families, Lamination Colony* and *Spork,* while working on a new novel, "sickgirl101," a thriller which delves into the online Alt Sex underworld, exploring and exposing the darker side of contemporary sexuality as perhaps no one else has done before.

About Schaffner Press:

Founded by former literary agent Tim Schaffner in 2000, Tucson, Arizona-based Schaffner Press is an independent publisher of general trade books in the area of fiction, and non-fiction with a particular focus on mysteries, literary fiction, memoir, biography and autobiography. Its mission is to provide the general reader with works of quality that address major social issues of our time, and to inspire and challenge audiences with new thoughts, ideas and perspectives on the world.

LOOK FOR **TODD GRIMSON'S** NOVEL

STAINLESS

FROM **SCHAFFNER PRESS/ FEBRUARY, 2012**

In Paperback: $14.95

ISBN: 9781936182237

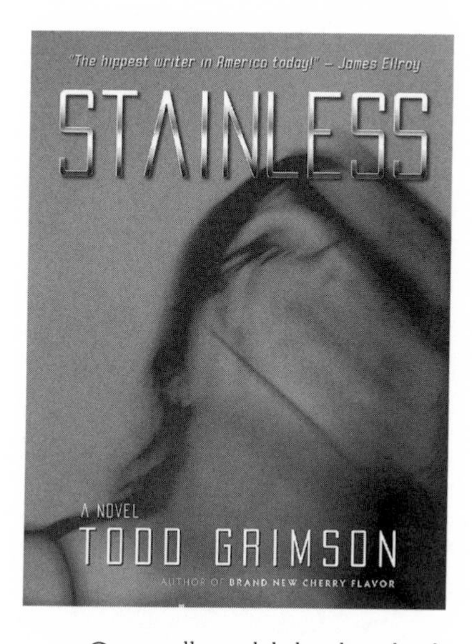

"The hippest writer in America today!" – James Ellroy
STAINLESS
A NOVEL
TODD GRIMSON
AUTHOR OF BRAND NEW CHERRY FLAVOR

"The finest vampire novel since, well, 'Dracula'"
—RICHARD MELTZER, PDXS

"An erotic confetti-shower that leaves you thrilled and unclean"
—KIRKUS REVIEWS

"A Satanic 'Less Than Zero'"
— THE NEW YORK TIMES

Originally published in the late 1990s, Todd Grimson's "**Stainless**" breaks fresh ground for the supernatural thriller genre by setting a vampire novel in contemporary Los Angeles, the pleasure dome of sex, drugs and rock n' roll culture, in which a 400 year-old female vampire, Justine, becomes entwined in a very human relationship with Keith, a down-on-his-luck rock guitarist whose hands have recently been mangled by a gang of drug dealers. The relationship between the undead and the living is realistically and tragically portrayed; Justine nurtures Keith and helps him to restore his self-esteem, while Keith acts both as Justine's enabler and unwitting nemesis, and in this classic role reversal, ends up having to destroy the one he loves in order to save her.